Also by Antoine Vanner

Britannia's Wolf

The Dawlish Chronicles, Volume 1

September 1877 - February 1878

Britannia's Reach

The Dawlish Chronicles, Volume 2

November 1879 - April 1880

Britannia's Shark

The Dawlish Chronicles, Volume 3

April – September1881

Being accounts of episodes in the life of

Nicholas Dawlish R.N.

Born Shrewsbury 16.12.1845

Died: Zeebrugge 23.04.1918

Britannia's Spartan

The Dawlish Chronicles, Volume 4

June 1859

and

April - August 1882

by

Antoine Vanner

Britannia's Spartan - Copyright © 2015 by Antoine Vanner

Library of Congress Cataloging-in-Publication Data:

Antoine Vanner 1945 -

Britannia's Spartan / Antoine Vanner.

(The Dawlish Chronicles Volume IV))

ISBN 978-1-943404-04-9 (pbk.)—ISBN 978-1-943404-05-6 (Kindle)

Cover design by Sara Lee Paterson

Published by Old Salt Press

Old Salt Press, LLC is based in Jersey City, New Jersey with an affiliate in New Zealand

978-1-943404-04-9

For more information about our titles go to www.oldsaltpress.com

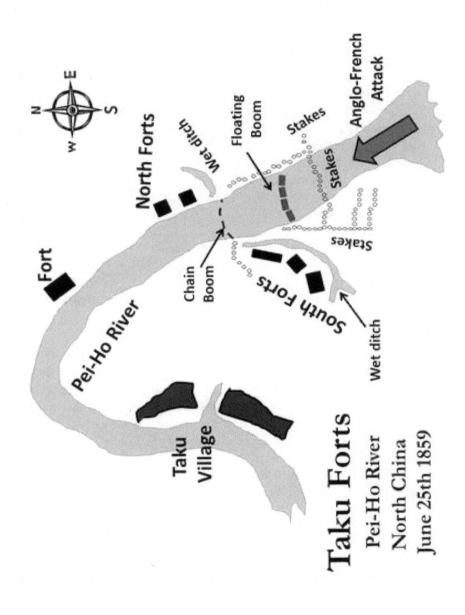

Taku Forts

Pei-Ho River
North China
June 25th 1859

Fort

North Forts

South Forts

Taku Village

Pei-Ho River

Wet ditch

Chain Boom

Floating Boom

Stakes

Stakes

Stakes

Wet ditch

Anglo-French Attack

N E S W

5

1

The *Plover* and the *Opossum* nudged cautiously towards the first barrier, a row of iron spikes that rose six feet above the foul mud-brown waters of the Pei-Ho River in North China. It was after midday, June 25th 1859, steaming hot, high water. The wooden gunboats held to the centre of the channel, clear of the now-unseen mud banks to either side which low tides uncovered.

"Still no sign of life, gentlemen." Rear-Admiral Hope gestured from *Plover's* exposed bridge towards the row of earthworks that lined the shore to port, six hundred yards distant.

"Not even a banner, sir, though God knows they're addicted to them." Rason was a young lieutenant, the gunboat his first command.

"They may even have abandoned the forts, sir." McKenna was an army captain attached to Hope's staff. "There's no guessing what these fellows might do."

Hope turned to his Flag-Lieutenant. "What do you think, Douglas?"

"Better for us to hold fire, sir."

Hope nodded. "No need to antagonise John Chinaman if he doesn't want to fight." He handed his telescope to Dawlish. "Here, lad," he said "take a look for yourself."

Intimidated by his proximity to an admiral, even a genial one, Dawlish stammered thanks. As he sharpened the focus he saw that the earthen ramparts were deeply embrasured at intervals along their fronts. The three separate batteries that constituted the Taku forts lay off the port bow in an almost continuous line for a quarter-mile. The guns that must lie inside those embrasures were hidden from view by what looked like thick rope curtains.

And those guns might well fire not just at *Plover*, but at himself, Dawlish knew. He was more afraid than he had ever been in his life, more than when the order "midshipmen aloft" had first sent him to the main-top, more than when he first ventured out along a yard and leant forward to gather in the canvas, feet braced on the footrope, only terror of showing fear in the presence of enlisted men driving him on. It was little more than a year since he had been introduced as a cadet in Britain to the rudiments of seamanship, navigation and gunnery. It had been scant preparation for the rigours of the voyage to China, for a war whose purpose he could scarcely understand, and none for the ordeal he knew he must now face. At thirteen on his last birthday he was old enough for the Navy to expect a man's role of him as Rason's messenger.

Plover's screw was thrashing slowly, barely sufficiently to hold her stationary against the current. The 68-pounder at the bow and the 32-pounder aft were ranged on the closest embrasures, the weapons charged and shotted, their crews at their numbered positions. Silence reigned on deck, every eye fixed on the glowering forts. *Plover* was to provide cover for *Opossum*, to starboard, which had now gently pushed her bows against the centremost of the iron stakes blocking the river. Men had been lowered to wrap a chain around it and, once secured, *Opossum* would drift back, set her screw in reverse, and drag it free. Removing it would provide just enough room for the two gunboats to slip through towards the next barrier, a floating boom of stout timbers – and closer still to the as-yet silent guns of the Chinese forts.

Nine other gunboats, similar shallow-draught units built for Baltic service five years before, hovered downstream and were ready to follow when the obstacles were cleared. Two French vessels lay beyond, their draughts too deep to venture up the channel. Enemies so often before, the French were now allies against the Chinese. They too were committed to forcing passage of the Pei-Ho River, essential as it was if land forces were to be launched towards Peking. Moored close was a warship of another old enemy, the United States, the *Toey-Wan*, no party to this particular quarrel but closely observing the drama now unfolding.

Three times the chain was drawn taut and *Opossum* thrashed astern, and three times the chain slipped and flailed and the iron stake still stood defiantly. Dawlish could identify *Opossum's* captain, Willes, up in the bows himself, urging his men on. The previous night, under cover of darkness, he had taken three boats upstream on muffled oars to investigate the barriers. Passing the row of spikes undetected, Willes had placed explosives on the boom there. A breach had been blown in it but the blast had alerted the defenders so that the small expedition had been lucky to slip back downriver alive. The Chinese had the boom repaired by mid-morning. Breaching that boom again, permanently so, was now a personal challenge to *Opossum's* commander and yet another effort was being made to secure the chain.

And this time, as foam boiled under the gunboat's counter, the chain held, bar tight. *Opossum* suddenly leapt astern and the stake arced down and was lost below the surging waters as it was dragged free.

"He's done it, By God!" Hope waved his cap towards *Opossum*. A cheer rose unbidden from the crews of both vessels. Willes had bounded to his bridge and was bowing towards the admiral, his own cap swept off in salute, a smile of quiet triumph on his face, an obstacle overcome, yet accepting, undaunted, that the worst might yet lie ahead. And Dawlish realised that Willes was the sort of man he wanted to be himself.

Plover moved into the narrow gap, the remaining stakes to either side all but brushing her flanks. *Opossum* followed and both gunboats ploughed towards the boom four hundred yards ahead.

Suddenly a flash from the rampart to port, an instant later the crash of the gun's report and a roundshot whistling low, though harmlessly, above *Plover's* bridge. Garish banners were rising above the earthworks amid a crash of drums and gongs. Black muzzles were appearing at the embrasures as cannon were run out. Another blast, and another, and then the entire wall of earth was half-obscured by a rolling wall of flame-shot smoke. Mud-streaked white plumes were rising around the gunboats. Dawlish heard a crash, felt a tremor through the deck beneath his feet and realised that *Plover* had been hit somewhere below the bulwark. He was trembling now and he found his bowels loosening. He tightened every muscle and somehow kept control.

"Signal *Engage the Enemy*, Lieutenant Rason." Hope's voice was calm. He made no move for cover and remained standing exposed on the bridge. The flags were already climbing the signal halliard to summon the other gunboats into action as *Plover's* bow and stern weapons blasted in response to Rason's shouted orders.

Now Hell engulfed the *Plover*.

It was nothing like what Dawlish's childish reading of the life of Nelson, or familiarity with engravings of Trafalgar or the Nile, had prepared him for. Huge rents were torn in the bulwarks as a succession of solid balls smashed into them, showering splinters across the deck and cutting down anybody in their path. *Plover's* 68- and 32-pounders were in continuous action with bursting-shell, their reports deafening, their crews already depleted by splinters, replacements summoned from the engine room. Choking smoke churned across the deck and through the murk Dawlish saw a boy of his own age lugging a bagged charge towards the bow weapon, then sway, headless, before he dropped, the open neck fountaining scarlet. Others, dragged aside and disregarded in the tumult, lay mangled on the decks, some still, some crawling towards an impossible succour.

But still the small group on the bridge stood immobile. Hope scanning the forts through his telescope as if he were viewing a regatta. Douglas concentrating on signals to the gunboats downriver. Rason calling commands to *Plover's* crew. McKenna calmly sketching the forts in his notebook. And Dawlish trembling, but somehow enduring, though feeling that this could not be happening, that he was a remote observer of someone else's nightmare.

Now *Plover* – or maybe *Opossum*, for she too was firing continuously – drew blood, a shell bursting in the nearest embrasure, the sudden sight of a black canon-barrel hurled upwards, and what might have been bodies too, and an instant later a larger flash as the weapon's munition store exploded. A cheer rose from the gunboats' crews, hastily silenced by the gun-captains as they urged reloading. Unable to manoeuvre in the narrow channel, the two gunboats could only endure, or retreat, and Hope was showing no inclination to fall back. But several of the other gunboats were now moving cautiously forward – *Lee* and *Haughty* had already manoeuvred through the downstream barrier – and their bow-mounted weapons were already in action, and *Banterer's* too, from further downriver. Plumes of mud were rising before the earthworks as their shells fell short, but some were gouging into the ramparts or falling beyond them to do unseen damage.

Dawlish suddenly felt a gale lashing past him and saw Rason exploding in a spray of blood, his features locked in surprise for an instant before his fragments were sucked away in the roundshot's wake. Himself spattered with Rason's flesh, Hope was already regaining his composure.

"You take command, Douglas," he gasped to his flag-lieutenant. Then he noticed Dawlish, pale and shaking, grasping the splintered rail before him. "Go forward to the bow-chaser, lad," he said. "Present my compliments to the gun-captain and congratulate him and his crew on their excellent shooting."

Dawlish descended – his knees were trembling – and somehow made his way forward across the debris-strewn deck. He clambered over fallen spars and shattered boats, ducking and cringing at every report, choking in the rolling smoke, ignoring cries of agony, jerking his gaze away from the mangled remains of what had been living beings only minutes before. He found the 68-pounder being served by half its crew, some bloodied, all smoked-grimed and sweat-sodden, with red-rimmed eyes and blackened faces, yet still following the rhythm of firing, sponging, loading and firing again with faultless precision. Their mates lay dead or moaning in the scuppers. As the massive weapon vomited and recoiled again the gunner noticed Dawlish hovering at his side, speechless, aware that it was not an appropriate time to deliver the Admiral's compliments.

"More men, lad! Tell 'em I need more men! Anybody!"

As Dawlish scrambled aft the entire vessel shook again – another hit on the hull – and shrouds snapped and whipped. The mainmast lurched to starboard, but it held. The spindly funnel was already rent in a dozen places and spewing choking coal-smoke through them. Deafened by the report of the 32-pounder still in action at the stern Dawlish suddenly saw, through a jagged gap in the starboard bulwark, through the drifting murk, a smart-looking cutter stroking towards *Plover* on rhythmic oars. A flag streamed from the staff at the stern. It took him a moment to recognise it for what it was, a white-mottled blue rectangle at one corner, and red and white stripes below – American. The boat glided alongside as the oars were tossed and a seaman in the bows pulled it alongside with a boathook. An elderly officer in immaculate full uniform, epaulettes on his shoulders, spotless linen at this throat, handsome and white-bearded, hauled himself on board.

"I want to see the Admiral, son." His tone was one to command instant compliance.

Hope had been hit in Dawlish's absence and one trouser leg was torn. A blood-soaked bandage was bound around his thigh. His face was white, his features drawn in pain, and he was supporting himself against the rail. The soldier, McKenna was slumped behind him, obviously dead, and Douglas was shouting to the 32-pounder to shift its aim. The Admiral did not notice the newcomer until he had mounted the bridge but he flushed with surprise when he saw him.

"Commodore Josiah Tattnall, United States Navy." The white-haired officer bowed.

"I know who you are, sir," Hope said. "You must forgive my appearance, but in the circumstances..."

"No matter, sir," Tattnall flinched slightly as another round screamed overhead. "And taking account of those circumstances I thought it neighbourly to offer some assistance."

"But you're no party to this quarrel, Commodore. Your nation is neutral in the matter."

"Blood is thicker than water, Admiral," Tattnall said. "We share a heritage, sir, and nobody could take offence if I were to take off your wounded."

Hope paused for a moment, then extended his hand. "I would be in your debt, sir, and in your country's."

Their voices had never risen and they might have been engaged in drawing room courtesies. Then Tattnall looked down towards Hope's bloody leg.

"You are wounded yourself, sir. Do you desire..."

"A trifle, Commodore, the merest trifle," Hope said. "Some other poor fellows deserve more attention."

Dawlish was detailed to supervise the evacuation process, moving across the deck with the American seamen. They dragged injured men from under debris, shaking torn and inert bodies for signs of life, ignoring the cries of the wounded as they were lifted on to hammocks or sheets of torn canvas, carried to the side and lowered into the waiting cutter. Busy now, Dawlish found himself becoming calmer and he kept count, realising with horror that almost three-quarters of *Plover's* crew of forty were dead or wounded. The cannonade continued throughout, the bow and stern-chasers still in action, but now at a slower rate. Chinese balls were still crashing into the hull and bulwarks, the noise deafening.

The last of the pathetic burdens were in the cutter and the American commodore was descending from the bridge after an exchange of salutes as formal as if they had been in a peacetime harbour. He paused before he disembarked and laid an arm on Dawlish's shoulder. "Well done, son," he said, "and good..." He stopped as three men came hurrying aft, their faces powder-blackened, their uniforms obviously American despite scorching and smoke marks.

Tattnall's features broke into a grin. "What have you been doing, you rascals?" He did not sound displeased. "Don't you know we're neutrals?"

"Beg pardon, sir," said one of the men, "but they were a bit short-handed with the bow-gun. We thought it no harm to give them a hand while we were waiting."

"Get in the boat, boys," Tattnall said. "It's getting a mite too hot round here."

Dawlish had a glimpse of the cutter disappearing downstream with its cargo of misery, threading its way between the British gunboats, all now in action, though *Kestrel* seemed to have been pounded to a hulk. *Plover* must look little better. Hope must have thought the same, for when Dawlish returned to the bridge he was ordering Douglas to take the stricken gunboat downriver after transferring him – and his flag – to *Opossum*. Willes's vessel was still valiantly in action and apparently less damaged. The two gunboats drew briefly together and the admiral, obviously pain-racked, was helped across. Dawlish saw a chair carried to the bridge and Hope propped in it, waving away further attention.

Plover dropped downriver, passing *Lee* and *Haughty* steaming up to take her place. A cheer rose from their decks as she passed. The quartermaster was wounded – he had one good arm, and the other was in an improvised sling – but with only nine men still active, including boiler and engine-room crew, there was nobody to take his place. He managed to negotiate the gap in the downstream barrier and *Plover* finally dropped anchor a mile further on, where the estuary widened, out of range of the still defiant forts.

There was no rest, just a few minutes to slurp water down dry throats, to bind up minor wounds, to realise that familiar faces were gone forever. Then clearing of the wreckage began, dumping shattered spars and woodwork overboard, hacking away fallen cordage, dragging further charges and shot to the cooling guns. Worst of all was sluicing away the blood – and worse – with buckets of water hoisted from the foul river. There were too few men for the job but Douglas left them in no doubt that his new command would be returning to the fray. Dawlish laboured with the rest, muscles aching, vomiting once when confronted with something unspeakable in the scuppers, yet somehow resisting the continuous urge to throw himself down and weep. Another American boat, already all but full of wounded, came by and took off the last of *Plover's*. All the while the crash of gunfire rolled down from the forts, but it was slackening, as if both sides were nearing exhaustion.

It was late in the afternoon when a call from the leaning maintop arrested Dawlish. He looked up to see Douglas beckoning to him, telescope in hand. His climb was painfully slow, frightening even, for the shrouds were sagging and many of the ratlines had been torn away. Douglas reached a hand to him and pulled him on to the tiny platform.

"Take a look, Boy," he said. "You may never see the like again."

He hoped he never would. The tide was falling, exposing wide mud banks to either side of what was now a narrow channel. The gunboats had finally retreated downriver past the row of spikes, smoke dying around *Opossum's* stern as a fire there was extinguished, *Kestrel* seemingly stranded, her decks awash, *Haughty* listing, *Lee* hardly more than a wreck, *Cormorant* scarcely better. Beyond them great craters had been torn in the earthen walls of the Taku forts but the gaudy banners still hung above them. As the last gunfire died the sound of gongs and cheering washed across the waters. Dawlish found himself weeping.

"What now, sir?" He hoped his tears were not noticed, was ashamed of them.

A call from the river cut off Douglas's answer. A cutter had drawn alongside, a lieutenant shouting up from the sternsheets. Douglas swung himself down from the maintop and Dawlish followed. The newcomer had already climbed aboard. His uniform was filthy and a blood-streaked bandage covered one eye. Dawlish stood at a respectful distance as the two officers spoke but he saw Douglas shaking his head as if in disbelief and heard him say "It's madness. It's madness and it's murder."

The other lieutenant shrugged, raised his hands in a gesture of powerlessness. It had been agreed. Nothing could change it.

"Volunteers then," Douglas said. "Volunteers only, though God knows I've few enough to call upon."

The nearest of the forts was to be stormed. Hope was convinced that it was so badly battered, its defenders so reduced, so dazed, by the cannonade they had endured that an unexpected assault before nightfall would take it. Boats were already moving from the transports moored downriver, all laden with marines and army personnel as well as seamen. The French too were sending men and every vessel that could spare uninjured men was being called on for support. Boats like that now moored alongside – it was from *Cormorant* – were collecting men from the stricken gunboats.

Douglas refused to let stokers or engineers volunteer – they were now the majority of *Plover's* remaining complement – but three seamen did, survivors of the gun-crews. One was a grey veteran, the others in their twenties, men whose coarse humour and foul language had shocked Dawlish when he had first overheard them, men who were poor and possibly illiterate, but men who had come unbroken in spirit through the afternoon's hell and were ready for more. Their resolution shamed him and he too stepped forward. He shook as he did so but knew he could do nothing else.

There was little over an hour of daylight left as the small flotilla of boats headed for the shoreline, some under oars, others towed by steam launches. Relative cleanliness of clothing distinguished the seamen from the unengaged vessels downriver from those who had been in furious action. The marines, in boats to themselves, looked especially smart, even if their tunics had been left behind. Several craft carried scarlet-coated soldiers, sappers, their hastily-fabricated scaling ladders encumbering the rowers. The French had contributed two cutters full of seamen, unmistakable in their white and navy striped shirts. There was absolute silence, broken only by the dipping of the oars, the landing parties eyeing the ominously quiet earthwork ahead with quiet dread. The banners still drooped there on their poles but there was no sign of life. It was close to low water and two hundred yards of fresh mud had been exposed even before the normal marshy shoreline, seamed with channels, could be reached. Sharpened stakes had been closely spaced along it to form an almost continuous obstacle, their points inclined towards the river. The base of the earthwork lay two hundred yards beyond.

Dawlish found himself packed with forty others in *Cormorant's* cutter, all men gathered from the damaged and disabled gunboats and with little sense of shared identity. "Move fast once we land! Head for the fort! Then help the sappers get the ladders up," were the only instructions given by the lieutenant who had come for volunteers. He said nothing about what should happen next, but perhaps it was obvious. Dawlish had a sick realisation that the boatload he found himself in was only there to make up numbers. The marines and sappers, and the bluejackets from the ships that had not seen action, represented the real attack. The *Cormorant's* lieutenant stood now in the bow, one foot resting on the prow, a revolver in his left hand, a cutlass in his right, his ostentatiously heroic stance all too obviously adopted to quell his own fears. A grizzled bosun was steering, growling to the rowers if the pace slackened and keeping the craft level with the marines and sappers to either side. Dawlish was grasping the cutlass he knew he was still inexpert at handling, but aware that he would have been even less so with an Enfield musket. He could sense the fear around him, noticed other hands as well as his own trembling and men endlessly checking bayonets, running fingers along cutlass edges, feeling the balance of boarding axes.

The mud exposed by the falling tide was fifty yards ahead now, glistening as it caught the rays of the setting sun. There was still no movement at the forts and somebody said "The buggers have gone home. They've had enough!" and a few laughed nervously. A west-country voice, quavering, began to recite "The Lord is my shepherd…" and another joined in. Not to be outdone, an Irish voice began "Hail Mary, full of grace…"

"Belay that talk!" the bosun yelled, and at that moment the bows grounded. The lieutenant was pitched forward, head-first, into the water and then everybody seemed to be leaping over the gunwales. Other boats had also grounded in shallow water, and their occupants also were jumping overboard. Dawlish hesitated – the water could be no deeper than two feet but the boat seemed surrounded by struggling, floundering men and few seemed to be making any progress towards the shore. He levered himself over and dropped, realising too late what the problem was. His feet had plunged a foot or more into soft, warm mud and when he tried to extricate them he failed, and fell forward, head and shoulders submerged. He tried to push himself up with his arms – and somehow he was still holding the cutlass – but they too plunged into the slime and failed to support him. He breathed in water and began to choke. He felt panic rising in him, knew he could not let it master him. He paused for a moment, dragged his hands free, straightened his back and broke surface again. He managed to pull his right foot from the ooze, though he left his canvas shoe behind, advanced a pace, felt himself sinking again and yet succeeded in dragging the other foot free. He was making progress, slowly, painfully, falling, struggling to his feet again, and so too were scores of men who advanced in a ragged line through the shallows to the exposed mud bank ahead.

The entire wall of the Chinese earthwork erupted into flame, cannon blasting from the undamaged embrasures, their barrels depressed so that their balls skipped across the mud in running plumes. Gaps were torn in the advancing line, but still it moved on, slowly, painfully, step by sucking step. Figures were appearing on top of the fort's ramparts, hastily erecting small-calibre swivel guns, and others were despatching rockets that weaved and undulated and whistled before exploding among the attackers.

Dawlish had gained the drier mud now and his progress was easier. Bodies lay slumped ahead and wounded men were struggling back towards the boats. The noise of the cannon was deafening and he moved in a daze. A ball raced through the mud to his right, spattering him, and he heard a scream behind but did not turn, then ducked as a rocket corkscrewed overhead, showering sparks. He was intent only on reaching the row of sharpened stakes which the majority of the attackers had now gained. Men were chopping at the wooden spikes with axes and cutlasses, and others were trying to wrest them from the mud by main force. Over to the right the sappers seemed to have hacked a gap, and were dragging ladders through. The crowding at this barrier and the funnelling of the attackers through the breaches now being torn in it were providing the fort's defenders with an ideal target. The deadly cannonade of the larger weapons was continuous, but slow. It was the lighter, long-barrelled, fast-loading swivel weapons on the parapet which were scything down the mud-plastered assault force, marines and sappers and seaman, British and French, all indistinguishable from each other under their filth.

Heart pounding, lungs bursting, muscles screaming, his mind numb with terror, Dawlish passed through a gap, still sinking to his shins with every step. He was aware remotely that his one bare foot was giving him agony but recognised that stopping here in the open would mean certain death. The mud bank was laced with rivulets that spread out in places to wide pools. Some patches were softer than others and in them wounded were crying out not to be abandoned, their fear of sinking into the ooze all too obvious. He was conscious of others moving forward with the same laborious haste to his right and left but there was no feeling of being part of a concerted effort. Several of the gunboats had opened on the earthwork, and they had the range. Their shells screamed overhead and threw up great fountains of flame-shot soil as they burrowed into the sloped ramparts. The swivel-gunners were being driven from the parapet and the fire that still lashed the open ground still to be crossed was slackening.

Dawlish saw a deep ditch lay ahead, running parallel to the fort's walls. The low tide had reduced the water in it to a trickle so that it offered a degree of shelter. In it the assault force was cowering, officers and petty officers moving among the men in an attempt to separate them into individual parties, checking weapons and ammunition, detailing groups to carry the ladders that the sappers had brought this far by so much effort, gesturing towards the damaged ramparts that lay still almost a hundred yards distant. Dawlish saw no sign of the *Plover's* volunteers and found himself hustled into a mixed group of marines and seamen. He realised that he had dropped the cutlass somewhere and somebody shoved a mud-caked Enfield, its bayonet fixed, into his hand. It had been fired and he was too dazed to ask for cartridges to reload it. He took it mechanically, then slouched, panting, against the side of the ditch, his brain refusing to accept that in minutes he must rise and launch himself forward. He looked down and saw that his unshod right foot was bleeding, but the pain seemed distant. A few yards away he recognised Fisher, another midshipman, perhaps five years older, whom he had met once when he had delivered messages to *Banterer*, and who looked as exhausted as himself. Fisher lifted his head and recognised him.

"Good to see you here, Young Dawlish," he called. "Good for *Plover!*"

Dawlish nodded mutely.

"I know I'm not born to be shot," Fisher shouted. "You neither Dawlish, I'll wager! We'll laugh about this when we're admirals!"

"Two minutes!" The word was passed along the line. "Two minutes! Ready!"

Frantic flag signals were being waved back to the gunboats to cease firing. Dawlish was shaking, his breath rasping, and the thought of sucking mud ahead was even more dreadful than of the gunfire that must be faced. His suddenly felt his bladder emptying. The wet warmth brought a surge of shame – and something worse, a fear that he might not be able to force himself from the ditch, that he might still cringe here when others surged forward, that he might prove what he suspected he might be, a coward.

He felt an arm on his shoulder, looked up to see a mud-smeared seaman he did not recognise, grey haired, middle-aged. His eyes

17

showed understanding and no contempt. "You'll be fine, lad," he said. "Stick with me and you'll be fine."

The fire from the gunboats died. There was dead silence for a moment that seemed to last a hundred years, then yells of "Forward!"

And at the word Dawlish somehow forced himself to scramble up the bank, conscious of a wave of men to his left and right doing the same. His feet slipped on the wet incline and he found himself sliding back, but the unknown seaman was grabbing his arm and dragging him up. The attackers were plodding slowly ahead, a continuous line initially, but then forced into separate groups, as some encountered softer mud. Dawlish and his companion were advancing over harder ground, part of a cluster of seamen. They were catching up with the leaders and the base of the badly damaged wall was perhaps fifty yards ahead. A shell's crater had torn a gap in the hedge of sharpened stakes, a focus for the advance. There was still no sign of defenders. Over to the right a knot of sappers and marines were dragging scaling ladders forward and another group – Frenchmen, led by an officer who was waving a tricolour flag – had almost reached the rampart.

Eyes fixed on the silent wall, careless of what was underfoot, Dawlish suddenly found himself sinking to knee height. He tried to kick free, sank deeper and he cried out in rising panic. The seaman was to his left and he came over, careful of his own footing, and reached out his musket, butt first. Dawlish, gasping thanks, grasped it and was pulled free. At that moment the earthwork once more erupted in flame and smoke. The attackers were too close for the cannons to depress sufficiently and their balls screamed uselessly overhead, but through the drifting smoke Chinese troops were surging on to the parapet, dragging swivel guns again or lining up with muskets.

The full blast of the defenders' fire smashed into the attackers, tearing down the nearest, giving pause to those following behind. Flame lashed from the swivel guns, hurling dozens of small balls with each report, and the musket-armed troops on the parapet were firing by volley, and with a rhythmic discipline none had expected of the Chinese. Rockets rushed from the smoke, their tails blazing, and fireballs, burning with white intensity, were being thrown down from the wall. A seaman ahead of Dawlish went down to one of them, the burning substance clinging to him as he rolled screaming in the mud. In the midst of the crashing noise Dawlish heard what might have been a loud sigh by his side and turned to see his own unknown seaman helper falling, his chest bloodied, red fragments spraying from his back. Others were going down all around. Men were falling back from the wall and as Dawlish himself turned away he saw the a scaling ladder arcing away from the wall, thrown back by the defenders, men clinging to it as it fell.

All along the front officers were shouting orders to retreat. Now a new agony commenced. Still scourged from the walls, the return through the clinging mud was even more terrible than the advance. The pleadings of the wounded were more urgent now, more pitiful, and Dawlish found himself helping a marine carry a seaman with a hideously burned face. "I'm blind, I'm blind," he was crying. Twice they dropped him in the sludge and he screamed in despair that they might abandon him before they could pull him free. Men were still falling to the goading fire from the earthwork, but the light was fading and promising some degree of cover.

Somehow they reached the shelter of the ditch with the burned man. It was full of exhausted, bitter, wounded men and somebody was shouting "It was murder! Murder I say!" until a blow silenced him. Dawlish saw Fisher come lurching down the bank, one of the last to return and supporting a white-haired officer with a wounded leg. A cold light illuminated the mud between them and the fort as the Chinese burned blue fireballs along the wall. At intervals rockets came snaking over, showering sparks and mostly bursting harmlessly. A mocking cacophony of gongs celebrated the Chinese triumph.

It was in the early hours of morning when Dawlish was taken off with the last of the attackers. They had stood up to their waists in mud and water as they waited, passing wounded overhead to the boats that had come for them. He was cold and exhausted, numb with pity and sorrow and horror. He had seen his first action, and it had been the Royal Navy's first defeat in over forty years. But he felt satisfaction too.

For though he had known terror he had not broken.

HMS Leonidas

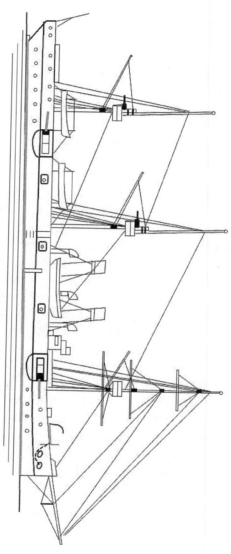

Builder: Pembroke Dockyard
Launched: February 1881
Completed: September 1881
Displacement: 4300 tons
Length: 315 feet overall
Beam: 46 feet
Draught: 20 feet
Armour: 1.5" deck, 1.5" gunshields

Machinery: Compound Engines, Twin Screw
5500 Horsepower
Speed: 17 Knot (Max.)
11 Knots (Cruising)
Armament: 10 X 6" Breechloaders
4 X 14" Torpedo-launchers
3 X .45" Gatlings in Fighting Tops
Complement: 280

2

He had achieved it at last, his heart's desire for three decades, command, as Captain, of his own ship of the Royal Navy. Nor was she some workaday gunboat or outdated sloop, nor an aging ironclad cruiser, but a lithe and powerful first vessel of a new and innovative class. He had loved her, had lusted for her, ever since he had seen her on the stocks at Pembroke Dockyard, when she had been a bait. Topcliffe had laid her before him to induce him to accept another assignment, one that had almost cost his life – and his wife Florence's also. But now, in early April 1882, HMS *Leonidas* was his. He had supervised *Leonidas's* completion and fitting-out at Pembroke and, after his promotion seven months before, her acceptance trials also.

The commissioning ceremony at Portsmouth Dockyard had been a strictly naval occasion but the celebration that afternoon in his own on-board quarters was personal, Dawlish's family and friends present as well as those of his officers. His father was there, slightly tipsy but not yet embarrassingly so. His step-mother – no older than himself – had met Florence today for the first time and was treating her with politeness icy to the point of insult. She seemed all the more angry because his four-year old half-brother Edgar – clad in a new sailor suit for the occasion – had taken to Florence and had not left her all afternoon. And Mrs. Rowena Dawlish's scarcely disguised contempt for a woman who had once been a servant was not the only scarcely-veiled disdain that Florence ignored. The wife of Commander Edgerton, Leonidas's executive officer, had been pointedly unavailable when she had been invited to tea previously and even now was keeping aloof. Edgerton himself was pleasant enough. He was in his forties and had come recommended as stolidly competent. He did not seem to resent a younger man's promotion and Dawlish suspected that he was reluctant to take on ultimate responsibility for a vessel.

The cabin was large – it occupied the entire stern of the cruiser, its after-side the port-holed transom. It was plainly furnished, by Dawlish's choice. A desk, bookshelves, four armchairs and a dining table large enough to seat his officers when he invited them – not more frequently than once a fortnight, he had decided. Frowning down from one bulkhead was the large official portrait of the Queen. Above his desk were three framed photographs. Florence in white, smiling. The faded sepia of the only image he had of the mother he only half-remembered. And his nurse, Mrs. Gore, who had died the year before and who would have been more proud of this moment than Florence herself. His sleeping berth and washing facilities were located just forward on the starboard side, a steward's pantry similarly placed to port. In the coming months – and years perhaps – this cabin would be his private office, his library, his dining room and his home, isolated from officers and men alike, an invitation to it to be either feared or hoped for, no visitor to it a casual one. But for now it was thronged and he moved through the guests with forced ease of manner. He had never enjoyed large social gatherings but it was now his duty to seem to do so.

"Adolphus is drunk." Florence spoke in an undertone and nodded towards his brother-in-law. "Can somebody get him out, Nick? Show him the guns or engines or something?"

"I'll ask O'Rourke."

He did, and his sister Susan, old before her time and yet again in an interesting condition, flushed with relief when the torpedo lieutenant approached her husband good-humouredly and bore him off to admire the compound engines. Susan's was not the only unease. In a far corner the staff engineer, Latham, was standing silently with his wife, a homely-looking woman who seemed bewildered by the company. A group next to them, Sub-Lieutenant Leigh and his parents and sisters, were laughing with Tadley, the surgeon, and ignoring them completely. Dawlish sought out Florence. He found her trying to make conversation, unsuccessfully for once, with Lieutenant Takenaka Katamori, a Japanese officer on temporary assignment to the Royal Navy. Florence looked perhaps more beautiful than he had ever known, pride and happiness rather than countenance alone making her so. He disengaged her.

"Latham and his wife," he said. "That couple over there. It's difficult for them."

She saw it immediately, the patient endurance of decent people who were never allowed to forget their origins, the artificer who against all odds had raised himself to commissioned rank, the woman with work-worn hands and a kindly face who was conscious of her accent, her imperfect grammar.

"I'll ask Miss Weston." The cheerful spinster who had founded the Sailors' Rest at Devonport, and whom Florence had helped set up another in Portsmouth, was in animated discussion with Purdon, the gunnery-lieutenant. She was no doubt impressing him with the need to provide clean lodgings, cheap meals and freedom from temptations for seamen when they came ashore. A moment later Florence was bringing her to meet the Lathams. For Miss Weston, Dawlish knew, neither rank nor class counted.

A slight commotion. A large woman, untidily but richly dressed, her pince-nez twinkling in the light, a broad smile on her great, friendly sheep's face, was pushing through the throng towards Florence. They embraced in obvious affection with no indication that the one's father and brother were employed by the other's as coachmen, nor that they had once been mistress and maid.

"So late! So unforgivably late! The wrong train, I'm afraid! But you'll forgive me, Florence? Yes – I knew you would!" Lady Agatha suddenly noticed Dawlish coming towards them. "And congratulations, Commander! No – I mean Captain! Captain Dawlish now! And so well deserved! Such happiness! For you, Captain, for Dear Florence!"

"And your brother, did he come with you?" Dawlish had invited Lord Oswald for the sake of propriety but neither wanted nor expected that he would come.

"Dear Oswald!" Agatha said. "He sends his apologies, would have loved to have been here. But he's been so busy since he got back from Washington! And not just at the Foreign Office! What with the preparations for the wedding he hasn't got a moment!"

The story had filled the society columns, yet another American heiress marrying into an ancient and noble British family. A glance passed between Dawlish and Florence but neither commented. Miss Rebecca Brewster was the first woman Oswald had ever shown any interest in.

Lady Agatha would be staying for a week, as often before, at their villa in Southsea's Albert Grove and assisting, as she always did, at the Sailors' Rest. She blinked through her thick lenses. "And there's Miss Weston too! I must speak to her! So much to be done! So little time to do it!" She pushed through the crowd as resolutely as an ironclad through a stormy sea.

Dawlish passed from group to group, accepted congratulations, exchanged small-talk with wives and parents, spoke about the voyage ahead and saw that his father had cornered Ross, the marine lieutenant. From what he had seen of him so far, the godly young man would be unlikely to welcome the smoking room stories his father was almost certainly regaling him with. If O'Rourke was not already engaged he would have asked him to take his father also to admire the guns. He saw too that his step-mother and Mrs. Edgerton had found each other and they looked quickly away when he noticed that their gaze – cold resentment incarnate – fixed on Florence.

Time for action.

He drew Florence aside, nodded towards the two ladies. "I think Miss Weston might need some help this week," he said.

Her eyes sparkled with delight. "I do believe she might." She supressed a smile.

He watched her approach the two women – that Edgar was firmly holding her hand seemed to add fresh venom to his step-mother's glance – and they reluctantly followed her. He joined them. Mrs. Latham was laughing now at something Lady Agatha had said and her husband's smile was unfeigned.

"Agatha," Florence said. "I'd like you to meet Nicholas's step-mother and ..." she paused, "It is Mrs. Edgerton, isn't it? That's right – I was sure it was." She made the introductions. "Lady Agatha – Lord Kegworth's daughter, you know – Mrs. Edgerton. Lady Agatha – the other Mrs. Dawlish." The elocution lessons that Dawlish was never supposed to know had been paid for from housekeeping money were never better employed.

"It's so good to be here with my oldest, dearest friend," Lady Agatha said. "You know that we were girls together? And all that we came through in Thrace! The snow! The Bashi Bazooks!"

"We can laugh about it now, Agatha," Florence said. "But let me introduce Miss Weston too. Founder of the Sailors' Rest, you know. And Mrs. Edgerton, and Step Mother – I may call you that, mayn't I? – allow me to introduce Mr. and Mrs Latham."

He could leave it to Florence now, Dawlish thought as he moved away to speak to other guests. Her two enemies would be flattered to agree to helping Lady Agatha in her charitable work while she was in Portsmouth. Only too late would they find that it would involve carbolic soap and lye and mops and floor-scrubbing in the new extension to the Sailors' Rest. Lady Agatha, earl's daughter and first woman to be elected to the Royal Society, never hesitated to roll up her sleeves, whether in a haven for Balkan refugees or in a hostel in Britain.

And soon it was time to rescue Ross – there was no help for it, for Dawlish's father was now seriously drunk. The bosun, Egdean, reliable in any circumstance, must be sent for and instructed to steer him out to admire the ground tackle.

*

"She's beautiful," Florence said.

"And I think she's beautiful too!" Edgar was still holding her hand.

They were standing on the bridge as the winter day's grey light faded. All the guests had left other than Dawlish's relations.

"As beautiful as the *Victory*, Ted?" Dawlish had brought him out the previous day to see Nelson's flagship. It still rode proudly at anchor more than seven decades after Trafalgar.

"More beautiful," Edgar paused, then added "Nicholas." He was still unsure if he could call an adult with grey streaks in his dark hair and beard by his Christian name, even if he had been assured that he was his brother. He had been in tears when he had been told of the significance of the silver plate embedded in the *Victory's* deck. "It won't happen to you, will it, Nicholas? Not like Lord Nelson."

"No. Ted," Dawlish had said. "Nobody's going to shoot me."

"Not ever?"

"No, Ted. Not ever."

Florence was no less impressed by the ship.

"You deserve her, Nick." Her voice had the slightest hint of sadness, sadness he knew she would never admit to him. And he felt the same, though he too would not admit it. A long parting was imminent. "You deserve her and she deserves you."

Even in the deepening gloom she was indeed beautiful, all 4300 tons of her, all 315 feet from stem to stern. *Leonidas* looked exactly what she was, a lean, fast greyhound, first in a new breed of cruiser. Her frames and plating were of steel, her unseen armoured deck within domed to protect the vital spaces beneath, her powerful but economical engines guaranteeing not just speed but endurance, her sailing rig the merest concession to tradition.

Dawlish regretted only one feature of which modernity had deprived *Leonidas*. He would have liked a figurehead of the unyielding Spartan king whose name she bore, a reminder of Thermopylae, of what discipline and loyalty demanded, of what skill at arms could deliver. But the guns more than compensated, the ten six-inch breechloaders on the open deck, the most modern and most accurate available. Four were mounted on turntables, two forward, two aft, and projected from the sides of the vessel on sponsons to provide fire ahead and astern as well as on the beam. The other six, three a side, were positioned to fire through broadside ports. Hidden from sight were the ports on the lower deck, two per side, through which fourteen-inch Whitehead torpedoes could be launched. Dawlish loved these weapons too. He had perhaps more confidence in them than any other man. It was not just because he had used them successfully in action – though the circumstances of their use must remain secret – but also because he had engineered improvements in them, was proud that they incorporated the Dawlish Cam, a refinement of his own invention. It was reassuring that O'Rourke, the lieutenant responsible for them, was as fascinated as himself.

"Will you sail her… Nicholas?" Edgar was looking uncertainly to the masts and yards above and then towards the two high funnels, surrounded by the cluster of ventilator cowls that rose between the fore and mainmasts. They were reminders that *Leonidas's* barquentine rig – square on the foremast and the fore-and-aft on the main and mizzen – represented coal-economy on long cruises in distant waters, and not the primary propulsion.

"No," Dawlish said. "Not on this voyage, Ted. We'll be steaming all the way. I'll show you the engines presently." For the purpose of sending this first ship of a class of five across half the world was to test the reliability and economy of engines and boilers and to identify possible refinements which could be applied to her sisters – *Leander* and *Phaeton*, *Arethusa* and *Amphion* – which were still under construction in Glasgow and Pembroke. Unlike the black-hulled ships lying here at Portsmouth, *Leonidas* had been painted white to repel the scorching heat she would encounter in the Red Sea and Indian Ocean.

"And this is where you would stand if it ever came to a fight, Nicholas?" Florence could see that the open-backed wheelhouse at its centre bridge spanning the beam ahead of the funnels offered little protection. "It seems so exposed. Thank God there's no chance of that."

It was exposed, just as *Victory's* quarterdeck had been on the day of her tragedy and glory, but Dawlish knew that he would never make use of the cylindrical armoured conning position that supported this bridge. As the only Royal Navy officer to have taken an ironclad, albeit not a British one, into battle, he knew that under fire he could not bring himself to seek the shelter of a metal citadel while others must be exposed on open decks. His place would be on the open bridge. He suspected that most other commanders would take the same decision.

The light was almost gone, lights winking onshore and across the harbour, the evening's chill growing. Dawlish would have to ask O'Rourke to get his father and his brother-in-law to their hotel as inconspicuously as possible. Egdean could provide discreet support. His sister and his step-mother could follow in a separate cab and take Edgar with them.

He felt a surge of love as he hoisted his little half-brother in his arms and hugged him to him.

"May I see the guns again?" The child asked.

"A last time then. And you like the ship?"

"I want one of my own... Nicholas"

"One day, Ted," Dawlish said. "One day perhaps."

*

Dawlish spent the following day in London. He wondered why Admiral Sir Richard Topcliffe had invited him to lunch at his club. Topcliffe always had a reason, even if was not immediately apparent. And as always, he was in mufti and his role in the Admiralty – or perhaps elsewhere in Government – seemed as unclear, though probably as powerful, as ever.

"Just a small celebration of your promotion, Dawlish," he said over coffee.

Conversation during the meal had been stilted and Dawlish did not think that the admiral needed his confirmation of *Leonidas's* trial results. They had probably been on his desk within twenty-four hours of her all but touching seventeen knots on the measured mile.

"Well deserved promotion too, Dawlish." No reference to the service the cruiser's command rewarded. Well-deserved the prize had been but had Dawlish failed, Topcliffe, and the government he served, would have had no hesitation in repudiating him.

"And I'm pleased too that you liked my suggestion to take Takenaka, Dawlish."

On secondment from the Imperial Japanese Navy, Lieutenant Takenaka Katamori, was now *Leonidas's* navigating officer. Dawlish knew better than to refuse the admiral's suggestions. Compliance with them in the past had earned him the advancement that he craved. They had also come close to killing him.

"He's made an excellent impression, sir," Dawlish said. "His work's meticulous." He could say nothing more, for it was impossible to gauge what went on beneath Takenaka's impassive exterior.

"It's important to be well in with the Japanese," Topcliffe said. "They're stronger by the year and they'll be the best ally we can have for keeping the Russians in check in the Far East. People like Takenaka, they'll be their leaders of tomorrow. Best to have them on our side."

"I can see the sense of it, sir." Dawlish's tone was neutral. More would be coming.

"It's not so straightforward, I fear. Other players, Dawlish, other players. The Chinese most of all. They've got to be taken into account even if they're not sure what they want themselves. Too disunited, too corrupt, too wedded to the past. And weaker than they want to admit to themselves."

"I doubt if I'll see too much of them, sir." Dawlish tried not to make it sound like a leading question. His orders were to take *Leonidas* to Hong Kong, testing boilers and machinery to the limit on the way, subject her to a quick refit there, and to return just as quickly. The only Chinese he would see would be dockyard coolies.

"I doubt it too, Dawlish." Topcliffe looked him straight in the eye and his voice was even. "But if you had to deal with the Chinese – or with our future Japanese allies, or anybody else – I've no doubt that I could rely on your initiative and on your judgement. And on your willingness to take hard decisions. I'm thinking of unexpected situations, Dawlish, the sort of thing that can't be predicted. They happen."

"I'd do my best to live up to your trust, sir." It was obviously not wise to probe further.

Topcliffe was gesturing to the waiter to bring him the bill for signature. "It can be lonely, damn lonely, as a captain, Dawlish," he said. "Long weary hours alone in one's quarters. I'm sending a few volumes to *Leonidas* to help you while away your leisure hours. No! No need to thank me! Just a small token of esteem."

There were more than a dozen when they arrived. All recent, all related to China and Japan.

And only one about Korea.

It seemed that nobody knew much about the Hermit Kingdom.

*

Another interview was more painful, not for Dawlish but for the young officer who was invited to meet him alone in his quarters. Sub-Lieutenant Leigh was clearly mystified as to why he was summoned but he relaxed somewhat after Dawlish sat him down and asked if he would like coffee. Leigh did, and before the steward brought it he was confirming that he had enjoyed his role in the preparations for departure. He was also looking forward to the voyage, had never been East of Suez so far. Dawlish mentioned that his own first experience overseas had been in China and that Leigh would find it interesting there.

The coffee came. Leigh took two lumps of sugar. Dawlish took none. They sipped.

"There's just one point I'd like you to clarify." Dawlish set his cup and saucer down.

Leigh looked alarmed. There was always something that a young officer knew that he had left undone or something he could have done better. "Yes, sir," he said.

"Mr. Latham and his wife," Dawlish's tone was even. "I got the impression that you ignored them pointedly the other day. That you saw they were embarrassed. But that still you made no attempt to put them at their ease."

"I, I mean, it wasn't meant, it…" Leigh was blushing with obvious guilt. Words failed him.

"Would you like to tell me why, Mr. Leigh?" A slight edge now to Dawlish's voice.

"It's because…"

"Yes, Mr. Leigh?"

"He's not a gentleman, sir. He's a tradesman." The words came out in a rush. "And his wife – my mother said that…"

Dawlish cut him off. "After myself, Mr. Latham is the most important man on this ship – you understand? I can do without you, but not without him. Do you realise what that man endured to earn his position? And his wife also? A splendid lady, from what I've seen of her."

"I could hardly introduce her to my mother, sir." Leigh was grasping at any straw.

"And why is that, Mr. Leigh?"

"My mother's cousin is the Duke of Holderness."

"First cousin? Second? Third? Maybe even fourth, fifth, sixth?"

"Fourth cousin." Leigh's head dropped and his voice was a whisper.

Dawlish guessed that His Grace probably didn't know of her existence. No need to press that point further. It was perhaps unfair to blame Leigh. Many more senior officers had probably set him an example. On many ships the presence of engineers in the wardroom was deeply resented, their exposure to thinly-veiled ridicule a daily misery. Real naval officers still sailed their ships and only steamed them when they had no option.

"Could you explain to me the advantages of a triple expansion engine over a compound?" Dawlish asked. "Or the purpose of a condenser or an economiser?"

Leigh looked wretched now. "No, sir."

"Could you tell me how an electric dynamo functions?"

"No, sir."

"But Mr. Latham could."

Dawlish stood up, went to his desk and opened the drawer. He extracted a thin object six inches long and wrapped in paper. He handed it to Leigh.

"Take it out. It's greased, so be careful not to get it on your uniform."

It was a steel shaft, its diameter varying in steps along its length.

"Every dimension is accurate to within two-thousandths of an inch, Mr. Leigh. Who do you think made it?"

"Mr. Latham, sir?"

"No, Mr. Leigh. I did. On a lathe." He had and he prized it. It was the drive-shaft for the original Dawlish Cam, his invention that had improved torpedo depth-keeping. There had been half-a-dozen earlier attempts before he got it right.

"I've heard of a lathe, sir."

"Good, Mr. Leigh! An excellent start! So do you know what you're going to do now? You're to approach Mr. Latham once we're at sea — no need to mention the other day, or this conversation, which remains confidential between you and me — and you'll ask him how to operate a lathe. And ask him to explain the ship's machinery to you until you're almost as familiar with it as he is himself. You'll have spare time enough for it."

"Yes, sir." Realisation that it could have been worse.

It was time to go, but as he reached the door Dawlish called him back.

"Take this shaft with you, Mr. Leigh. I'm looking forward to receiving a copy."

"Thank you, sir."

Dawlish had endured more painful interviews in his own youth.

*

And finally departure, last signals and acknowledgements exchanged, *Leonidas* slipping her moorings and heading slowly towards the harbour's narrow entrance.

Past *Victory* to starboard, the dockyard and town quays to port. Then past the Point and the Square Tower beyond it where for centuries families had stood to wave welcome or farewell to their menfolk. They were there now, a ragged knot, officer's wives and children and parents indistinguishable at this distance from those of enlisted men. Florence would be there, Dawlish knew, and Lady Agatha with her, opera glasses trained on the bridge where he stood so impassively, so proudly. He allowed himself to turn, to raise his hand in salute, in silent gratitude and love, knowing that they would see him even if he could not distinguish them among the flutter of waving handkerchiefs.

Out then into the broadening waters of Spithead, engines building to half-revolutions, the bows nudging slightly to port to pass the great artificial islands of the Spitbank and Horse Sand forts, past their grey bulk and dark gun-muzzles, swinging south five miles further on, and afterwards arcing over to the South West.

HMS *Leonidas* was on her way and Dawlish was in command.

His heart's desire.

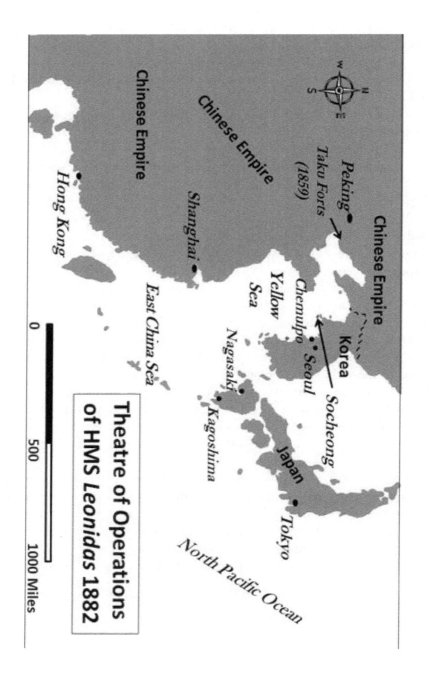

Theatre of Operations
of HMS *Leonidas* 1882

3

In the mid-morning of July the fourth 1882 Dawlish's newly painted gig came alongside *HMS Iron Duke*. Egdean, *Leonidas's* bosun, had ensured that the crew's turn-out was impeccable, their boat-drill even more so. In the steaming humidity Dawlish found the weight of his full uniform a torment.

As he climbed to the entry port he glanced back to see *Leonidas* swinging at anchor a half-mile distant in the broad expanse that separated Hong Kong from Kowloon. He felt a thrill of pride for her smartness – her hull and upperworks gleaming white, her funnels and masts deep yellow – and clean again despite the black dust-cloud that had enveloped her during coaling two days before. He and his officers had laboured with the crew to load the endless sacks from the lighters alongside, back-breaking and filthy work, their participation a lesson that no task was too menial to be important. She had been towed to her present mooring after her brief refit in the Hope drydock at Aberdeen, a few miles to the south.

A bosun's pipe trilled as Dawlish came on *Iron Duke's* deck and he returned the salutes of the officers awaiting him. Immediate formalities complete, the captain led him aft in silence. Dawlish guessed that he was older than his own thirty-six years by at least fifteen and he sensed a hint of the resentment that so many felt against his own early promotion to captain and his immediate appointment to such a desirable command.

Iron Duke was the flagship of the China Station and since last evening, since the despatch-vessel *Vigilant* had returned him from Chemulpo, she was once more flying the flag of the Station Commander, Admiral George Willes. He had been absent in recent weeks, since before Dawlish's arrival. Dawlish had hoped to pay him his compliments before *Leonidas,* not assigned to the China Station, would start in two days on the first leg of her return to Britain. He had seen Willes on one occasion only, twenty-three years before, but he had never forgotten him.

The sort of man he wanted to be himself.

They met in the Willes' elegantly panelled and furnished saloon, a remnant of an age already dying, at stark variance with the austere functionalism of his own quarters on *Leonidas*. Though the glass casements had been thrown open it was still oppressively warm. The air carried a faint odour of the night-soil that fertilised the fields on the northern shore.

Willes had aged – but so too had Dawlish. He realised that he himself must look now rather as Willes had looked then, still young, yet old and senior enough for midshipmen to approach with caution, aware that he was first and foremost their captain, no matter how relaxed his manner might sometimes seem. He hoped too that he conveyed the same impression of quiet competence, resolution and toughness that Willes had demonstrated on the *Opossum* that day on the Pei-Ho River.

The usual courtesies followed and a steward brought wine. "I understand you made a fast passage, Captain," Willes said.

"Fast, and more uneventful than we could have hoped, sir, and under steam all the way. Eleven point one knots average speed." It was hard to keep the pride from his voice. Nine and a half thousand miles, two hurried re-coaling stops, never less than one hundred and eighty-four tons per hour loaded even in the steam-oven that had been Aden.

"Steam all the way!" Willes was visibly impressed. "It's a new navy, Captain. Perhaps too new for many officers ever to adapt to easily."

"Yet one that demands as much courage and initiative as ever," Dawlish said, He hesitated, afraid that his next words might sound sycophantic. But he had waited twenty-three years to say them and now he did. "I remember you at the Taku forts in '59, sir," he said. "You inspired me then. You inspired us all." And so Willes had, though he was not the only man that day whose example Dawlish had tried to live up to ever since.

Willes was obviously embarrassed. "Just my duty," he said. "Just my duty – you'll understand that now, Captain. But I'm afraid I didn't know you were there and I can't remember seeing you." He smiled. "I was somewhat preoccupied that day. So too were you, I imagine. You must have been young. Very young."

"Thirteen and a half, sir" The half had seemed very important at the time. "It seems like yesterday."

"None of us are going to forget the Taku forts." Willes shook his head. "Some hard lessons learned there that day, some very hard lessons. And I'll wager you've learned a few more yourself since then." He smiled, and his look conveyed recognition that they shared a brotherhood of duty, skill and courage, a pleasing look. He moved to the open stern casement, looked out towards *Leonidas*.

"I understand that you're almost ready for sea, Captain Dawlish," he said.

"In two days, sir, we'll be heading for England, Home and Beauty." *And Florence embodies all three*, Dawlish thought, and his heart soared.

"There's going to be a slight change of plan," Willes said. He moved to his desk, put on his spectacles – Dawlish noticed that he seemed discomfited by being seen with them – and picked up a small sheaf of papers. The uppermost was a telegram.

"You know I've been to Korea, Dawlish?" he said. "Diplomatic stuff, the sort of thing we bluff sailormen are called upon at times to undertake?"

Dawlish nodded. Discussions that started like this, especially if they involved telegrams, tended to lead to something usually onerous, often difficult and occasionally dangerous. Reunion with Florence might already be receding into an uncertain future.

"Korea's opening up, and not before time either," Willes said. "Everybody – French, Americans, Germans, Russians, even the Japanese – has been negotiating for access. You know the sort of thing, free trade especially. Our own efforts to secure a treaty were being conducted by staff from the Embassy in Peking. Damn slow they were about it too. Protocol had to be observed, endlessly observed, because the Chinese still think they've got feudal rights in Korea, even if they haven't exercised them for years."

"But I understood you'd been to sign a treaty, sir?" Dawlish was less concerned with diplomatic niceties than with the content of that telegram.

"I was," Willes said. "We had to, and fast, because the Americans had beaten us to it and we couldn't let the French and the Russians and God knows who else to do the same. While our diplomatic people were shuttling between Peking and Korea and worrying about forms of address and degrees of precedence, our Yankee cousins ignored the flummeries and negotiated a concise business-like treaty. So our own diplomats got into a lather. Their man at the Korean court secured a copy of the American treaty. It proved to be precisely what we needed if we'd cross out 'United States' and fill in 'Great Britain' instead, but we'd need to get it signed before everybody else demanded the same, and before the Koreans started to suspect that it might not all be wholly to their benefit. So a telegram arrived from Peking requesting me to repair to Chemulpo with all despatch, put on my best bib and tucker to look suitably impressive as Her Majesty's representative and to sign as close to dammit a duplicate of the American document. Which I did, in a tent on the beach that looked like something from the Arabian Nights. A Chinese mandarin – a good fellow, very helpful – also signed so that honour was served on all sides."

"So Britain now has free access to Korea, sir?"

"Access yes – trade and the rest of it. But we need more if our interests are to be secured, just as we secured them here forty years ago." He gestured towards the crowded Hong Kong waterfront and the mass of merchant shipping and the lighters moving between them. "The Japanese gained special rights at three ports. We need the same. And they're ambitious for more. They've got a small military mission there already, training Korean troops to Japanese standards." He paused, then said "They're damned impressive too."

"If they're like my navigating lieutenant then they're likely to be very impressive indeed," Dawlish said. "He's Japanese, on secondment." In less than a generation Japan had emerged from medieval isolation and was not only industrialising but also creating powerful and modern armed forces. Their most promising naval officers were training in Britain, their army counterparts in Germany.

"Does your man speak Chinese? Or better still Korean?"

Dawlish shook his head. "I don't know, sir," he said, "but if it's needed he'll learn, and fast." For the Japanese secondee brought an intensity to all he undertook that seemed almost superhuman.

"He could be useful," Willes said. "There's some unfinished diplomatic business. Routine stuff, but important, starting with the right of entry for any British warship to any Korean port to take on water and supplies and to conduct maintenance. And we need the right to survey the coast – it's a dangerous one and we need detailed charts. So codicils have been drawn up to cover these items and they need to be signed. And it's been decided – instructions from London – that you're to sail to Chemulpo, impress everybody there with the Navy's most modern ship in the Orient, present yourself at the court in Seoul and obtain the signatures. It should be a formality."

And Dawlish knew that it wasn't. Not if London had specified his involvement. Because London probably meant Topcliffe.

"I can see you think it's dull stuff, Captain," the admiral said, "But nothing's straightforward in Korea. The court is divided as to whether they should invite foreigners in or not." He nodded towards three thick files on the desk. "You'll find as much there as I can give you on the background. You'll need to familiarise yourself with it before you sail – it's confidential, so confidential that you can't take it to Korea with you. I'll do my best to answer any queries you may have, not that I'm an expert on the place. I don't think any outsider is except the Foreign Office man there. He's quite junior but he seems as good a fellow as any diplomat could be. A chap called Whitaker."

Dawlish glanced towards the files and saw a long night and plenty of black coffee ahead.

"And there's something else. You'll find it interesting," Willes glanced at the telegram. "There's concern in London about the possibility of our Russian friends establishing a base somewhere in the North China Sea. And that could be damn inconvenient if we ever had a re-run of the Crimean affair. So we might need to be there first with something similar. There's a suggestion that a small island off Korea's west coast could be suitable – a place called Socheong. There's already a small British commercial presence there – a coaling station – and you're required to provide an assessment of its suitability."

"A coaling station, sir? In Korea?"

"Never be surprised by Scots enterprise, Captain." Willes laughed. "You've probably heard it said that trade follows the flag but in this case it's the other way round."

"I'm honoured by the assignment, sir," Dawlish sensed there was more to it than Willes himself knew. And then the admiral confirmed it.

"One other point, Captain," he said, "and it's a damn strange one – not that I'm objecting, not in the least. I've no doubt there are good reasons for it." He reached the telegram across.

The printed strips pasted to the paper bore a jumble of random letters but it was the handwritten decoding below them that drew Dawlish's attention.

"*Afford Captain Dawlish every support. He is entrusted with full discretion and full freedom of action. He will be held accountable to T alone.*"

"It's a roving commission," Willes said. "Not common these days."

"No, sir, not common at all."

"Ready for sea in two days, Captain?" Willes asked.

Dawlish nodded. "Ready for sea, sir."

But he was uncertain about whatever else he must be ready for.

*

Dawlish made his pre-departure inspection that afternoon, not the formal full captain's inspection he would make later, but informal, outwardly random and unstructured, and all the more effective for that. Edgerton was noting down his comments.

There was little to complain of – *Leonidas* was a smart ship, a credit to the two hundred and eighty officers and men who crewed her. Young for a captain, and entrusted with a crack ship, Dawlish knew that many begrudged his success, would be glad to see him fail. He could afford no shortcomings, must make no allowances, least of all for himself. He had made it plain since commissioning that he would accept nothing less than excellence and that even in these days of peace he considered *Leonidas* first and foremost a fighting machine, ready for action at short notice. He might not share the obsession of so many officers with outward appearance alone but he still demanded immaculately holystoned decks and gleaming brass and fresh paintwork. But all that, he knew, must be subordinate to the cruiser's ability to bring ten six-inch breech-loaders and four torpedo-launchers into action at short notice and to steam or sail long distances, in no company but her own, and far from any base, to protect trade routes.

He started, having arrived barefoot on deck, at the fore-top, hauling himself nimbly up the shrouds and disdaining the lubber's hole, knowing that the eyes of every crew-member were fixed on him. On the deck below, Edgerton, taken by surprise, was quickly stripping off his footwear so he could follow, for there was no safer way to climb. A five-barrel Gatling had been hoisted earlier to its position in the top – it normally remained under cover on deck until required. The gunner supressed a smile as Dawlish, finding it perfectly cleaned and lubricated, nodded approval. He spun the barrels and as they clicked over he had a fleeting memory of the slaughter he had once seen such weapons accomplish on a far-off river. Mounted on the top, and supported by an identical piece on the mizzen, the Gatling represented a lethal defence against small-boat attack.

38

Edgerton's face registered surprise, almost alarm, as Dawlish edged out along the main-yard to starboard, his bare feet on the footrope, systematically checking fastenings and stirrups, chafing-grommets and strops, goosenecks and trusses, all unused on the race from Britain. He wondered silently how long officers would remain familiar with this intricacy of wood and rope and canvas that had reached this peak of perfection years before. Was it not already time to abandon this expertise to honourable oblivion, to stake all instead on the boilers and machinery unseen beneath the deck below? Impressive as this ability to harness the wind might be, the masts and yards and cordage it demanded could only represent vulnerability in any serious action. But for now there was nothing to find fault with and as he moved back along the yard he called his approval for Edgerton to jot in his notebook.

The gunnery lieutenant, Purdon, was waiting expectantly on deck.

"Starboard aft," Dawlish said.

"Man her, sir?"

Dawlish shook his head – no need. He knew that he would find the six-inch there in perfect condition, that his inspection would be all but superfluous, but he took a secret pleasure in looking at these beautifully crafted weapons whenever he could. As he expected, the turntable's rollers and gearing were well greased, the gun rotating and elevating smoothly as he spun the hand-wheels. The breech-block swung open smoothly as a single throw of a lever unlocked its interrupted screw and a glance up through the barrel towards a disc of sky revealed immaculately clean rifling. It was a world removed from the rows of muzzle-loaders, all but unchanged since Nelson's day, which had lined whole battery decks when he had joined the navy, different even from the enormous hydraulically-served muzzle-loaders which were still mounted on large ships. And on a few small ones, and especially on a certain Rendel gunboat which Dawlish could never forget. The memory was not a comfortable one.

"We would have welcomed this on the San Joac, Mister Purdon." The words slipped out and Dawlish knew already that he should not have said them.

"But we did well enough without it, sir," Purdon was obviously unwilling to say more. He must know, though neither ever alluded to it, that Dawlish had sought him for this position on the basis of the skill and loyalty he had demonstrated on that terrible river in the heart of South America.

Dawlish left it at that. They had been no more than mercenaries there and he suspected that Purdon was as ashamed of the cause they had served there as he was himself. He wondered if, like himself, Purdon had refused remuneration afterwards. The question could never be asked.

"We can conduct live firing drill once we're at sea." Dawlish was glad to change the subject. "I want us to take full advantage of the range."

For the six-inch's range was unprecedented, ten-thousand yards maximum, the effective range less, though extending with each practice-firing at a target raft. It could not be a greater contrast with the smallest weapon *Leonidas* carried, the seven-pounder field gun for use by landing parties. The wheeled muzzle-loader could be broken into separate loads and reassembled wherever needed. Gunners prided themselves in the speed with which they could break it down or reassemble it.

Lieutenant Takenaka Katamori snapped to attention and bowed as Dawlish entered the charthouse. His face showed no flicker of emotion, neither pleasure or annoyance, at the interruption. He remained rigid as Dawlish took in the precision with which the charts and instruments had been arranged on the table. There were two note pads, the characters on one in neat vertical columns, the handwriting on the other in equally neat horizontal lines. The lettering in each had the sharpness of printer's type. Takenaka did his calculations in Japanese, then transferred them into English.

"We can expect a fast passage, Lieutenant?" Dawlish hoped to put the navigator at ease, for he found his remoteness unnerving. As captain, with his own quarters, and only entering the wardroom by invitation, he had to preserve a degree of distance from all his officers. They in turn respected it, but never to this degree.

"I must apologise, sir." Takenaka bowed again, stiffly, from the waist. Dawlish had heard that he did the same towards the portrait of Queen Victoria every time he entered the wardroom.

"You must apologise, Lieutenant?" It was hard to imagine the navigator ever guilty of any dereliction.

"I have not sufficiently thoroughly ascertained your wishes, sir. My work may therefore not satisfy your expectations." And still the face conveyed nothing.

"I find that hard to believe, Lieutenant. Your work has always been exemplary."

"I understood you to request a fast passage, sir," Takenaka's voice, normally quiet, began to break into a staccato bark. "I did not request clarification regarding fuel economy consistent with that, nor whether I should take into account cleaning of the hull in drydock. On the basis of information accumulated on the voyage here from Britain I have therefore prepared three plans, one aimed at shortest passage time, a second balancing speed and fuel economy and a third – for comparison only, sir – guaranteeing minimum coal usage." He bowed again.

Dawlish suddenly realised that Takenaka had seen a barrier that did not exist, but which might well be absolute in his own society. Because of a reluctance to seek clarification – perhaps even a fear to speak freely to a superior – he had undertaken a huge burden of extra work. His adaptation to the Royal Navy's bewildering mix of rigid discipline and often easy communication between commanders and commanded must be a constant nightmare. And Dawlish recognised that he himself had perhaps not done enough to put the Japanese at his ease.

"I look forward to examining your proposals, Lieutenant," Dawlish kept his own face expressionless, "and in future, I would be pleased if you were to feel free to request clarifications. And more than that, I will value your observations and your recommendations."

"Thank you, sir." There was the first hint of a smile.

Dawlish mentioned his concern about Takenaka to Edgerton when they returned on deck.

"When he's off duty he spends his waking hours either studying mathematics or practising sword-exercises," the commander said.

"I've seen him." Stripped to the waist, and regardless of weather, armed with a gently curved sword that was a thing of beauty, Takenaka's ritual never faltered. His dedication to cutlass-drill and bayonet practice was similarly intense. The half-concealed amusement of the crew had ended with the first mock-combat he had engaged in. He was invincible.

"Has he made friends?"

Edgerton shook his head. "None. Perhaps none even since he left Japan."

The inspection continued – deck fittings, the cleanliness of the scuppers, the absence of the slightest sign of rust. Sub-Lieutenant Hamilton, the most junior officer on board, proved to have been punctilious in his duties. Dawlish swung himself down on a line to a painting float, surprising the men busy there with chipping hammers and wire brushes and paint pots. He had the float dragged along the side to confirm that touch-up activity since the vessel had left the dockyard had been effective. Only a few inches of the wood-backed copper sheathing that protected the hull below the waterline against marine growth were visible but he had already inspected that in the drydock.

Once more on deck, and shod again, he continued the inspection and found, much as he expected, little to admonish. Watch in hand, he ordered the lifeboat away – thirty-five seconds – and then all boats away, their crews racing to get them moored to the boom.

"Ten seconds too long," he dictated to Edgerton. "I want all away – all, you understand – in seven minutes at the very most."

Then below: the sailmaker's and carpenter's workshops, the heads and washing facilities – spotless these, and smelling of carbolic, a welcome contrast to the squalid discomfort he had endured as a boy – and the mess decks, more comfortable now when a handful of breech-loaders had taken the place of the ranks of broadside cannon between which crews had eaten and slept for centuries. Tadley, the staff surgeon came with him to the galley. It was steaming there as the huge range added to the day's humid warmth but the pans were scoured and gleaming. The cook and his assistants were nervous as Dawlish pulled on white gloves and ran his hands beneath tables and inside cold ovens but their faces showed relief and pride as he found nothing to reprove. The sick berth, Tadley's own domain, was no less pristine. Aft then through the storage area where the seamen's bags were stacked on shelves in neat white rows. He spent twenty minutes at the issue room, checking through the ledgers, selecting specific items at random to confirm that actual stores tallied with records. He had few concerns about honesty in this area, but temptation was never far away and it did no harm to show close interest.

And then down into the vitals. He descended though a hatchway – one of only five accesses through the armoured deck, an inch and a half thick, that protected the engines, boilers and magazines beneath. Along the ship's centreline this deck was positioned just above the normal waterline but it sloped down to either side to deflect any shot that might punch through the vessel's unarmoured sides. Above it, ranged along the flanks, were the coal bunkers and from these it was the trimmers' unenviable job to shift the fuel by wheelbarrows and chain hoists to the furnaces. Dawlish passed through the boiler and engine rooms. The fires had been lit two days previously and the furnaces had been carefully stoked since then to avoid stressing. All twelve boilers were at harbour-pressure and the engineers and stokers were once more accustoming themselves to the hell that was even hotter here than in Northern waters. Every bearing had been checked and oiled, every lubrication-cup filled and the twin compound engines were again ready to deliver over five thousand horsepower when called upon to drive *Leonidas* at her maximum seventeen knots. Latham took special pride in demonstrating the efficiency of the dynamo that delivered electricity to the searchlights and in his knowledge of this new, arcane, area of expertise. Dawlish was soaked in sweat after a few minutes but he spent over an hour below here, sometimes asking questions he might already know the answer to, sometimes levering himself into confined spaces to examine details, always conveying the value and importance he placed on the men who were so often ignored, so often resented.

The light was fading when he came on deck. It was time to bathe – not the least benefit of promotion to his own command was his private bathroom – and then he must settle down to the three files that Willes had given him.

It was going to be a long night.

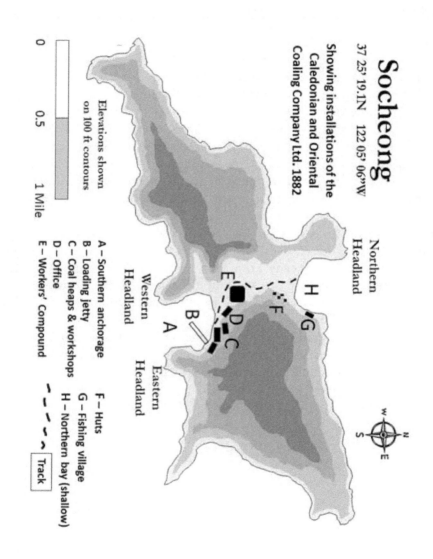

Socheong

37 25' 19.1N   122 05' 06"W

Showing installations of the
Caledonian and Oriental
Coaling Company Ltd. 1882

Elevations shown
on 100 ft contours

0   0.5   1 Mile

Northern
Headland

Western
Headland

Eastern
Headland

A – Southern anchorage   F – Huts
B – Loading jetty   G – Fishing village
C – Coal heaps & workshops H – Northern bay (shallow)
D – Office
E – Workers' Compound   〜〜〜〜 Track

N
W   E
S

44

4

Leonidas was forging north-north east and the sun was dropping astern like a scarlet ball that would race for long hours more across the vastness of China.

The scuttles were open but it was still uncomfortably, suffocatingly warm as Dawlish, alone and restless in his saloon, pulled one volume after another from his bookshelf, then thrust them back unopened. He rummaged through the four boxes of second-hand books that Florence had bought for him – the habit of her days of proud penury had not left her and she had sought out what amounted to a small library to take with him. Nothing matched his mood, not history, exploration, scientific enquiry, not even the Trollopes that so often entertained him, as he waited for his steward to bring him dinner. It was not the mission ahead that unsettled him – for nothing in the files he had studied worried him unduly – but he could not deny that he felt another unease. It was one he had felt since *Leonidas* had left Britain, a nagging concern that the goal of command he had sought so long and gained at last might not bring satisfaction.

For it was not easy to come to terms with solitude. He had expected it – had known from boyhood that it was the burden every captain must bear – yet he had never thought that it would be as intense as this. He could not betray external sign of it, could not even bring himself to mention it in the letters he had sent to Florence from Suez, from Aden, from Singapore, from Hong Kong. He had known sole command before, but then briefly, weeks only, in the Ottoman Navy. Barriers of language and religion and culture had made isolation seem natural then and the pace of action had been too relentless to allow time for introspection. But now he was with his own kind, in the society that had nurtured and formed him – and sometimes almost killed him – since boyhood. The gunroom had provided rough companionship and the later fellowship of the wardroom had much of a brotherhood about it. But now he had crossed a barrier that had brought him to the austere glory of the captain's saloon, separated by rank and custom from every other being on the ship, his power all but absolute once land had dropped over the horizon astern, his slightest frown feared, his approval eagerly sought. He had no friend on board, could have none, was himself nobody's friend. He was their captain.

He had known every sort of captain, the efficient and the careless, the abstemious and the drunken, the martinet and the slack, the pompous and the over-familiar, the leaders who brought out more in men than they knew they had, the others who had destroyed spirit and crushed initiative. From all of them he had learned.

He had told himself for years what sort of captain he wanted to be – strict but fair, never demanding less than excellence, never sparing himself, ready to praise as well as censure, tempering discipline with humanity. Now, not always easily, he was largely living up to that vision of himself. He dined in the wardroom only by invitation and when he returned the compliment the officers round his table were cautious in what they said, about how much they drank, about how far they might dissent from any view he might express, no matter how trivial or unrelated to the navy that the topic might be. When he conducted the Sunday service on the quarterdeck – *Leonidas* did not rate a chaplain – he knew that the reverence shown by many was motivated by fear of him rather than of the Almighty. There might be more genuine piety present in the prayers which O'Rourke led for some thirty or so Roman Catholics, mostly Irish, in the crew quarters forward.

The solitude was the price of command. He had now what he had aspired to from boyhood, to stand on the bridge of his own ship, to revel in the challenges she brought, to accept gladly the responsibility for her and all who served in her.

And yet...

There must be more. He was almost thirty-seven years old and decades might still stretch before him. Command of other ships, ever larger and more sophisticated, was now all but inevitable. Promotion to Rear Admiral, as a minimum, was not inconceivable.

But he wanted more. He did not want like other officers to find the North West Passage or explore the Antarctic, nor yet map coasts in worthy hydrographic effort that would benefit mariners for years to come. He wanted command – high command, not ships and men alone but strategy, policy, the capability to deal with statesmen and politicians on equal footing. Like Admiral Sir Richard Topcliffe. But without war, a great war, he would retire as just another senior officer who might have been an Anson or a Rodney or a Nelson. War with France or Russia, perhaps with both, was always a possibility. There were less likely possibilities – the United States, with which Britain had come close to war twenty years before, maybe even, however farfetched the idea, with the German Empire if it decided to match its strength on land with power at sea.

And in that light he could see that the roving commission Topcliffe had secured for him was no gift. It was a test of his ability to manage diplomatic and political complexities. He might be one of half-a-dozen promising officers of his age, all hungry for advancement, all unknown to each other, whom Topcliffe was evaluating. The outcome of the Korean mission might move him up one step on the ladder to high command or it might condemn him to a steady, worthy, undemanding career that would never satisfy him. This opportunity was to be welcomed – and to be feared.

His feeling of isolation had never seemed so intense as now, the more so for his separation from the wife from whom he had gained so much strength, with whom he had known such quiet joy as well as such moments of terror. He missed the smile that transformed Florence's face into a thing of beauty, and her enthusiasm for books, and her capacity for laughter, a capacity he knew he was deficient in himself without her. He missed her generosity and the energy with which she had flung herself into organisation of the Sailors' Rest at Portsmouth. He missed the courage with which she ignored the subtle slights aimed at her for having once been a servant, however much they might wound. He missed...

He stopped himself. Memory and longing could be insidious enemies, subtly capable of eroding focus and commitment. He thrust them from his mind. Korea, closed and mysterious until a few years before, and still unknown to him, must have his full attention.

*

Socheong Island grew slowly above the horizon as *Leonidas* approached cautiously from the south-west. Only the main features of the island-dotted west coast of Korea had been charted and there was good reason why gaining the right to survey it more thoroughly was one of Dawlish's diplomatic objectives. He was taking no chances and the leadsman was positioned near the bow, monotonously confirming that there were at least twenty fathoms beneath the cruiser's keel. It was midday, hot and humid, the sea oily calm. Further north the humped outlines of two larger islands were also revealing themselves. In the haze to the east the mainland was a long, rolling streak. Seen end on –

47

for its long-axis lay almost south-west to north-east – Socheong showed itself as like a mountain-top thrusting up from the sea, its steep cliffs capped with green.

"It doesn't look promising." Edgerton was the only officer who had been told that the island was being considered as a base.

Dawlish shook his head and braced himself against the bridge wing to steady his telescope. "It's too early to say. We'll follow the south coast, allow a mile sea room. We should see the coaling station soon."

Leonidas crept forward, her screws churning to drive her at dead-slow, the coast to port a succession of cliffs of varying height, never less than seventy or eighty feet, often much higher, no sign of life on the scrub-covered hills above. The island was long – the poor-quality chart available indicated three miles, and it was apparently nowhere wider than a mile. The high ridge that lay along it like a spine was its most obvious feature. Deep clefts gouged into the merciless shore which had so far not revealed a single landing place for even a small boat. The leadsman's calls were still confirming deep water. Lieutenant Takenaka stood by the helmsman, his instructions, as ever, terse and precise. He was sketching the shoreline on a pad with quick pencil strokes.

High above, a lookout called out, drawing Dawlish's attention away from the coast and past the steep headland that jutted out maybe a mile ahead. A small craft with a spindly funnel and wreathed in dark smoke was crawling southwards into view from behind the outcrop. A long barge strained on a cable in her wake, its deck laden with a black mound.

Almost simultaneously, and as *Leonidas* passed another high and rocky promontory, the shoreline to port fell away to reveal a semi-circular bay, eight or nine hundred yards across. The cliffs ran down to a small beach and died there. A broad valley, little higher than sea level, lay to the north, dividing the island's spine. And in this bay, bizarrely, was a scene of industrial activity that might have been more appropriate to some northern British port. A long wooden jetty jutted out into the bay and alongside it lay two small steamers – five-hundred tonners or less, typical of the traders that plied the Chinese coasts and penetrated its rivers. Two similar craft lay at anchor further out, a red ensign drooping at one poop and what looked like a French one at the other. On the jetty itself Dawlish could make out clusters of men pushing coal-laden trucks along what seemed to be a rail track. White vapour drifting around a crane there showed it to be steam-driven. Bent under sacks, a stream of men was running up a gang plank from the jetty to one of the ships, dumping their loads in a cloud of black dust and running back along a second plank. Their speed seemed superhuman and unsustainable. Two coal-laden barges were moored in the centre of the bay, obviously waiting for the jetty to be vacated and a third was being manoeuvred by a small tug similar to the one sighted off the headland. A row of low corrugated-metal sheds and high coal heaps lined the shore beyond. There too, like ants, men were scurrying and loading trucks and pushing them towards the jetty. Further up in the valley Dawlish could make out two twin-storey wooden houses, the sort that could be assembled in days from readymade sections. Under their dark pallor of dust it looked as if they had once been whitewashed. Behind them lay a large walled compound with a mass of thatch-roofs within.

"That must be the Caledonian and Oriental Coaling Company's station." Dawlish knew from Willes's documents that it was a large undertaking, but the actuality far exceeded the mental picture he had created of it. And the sight of those scurrying men was disquieting. The company had apparently operated such stations along the China coast for two decades, but this – and the coal mine on the mainland that fed it – was a new venture. Takenaka had turned towards him, as if awaiting an order to heave to. Dawlish shook his head. "We'll complete the circumnavigation, Lieutenant" he said. "We'll anchor here on return." Takenaka bowed.

"The anchorage looks small, sir" Edgerton said. "Useful enough for smaller craft though."

"But small craft can be deadly, Commander, and more deadly by the year." Certain of Dawlish's experiences which could never be discussed, no less than the insights he had accumulated as an expert at HMS *Vernon*, the navy's torpedo school, had confirmed that view. The future did not belong to guns alone. And the island ... a flotilla of torpedo boats might shelter safely here from north-westerly winter gales howling down from the heart of Asia, he thought. Batteries on the cliffs above could provide protection and a depot ship could furnish them workshops, stores and medical support. The tip of the Shantung Peninsula that thrust eastwards from the Chinese coast was little over a hundred miles to the west. A force based here could menace the entrance to the Bohai Sea and the approaches to Peking and to Southern Manchuria, on which Russian greed was so blatantly focussed. Socheong might well have possibilities…

No signal of welcome came from shore, even though the sight of the immaculate white cruiser must have come as a surprise. But *Leonidas* steamed slowly on, past the jagged cliffs that rose again beyond the bay's eastern extremity, the land behind once more high and scrub-clad. She drew level with the oncoming tug and barge, passing to seaward of them. Dawlish's glass picked out a florid European on the tug's open bridge, his shirt filthy, unkempt hair straggling beneath an equally dirty cap. He was examining *Leonidas* through his own telescope and for a long moment his gaze was locked on Dawlish's. Though he raised a hand in greeting, Dawlish elicited no response. The few crew who were on deck seemed to be Asians and there were others slumped on the coal on the barge astern, apparently sleeping. The labouring, grimy, smoke-engulfed tug and the burden it dragged looked out of place against the blue sea and clear sky and the majesty of the cliffs.

Past the headland now. *Leonidas* swung to port, her bows just east of north as she continued along the mile of coast that extended to the island's tip. The cliffs here were even higher than before, deep gullies thrusting deeply in places into the rock behind. As at the western end of the island there was no sign of life on the hills above, in stark contrast to the frenetic activity at the anchorage so close by. The eastern extremity proved no less precipitous and as the cruiser swung over to head westwards along the northern coast the same vista persisted of high cliffs, without even the narrowest beach at their base. Northwards, to starboard, four miles distant, rose the equally forbidding mass of the larger island of Daechoeng. A rocky peninsula reached out towards it from Socheong, obliging *Leonidas* to curve north and west around it. Just east of the peninsula lay the northern exit of the valley that had been seen earlier from the southern coast. Here, in a break in the cliffs, was another semi-circular bay, larger this time, beach-fringed and obviously shallow, judging by the lighter blue of the water nearer the shore. A few small fishing boats were drawn up on the sand and beyond them, all but blocking the valley, Dawlish could just glimpse the thatched roofs inside the walled compound he had previously seen from the south.

The cruiser ploughed on towards Socheong's western end, the coast no less forbidding than before, and rounded it, heading back towards the southern anchorage.

"I would appreciate seeing your sketch, Lieutenant Takenaka," Dawlish said. The navigator had been observing the island with almost painful concentration for minutes at a time, his hand then moving rapidly for three or four short pencil strokes before falling still again.

"I am honoured, sir." As he presented the pad with an inevitable bow there was something like a smile of pride around his lips.

Dawlish wished immediately that he might keep it, frame it, treasure it for the work of art it was. With his eye alone to guide him, with only his awareness of time and of ship's estimated speed to provide any approximation of distance, and of compass references to indicate direction, Takenaka had produced a map that recorded every curve of the shoreline, every headland, every cleft, every jagged spur. He had even indicated the contours of the hills and crags above, their closeness indicating the steepness of their slopes, close hatching identifying where the scrub appeared most dense. It was executed with a deftness and an elegance that were obvious in every confident stroke. Seen now as a whole, the island suggested a leaping fish, its narrow western end flaring out into a small tail, the centre long and thick, the southern bay and the headland to its east emphasising the belly's concave curve, the eastern mass the head that tapered to a nose, the transverse valley in the centre the gills, the small peninsula to the north jutting like a fin from the back.

"Congratulations, Lieutenant Takenaka. And you may be able to add some further detail when we go ashore. I want you to accompany me." Dawlish had already ascertained that Takenaka understood Korean, even if he was not fully fluent in it, and that he could communicate, but not easily, in Mandarin Chinese. Given the painful modesty with which the Japanese officer normally referred to his own achievements, Dawlish suspected that he might be fully competent in both languages.

A half-hour brought *Leonidas* along the southern coast to find good holding ground in ten fathoms on the western edge of the coaling station's bay, well clear of the other moored craft. Dawlish's gig was dropped. Takenaka and Purdon accompanied him as he swung himself down to seat himself in the sternsheets. As the craft stroked towards the jetty he noticed that the still waters were scummed with coal dust and that when the seabed came into view through the otherwise clear water, it was paved with black. A barge had been secured alongside the anchored French ship and coal was being carried on board in sacks by half-naked coolies. Coaling was never a pleasant activity – which was why Dawlish insisted that he and his officers be seen to shoulder part of the load themselves – but the insistent shouts of the overseers and their flourishing of cudgels made this frantic activity worse than normal. A warship coaled only at intervals – but this was a daily task.

A short European in duck shirt and trousers that had once been white stood at the top of the ladder the gig made fast to. The face beneath his pith helmet was bloated and covered in white stubble. His expression conveyed no welcome. Dawlish called up a greeting, requested permission to land, got no response. He did so anyway, pulling himself up the grimy steps.

"Captain Nicholas Dawlish," he said, extending his hand. "Royal Navy, HMS *Leonidas*."

The other man glared at him and made no movement. Behind him stood two short Asians in semi-military blue cotton uniforms and peaked caps, both with rifles slung on their shoulders and whips in their hands. The stream of men running with coal sacks on to the nearer of the ships moored at the jetty never ceased and there were other uniformed figures there also, counting off those returning empty-handed.

"Do I have the honour of addressing Mr. Robert Wishart?" Dawlish said.

"You're addressing Mr. McIver." The accent was unmistakably Scottish. "And ye can state your business. You and that damned Chink with you." He nodded towards Takenaka, who was now standing behind Dawlish with Purdon.

Dawlish advanced, put his face close enough to McIver to smell the alcohol he seemed steeped in, and spoke in a near whisper. "I don't give a damn who or what you are, Mr. McIver, but I'm here to speak to Mr. Wishart. There's a boatload of bluejackets below me who'd have the greatest pleasure throwing you off this jetty. So just be a sensible man and bring me to Mr. Wishart."

McIver pulled back. "If that's what ye want then we'd better be moving." His voice was a snarl. He turned away, pushing past his guards.

"Mr. McIver!" Dawlish's raised voice halted him

"What's it now? I thought ye wanted to see the boss?"

"You'll address Lieutenant Takenaka with courtesy, just as you'll address me. You understand?"

McIver growled what might have been assent and started back along the jetty. Dawlish and his officers followed. Two rail tracks, eighteen- or twenty-inch gauge, had been laid along the planks, and on these straining labourers were pushing open wagons, one side for laden, the other for empties. As each wagon stopped in turn by the receiving ship a small mob fell on it, furiously shovelling the coal into sacks and emptying it in a minute, and it was just as quickly replaced with the next as it was dragged away on the other track. Streaks of black sweat gleamed on bare torsos and heads and faces were swathed in rags to escape the enveloping dust. Under their grime they might have been of any race or colour but Dawlish assumed that they were Koreans, the first he had encountered. The overseers were little cleaner but their free use of their cudgels on any exhausted laggard identified them as what they were. Several more armed men in uniforms stood aloof, not many, but enough to inhibit any protest.

Coal fragments crunched underfoot as Dawlish and his officers followed McIver past the high heaps along the shoreline from which the wagons drew their loads. The heat was intense, the air heavy with humidity. Dawlish, conscious of his dignity, resented the patches of sweat that were already darkening his white uniform. They passed the corrugated sheds. Through the first's open sides a small steam engine could be seen driving overhead shafting, leather belts slapping as they drove lathes and drill presses. The other sheds appeared to be stores. A few more Europeans were seen, none any cleaner than McIver, and they showed little curiosity in the newcomers. Asian guards stood by at each building, uniforms neat and perhaps even pressed, faces wholly expressionless.

They stopped before one of the wooden houses. Steps led up to a veranda. McIver turned to speak for the first time since they had left the jetty. "Mr. Wishart's office," he said.

"I'll be able to find my own way then, Mr. McIver," Dawlish said. "My officers will be taking a little stroll while I'm seeing Mr. Wishart. You might like to accompany them."

He did not wait for a reply and mounted the steps without looking back. He pushed the door open and entered an office with six desks, the walls lined with file-stacked shelves. Another door beyond.

Five Asian clerks were writing in ledgers and the sixth, a young European, was in discussion with what looked like officers from one of the ships being coaled. One of them half-turned, saw Dawlish in full uniform, then turned away again, saying something that made the others laugh.

Dawlish ignored them – merchant officers frequently resented perceived or actual naval assumptions of superiority – and he went straight to the door beyond. The young European clerk was rising to his feet in protest. "You can't just ..." he stammered but Dawlish turned the knob and stepped inside.

A large man sat behind a writing desk, his head down as if studying intently the document before him. A tonsure of coarse ginger hair encircled a livid crown and Dawlish could not see his face. He did not look up, though he must be aware of his visitor.

"Mr. Wishart, I presume" Dawlish said. "Captain Nicholas Dawlish of Her Majesty's Ship *Leonidas*." He was aware that the clerk was in the doorway behind him and stammering excuses for not barring entry. Without looking up or speaking the man at the desk dismissed the clerk with a wave of his hand and the door closed. He ignored Dawlish's presence.

Dawlish forced himself not to rise to the bait. "You've got an impressive establishment here, Mr. Wishart," he said as pleasantly as he could.

Wishart still did not look up and the discourtesy was obviously deliberate. Dawlish felt his anger rising and knew he must control it, but he was damned if he was going to accept insult meekly. He saw several chairs along the wall, picked one up and planted it in front of the desk. Then he sat in it and tilted back slightly. Still no reaction. Dawlish noted that the window was open and that a telescope on a tripod was directed towards *Leonidas*. There could be no doubt as to who he was. He reached inside his jacket for his humidor, extracted a cheroot and was lighting it when Wishart looked up.

"You can state your business and ye can be gone." Another Scots accent. The features were gaunt, the skin red and peeling. A huge ginger moustache was not enough to conceal the yellow buck teeth.

"My business?" Dawlish savoured the cheroot. "My business, Mr. Wishart, among much else, is the protection of British trade and enterprise. And I think we'd agree that your undertaking here falls under that description. So my call here, Mr. Wishart, is purely one of courtesy, to see how Her Majesty's subjects are prospering in foreign parts. And courtesy, by the way, is something I've seen damned little of since I landed here."

"You're on Korean soil, Captain... whatever your name is. Our activities here and in the mine on the mainland have the full support of the provincial governor. State Councillor Choi Haung," he pronounced the name slowly, as if for a child. "So if you've got concerns you can address them to him. And we don't need your protection, so Good Day to you."

"I trust that your miners are treated with somewhat more humanity than those men on the jetty," Dawlish said. He found himself loathing this man, and all the more so because of the shame he still felt for having once helped restore a similar regime of exploitation.

"Don't you come here to lecture me, man!" Wishart flushed even redder. "There's no law here against indentured service! These people don't ask more than a bellyful of rice and generous payment after two years. They're housed well enough and they even get a woman every month or six weeks." He had risen to his feet and now he sat down again. "You can close the door behind you when you leave." He picked up a document and made as if to read it. Without looking up he said "And you can remove that ship of yours from our anchorage."

There was nothing to be gained by continuing the conversation. "I may be back, sir," Dawlish said, rising, "and I'll hope then for a more civil reception."

"You can wish for what you damn-well like, Captain, as long as you pay for it," Wishart said. "If it's coal you need ye'll be welcome as long as it's cash on the nail and if ye don't then I'll thank you to stay away. So Good Day to ye again."

Dawlish left. Outside he cast his cheroot aside and looked up into the valley behind the house. He spotted Takenaka and Purdon there with McIver. As he began to walk towards them two of the armed guards fell in silently behind him. He ignored them and as he advanced he saw that that wall of the compound ahead was of dried mud and stone. There was one gate only, and open. Through it he could see a squalid alley lined with thatched hovels. Even at a distance the smell drifting towards him was foul. He felt no urge to investigate further and was relieved to see Takenaka and Purdon returning to meet him.

"Four hundred workers, give or take, sir, he tells us," Purdon nodded towards McIver, who was following at a distance. "It's somewhat of a paradise, he says, compared with what they're used to."

Dawlish noticed Takenaka looking intently at the guards who had stopped several paces away. "Excuse me, sir," he said, then moved towards them. He spoke quietly to them, and Dawlish was unsure what the language might be, but both men seemed to stiffen into attitudes of respect, their entire demeanour changed. Takenaka seemed to be questioning them and they were answering in what might have been an ingratiating tone, bobbing in half-bows as they did. It was better to leave them to it and Dawlish intercepted McIver, who was hurrying towards them with an obvious intention of breaking up the interrogation.

"Are you a seafaring man yourself, Mr. McIver?" he asked.

"I'm not," he said, looking past Dawlish towards Takenaka.

"In the commercial line then? It seems to be a wonderful enterprise you have going here."

"It is."

"And a coal-mine on the mainland also?" Purdon came in, understanding the need to keep the conversation going. Takenaka needed time.

"There is."

"The most modern equipment, no doubt?" Dawlish could already imagine the medieval hell it must be there, picks and shovels and windlasses and overseers and guards like those here.

"All we need." McIver looked increasingly agitated as he saw Takenaka's questioning continue.

"Excellent relations with the Korean governor, I hear," Dawlish said.

"Good enough." McIver pushed past. "You!" he shouted towards Takenaka. "What are ye talking to my men for? Don't you know ye've no business here?"

Takenaka turned and for a moment Dawlish saw a flash of cold fury in his black eyes even if his face was wholly impassive. He stepped towards McIver, who seemed to be already realising his mistake, and although he carried no weapon Takenaka's whole demeanour was like that of a cobra about to strike. McIver paled. Purdon sensed the danger and moved forward, as if to restrain his colleague, only to have Dawlish lay a restraining hand on his arm. "Leave him to it," he said.

Takenaka's English enunciation was perfect. "I will not forget you, Mr. McIver," he said, nothing more. Then he stepped back and bowed towards Dawlish. He smiled slightly and it was as if the cobra had uncoiled and slipped away.

"You can find yer own way to the jetty, and be damned to ye," McIver's voice had a quaver. He called to the two guards. "You two! Make 'em go! No talk! You understand? No talk!" He stalked off.

Dawlish passed round cheroots and slowed their pace to the jetty to a saunter. The two guards followed at a respectful distance. He glanced back, took in their clean blue tunics, the rifles – Sniders, metal gleaming, wood polished – the single diagonal bandoliers, the air of confidence and alertness, even the straw sandals, all impressively neat and well maintained, at variance with McIver's squalor. And the whips.

The pace of work at the jetty had not slackened. The barge which had previously been seen under tow from the mainland was now being offloaded. Black dust hung in a cloud over labourers and overseas alike. Dawlish felt it settle on his own uniform, felt soiled by it, but even more by his contacts with Wishart and McIver.

*

Leonidas was underway again within the half-hour. Dawlish delayed questioning Takenaka until the island was dropping astern. He invited him, alone, to his own quarters, ordered the steward to bring coffee and had him sit down. He failed however to put him at his ease and he sat stiffly.

"I'm impressed by your Korean," Dawlish said. "What did those men tell you?"

"Not Korean, sir. They're Japanese."

"Japanese, you said?" Dawlish was surprised. He knew that there was already a strong Japanese presence in Korea, not just diplomatic and mercantile, but a military training mission – just as European advisers had once helped modernise Japanese forces. "You mean Japanese troops are guarding the station here? A British commercial enterprise?"

Takenaka shook his head. "Not troops, sir. Civilian guards, but recruited in Japan."

Dawlish senses a reluctance to say more. "Is the engagement – the contract, I presume – officially sanctioned by the Japanese government?"

"These men would not know, sir. They are peasants, pleased to have this work. It is not for them to question their superiors."

"How many of them, Lieutenant?"

"They said eighty, sir. Including their superiors."

"And the labourers? What are they?"

"Koreans, sir. Provided by the provincial governor."

There were four hundred of them, Dawlish thought, and one guard to every five. It was no wonder that they seemed cowed and subservient even if they did get a bellyful of rice daily and a woman every month or six weeks. And he could sense a greater unease in Takenaka than his clipped answers conveyed.

"Is there something more you need to tell me, Lieutenant?" Dawlish said.

Takenaka hesitated, then said "They are all recruited in Satsuma, sir. All from around Kagoshima."

Dawlish recognised the name, knew that it was somewhere in Southern Japan, that almost twenty years before a small Royal Navy squadron had bombarded forts there during a squabble with a local warlord. It was one of those small incidents which were often so deadly for the participants, but soon half-forgotten even in the service.

"From Satsuma, you say, Lieutenant Takenaka? Is that a district?"

"A province, sir. But more – a domain, like a ..." He searched for a word. "... a territory that a daimyo, a lord, holds under His Majesty, the Emperor." He bowed when he uttered the words.

"And is it significant that they all come from Satsuma?"

Takenaka shook his head. "I do not know, sir. I do not understand it."

And Dawlish believed him, and saw that he was troubled by it.

As he was himself.

5

The water was yellow with silt for miles offshore before Chemulpo came into view. There was no harbour, just a roadstead a mile or more from the coastline with slimy mud flats in between. Three small coastal steamers lay moored there, offloading on to lighters, and beyond them sampans bustled around a cluster of junks. Two large warships were anchored further out, the red and white ensign of the rising sun flapping gently at each stern. One vessel also bore an admiral's pennant. Scanning the scene from *Leonidas's* bridge, Dawlish remembered warnings that the tidal range here could exceed thirty-five feet. He ordered mooring just seaward of both warships.

"Do you recognise those vessels, Lieutenant Takenaka?" Dawlish passed him the telescope he had been studying them through. They was larger than *Leonidas*, also equipped for both steam and sail propulsion. The Japanese characters that disappeared around the curve of the sterns meant nothing to Dawlish but the ships looked as smart as any of the Royal Navy.

Takenaka's pride was palpable as he scanned the nearer vessel. "His Imperial Majesty's corvettes *Haruna* and *Kirishima*." Despite the telescope he made the inevitable effort at a bow at the mention of the emperor's name. "*Haruna* is the flagship." He stopped, frowning in concentration, then continued: "Sisters, iron-hulls, built in Britain, sir, at Earle's yard in Hull, launched four years ago. A near-sister was completed last year, the *Tatsuta*, is due to be delivered around now. Two thousand, two hundred tons, sir, and as many horsepower, fourteen knots, ten six-inch breech-loaders and ..."

As Takenaka continued to reel off statistics with undisguised pride Dawlish suspected that he could probably do the same for any ship in the expanding Imperial Japanese Navy. He had read of these vessels, the largest so far in Japanese service, as well armed as *Leonidas* though without her armoured deck. They were all the more so because of the two long, narrow craft stored on chocks abaft the mainmast of each ship. For the twin funnels and slim lines and raised forecastles of these slim craft identified them for what they were. Torpedo boats, Thorneycrafts, built in Britain, each carrying at least one fourteen-inch Whitehead fish-torpedo.

Salutes were exchanged, Japanese precision matching *Leonidas's* own.

Dawlish turned to Takenaka. "You'll oblige me by crossing to the *Haruna*, Lieutenant. Present my compliments to the admiral and advise that I wish to visit him myself in two hours." Protocol was a tricky matter, he thought, and many a British captain might find excuses not to pay his respects personally to a more senior officer of an upstart navy, and an oriental one at that. But he was now temporarily a diplomat as well as a naval officer and he needed to know more of the significance of the presence of these splendid ships.

Leonidas was at anchor, her hull's whiteness insufficient to repel all of the sun's humid warmth, when Takenaka returned. He seemed to carry himself with a confidence, almost a swagger, which Dawlish had not seen before. He had known him as competent, dedicated perhaps to the point of obsession, but always reserved, a man apart whom all respected but no one knew. But this was a new, smiling, relaxed Takenaka, obviously proud of what he had seen on the *Haruna*, eager perhaps that Dawlish see it too.

"Rear Admiral Hojo Ujinao invites you and your senior officers to dine, sir, and he will be honoured by your visit," Takenaka said. "He will be happy to employ his English and to recall his own days in Britain. Admiral Hojo was one of the first Japanese officers to be so privileged."

And Dawlish knew of them, young men plucked from a medieval society some twenty years before. They had arrived without knowledge of any language but their own, the butt of jokes and contempt, at first patiently mastering English as lodgers in rectories where needy clergymen tutored them, passing on, by then fluent, to formal training in the Royal Navy, challenging and matching their British contemporaries by their dedication, speed of learning and, above all, competence, shaming and silencing the petty slights they had initially encountered. And now these men were forging a power in the Far East that defied all notions of inherent European superiority.

"Commander Edgerton, Lieutenant Purdon and you yourself will accompany me," Dawlish said. "Please advise these officers accordingly. I trust that the two Japanese captains will also be present?"

"The *Haruna's* captain will welcome you, but Captain Shimazu Hirosato of the *Kirishima* landed this morning." Takenaka's manner suddenly seemed cautious. "He is on his way to the capital, to Seoul"

"Any indication of why, Lieutenant?"

"The same reason as for your journey, sir. A diplomatic task. No details were provided."

Dawlish had already informed Takenaka of the purpose of his own journey and had asked him to act as interpreter. "Perhaps we'll catch up with him on the way," he said. "Do you know Captain Shi … Shi … … I mean the *Kirishima's* captain?"

"I know of him, sir. He too trained with the Royal Navy. But he…" Takenaka stopped, his face set in an unreadable mask. "I have no direct experience of this officer," he said.

Dawlish sensed even greater caution and risked a wild shot. "Another Satsuman perhaps?"

"I understand that Captain Shimazu is from Kagoshima." Still impassive, no flicker of emotion. "So yes, sir. From Satsuma."

"And you, Lieutenant Takenaka. Where are you from?"

"From Mino, sir. In central Japan."

"A different…" Dawlish tried to remember a word used back at the island. "A different domain?"

"A very different domain, sir."

"And Rear Admiral Hojo? Where does he come from?"

"From Kanto, sir. From central Japan." Takenaka paused, then said. "Rear Admiral Hojo is especially esteemed for his loyalty."

And loyal he should be, like any officer, Dawlish thought, so why mention it? But he knew that he'd be damned if he'd get anything more of substance from Takenaka, and damned also if he knew what Takenaka would like to tell him, but could not. It could hardly matter. *We need spend no more than a week in Korea, a fortnight at the utmost*, he reminded himself. *We'll get the signatures we've been assured are a formality and then we'll start the long haul home.* It seemed simple.

But it sounded less simple two hours later after Matthew Whitaker, third secretary at the Peking embassy, and assigned temporarily as Her Majesty's envoy in Korea, was rowed out over the now-flooded mud flats. He had sent a message ahead respectfully requesting that he meet Dawlish on deck, and not below, adding "You will understand why when you see me."

And Dawlish did understand when they met under the canvas awning stretched over the quarterdeck. Whitaker, a short dark man of his own age, not only looked unkempt in a sweat-soaked cotton jacket with grimy linen beneath, but had a fading bruise on the side of his face and he walked stiffly. His exposed skin was covered in tiny livid spots.

"I was robbed on my way from Seoul," he said. "The scoundrels beat two of my servants, buffeted me around somewhat, took everything, left us like beggars. I'm relying on you to settle my expenses at the inn I'm lodged at – a wretched place – and for the horses I've arranged for you." He scratched under his armpit and forced a smile. "Not a dignified state for Her Majesty's representative, is it? The villages are dirty here, worse even than China, and Chemulpo's worst of all."

"And you're lousy?" Dawlish recognised the spots and found himself liking Whitaker. "It's nothing to be ashamed of. But bad, isn't it? I've known the same." The memory of lice chewing into him and of the feeling of degradation they brought with them was an unforgettable part of that terrible winter in Thrace four years before. "We'll soon get you cleaned up," he said, "and if you don't object to sharing somebody's clothing we'll find an officer of your size on board. I fear that what you're wearing belongs in this ship's furnaces."

A canvas screen provided a degree of privacy as Whitaker sluiced down with seawater. Wrapped in a blanket, Dawlish conducted him down to his own bathroom to complete the process while a steward was sent to borrow suitable clothes. Lieutenant Hamilton would temporarily relinquish his quarters to provide decent overnight accommodation. By the time they met in Dawlish's own saloon Whitaker looked like a different man and was smelling strongly of carbolic soap and zinc ointment. He waved aside Dawlish's concerns about the beating he had taken from his attackers and was thankful that his two servants, more badly injured than himself, had been taken on board for treatment. The surgeon had already decided that one was going to have to lose an arm before the gangrene rose too far up it.

"We'll need to start as soon as possible for Seoul, Captain" Whitaker drained his glass. "You're comfortable with horses? Good! Not that they're more than miserable little ponies, I'm afraid. And I trust you can supply an escort – a dozen of your men would be just the thing and if we run into my late assailants again then so much the better. Summary justice would be most appropriate."

"You've been long in Korea?" Dawlish asked.

"Too damn long! Peking is like Cheltenham by comparison. And what with the King, and the Queen, and the King's father all busily intriguing against each other, and the Japanese stirring the pot and the Chinese realising too late that they're losing whatever influence they ever had, Seoul is like a snake pit."

And for Dawlish the phrase recalled Hobart Pasha, the flamboyant English head of the Ottoman Navy, using a similar term, warning that Istanbul was a pit of serpents. As it had so lethally proved.

"I understand that the treaty codicils are ready for signature?" Dawlish was feeling uneasy.

"Ready," Whitaker said, "but that doesn't mean that anybody from the Korean side will be in a hurry to sign them. Not when there's so much unrest at present, what with a drought, and rice dying in the fields. With so many peasants starving and turning to banditry, like those fellows who robbed me. The Japanese aren't helping, not when everybody doubts the loyalty of the Korean army unit that they've undertaken to arm and train to modern standards."

"We called in at Socheong Island to see the Caledonian and Oriental enterprise," Dawlish said. "I'd been led to believe that just some enterprising Scots had done a deal with Korean officials to open mines and set up a coaling station. I was surprised to see so many Japanese there also."

Whitaker shrugged. "Good luck to Caledonian and Oriental, say I. The Japs get things done when they put their minds to it. That's one reason why the Koreans resent them."

"So the Japanese aren't trusted here?" The files Dawlish had read before leaving Hong Kong had stressed, like Topcliffe had done, the potential for Japan to counterbalance the Russian menace in the Far East. The Muscovite armies that had conquered much of Central Asia in the last two decades, were an ominous presence north of Britain's Indian Empire. They might next dominate Manchuria and North China and exclude all other powers from trade there. And Dawlish himself had fought to resist Russian expansion...

Whitaker shook his head. "King Gojong – somewhat of an idiot, by the way – and Queen Min, who's worth ten of him, both rely on the Japanese, though I doubt that they fully trust them. But the Japanese-trained companies, stiffened by Jap officers, are their best protection against the King's father, the *Daewongun*."

"He's not the King himself?" Dawlish felt bemused.

"It's complicated. The succession is labyrinthine," Whitaker said "But no, the *Daewongun* isn't king, and he hates his son because he is king, and he hates the queen even more because she has his measure. He tried to have her killed, have her blown up, a few years ago and he'd do as much again if he got the chance. And every Korean – and there's a lot of them – who resents their Hermit Kingdom being opened to foreign influence is looking to the *Daewongun* for leadership."

"So what do the Japanese want?" Dawlish said.

"Korea. Simply that, Captain Dawlish, all Korea, with or without a puppet monarch. They damn nearly took it three centuries ago and they still resent that they didn't succeed. But Korea's for the taking now and as far as we're concerned it's better that the Japanese rather than the Russians have it."

"The Japanese don't resent us signing treaties here?"

Whitaker shook his head. "They want an alliance with Britain just as much as we want one with them. They'll be glad if we sign. So will the Chinese, but for different reasons. When you arrive in Seoul in your best uniform with a full escort, and all due respects paid to the Chinese and Japanese ambassadors, and an obvious unwillingness to accept any delay while you've got a powerful warship lying off the country's biggest port, miserable though it is, then, Captain Dawlish, we'll have the signatures before you know it."

"I'm dining with the Japanese admiral tonight," Dawlish said. "My senior officers are invited as well. I can include you in my party."

"You'll be impressed. Whatever they turn their hand to they do well, frighteningly well – Army, Navy, commerce, even manufacturing. They're starting to dominate trade here, you'll see that when you get ashore. Depend on it, Captain, you'll be impressed."

*

Dawlish was impressed.

Few ships of the Mediterranean Fleet, that epitome of naval smartness, could have surpassed the *Haruna* for the brightness of her brass, the smoothness of her holystoned decks, the sheen of her freshly washed paintwork, the tautness of her standing rigging. Her crew, drawn up in die-straight ranks, wore spotless uniforms that were uncannily similar to those of the Royal Navy, though the faces above them seemed blandly expressionless. When her marines crashed to attention it was with a precision that the Coldstreams might have envied. As Dawlish and his officers saluted and were saluted, as Japanese officers jerked into bows that seemed even more precise than Takenaka's, as hands were shaken afterwards, the overall impression was of a machine in which each human had a function as exactly defined as that of a cog or cam or gear.

And yet all changed when they went below, when Dawlish joined Admiral Hojo in his saloon, accompanied by Takenaka and the ship's captain, while *Leonidas's* other officers were welcomed by their *Haruna* counterparts in their wardroom. Ensconcing Dawlish in a luxuriously padded armchair, settling himself in another, with Takenaka and the captain seated a respectful distance behind, Hojo's impassive mask broke into a warm smile.

"It is a pleasure to welcome you on board, Captain," he said, and Dawlish felt that he meant it. Hojo's English was accentless and he spoke with the assurance of someone who thought as easily in the language as he did in his own. He gestured round the comfortably furnished saloon, different only from a British admiral's in that the portrait hanging there was of the Emperor Meiji rather than of Queen Victoria. A lamp burned before it. Along one side a small forest of plants topped what looked like a large, exquisitely carved, sideboard with a sword in a decorated scabbard suspended above it.

"Better quarters I'll warrant than when you and I joined as lads, Captain," Hojo said, "and I'll wager you have as good yourself today. But it was hard-lying for a youngster in those days, was it not?" Behind him Takenaka's face had also broken into a smile and the captain – who alone seemed to have no English - was gesturing to the steward to come forward with a tray carrying four porcelain cups.

"Saké," Hojo laughed. "Rice wine! You've never tried it? Better even than Scottish whiskey, but the results are the same."

They turned towards the portrait of the darkly bearded, intense and intelligent-looking Emperor in a European-style uniform and drank his health. Then they drank the Queens's health. The steward glided forward with refills.

"And now a good British toast, Captain," Hojo beamed. "Wives and Sweethearts! May they never meet!"

They drained the cups and Dawlish was already wondering how he could, with courtesy, slow the pace of drinking. He needed a clear head. Already sounds of rising conviviality were drifting aft from the wardroom. Here in the admiral's saloon Hojo was launching into almost wistful reminiscences of a global circumnavigation in HMS *Hampshire* and laughing about how his stomach had accustomed itself to salt beef and ship's biscuits. Dawlish held his hand, palm down, above the cup when the steward next came forward and no offence seemed to be taken.

The dinner was eaten at a round table with silver European cutlery. Dawlish guessed that Takenaka had hinted previously that bowls and chopsticks might occasion embarrassment but the brown soup and the roast pork – which the Japanese discreetly pushed to one side of their plates – and the plum duff afterwards were almost as unappetising as a British cook could have managed. It was slightly reassuring that not everything was perfect on this ship.

They talked weapons, Hojo keen to hear details of *Leonidas's* 6-inch Armstrong breech loaders, and clearly envious of them, for both Japanese ships, though British-built, were armed with Krupps of the same calibre. Dawlish remembered the devastation he had unleashed in a Black Sea anchorage with similar German weapons but he said nothing of it. That had been in the Ottoman Sultan's service, his secondment unofficial and better not discussed. Hojo added with pride that the *Tatsuta*, the new near-sister due soon to arrive in Japan from Europe, would be armed with similar, but yet-further improved, weapons.

They were drinking French brandy now. Hojo's conversation was again of early days, of his arrival in Britain, of his initial struggles with English, of his surprise at the number of stone buildings, of his shock at seeing so much meat hung in butchers' shops. He pressed Dawlish for accounts of his own service, seemed genuinely fascinated by his account of the rocket battery in Abyssinia, of fighting in the dark Ashanti bush, of chasing Arab slavers off East Africa. Dawlish avoided any mention of more recent, more sensitive, service.

Hojo was sweating heavily now, his face flushed, his speech slurring slightly, and neither Takenaka nor the captain were in scarcely better shape, yet none of them seemed embarrassed. Within the confines of these quarters, during this period of hospitality, they had accepted him as one of themselves, Dawlish realised, linked by common experience and by the standards of a service they all revered. *They're like us,* a small, comfortable voice told him, *Englishmen with oriental faces.* And yet he realised that there had been no opportunity to enquire about the nature of the diplomatic mission that had sent the absent captain of the other Japanese corvette to Seoul.

For all his increasing inebriation Hojo noticed Dawlish's gaze drifting towards the long sideboard. "You have not seen *Bonsai* before, Captain?" he said. "It is an art peculiarly suited to life at sea – not just the delight its perfection affords, but the reward of triumphing over so many challenges. Let me show you."

There were perhaps a dozen of them, tiny trees, each a perfect miniature of a full-size species, each in its own shallow stoneware dish, some round and with only a single specimen, others rectangular trays that contained miniature landscapes.

"Here is an... an *ume*, " Hojo paused, searching for a word, then found it, ".. a plum." He lifted another carefully, and placed it in Dawlish's hands. "And this a *sakuru*, a cherry."

It was of flawless beauty and Dawlish realised that it must have taken infinite patience, infinite dedication, to have brought it to this state and to have maintained it on shipboard. He murmured his appreciation, knowing that no words in English were adequate for its excellence. As he replaced it in its position he realised that there was a water-filled rectangular tank set into the surface behind. Something stirred sluggishly within and looking down Dawlish saw a small eel burrowing under the pebbles on the bottom.

"He feeds from my hand," Hojo said. "He is an old friend."

Dawlish must have looked surprised, for Takenaka said "It's common on our ships to keep small animals. It is an aid to rest and contemplation."

"You would like to see?" Hojo said. "The captain will be happy to conduct you to visit a mess deck."

And, as the admiral's quarters had been, so too was the mess deck very similar to a British one, practically identical indeed – and yet different in some undefinable way. There was once again the feeling of something beyond perfection in the neatness of the stowage, in the polish of the fittings, even in the men's smiles – and they seemed genuine – once they had been put at ease after laying down the paper fans they had been cooling themselves with and leaping to ramrod-straight attention when their officers entered.

"Kindly listen, Captain Dawlish," Takenaka was smiling. "Can you guess what that is?"

There was a low, steady noise, as if scissors were being ground on a whetstone. Dawlish shook his head.

The captain barked something – every command in Japanese sounded impatient, angry, even when no anger was involved. Several seamen moved to retrieve what looked like small boxes from above the personal lockers. At another word from the captain one came forward, the object held towards Dawlish on outstretched hands. It was a tiny cage, constructed of bamboo slivers, and within it a large cricket chirped, adding its voice to those held by others. The crew were crowding round, obvious pleasure on their faces. Somebody produced a small piece of melon and pushed it into the cage. The chirping stopped as the insect turned its attention to it.

"Would you like to see how they drink, sir?" Takenaka turned and spoke to one of the men.

A small cup of water was produced. The cricket's owner took a sip and then began to blow a light spray from his mouth, through the little bars, to wet the creature. It reared back, rubbing the moisture over its body with obvious pleasure. Somebody said something and there was a chorus of laughter.

"Seaman Kiyoshi says that his cricket also serves His Majesty," Takenaka explained. The captain said something else and everybody laughed again.

Then it was time to leave, the men leaping again to rigid attention and radiating something – more than competence, more than confidence and dedication, more than pride – that was indefinable. These men, these officers, this ship, this navy, all impressed, all demanded respect.

Hojo must have known that, though he did not allude to it directly.

"My father never saw a steamship," he said as they shook Dawlish's hand at parting. "He died the year before the Americans came with their black ships."

There was no need to say more. *We've come this far in twenty-eight years. Respect us. We're your equals now.*

But as Dawlish was rowed back to *Leonidas* he realised that he still knew as little about the reason for the Japanese ships' presence here as when he had arrived.

6

It took two more days to get on the road for Seoul, despite Dawlish's impatience, but he could not afford to be short of money when acting in the Queen's name. The problem was not the money itself – though it would need careful accounting – but the means of transporting it. Accompanied by Takenaka and a small guard of marines, Watkin, *Leonidas's* paymaster, had gone ashore with a thousand gold sovereigns.

The two Japanese banks operating in Chemulpo were between them able to convert these in *cash*, the standard currency, but with an exchange rate of over fourteen thousand to the pound, and no larger denominations available than single units, the quantities were vast. Hours were spent in telling out the coins, each with a hole in the centre, and stringing them on straw twine. Clearance of Whitaker's accommodation costs at an inn and advance payments for horse and rental made only a negligible impact on the huge weight involved. Not a single cart could be found for hire and there was nothing for it but to rent six draught oxen, great lumbering creatures, each with its own driver, to carry the sacks of coin on their backs. The journey to Seoul, little over twenty miles, was already beginning to sound like a long one.

Whitaker acted as Dawlish's guide around Chemulpo, what there was of it. The Chinese quarter was like a small Hong Kong, a hive of noisy trade in imported wares. The Japanese settlement, more recent, more ordered, was dominated by large rice warehouses. The Korean town contrasted with both, a confused huddle of mud hovels clustered around winding alleyways which Dawlish had no desire to enter. The city governor's residence looked down from a low hill above, its gate topped with double curved tiled roofs. Though *Leonidas* could be clearly seen at anchor, and though minor port functionaries had come on board, the town governor had made no effort to acknowledge her presence. Dawlish decided to ignore him.

Already he wished to be on his way, for the filth and squalor offended him, and the inhabitants seemed surly and unwelcoming. Most were clad in dingy white, the men wearing high black hats with circular brims, many of the women with breasts exposed despite the swathes that otherwise engulfed them, the children barefoot and dirty. There were few animals to be seen and Dawlish found the sight of porters bowed under enormous weights on wooden-pack saddles depressing. The contrast with the calm efficiency on the immaculate Japanese ships in the roadstead was striking. It was they perhaps who represented the better future, Dawlish thought, better perhaps for the Koreans that Japan should rule them. He was looking forward to the dinner on *Leonidas* that night to which he had invited Hojo and his officers. They had been good company the previous evening and he hoped for as much again.

*

They left for Seoul next morning. There was no road, just a track that ran through rolling, cultivated but sun-parched countryside. Only

69

Dawlish, Whitaker and Takenaka rode, for Watkin had elected to tramp next to the cash-laden oxen, but after the first two miles Dawlish was overcome with pity for his own wretched little pony and he dismounted. The others followed suit and resigned themselves to marching like the ten-strong Royal Marine detachment commanded by Ross, their Lieutenant. Several more oxen carried food and personal effects, which had been kept to a minimum, and it was their slow plod that set the pace.

The heat was intense and progress was uncomfortable, all the worse for the throat-searing dust thrown up by the animals. The slow, dawdling, advance was as exhausting as marching too quickly. Dawlish ordered a halt for five minutes in each hour and, even though the start had been in the cool of dawn, progress by mid-morning was scarcely six miles. At this rate Seoul could not be reached before nightfall and, considering Whitaker's early experience with bandits, he was reluctant to press on with a smaller group. Towards noon he permitted everybody to march in shirtsleeves, their tunics and accoutrements laden on the ponies.

Dawlish tried to ignore his nagging concern about leaving *Leonidas*, however temporarily. It had cost him dearly to win her and he disliked entrusting her to other hands. But Edgerton, for all his lack of ambition, should be well capable of taking her out to sea if unexpected weather were to endanger her on a lee shore.

Only a few spindly pines and stone slabs on the hillsides – which Whitaker identified as gravestones – broke the monotony of the landscape. Peasants in the fields looked up with little sign of curiosity as the column passed, then stooped again to their toil among the shrivelled crops. Wooden posts at regular intervals, each carved with a grotesque human face, marked some Korean unit of distance. Here and there an abandoned bullock cart was stuck in the track, as if half-submerged, sunk inextricably in the winter mud and locked there by the summer drought. There were other travellers on the move also, none moving any faster, but all protected to some extent even if this meant just two men with pikes or one alone with an ancient flintlock. They passed through a village, unwalled, fruit trees on its fringes, where the few emaciated half-naked children playing in the dust and tired-looking women scarcely noticed them.

There was a sudden guffaw among the marines, who were marching in easy step. "That's enough!" Dawlish heard Ross shout angrily. "We'll have none of that!"

"What's the problem, Lieutenant?" Dawlish fell in beside him and spoke quietly. A silence had fallen over the marines and several were looking shame-faced.

"A coarse remark, sir," Ross's face was blushing an even deeper red than the sun had burned it. He was a serious young man, much dedicated to reading his Bible.

"I'm shocked!" Dawlish said. Ross did not notice the tone of irony. "What was it?"

"It was about the Korean ladies' attire. It was about ..." Ross hesitated, embarrassed. "About the ladies' upper persons."

Dawlish glanced back and saw two women outside a hovel, both bare-breasted even though neither was suckling a child. However strange, it seemed to be standard dress here. And suddenly it didn't seem like a joke. Insensitivity like this had triggered the Indian Mutiny.

"You did right, Lieutenant," Dawlish said. "It makes no sense to give offence."

There was a well on the further outskirts of the village and they paused here for the midday break and to water the oxen. Several peasants were already drawing from it and Dawlish overheard Watkin, always the conscientious paymaster, ask Takenaka how much they should receive for supplying water to the column.

Takenaka laughed. "Nothing," he said. "They should be grateful for the protection we represent."

"They still deserve to be paid," Watkin said.

Takenaka shrugged and snapped a few words towards the Koreans. Their heads bowed and there was an immediate impression of fear. There was a sullen obsequiousness in the manner of the man who replied and he did not look Takenaka in the face.

"Fifty cash," Takenaka told Watkin. "Fifty more than they deserve." He turned and stalked away. There was an assertiveness, even an arrogance, about him now that had not been obvious on shipboard.

The marines had a small fire going and tea had been brewed. Dawlish saw Watkin sitting beneath a tree and sat down on the ground beside him to drink his own. "I think Her Majesty can afford a thousand, Lieutenant," he said quietly, and then, louder, "It's a fine day, is it not? I trust you're enjoying the journey?"

71

"Indeed, sir. A fascinating journey." Watkin, just as loudly, finding it hard to supress a smile.

The low hills on the eastern horizon, and the gap through which the track led to Seoul, were still five miles distant in late afternoon. There would be no option but to camp overnight in the next village.

"I was robbed near there," Whitaker gestured towards the knot of hovels. Dawlish already knew the story, sensed also that Whitaker felt guilty that he had failed to protect his people. "They'd clubbed them down – good fellows, Chinese, they'd been with me for two years – before I could even draw my revolver," he had told Dawlish apologetically. "When I did, and before I could cock it, they knocked it from my hand and had me on the ground." Whitaker suspected that the robbers dared not kill him because of the retribution the murder of a European might bring, but they had not hesitated to strip him and his men of all they had and to steal his horse. "A decent one," he said, "a good Manchurian pony. I'd brought her from Peking." Korean Good Samaritans had later found Whitaker and his servants dazed and beaten and had helped them to Chemulpo.

The shrivelled fields on either side now seemed deserted, no peasants bent here in endless labour. The land seemed empty, eerily empty, and Dawlish had noticed that for the last hour they had encountered no travellers moving in the opposite direction. He was about to remark this to Whitaker when a low roar rose from the village ahead, now no more than a half-mile distant. It came again, and then again, three times in all and measured in time. Then there was silence again. Takenaka had been walking beside Whitaker and Dawlish saw what seemed like concern on his face.

"What do you think that was, Lieutenant?" Dawlish asked the Japanese.

"Impossible to say, sir." Takenaka's features had already been rearranged in the same unreadable mask that Dawlish had seen before. He paused, then said "There may be Japanese troops in the village."

"In that case…" Dawlish began, but another low roar interrupted him, then another, as measured and as regular as before.

"I believe that it might be better if we were to be properly uniformed, sir," Takenaka said. He bowed very slightly and Dawlish sensed that it had taken a lot from him to make a suggestion to a more senior officer.

Whitaker was nodding. "Protocol is everything here," he said.

Though the sun was dropping it was still hot enough to make it oppressive to put on uniform tunics over sweat-sodden shirts, worse still for the marines as they buttoned up tightly and rearranged their kit. Hawley, Ross's sergeant, was urging frantic polishing of dust-dulled buckles and demanding parade-ground precision in the formation of a short column. Dawlish's tunic was crumpled and his cap was enveloped in cloud of dust when he slapped it on his thigh. It took time – too long, for another triple roar came from the village – to retrieve his sword from his baggage on one of the oxen and to strap it on.

"Stay here," he told Watkin. The paymaster had his revolver to protect the cash should the oxen-drivers, or any bandits, want to make off with it. Given the weight and the beasts' lack of speed the risk seemed minimal.

Dawlish led the column on foot – better that than the indignity of making an entrance on that pitiful little pony. Takenaka and Whitaker followed, the diplomat obviously uncertain as to whether he should adopt a more military step, the Japanese looking smarter in his Royal Navy uniform than Dawlish suspected he did himself. Ross followed with the marines, Martini-Henry rifles sloped on their shoulders, bayonet-scabbards slapping rhythmically on their thighs as they marched. Their trudge through the day's heat had been as listless as everybody else's but now their steady tread reflected discipline and pride.

The village was as squalid as the one they had encountered previously. As they entered another triple roar erupted from beyond the slight bend in the track the seemingly empty huts flanked. This time Dawlish could half-make out the word, an explosive yell that must come from a dozen throats. He turned to look questioningly towards Takenaka.

"*Banzai*," Takenaka said, face still unreadable. "Like your Hurrah. It means Long Life."

They rounded the bend and saw a crowd ahead, Koreans in dingy white, their faces fearful as they turned to see the newcomers. They stepped back, exposing a path, and Dawlish passed through to a square of beaten earth beyond.

And found Hell.

Seamen in uniforms not unlike those of their British counterparts, with Sennet hats and square collars and their trousers gathered in for marching by canvas gaiters, were disposed at intervals around the open space, their rifles bayonet-tipped. Even as Dawlish entered one turned to smash his rifle butt against the temple of a peasant crowding behind and knocked him down. The crowd was silent, silent with terror, their gaze fixed in horror on the three bodies sprawled on the ground, their heads several feet away, dark puddles running from the terrible craters that had been their necks. They lay in a straight line and two men, still living, their torsos bare and blood-streaked, were crouched on their knees at the end of it. Their heads were bowed and one seemed calm with the dazed incomprehension of a bullock awaiting slaughter while the other was moaning and shaking uncontrollably. Two officers, Japanese, though their naval uniforms were almost British, were standing over them, both with blood-streaked, slightly curved swords, both relaxed, one smoking a cigarette, the other laughing and nodding towards the calmer of the kneeling men. Neither seemed in any hurry to get on with the business.

Dawlish advanced towards them and they saw him for the first time. One, by his uniform a captain, smiled and moved forward, transferring his sword to his left hand and extending his right as if to grasp Dawlish's in greeting. He was as tall as Dawlish himself and his features, by the standards of any society, could not have been more handsome. His lips were drawn back in a smile. But it was not on him that Dawlish's gaze rested, but what he now saw on the far side of the square. An X-shaped cross made of two stout poles lashed together was propped against the side of a hut and on it a man was bound, stark naked, red slashes down his front, his head lolling feebly. Two seamen stood by him, their bayonets dissuading the onlookers from coming any closer.

"Captain Shimazu Hirosato of the Imperial Japanese Navy." The officer bowed, still smiling, Dawlish saw him counting the rings on his own sleeve. A single drop of blood fell to the ground from the sword in Shimazu's left hand. "I see I have the pleasure of greeting a British officer." His English was perfect. "I have warm memories of my own training and service in the Royal Navy."

Dawlish affected not to see the outstretched hand. "Captain Nicholas Dawlish, Her Majesty's Ship *Leonidas*," he said. He bowed. Over Shimazu's shoulder he could see the figure struggling feebly on the cross. Behind him he heard Whitaker exclaim "Oh sweet Jesus!"

74

"I would be honoured if you would introduce me to your officers, Captain." Shimazu's smile faded briefly as he saw Takenaka.

Dawlish ignored him. "What's happening here, Captain Shimazu?" He could not keep the disgust and anger from his tone, knew too that he must control it. *They want an alliance with Britain just as much as we want one with them,* Whitaker had told him. He was here as a diplomat.

"A small contribution to pacification," Shimazu said. "We were returning from Seoul to Chemulpo and lodged here last night. There was a theft of rice from one of my men's cooking pots. We questioned the villagers and found that several of them have reputations as bandits. It wasn't hard to identify them – one had a revolver, a British revolver, he couldn't explain – and there they are." He gestured towards the prisoners behind him, living and dead.

"This is justice, Captain Shimazu?"

"This is Korea, Captain Dawlish. And Korea needs a firm hand." He turned and barked a single word.

The officer by the kneeling man threw down his cigarette, bowed towards Shimazu and then, in a single fluid motion almost too fast for the eye to register, he swept his sword up in two hands and swung it. His victim had no warning of what was coming. His body was suddenly pitching forward, blood fountaining from the severed neck, the head dropping and rolling, the eyes locked open. A moan rose from the crowd. A Japanese petty officer was striding forward and raising his arms and his bayoneted rifle. "*Banzai!*" he shouted, the other seamen joining so that the cry was as if from a single throat. The swordsman was smirking with pride. Twice more the shout was repeated.

"Lieutenant Yamada is renowned for his skill with the sword." Shimazu said it in the tone an Englishman might use to praise a batsman's stroke on the cricket pitch.

Dawlish supressed an urge to vomit. "That's enough, Captain," Dawlish said, and as he did realised that he should not have done so. Before this crowd Shimazu would never back down. And he himself was for the time-being a diplomat...

Takenaka stepped forward to Dawlish's side. He bowed, spoke in Japanese, his words staccato but the word "Satsuma" was clearly identifiable.

"Captain Dawlish, you must remind your lieutenant that he is only seconded to the Royal Navy." Shimazu's smile was gone and his anger was palpable. "Kindly inform him that he will be returning to service with the Imperial Japanese Navy in due course. That at all times, no matter what uniform he might wear, his loyalty must be to His Majesty, the Emperor, and that he must respect his superior officers."

Takenaka stiffened, glowing wordlessly with obvious fury. But Shimazu was turning back towards the other officer and Dawlish realised that the confrontation had doomed the last kneeling man. Shimazu nodded and Lieutenant Yamada, the swordsman, flashed a smile of acknowledgement. Again the motion was almost too quick to follow. The dazed victim died silently, his head tumbling into the dirt, his blood a scarlet flood. And again three *Banzais*.

Dawlish felt numb with impotence. This was worse than facing enemy fire, worse even than when Cossacks had once surged towards him, frozen clods flying from hooves, lances levelled, for though almost a dozen armed marines stood behind him now, ready to die at his orders no matter what the odds, they were of no avail.

"That man on the cross." It was Whitaker, by Dawlish's shoulder, his voice low, quavering. "He's the one who took my revolver from me. I'm sure of it."

"You wanted summary justice, you said?" Dawlish felt a wave of disgust.

"Oh Christ! No! Not this!" Whitaker's voice had risen, had the despair of a damned soul's. "We can't let him suffer this way!"

And though the crucified man understood nothing of the words he lifted his head and the expression of torment and entreaty was terrifying. He was trying to speak, but the pressure of his hanging body on his chest was choking off the words.

"So this is how he came by the revolver!" Shimazu had heard the exchange. "Stolen from an Englishman, was it? And I, Gentlemen, have a debt of honour to repay Britain for my training!" He barked an order and the two seamen at the foot of the cross raised their rifles.

Takenaka was shouting what might have been a counter-order even as both men drove upwards with their bayonets, gouging into their victim's belly and ripping outwards. He jerked rigid against his bonds and threw back his head, screaming – an animal sound, scarcely human – and shrieking again as they dragged their blades free before plunging them upwards once more.

Then silence, the scream cut off abruptly, the head falling forward on the chest, entrails hanging like glistening ropes, the body voiding blood and waste. The silence lasted long seconds, and then there was a collective intake of breath, the sound of moaning, of women sobbing, all to be drowned out in the three successive *Banzais* that thundered across the square.

Dawlish found himself shaking, not with anger now, but with shame. I've stood here and I've seen murder done, he thought, and I've done nothing to stop it. There's nothing I could have done, he was already telling himself, but he knew already that this was a disgrace he would reproach himself with forever, as bad as the infamy he had allied himself to on the Rio San Joaquin. And still I must not antagonise this smiling beast in uniform he told himself. Britain needs a Japanese alliance and I'm here as a diplomat.

A diplomat — a man sent abroad to lie for his country, a small voice reminded him.

Shimazu's look combined contempt of pity with smug triumph. "I don't think your party will lose anything else to these people, Captain Dawlish," he said.

Dawlish put his face very close to him and spoke low enough for nobody else to hear. "I've seen your pacification, and when you're gone, these people will see mine." As he stepped back he saw deep anger in Shimazu's eyes though his smirk never faded.

"I'm on my way to Chemulpo," Shimazu bowed, "but I'll be returning to Seoul in a few days to complete some unfinished business there. I trust I'll have the honour of meeting you there, Captain Dawlish".

There was no salute from Dawlish, nor from his marines, as the Japanese party left. Shimazu had approached Whitaker and handed over the revolver that had been found. Dawlish saw the diplomat flinch when he took it, only too aware of the price at which it had been recovered. His pony had been located also, through what questioning it was better not to ask.

The Japanese were gone in ten minutes, in perfect marching order, leaving only the headless bodies on the bloody earth, and the disembowelled figure hanging on the cross, and the sounds of muffled wailing behind them. The crowd still stood in terrified silence and immobility, eyeing the British group in fear and doubt. It was time now, Dawlish realised, for reassurance, for assistance in clearing the shambles, for simple humanity. He gave the necessary orders.

It was his pacification, inadequate, but the best that could be managed.

*

Dawlish's entire party stayed outside the village that night, bivouacking on the ground to avoid the fleas which according to Whitaker infested every inn. Only partly reassured that these newly-arrived armed men might not be as great a menace as the Japanese, the villagers had wrapped the butchered bodies in straw for burial and held wake for them through the night hours. The sounds of drumming, and a plaintive piping, and occasional snatches of singing reached the British campfires. Marine sentries were posted in turns. After they had eaten, four of them had been led in quiet prayer by Sergeant Hawley, a Methodist. Their lieutenant, Ross stood close by, as if casually, obviously reluctant to break the barrier of rank by joining them but his own lips moving soundlessly. Dawlish was aware of furtive but resentful looks towards himself as he passed them. He felt it keenly that they had probably expected more – and better – of him than he had been able to provide when faced with such cold-blooded savagery. He had no alternative, he kept telling himself, and yet knew that it was not answer enough. And there was more, a growing awareness that he knew little – knew nothing – of these potential Japanese allies and that the dinner on Hojo's flagship had blinded him. He felt at a total loss as to how to deal with these... he sought for the word... these barbarians in modern uniform.

He found Takenaka kneeling immobile on the ground just outside the circle of flickering light, staring out silently into the warm darkness. His sword – a Japanese sword – lay before him next to its ornate scabbard. Dawlish suspected that he was suffering something like the frustration and shame that he was enduring himself. He lowered himself beside him. Takenaka made to get up to bow but Dawlish restrained him.

"You must be open with me, Lieutenant," he said. He tried to make it sound as unthreatening, as little like an accusation, as he could. "There's something about Captain Shimazu you've been holding back. What is it?"

"Captain Shimazu is a loyal servant of His Majesty, sir." Takenaka's gaze was fixed on the darkness.

"There's more to it than that, isn't there? You spoke of him being from Kagoshima? From Satsuma? Is that important?"

"It is very important, sir."

"And you're from – where was it? From Central Japan?"

"From Mino, sir." The voice neutral, giving nothing away.

"Admiral Hojo is also from Mino. And he's especially respected for his loyalty?"

"That is correct, sir."

"So what's the significance of Satsuma, of Kagoshima?"

A long silence. Then Takenaka sighed. "There was a revolt in Satsuma five years ago," he said. "A protest against the abolition for the Samurai class." He paused. "The leaders were honourable men, loyal to His Majesty, but they felt that honour demand that they make a protest."

"And Shimazu was one of them?"

"No. He was in Britain, serving with the Royal Navy. But his father and three brothers were prominent in the rebellion. It was over before he even came to hear of it."

"And they died?"

"Two brothers in battle. The third, and his father, committed *seppuku*." He spoke the word with what might have been reverence.

"*Seppuku?*"

"They cut their bellies to prove that their actions were motivated by loyalty to His Majesty."

Dawlish's mind recoiled from the image. The memory of the crucifixion made it all too real. "So Captain Shimazu wanted vengeance?"

"No, sir!" The question seemed to shock Takenaka. "His father's wish was that his son should serve the Emperor. As he has done since, with loyalty and dedication."

"And as he still does, Lieutenant Takenaka?"

Again a long silence. Dawlish persisted. "You heard something the night of the dinner on the *Haruna*. What was it, Lieutenant?" He sensed reluctance. "Your superior officer is asking you," he said gently.

Silence again, Takenaka rocking slightly back and forth, his face set in what might be mental turmoil. At last he said "*Genyosha.*"

It meant nothing to Dawlish. "What is that?"

"*Genyosha* means Dark Ocean. It's a ..." Takenaka sought for a word. "It's a group, a society, but officially it does not exist. It wants to influence policy. Its loyalty to the Emperor is absolute even though his advisers oppose it. It wants the Empire to absorb Korea as soon as possible. And afterwards Manchuria, then China, then all Asia."

The idea seemed ludicrous – Korea alone would be challenge enough for the small island Empire, however rapidly it might have modernised. But Dawlish kept scepticism from his voice. "And the *Genyosha* – do I pronounce it correctly? – is centred in Satsuma?"

"That is correct, sir."

"And Admiral Hojo and you are from elsewhere?"

"We are all loyal to His Majesty, the Emperor." Takenaka, still kneeling, bowed forward and touched his forehead on the sword before him.

And Dawlish knew he would get no more from him. He left Takenaka staring into the darkness and lay down himself, a blanket drawn across him and his head cradled on a saddlebag. Sleep did not come easily. The day's memories saw to that.

7

A start in the cool of dawn brought the party through the gap in the hills ahead by mid-morning. Seoul stretched below, vast, bordered by hills, some wooded, a ragged outer ring of low dwellings surrounding the walled centre. Rising above the sea of meaner single-story buildings within it were tall pagoda-style roofs that marked the palaces. Dawlish left Watkin with the plodding oxen and pushed ahead with Whitaker, Takenaka and the marines, their baggage carried on the ponies. Noon saw them crossing the broad Han river by ferry, the boatmen responding morosely to Whitaker's request for passage in what seemed to be fluent Korean but all but cowering at the sight of Takenaka.

"They don't seem to be a cheerful lot," Dawlish said.

"They told me that one of them was carried off by a tiger last night," Whitaker said. "He hasn't been found yet." He noticed Dawlish's look of incredulity. "It happens here occasionally," he said.

On the far shore they followed the rough, winding street that passed for the western entrance to the city. Both sides were lined with thatched hovels, some with wares for sale, the ditches outside them scummed with filth. Progress was slowed by oxen laden with mountains of brushwood plodding into the city and by others coming away from it with foul loads of night soil. There was no hint of curiosity, no sign of welcome or of distrust on any face Dawlish saw, not even on the barefoot children's, nothing but a blank impassivity he found unnerving. The impression that had grown since Chemulpo was that these people were all but broken in spirit and submissive beyond hope.

The city wall, of rectangular stone blocks, was almost engulfed by houses built right up to it. The gate was set in a single narrow archway in a massive structure with an ornate roof of upward curving wings above it. A half-dozen blackened objects hung there in basketry cages. Dawlish looked away quickly. Similar reminders of the price of treason had once graced London Bridge.

"The *Donuimun* Gate," Whitaker had followed his gaze. "It means Loyalty."

"I've never before heard so much about loyalty." Dawlish realised that he had always taken it for granted, had seldom spoken of it. And yet it had ruled his life since childhood, to those above him, and to those below. Perhaps those who talked most of it practised it least.

Several soldiers in dingy knee-length red tunics, and with the tall, brimmed, black hats that no Korean man seemed to venture out without, lounged by the gate. None of their weapons was more modern than a flintlock. They stood aside, dull-eyed, as the small column approached, *Leonidas's* marines marching in impeccable step, and they gave no sign of recognition as it passed through, even as Ross called for his men to bring their rifles to the salute. A little further on two soldiers were pulling its load from an ox as its cringing owner protested weakly, already resigned to paying whatever they demanded to allow passage.

"Not much vigilance here," Dawlish could not disguise his contempt.

"They haven't been paid for months." Whitaker sounded sympathetic. "They're probably hungry."

"Worse than normal?"

"Much worse. Because of the drought. Rice is almost unaffordable. And the Japanese buy up whatever is available."

They pressed on through a labyrinth of narrow streets, passing the occasional sumptuously dressed official on a pony led by retainers and others in palanquins, their sweating bearers carrying them with

81

dumb resignation. The overall impression of others on the streets – mainly men, with very few women visible – was of sullen indifference.

Whitaker's residence proved to be near the summit of a hill that gave a view across the sea of tiled and thatch roofs towards the huge palace compound to the north. He had rented what had been an inn, had got it cleaned thoroughly and had installed a small staff of servants, mainly Chinese whom he had brought from Peking. A small lion and unicorn crest was mounted over the gate and a union flag hung limply from a pole within. The small compound was surrounded by eight-foot brick walls though Dawlish thought little of the pike-armed watchmen who guarded it. Everybody would sleep better for the presence of *Leonidas's* marines. Within, the residence was furnished pleasantly in Oriental style with only a shelf of English books to indicate its tenant's origins. The faintest whiff of opium hung about it and Dawlish wondered if some unseen Chinese lady was not overseeing the establishment as well as providing other comforts. Whitaker's first task was to tell his servants of the injuries of the two of their number left in Chemulpo. They heard the news with a dignity that was all the more moving for a quiet acceptance that Dawlish found almost inhuman.

The tragedy did not prevent Whitaker's cook preparing a Chinese-style meal that Dawlish found excellent. He was embarrassed by Whitaker's and Takenaka's ability to pick up each morsel with sticks and by the steward's provision of a knife and fork and spoon for him. He swallowed his pride and asked Takenaka to instruct him. The Japanese seemed delighted by the request and showed genuine pleasure when Dawlish found the skill easier than he had expected. They were all three in silk dressing gowns provided by Whitaker, he and Takenaka wearing them easily, Dawlish initially self-conscious. The clothing they had worn was already being washed and guaranteed to be back, fully ironed, by morning. The crumpled dress uniform Dawlish would need in the coming days was receiving special attention.

As they ate Whitaker outlined his plans. He had already sent his Chinese clerk to give notice that he would visit the Foreign Ministry – "And don't think of it as being like Whitehall" – the following day to arrange an audience at which Dawlish could present his credentials. Only thereafter would come discussions about when to sign the treaty codicils.

"More important still, you'll need to see the Chinese ambassador and his Jap counterpart," Whitaker said. Then, catching himself, he looked towards Takenaka. "Sorry, old chap." His voice was apologetic. "No offence meant, none taken, I hope. I've come to think of you as one of us. I should have said that we'll need to speak to the representative of His Imperial Majesty."

Takenaka bowed but said nothing. Dawlish realised that he must have endured months of this in British wardrooms. The moment of uneasiness was interrupted by a deep boom from outside.

"The curfew bell," Whitaker said. "It's a sight to see, Dawlish. You'll be surprised."

He led them up to a small platform built against the compound wall and from it they could see across the city. A soft moonlit darkness had fallen and the air was warm. The noises of the day were gone and only a distant barking dog broke the silence. Few lighted windows seemed to open on to winding streets and alleys that were plunged in deep shadow with no sign of life. And then, slowly, at first as single pinpricks, then in tens, and then hundreds, and at last innumerable, lights were appearing and bobbing gently through the dark thoroughfares. They moved haphazardly, like glow-worms in a wood by night, some suddenly extinguished as they entered a dwelling, others just as quickly appearing elsewhere. The sight was at once pleasing and perplexing.

"It's the ladies' time," Whitaker said. "From now until midnight the streets are theirs. The men must remain indoors, as the ladies must all day, and unless a man's blind, or an official, he'll be thrashed by the night-watch if he's found outside. It's the only chance ladies have to visit their friends."

"But we've seen women enough," Dawlish said. "In fact Ross's men were appreciative of the sight."

"They saw women" Whitaker said. "Now you're seeing ladies. And in Korea the difference matters."

And not just in Korea, Dawlish thought bitterly. He wondered how Whitaker might react if he knew that his own wife was a coachman's daughter. He thought of her alone now in their villa in Southsea, selfless and busy as always at the Sailors' Rest home she had helped establish, outwardly immune to slight and yet feeling it keenly. Now, more than ever, he wished that *Leonidas* was headed homewards.

But first those codicils, those damned codicils, must be signed. It was now July the 19th and he had given himself a mental target to be gone from here by the month's end.

Whitaker was absent most of the next day and Dawlish toured the city on foot with Takenaka, guided by one of the Chinese clerks. They wore civilian garb and Dawlish decided not to take an escort. From what he had seen the previous day a stout stick should be enough for protection and he did not want to draw attention to himself.

He had hoped to buy gifts to add to the silk shawls he had bought in Hong Kong for Florence and for his sister Susan, but every stall, every shop, seemed bare, as if all of value had been removed from display. There was little of note other than the exteriors of the royal palaces and they viewed these from a distance. By early afternoon they had exhausted their interest in the giant bell they had heard the night before, in a pagoda defaced in the Japanese invasion three centuries before and in a huge inscribed tablet standing on the back of a granite turtle. Everywhere they met the same blank looks and everywhere men stepped aside, careful, eyes downcast, when they recognised Takenaka as Japanese. Whitaker's residence was again close by when a crowd ahead blocked the street and the sound of shouting – angry shouting – reached them.

"We had better step inside here, sir." Takenaka motioned to an open-fronted shop selling ugly brassware. The owner shrank from them.

The crowd had the makings of a mob and it was crying out and gesticulating as it came down the street. It was moving reluctantly ahead of a phalanx of a half-dozen soldiers in the same red tunics and black hats that Dawlish had seen the previous day, but these troops had an alertness about them now, a consciousness that they themselves might be at risk, that had been absent then. They were prodding the protesters before them with levelled pikes and a few were sweeping flintlocks menacingly towards the most vocal. Behind them other soldiers were dragging three half-naked men, hands bound behind them, their backs blood-striped, who stumbled along with their heads thrust though holes in massive wooden planks that dragged on the ground before their feet. Characters daubed in front in running black paint proclaimed their crime. One fell, struggled unsuccessfully to rise, was kicked and beaten and then hoisted to his feet again. Another half-dozen soldiers made up the rear-guard, protecting the procession from the anger of the crowd behind.

"What's happening?" Dawlish was sickened by the sight, by the mute resignation of the suffering men. The road to Calvary must have been like this.

The Chinese clerk directed a torrent of questions at the trembling shop owner. The man stammered answers and kept looking fearfully towards Takenaka.

"They tried to steal from an army rice store. They were hungry. Everybody is."

"What's going to happen to them?"

"Their heads will be cut off." The clerk stated it without emotion. "Do you want to see it, sir? The execution ground is near."

Dawlish shook his head. "That won't be necessary." He kept silent all the way back to the residence, offended that the clerk should even think he might want to see such a sight. He was reluctant too to let Takenaka suspect how much he had been moved, how much he already loathed this place and longed for the ordered certainties of routine and duty on his own ship.

Watkin's cash-laden oxen and the remaining baggage had now arrived and Ross was busy turning the now-crowded compound into a well-run garrison. Whitaker had been successful in arranging an audience for the morrow. "You're lucky, Dawlish," he said. "There's a chance you'll see the king, and better still the queen perhaps. Not that they'll say anything, but the recognition is all you need." In three days they would see the Japanese ambassador but there was no appointment yet with the Chinese envoy. "But I've had a message sent to Fred Kung," he said. "He'll see to it."

"Who?" Dawlish was growing accustomed to unusual names but this seemed wholly outlandish.

Whitaker laughed. "He's an original," he said. "A Yankee Chinaman. Went to America as a railroad labourer and came back educated from some Presbyterian college. He speaks perfect English or, more accurately, American. He does things for the ambassador that he can't be seen doing for himself."

But that was the end of the good news. "The discontent's getting worse," Whitaker said. "The drought's bad and the crops have failed and food is short but up to now it's just been ordinary people suffering. It's been happening at intervals for centuries. But what's worse now is rumour of discontent in the army. Most of the troops are paid in rice and half of what they've been getting is chaff."

They saw the results that evening as once again they looked out over the dark city after the curfew bell had tolled. Though the glow-worm lights appeared again the darkness was also lit by the scarlet flickers of fires burning at three random places. The silence was broken by distant murmuring that rose and fell in waves, all too obviously the sound of rage. Another fire erupted, and minutes later, another, closer by. The glow-worms were disappearing now, scurrying for shelter and being replaced by blazing torches that marked the furious progress of angry groups down dark streets. A small flame-lit knot, thirty perhaps, passed below the compound walls, waving clubs and shouting, oblivious of Ross's marines posted above them, Martini-Henrys loaded and bayonet-tipped. The mob disappeared around a corner, its target some rice-store, but the sight was worrying nonetheless.

Another eruption of flame, perhaps a mile away, and with it a ripple of gunfire – muskets, by the sound, rather than modern rifles. It died, rose again, petered out.

"Has anything like this happened before?" Dawlish asked.

Whitaker shook his head. "Not this bad. And that looked like the barracks of the *Muwi* Regiment." He nodded towards the flame-shot smoke billowing from where the gunfire had sounded.

"Mutiny?"

"God knows. There's been a rumour of the *Daewongun* stirring up trouble in the *Muwi* – the regiment used to provide the King's bodyguard – and he's encouraging discontent about it being pushed aside. He might see it as his best chance to get his son off the throne. But without modern weapons they're an anachronism." He glanced towards Takenaka. "A lot of the Korean officers resent the special favour shown to that unit the Japanese are training. They want them gone."

But by midnight the tumult had died down, the fires too, the rioters slinking back to their homes laden with purloined food and perhaps shocked by the temerity of what they had done. Smoke dispersed lazily above the city and the smell of burning faded. The silence was only broken now by the shouts of those extinguishing the fires. Before he retired Dawlish accompanied Ross on his round of the marine guard – a word of encouragement here, of a joke there – and knew he could sleep securely. Yet on every face, on Whitaker's and Takenaka's most of all, he detected unease, of unspoken fear that a boundary had been crossed.

A people who had endured so hopelessly for so long were at last stirring.

*

The dress-uniform was uncomfortable in the steaming heat but there was no option but to wear it for the visit to the palace. Dawlish hoped he looked sufficiently impressive, not just for the Navy's honour but as the representative, however briefly, of the Queen-Empress. He regretted that his medals lay in a safe-box in a bank in Southsea – his two bejewelled Turkish orders would have looked especially well – but he had pride enough in his row of British campaign ribbons.

A Korean escort had been provided, pike-armed palace guards in red or blue knee-length tunics who pushed resentful onlookers aside as the small procession moved through the streets. As a special mark of favour richly decorated horses had been sent from the royal stables for Dawlish and Whitaker. Led by grooms in faded robes that had once been brightly coloured, they balanced uncertainly on high wooden saddles and saw nothing but squalor and resentment. Here and there a shop had been burned and distraught owners were rummaging in the smoking debris.

Only at the palace's south gate, the main one, was Dawlish confronted for the first time with what had been the majesty of a once-great nation. Three arches passed through a massive wall of white stone. Above them rose a high wooden structure with a double roof, one carried high above the other, their tiled wings extended like birds'. The entire surface seemed covered by intricate carvings and painted in red or gold or turquoise. A stone-flagged roadway led towards it across open ground, the hovels bordering it looking more wretched for their contrast with the gate's splendour. Close to the gate troops lined the roadway's sides in uniforms and with weaponry that must have been unchanged for centuries. Some court functionary, flanked by a small entourage, was waiting by the gate in silken robes. Bowing and greeting and compliments followed which Whitaker seemed to carry off flawlessly but which left Dawlish bewildered. He hoped that maintaining a stonily impassive face might impress and he returned the bows as frostily as he could manage.

At last they passed into a huge flagged courtyard. Dawlish had been warned by Whitaker that the palace compound was vast, but only the eye could confirm what this actually meant. The inner wall ahead was low, white, with what looked like a tile-roofed cloister built above it. The double-roofed gate at the centre was even more impressive, more exquisite than the first. More troops lined the way to it. They looked decorative rather than effective, Dawlish thought as he viewed their medieval arms. He wondered how many were hungry, how many resented the dilution of their rice with chaff, how many could be relied upon. There was more ceremonial here, courtly and interminable, long enough for Dawlish to broil inside his uniform and to yearn for passage into shade. Whitaker was effortlessly passing and receiving compliments, bowing and receiving bows, and Dawlish took his cue from him and bowed himself when it seemed appropriate.

And as he waited it seemed half-familiar, reminiscent of Peking twenty-two years before. The Summer Palace there had been as beautiful, as fine, as this but Dawlish felt no remorse about having participated in its deliberate destruction by fire and explosive. It had been some compensation for the slaughter at the Taku Forts, not just for the first assault's bloody repulse in the mud but for the storming a year later that bought success at a fearful price. But it had been more than that, some recompense for the prisoners' tortured, hideously mutilated bodies he had never forgotten. The palace's ruin was a revenge that had hurt the imperial rulers more keenly than any mere loss of thousands of their subjects. He was not yet fifteen at the time but it was then when his heart began to harden.

"It's better than we could have hoped." Whitaker's low tone shook him from his reverie as they passed through the gate at last. "We'll see the King in the *Geunjeongjeon*, the throne hall. It means they're according you full status."

Through the gate was another courtyard, vast and cobbled, also bordered with cloistered walls. Above them, to the left, was a glimpse of the flowering shrubs and pagoda-like pavilions of the gardens beyond, but ahead lay a huge two-tiered stone platform, blindingly white in the sunshine and topped by a stone balustrade and dragon statues. On it stood a huge and intricately decorated wooden building, its walls carved and painted, its double-roofs soaring out and curving up in the style that Dawlish now recognised as typically Korean. The path leading to it across the courtyard was flanked at intervals by carved stone pillars, not unlike English gravestones. By each a court official stood, their clothing ever more colourful and lavish the closer they were to the hall beyond, bowing as the delegation passed. The silence, broken only by the sound of feet on flagstones, was unnerving and Dawlish looked neither to the right or left as he advanced, Whitaker slightly behind. They began to climb the platform steps towards the hall. Large doors stood open in the side facing them but the interior beyond was dim.

And then, at the top of the steps, Dawlish was surprised. He had expected to see more officials in silken grandeur, a royal guard perhaps in medieval garb, but instead the twenty yards to the central door were lined with troops in European-style blue uniforms, peaked caps ringed with red, whitened canvas gaiters drawing in sharply-creased trousers over shining black boots. A single barked word of command from an officer brought a hundred modern rifles as one to the salute as he swung up his own gleaming sword.

Dawlish continued to move forward as Whitaker spoke in a voice that was almost a whisper. "It's the *Pyolgigun*, the Korean unit the Japanese train," he said. "That officer's a Jap. I know him, Lieutenant Horimoto Reizo. Don't be fooled by his rank. He was military attaché at their embassy. And now he's cock of the walk here." He paused, as if shocked. "I didn't expect it so soon. They've damn nearly taken over."

They entered the gloom. As Dawlish's eyes recovered from the glare outside he found himself in a high and all-but-empty hall, with only a handful of officials ranged to either side of the approach to a high, red-painted dais. Seated there, swathed in silken robes, a slight figure sat immobile on a throne, his face blank, his eyes staring at some point above the heads of his courtiers. A carved wooden screen stood behind, an opening in it large enough only to allow a single person to pass. Dawlish, well-rehearsed by Whitaker, advanced to the bottom of the dais as a court official, whom he had been told would be the chamberlain, announced him. He bowed and, as he had been warned, saw no reaction from the figure above. The chamberlain was speaking again and Whitaker was coming forward and handing Dawlish the accreditation he must present. Whitaker spoke, his Korean again sounding impressive. It was, he had told Dawlish a formula that had been used, unchanged, for centuries. The chamberlain answered. At a murmured prompt from Whitaker Dawlish bowed again and handed over a document heavy with red sealing wax. Its pompous phrasing in English and French had also been translated into Chinese characters. Bowing low, the official mounted the dais, knelt before the king, held up the accreditation, and spoke inaudibly. The king's nod was all but imperceptible. The chamberlain descended again and raised his voice as he made a short speech. Whitaker translated in a loud whisper – part of the protocol too, he had warned Dawlish – and told that His Majesty, King Gojong, had been overjoyed by the arrival of the representative of Her Majesty, Queen-Empress Victoria, and that he sent her fraternal greetings. Dawlish's assurance that this joy would be relayed to Her Majesty, who would most surely be delighted by such a communication, was duly translated.

Then the audience was at an end. Except for his nod the king had not moved and his face had not shown a flicker of interest, understanding or emotion. But just as Dawlish lowered his head and began to pace back as he had come he glimpsed a movement in the opening in the screen behind the throne. For one instant he saw a woman's face, small, delicate, obviously intelligent, full of the energy and understanding her husband so clearly lacked. Even as his eyes dropped Dawlish realised that Queen Min must have witnessed the whole exchange, must have been weighing the significance of his presence.

Dawlish thought he saw the slightest smirk on the Japanese officer's face as he again brought the guard to the salute, a smug awareness perhaps of the emptiness of the rituals just completed, of where the real power now lay. Sweltering ever more uncomfortably in his dress uniform Dawlish retraced his steps through the courtyards, past the bowing officials, through the near-silence and the ornate gates. He felt himself oppressed by the sense of progress frozen for centuries, of mental challenge smothered, of minds resigned to weary and unquestioned repetition of meaningless ceremonial. He wondered how Whitaker could endure such formalities year upon year, could build a career on them, could face their tedium. It seemed even worse when Whitaker, apparently genuinely pleased, said "That went off well".

It was a relief to pass into the squalor of the half-starving city beyond the palace walls.

At least there seemed to be some life there.

8

There were no glow-worms that night and fires broke out at a dozen places and more, smoke rolling across the flame-crimsoned roofs, the sounds of angry voices and of shooting rising and falling in irregular waves. Whitaker was more worried than on the previous night. "I thought it would have died down by now," he said. "I thought it would have burned itself out."

The angry throngs that surged past the British compound, ignoring it, confirmed his fears. The protesters seen the previous night had been intent on looting food but now there was a bloodlust about them, a frenzy, emphasised by the impaled heads that one group bore before them by and the two bruised and terrified, half-naked figures who were being dragged with them. And worst of all there were soldiers among them, not resisting the mob but part of it, all semblance of discipline gone, screaming fury like the rest.

Ross's marines had been posted on the walls. The young officer had served only in home waters and in the Mediterranean previously and had no experience of combat, but his quiet efficiency so far was reassuring. Dawlish was uneasily aware that if a large mob, however poorly armed, turned its ire on this compound its defence could only be short-lived.

"Can we find out what's going on?" he asked Whitaker.

One of the Korean compound guards was sent out to speak with a straggler after the main body of rioters had passed. He had been given cash and – probably more valuable – rice to buy the man's cooperation. With the gate closed behind him the guard huddled in the shadows with the rioter.

Whitaker translated for him when he returned. "*Muwi* troops stormed a government rice store earlier. They killed officials – apparently tore them apart – and then they were arrested themselves. It seems that groups from all over are heading for the prison to free them. And most of the *Muwi* have joined them." He dropped his voice so that only Dawlish could hear and glanced uneasily towards Takenaka. "They killed several Japanese they caught on the street," he said. "It's better that they don't know that our friend is here. Keep him off the walls."

"Are we at risk here?" Dawlish spoke calmly but found the idea of a hopeless defence, or of a fighting retreat through this labyrinthine city, appalling. If it was necessary to leave then it would be better to do so now.

Whitaker paused before answering. "Safe enough for the time being," he said at last. "It wouldn't do British prestige any good to lower the flag. These people may not like foreigners but they'll hesitate to attack them." Then he added "Except the Japanese. They hate them enough to risk anything."

There was no let-up in the violence through the night but as the sky lightened the sounds of anger and shooting petered away to leave only a pall of smoke swirling lazily over the city. The streets and alleys seemed eerily empty. Dawlish had slept fitfully and wondered again if there was any sense remaining here, whether it was not better to retreat to the security of *Leonidas* and return when the situation calmed – if indeed it would. There was no telegraph here to link him to the world outside, no way of securing advice. The decision was his alone. Back in Hong Kong he had felt proud to have been entrusted with full discretion, full freedom of action. Now, the reality of such empowerment was a burden. Yet Whitaker's reference to lowering the flag had made the idea of retreat repugnant. He had come here for a purpose, to get a signature on the codicils, and get it he would.

The morning passed slowly, the city sweltering under the same pitiless sun that was shrivelling crops and inflicting hunger. A measure of life returned to the streets, then halted again as shooting rattled briefly from some unseen source, then died again. There was no need to venture out into the city but Dawlish felt the sense of isolation and threat intolerable, all the more for the knowledge that the massive force at his disposal afloat was worthless here. He could only inspect Ross's deployments once more and satisfy himself that the compound was as secure as it could be made with what was available. He hoped nobody recognised his unease, for he was inwardly recoiling from the memory of a compound in Thrace where a human torrent had all but overwhelmed resolute defenders.

When the arrival of the Chinese ambassador's representative was announced in early afternoon Dawlish expected a silk-clad mandarin with long sleeves and longer fingernails. But the man who spoke for the envoy of the Son of Heaven wore a shabby European-style jacket with a Paisley scarf at his throat and whipcord riding breeches stuffed into dusty boots. He wore no queue beneath his broad-brimmed hat – his hair was cropped as close as Dawlish's own – and a revolver butt protruded forward from a holster belted over his jacket on the right side. When Dawlish entered Whitaker's office after hurriedly donning his uniform, having trusted Whitaker to delay with polite compliments, the newcomer advanced with extended hand – his left hand, for the right seemed tucked away – and smiled broadly.

"Good to meet you, sir," he said. The accent was unmistakably American, the delivery wholly relaxed. "I guess you're Captain Dawlish." He grasped his hand and the grip was powerful though the shake was clumsy, left to right. "And I'm Kung, Fred Kung, here for a little man-to-man discussion." He turned to Whitaker. "You'd better translate this for the Captain – proves what I say I am." He reached inside his jacket, produced a small roll of parchment and handed it to him.

Whitaker unwound it and showed Dawlish the black characters, the red seal. "Mr. Kung's formal accreditation," he said, "but we hardly need it. We're old friends" He turned to Kung. "His Excellency is well?"

"Well enough until the rioting started. But yeah, he's fine, sends his greetings."

"Won't you sit down, Mr. Kung?" Dawlish had been preparing meaningless diplomatic phrases but they now seemed inappropriate. This man spoke English as fluently as he did himself. Kung was already seating himself on the rosewood couch beneath the lithograph of Queen Victoria. Dawlish and Whitaker took chairs opposite.

"Did you have any trouble on the street?" Dawlish estimated that Kung might be his own age, maybe slightly older, taller and heavier than most Chinese. His total self-assurance and easy manner were somehow attractive.

"Trouble, Captain? Not when I had that bunch out there with me." Kung jerked his head towards the window. "Take a look for yourself, sir."

Curiosity roused, Dawlish did so. A half-dozen men, all larger and heavier again than Kung, were lounging just inside the gate and taking no notice of the marines Ross had set to watching them. They too were clad in a mix of Chinese and European clothing, each different, with only blue turbans in common. Bandoliers slanted across their chests and they were carrying what looked like Spencer repeaters as well as short broad-bladed swords hung on their belts without scabbards. They all looked vicious and one's blade seemed smeared with red.

"Uighurs," Kung said. "From Western China. Muslims from Tianshan. Loyal to nobody but me, and that only because I pay them well. Mean sons of bitches."

"I don't doubt that you've had no trouble, Mr. Kung." Dawlish said. "And I understand you may have a message for me?"

"Here to do some plain talking, Captain, straighter than His Excellency himself can permit himself. That's why he keeps an Americanised Chinaman, a Chink as you might call him – No? You wouldn't to my face anyway, would you? – to tell in straight terms what would take too long to tell in diplomatic lingo. That's what I do for the ambassador, that and a few other jobs. Unofficially of course."

"So what's the plain talk, Mr. Kung?"

"Simple, Captain. You're here to sign a small extension to a treaty which my boss helped you Britishers get signed. It's in China's interest that you do and we'll see that the King, or better still the Queen, will be so advised. But in return we want you to talk some sense into your new friends"

"New friends, Mr. Kung?"

"Japanese, Captain Dawlish, Japs, Nipponese Sons of Heaven, Lords of the Rising Sun and what not. Korea is still our Chinese Celestial Empire's tributary kingdom – a nominal tributary, I grant you. And as long as face is satisfied on all sides, and a little hard cash is involved, there'll be Chinese hands-off as long as nobody else tries to dominate what's on our doorstep. But now the Japs are trying to do just that. They're already preening themselves that they have the King in their pocket and they're glad that his father, the so-called *Daewongun*, doesn't like it and that the country's on the edge of civil war. Because that's what they want – civil war, anarchy, an excuse to land a Japanese army to restore order. If they do they'll have no intention of leaving. And we don't want that, do we, Captain?"

"Does *we* mean China, Mr. Kung?"

"*We* means China and it means Britain, Captain Dawlish," Kung said. "China can't accept a Japanese Korea, and you Britishers can't afford a Russian one. The Empire that employs me is damned-nearly bankrupt and we'd be incapable of defeating Japanese forces – and that's plain speaking, Gentlemen, plainer than my boss can speak himself. So what happens if the Japanese take Korea? Do you think the Russians will sit back and ignore the fact? They need ice-free ports on the Pacific, they've got ambitions in Manchuria, and they'll be glad of the excuse, and the opportunity, to kick the Japs back to where they came from. For all their strutting and modernity the Japanese still aren't as strong – not yet anyway – as they'd have you believe. And if the Russians come in here, they won't be going home. They'll make the North China Sea a Russian lake. And that's the last thing Britain wants, isn't it, Gentlemen?"

"Captain Dawlish can hardly discuss hypothetical situations." Whitaker's glance towards Dawlish told him to hold back, to leave the talking to him.

Dawlish ignored him. "So what are you proposing, Mr. Kung?"

"Simple, Captain. You've got an appointment tomorrow with Hanabusa Yoshitada, the Japanese Ambassador – I know that as well as I know most of what's going on round here – and when you do you'll tell him to step back. As politely as you like, it's up to you, but tell them just that." Kung's relaxed tone was suddenly one of barely suppressed anger, even hatred, even though the accent was still American, the mastery of English perfect. "No more challenge to Chinese authority here, no more Japanese military advisers, no more Japanese-commanded Palace Guard, no more high-handed provocations for the King's father to rouse resentment over, no more stoking of civil war. They'll be welcome to trade, within reason, but not trade backed by armed ships moored off Chemulpo or any other Korean port. But we'll be damned if they think we'll accept them using Socheong as a naval base and…"

Dawlish started. "Socheong?" he said. "The coaling enterprise there is operated by a British company."

Kung smiled, almost tolerantly, as if a child had spoken naively. "Correct, Captain. And the coalmine at Songang-ni that supplies it is operated by it also. Do you think that Choi Haung, a Korean state-councillor, approved the concession out of goodwill to the Caledonian and Oriental Coaling Company? That he isn't in a Japanese pocket? That the bastards aren't playing the C and O like puppets?"

"You seem well informed, Mr. Kung."

"That's my stock in trade," Kung said. "Advice too – and you can have mine for free. You can tell the Jap ambassador that though Britain may want Japan as an ally, Britain has no inclination to be dragged by them into confrontation with the Russians at this time. That is the case, isn't it, Gentlemen?" He looked straight into Dawlish's eyes. "You're somewhat of an expert on dealing with the Russians, aren't you, Captain Dawlish? No illusions there, I'd guess."

Dawlish felt uncomfortable. Kung had conveyed an unmistakable message: *I know all I need to know about you, even though you did not know me until I entered this room.* Dawlish had not expected his Ottoman service to be known here. He ignored the reference and said "What if I don't care to relay this message?"

"Simple," Kung's voice had lost its fury and sounded quietly reasonable. "Things will get worse, a lot worse. Even before this rioting my bosses in Peking had already decided to send troops here to maintain order – they'll land at Chemulpo before the week's out, and more are coming overland from the north. But in Peking eunuch-ministers and court favourites – and please don't quote me verbatim in your reports, Mr. Whitaker – have not wholly come to terms with reality. They haven't realised that half-trained bannermen armed with muskets and pikes won't stand a chance against disciplined Japanese troops who believe they're invincible. And they probably are, against Chinese forces at least, once they've got modern rifles in their hands and modern artillery to back them. They'll whip us, no doubt of it, send us packing, but they still won't be strong enough to hold Korea if and when the Russians move. And I guess you won't take kindly then to Russian ports on the Yellow Sea."

Dawlish glanced towards Whitaker and saw the faintest shake of his head. "Can I take your views to be the same as those of His Excellency, the Imperial Chinese Ambassador?" Dawlish said.

"He'd express them so elegantly, and at such length, that you mightn't understand what he meant," Kung said. "He's hamstrung by protocol, which I am not, but yes, Captain Dawlish, his views are just the same as I've just told you."

"You know I can't commit to anything, Mr. Kung." From the corner of his eye Dawlish could see Whitaker nodding approval.

"Oh we're both practical men, Captain. We understand one another." Kung stood up. "I've other business to attend to," he said and reached for Dawlish's hand. Again the clumsy shake.

"I'm impressed by your English." Dawlish regretted the comment even as he spoke, realising that it might sound patronisingly offensive.

Kung turned and for the first time somehow extended the right arm that had been clamped against his body throughout the meeting.

He raised it as far as he could, for he gave a slight wince of pain, and still it was bent towards him in a grotesque curve and ended in a hand that bore only a thumb and little finger.

"Nitro-glycerine and Central Pacific Tunnel Number 6," he said. "One of the illiterate Celestials shipped across to drill and hack and freeze to drive the railroad through the Sierra Nevada." He looked at the mutilated hand. "I was careless," he said, "but I know now that I was lucky. They gave me a few dollars for it and I probably wouldn't have survived another blasting accident or rock fall. Hundreds didn't. I got enough to get started in business."

"What business, Mr. Kung?" His pause seemed to invite the question.

"Bodies, Captain. Corpses. Labourers who feared burial in foreign soil worse than they feared Death itself. Drudges who were ready to pay me monthly for assurance that they'd be shipped home to their ancestors. Good business too, because the supply never failed and it bought me an American education. Yet for all the talk about gentle Jesus sweet and mild, and brotherly love, I was still a Chinaman, a Chink, a Celestial, a jumped-up coolie, but now one who could talk and think and reason like an American as well as a Chinese. I came back with something to sell and today you've seen what I trade in. It's another type of business, Captain. An even more rewarding one."

They parted at the gate. There was further shooting in the distance but it did not seem to worry Kung or his Uighurs. He jerked his head in its general direction. "When this dies down I'd welcome you at my place on the Ingwan San Hill, Captain," he said. "Sample some rye whisky, maybe a cigar. Informal, the way I like it and I guess you do too. One man to another. Just don't bring with you that goddam Jap you've got hidden here."

As they marched away Dawlish saw that one of the sword blades was indeed bloody and that a drop had congealed at its tip. There was no need to worry about Fred Kung getting home safely.

*

"Can he be trusted?" Dawlish was sharing a cheroot in Whitaker's study afterwards.

Whitaker shook his head. "Nobody is ever to be trusted, not completely. But it doesn't matter as long as you've no illusions and if they're useful. And Fred Kung's useful to us for now."

"And we to him?"

"And we to him, Captain."

"He wants us to tell the Japanese what the Chinese want to tell but can't." Dawlish could feel the burden of decision weighing on him, heavier than the responsibility for his ship, for the lives of his men.

"Face matters," Whitaker said. "No Chinese, not even Fred Kung, could relay that message. But he's correct in his assessment. Especially about the Russians." He paused. "I'd be damned careful about what I'd say to the Japanese ambassador and how I'd say it. We're going to need them as allies and they're as sensitive about face as the Chinese are." He was avoiding Dawlish's eyes now. "I wouldn't like to be in your shoes, Captain."

Dawlish realised that there was nothing more to be got from Whitaker, no offer of advice, or of opinion that the Foreign Office might later count against him. It was obvious now to Dawlish that it was no accident that first Willes, now he himself, naval officers both, had been saddled with securing this treaty and its codicils in what Whitaker had identified as a snake-pit. To him and to his masters it mattered only that the professional diplomats would emerge unscathed. For Dawlish himself success might earn faint praise, perhaps even another degree of advancement, but failure would certainly result in repudiation. It was the old pattern, the one he had lived with since he had first been singled out by Topcliffe.

Seoul rioted and burned through the evening, peace of a kind only restoring itself after midnight. There was still no direct threat to the British compound, though angry groups still surged past at intervals, and the nearest major fire, one of the tens that blazed in patches across the city, was no closer than half a mile. But the knowledge that he might need to remain here longer than expected weighed upon Dawlish, that and awareness that the force for defending the compound was so meagre. There were reinforcements aplenty on the *Leonidas.* A forced march could have them here in a day as there was still no indication of major unrest outside the city. But first a message had to be got through to the coast, ideally by an officer, even though doing so would temporarily reduce the small garrison. Decision made, he called in Watkin and Ross in the early hours, told them what was required. On foot, accompanied by two marines, carrying only the bare minimum and guided by one of Whitaker's Chinese servants, the paymaster was to set off at first light. The twenty-five miles to Chemulpo should be covered by nightfall, the ferry at the Han river the only serious potential obstacle. A rope loop strung with cash and slung over a marine's shoulder would buy passage. If all went well another dozen more marines could be here at the latest two days from now.

But first there was no alternative to venturing out into the city tomorrow, to see the Japanese ambassador, not if face was to be upheld. An appointment had been made and Dawlish would keep it. Oppressed by knowledge of the risk, he slept only fitfully. He had himself woken before the small group set off and pushed a note into Watkin's hand. It was addressed to Florence and was numbered in sequence like all the other letters that awaited forwarding by mail steamer once *Leonidas* docked again at Hong Kong. It contained nothing but trivia about the sights of Seoul, nothing of the horror on the road from Chemulpo, nothing of what was now happening, nothing that could compromise Watkin if it were captured. Only the last line was important, the same as he had written countless times to her, the simple statement that he loved her. If the current situation developed badly then it would be the last she would have from him.

9

Dawlish, accompanied by Whitaker and Takenaka, set out, on foot, for the Japanese mission soon after sunrise. He left Ross at the British compound, three marines with him, enough to deter any casual looters. Dawlish brought the four other marines with him as escort, one of them Sergeant Hawley. Their bayonets were fixed and there was a round in each chamber but Dawlish would have preferred magazine repeaters – ideally Winchesters – to the single-shot Sniders. He had learned their worth in a night of rapine and slaughter in the streets of a Turkish town.

But now the streets they passed through were mainly deserted, residents cowering inside, though in places acrid smoke still drifted from the remnants of the night's fires. Several times they encountered bodies, some mutilated, some already worried by dogs and picked by birds. A cluster indicated a short clash between opposing groups while individual corpses told of what might have been some personal account settled, some wretch dragged from his home and butchered before his terrified family. The sound of distant shooting – the sharp bark of modern small arms mixed with the duller report of flintlock muskets – was intermittent but distant. Dawlish wondered if it was not wise to abandon this attempt to reach the Japanese Ambassador, if it was not better to retreat to the security of Whitaker's small fortress and sit out the unrest there. Yet he knew that were he to do so he could never gain the respect or the trust of these allies Britain needed. There was no option but to press on.

Whitaker, familiar with the city, was leading. They wove through a warren of small streets and alleyways, heading towards the Nam San hill that was visible over the tiled and thatched roofs. On its green-forested slopes the Japanese had built their legation, and there too, was the separate compound in which most of Seoul's Japanese residents were housed. Even from a distance it gave an impression of order and cleanliness, its buildings spaced in a pleasing pattern on the slope and surrounded by gardens, the contrast with the squalid city it overlooked blatant.

There was a sudden sound of shouting behind, growing in volume, many voices, hundreds perhaps, still invisible, all raised in anger, and with them came the pounding of hurrying feet. Suddenly a scattering of figures was running from an intersecting alley some hundred yards to the rear, stumbling, falling, rising again in blind panic as a mob spilled into the street after them. Amidst the white-clothed horde red knee-length tunics told of soldiers having joined the crowd. A fugitive was caught and was immediately surrounded by a screaming, chopping, stabbing mass that was momentarily too intent on vengeance to take any notice of Dawlish's party. Another frenzied group were dragging more victims from the ditches and hovels in which they vainly sought shelter.

And Dawlish recognised – for he had seen it before – that the mob had crossed the boundary from being a crowd of individuals to a single living entity, driven by rage and intoxicated by release from all constraint, its joy slaughter, its delight fury. All reason had been abandoned and any victim would do.

Whitaker spoke, his face was pale. "It's worse than I thought." He looked beseechingly at Dawlish.

Dawlish ignored him. It was important now to hurry, yet not to run, not do anything that might appear either weak or provocative. "Sergeant," he said. "Watch our rear! Don't fire without an order!"

"Very well, sir." Hawley's men formed a pitifully thin screen, turning at intervals to face the mob as Dawlish led the party at a fast walk.

The street ahead was clear, bounded by a filthy ditch to either side, low hovels bordering them, the occupants unseen inside. A hundred yards ahead Dawlish could see an alley entrance that could offer cover. He had his revolver out now, Whitaker his also, and Takenaka had drawn his sword. The Japanese buildings on the slopes of Nam San were near enough to be lost to view behind the flanking roofs.

"How far…" Dawlish began to Whitaker but his words were cut off by a roar from behind. He glanced back to see a solid wall of men advancing down the street, hungry for new victims, pikes and spears and makeshift weapons brandished above them, sunlight flashing on their blades. Puffs of black smoke followed by dull reports marked wildly aimed discharges from muskets.

Dawlish halted, his voice low. "A single volley, Sergeant. Over their heads! Over their heads, mind you!"

Drilled on *Leonidas* to clockwork precision, undeterred by the wrath bearing down on them, the marines' Sniders crashed like a single weapon. Shocked perhaps as much by the immobility of the thin screen before them as by the rounds screaming over their heads, the rioters ground to a halt, those behind stumbling into those ahead. Several blundered into the ditches.

"Follow me!" Dawlish went forward at a fast walk, conscious that the respite could only be of seconds. The alley ahead would offer shelter, an opportunity if necessary to improvise a defence. The small group hurried on, Takenaka keeping pace to Dawlish's right, Whitaker a little behind, the marines in the rear. Forty yards, thirty…

And then another mob came surging out of the alley ahead, blocking the roadway. It halted suddenly, its leaders, red-tunicked soldiers, as surprised by Dawlish's group as his was by them. Others were piling up and jostling behind them, white-clad civilians, two severed heads waving above them on poles.

"Halt!" Dawlish's order was superfluous for there was no way forward or back, nothing to either side but the rows of thatched hovels along the ditches to either side. "Protect the rear, Sergeant!" he called. It was up to him, to Takenaka and to Whitaker to face the group ahead.

The mobs to front and rear, that ahead the smaller, had fallen silent. Neither was advancing, the sight perhaps of European uniforms a deterrent that might not last. And the soldiers, even if mutineers, might be amenable to some appeal to discipline and reason...

"Whitaker," Dawlish said. "Lower your pistol. Talk to them." He nodded towards the blockage to the front and slowly lowered his revolver. His heart was thumping, blood racing, and yet he knew that it was essential to remain calm.

Whitaker advanced, trembling. He began to speak in Korean, the words slowly and carefully enunciated. There was no flicker of reaction from the wall of faces. Dawlish glanced back – the rioters some eighty yards to the rear were edging forward slowly, the eyes in front locked in dread on the marines' rifles, but pushed onwards by those behind.

Still speaking, Whitaker was close to the group in front, his control of his fear all the more impressive for his being a civilian. Now a soldier was answering, lowering the flintlock he carried and gesturing to the others who flanked him to do the same. The words were incomprehensible but Dawlish sensed the beginning of a negotiation. Hope flickered in him.

"Steady, lads. Steady now." Hawley's voice was calm and low, reassurance that his men held the rear, bayonets lowered, their resolution slowing the advance towards them to a creep.

An eternity passed as Dawlish, cut off by language, tried to understand what Whitaker was conveying. He was pointing to Dawlish, to his uniform, to the golden rings on his sleeve, obviously explaining who and what he was. The soldier who seemed a leader was questioning Whitaker now – that was hopeful – and others in the front rank were turning to quieten voices from behind them. Whitaker was answering and gesturing forward – Dawlish's party wanted to go that way. He was shaking his head – no, they had no quarrel with the rioters. A brief consultation by the leading soldier with those close to him, the conversation low but voluble. He turned again to Whitaker with another question. Dawlish glanced back and saw that though the road behind was still blocked the mob there had come to a halt. Hope grew. Whitaker was going to talk them through.

A single yell of anger rose from somewhere behind the soldiers and a figure pushed through between them, a civilian in blood-stained white, his tall black hat askew, a cleaver in his hand. He stood there, his voice a scream, and he gestured towards Takenaka. Now others were shouting and gesticulating, and muskets were being raised and all attention had shifted from Whitaker. Dawlish glanced to his right and saw Takenaka's face tight, his eyes hard, and his left hand creeping slowly across his body to grasp the sword-hilt in his right. Whitaker had stepped back slightly but he was still trying to talk, to explain the presence of a Japanese. His voice was raised, though still calm, but nobody was listening. Every eye, every scream of hate, was directed towards Takenaka. Something – a mud brick – came arcing from the crowd and towards him. He shifted a fraction, a movement as graceful as a dancer's, and it shattered on the ground to his left.

"They want him," Whitaker said. "They know he's Japanese. They won't believe he's a British officer."

Dawlish, fighting down the cold terror he felt rising within him, shook his head. "Warn them that..." he began, but even as his spoke another brick came sailing across, clumsily and badly aimed. Then another, and another, one catching Whitaker on his left shoulder.

He gasped in pain. "It's hopeless," he said, "If they won't have him ..." His words were cut off as a soldier dashed forward, yelling, his levelled pike aimed at Takenaka. The Japanese stood still, his face devoid of expression, but his sword raised, grasped by both hands. What followed was almost too fast for the eye to register – the pike-head inches from Takenaka's chest, his slightest step to one side to let his attacker blunder past, the lighting sweep of the sword that bit between neck and shoulder and the fountaining blood as the body fell.

Muskets blasted from the front, uselessly, poorly aimed in the heaving mass, but several figures – soldiers – came lunging through their billowing black smoke, their pikes no less deadly for being antique. Dawlish brought up his revolver, cocked, then held aim on the chest of the nearest, fired, saw him go down, swung over and took down a second. Whitaker was firing also, wildly, but Takenaka was like a whirlwind, sword sweeping and slashing, severing an arm, biting into a waist and sending the last of the attackers scurrying back towards the mob ahead. A roar of anger erupted from behind – the crowd there was dashing forward but it died as the marines' rifles crashed out a volley. Four leading rioters tumbled to the ground but the throng behind them, though slowing, still came on across the bodies. Long-practised hands reached into ammunition pouches and slipped a round into each breech. As Hawley was about to shout the command to fire black smoke rolled from the advancing mass, musket reports rising above the screams of hatred, the shots unaimed and harmless. The marines' next volley crashed out, the aim low and deadly, tearing down four more in the leading rank and slamming the advance to a halt.

The only way was forward, speed and resolution everything. "Sergeant Hawley!" Dawlish called. "Face forward! Fire on my command then on with the bayonet."

There were half-a-dozen bodies in the roadway ahead, several still moving, but the mob beyond, though still shouting, was momentarily cowed. A soldier edged forward, calling for others to join him. He looked back nervously and realised that nobody was following. Dawlish saw the fear on the man's face but he drew a bead on him nonetheless, aimed for the sash around the waist and fired. The soldier fell, blood spurting, and the crowd seemed to jerk backwards. Dawlish reached into his pouch and forced himself to be calm as he pushed rounds into the emptied chambers. The marines had hurried forward, a thin four-man screen across the road, and Dawlish gestured to Whitaker and Takenaka to take places between them.

He glanced towards Hawley. "Ready, Sergeant?"

"Ready, sir!"

"Fire!"

Then the crash of rifle-fire, the range almost point blank, the revolvers adding their contribution. Bodies were falling ahead and then a shocked hush, broken only by moans as Dawlish called "Forward!"

What followed might have been seconds only, a minute at the most, but it was an aeon of stabbing and slashing, the marines thrusting with their merciless bayonets, Dawlish and Whitaker blasting with muzzles that several times touched their targets' bodies, Takenaka slicing and cleaving. Muskets exploded, their black smoke choking, and bodies squirmed underfoot and a head knocked off a pole bounced on the ground. The mob was dissolving, terrified figures stumbling and pushing each other aside, tripping over fallen pikes as they fled before the advancing phalanx, some rushing back into the alley they had come through, others plunging into the ditches or dashing back along the street ahead.

"Which way?" Dawlish yelled to Whitaker.

Speechless, white-faced, Whitaker pointed towards the alley. The street was clear to that point. A glance backwards confirmed to

Dawlish that the mob there was creeping forward again. And one of the marines was wounded, badly wounded, blood bubbling from his lips and soaking his tunic where a musket ball had torn into his right lung. Two men less, one the wounded man, another to half-carry him with his arm wrapped over his shoulder. Dawlish took one rifle – its bayonet was scarlet to the hilt – and gestured to Whitaker to take the other.

They reached the corner of the alley, saw it was empty until its winding blocked further sight some eighty yards further on. They paused, panting. The wounded marine was making a dreadful gurgling sound.

"Any way back to your compound?" Dawlish asked Whitaker.

"Too far. Too dangerous."

"Can you find our way to the Japanese embassy? This way?" Dawlish indicated the empty alleyway.

A nod. "Not easy. It's a maze. But once we see the hill we can find our way".

Dawlish peered around the corner. The mob was still there, eighty, a hundred yards distant, screaming anger, moving cautiously forward towards the bodies littering the street. One determined leader might embolden them to another charge. Dawlish called Hawley to join him. "Keep them back, Sergeant. Two minutes. Then follow us." Hawley beckoned to the fourth marine and crouched by the corner. He glanced around, then nodded back to Dawlish – the tiny rear-guard could be relied upon.

They started up the narrow alley, just wide enough to allow a laden ox to pass, Dawlish and Whitaker leading, Takenaka assisting the third marine to carry the wounded man. His face was drained of all colour and death must be close, but he was conscious and very frightened. "It's not far now, Bob," his comrade kept telling him, "not far at all now," his words repeated like a mantra as they stumbled forward.

At the sweep of the alley's bend Dawlish waved Whitaker back, advanced slowly, pistol drawn, its chambers again filled. The way beyond the bend was clear but for a single bloody heap in the centre of the pathway, an earlier victim of the rioters. Nan San Hill was visible over the roofs at the end of it, the Japanese buildings there now like a beacon of hope. Dawlish called the others forward and heard a rising roar from behind – the mob gaining confidence, perhaps surging forward – then rifle fire, two closely spaced shots, then two more, and then the mob's voice hushed again. Hawley and his companion were indeed securing the rear. Dawlish beckoned the others forward, the thatched roofs to either side extending down almost to head level, the pathway beaten earth. There seemed to be another intersection ahead and there must be occupants cowering in the houses for several heads emerged briefly from doorways and were hastily withdrawn. Progress was slow, little more than a fast walk since the dying marine's boots were trailing on the ground as he was dragged forward.

Whitaker gestured a turn to the left at the next intersection. Hawley and the marine with him re-joined them. "They're scared, sir," he said as he arrived. "They won't be following immediately".

Down this alley, even narrower and more winding than the first, a figure darting across the pathway and into a house as they moved forward, then another turn, another alleyway, and at intervals, depending on the twists, Nan San in view and getting closer. They paused at another intersection, bodies slumped there, hacked, several with heads missing, two dogs scurrying away with bloody muzzles, and to the left a building, a shop or rice store perhaps, burning furiously, more bodies outside but no other sign of life. They headed to the right through the labyrinth, Whitaker calling directions that were increasingly superfluous as the hill ahead loomed ever closer. And still there was no pursuit.

"He's dead, sir!" Takenaka called. Dawlish turned and saw the body hanging limply between the supporters to either side. The tunic front was sodden red. Dawlish raised the drooping head and when he saw the lifeless eyes he knew life was gone even before he held his fingers against the still-warm throat and felt no pulse. He saw to the unasked question on every face.

"We're taking him with us," he said and beckoned to the marine with Hawley to relieve Takenaka. The idea of leaving the body for mutilation was unthinkable. "Thank you, sir," the sergeant said.

Slowed even more now, they wound on through the alleys, once flitting across a wider thoroughfare, the slopes of Nan San now tantalisingly close. From this more open space they could glimpse smoke drifting skywards from several locations and hear the sound of irregular musket fire, the angry murmur of an unseen crowd. Then on again through the foul-smelling warren, their appearance sending terrified occupants darting for cover. Watchful for any threat,

Dawlish's mind was at the same time racing over the options now open to him. The rioting was worse than he had ever expected, worse than Whitaker had imagined possible. The chance that he would be isolated at the Japanese Embassy until calm was restored was unattractive – it would proclaim an alignment of interests that might antagonise the Chinese and threaten the treaty codicil. And he wanted that signed and then to be gone. And Whitaker's compound was too far off for safety. And …

A broad street ahead. "Slow down." Whitaker gestured for a slow approach to the corner. There to the right was the approach to the walled grandeur of the Japanese Embassy, a watchtower over the gate, a red and white sunburst flag drooping above and trees beyond. Four hundred yards…

They were almost at a run now, the trailing corpse notwithstanding, Hawley and his marine ever the alert rear-guard, Takenaka pushing ahead, hope surging in Dawlish. There were figures moving in the watchtower – they had been seen. It was two hundred yards now, scarce minutes only and then came the sound of tumult and another mob, red-clad, soldiers, was spilling out of a roadway to the left between them and the gate. They were few as yet ahead but the roar of voices told that more were following. And again the only way was forward.

The leaders of the mob had spotted them and were turning, momentarily surprised, enough to give precious seconds advantage. Dawlish yelled orders. The poor bloody corpse was abandoned in the roadway – there was no help for it – as the marines carrying it grabbed the rifles Dawlish and Takenaka had been carrying for them. Dawlish himself kept the dead man's rifle – there was a round in the breech – and he dropped to one knee with the marines, the better to aim. "Choose your target! Wait for my order!" he shouted.

The mob was surging towards them as Dawlish shouted "Fire!" He was conscious of bodies falling and of the crowd's momentum stilled as he leapt to his feet and charged forward, bayonet levelled. The marines were by his side and Takenaka's sword was laid across his right shoulder, ready for its first lethal swing. Whitaker was blasting with his pistol and crumpling down a pike-wielding soldier.

And then contact, bayonets rammed into squirming bodies and ripped from them for the next thrust, screams of pain and terror, Takenaka's blade whirling and biting, muskets exploding and black smoke rolling, men stumbling and falling over the pikes that were now more encumbrances than weapons. Dawlish's force was through and over the front rank now, boots slipping on the bodies underfoot but its onslaught was slowed now as it hit the mass behind. Many of the rioters were struggling to escape but others – soldiers – were standing their ground. There was no room now for another deadly levelled bayonet charge, only close-order thrusting and parrying and smashing upwards with the butt and following through with a short stab. A musket exploded close enough to Dawlish's head for its hot breath to scorch his face. He swung to the right to lunge towards his assailant but Takenaka was on to this wretch already, sword arcing down to cleave his head down to his terror-filled eyes. Cowering behind the Japanese, protected for now by his dreadful sword, Whitaker was thrusting new rounds into his revolver with shaking hands. Dawlish turned to meet a new threat, a soldier coming at him, shouting, with a broad-bladed sword. It was raised, ready for a downward sweep, but it momentarily exposed the man's face and Dawlish jabbed for it. The soldier swept his arm across to protect his eyes and as he did Dawlish dropped his bayonet and threw his full weight behind it as it crashed into the soldier's torso. The man twisted as he went down and Dawlish had to stamp on his chest to jerk the bayonet free.

Dawlish felt terror now for the mob ahead was still solid, unwilling to yield its ground, undeterred by the bodies strewn before them, the more audacious pushing to the fore to confront the small knot of desperate men. He glanced to his right – Takenaka and Whitaker, exhausted, bloodied but still defiantly facing the crowd that had stepped back but which was obviously steeling itself to surge forward towards them. To his left he saw that another of the marines was down and motionless, the back of his head a bloody mess. Sergeant Hawley was supported by the remaining marine, but his right leg was crimson and obviously useless. There too the crowd hung back but it could be seconds only before it gained courage enough to overwhelm them. Hawley was trying to reload his Snider and he raised his face to Dawlish. He knew what was coming, his nod told, and he would go down fighting.

As they all would, Dawlish told himself, and that could be the only satisfaction. The noise of tumult had died down, the silence palpable, as the panting, furious mob steeled itself to launch forward. He was past fear now, reduced to numb acceptance that he was going to die, as his men would too because of him, and he felt an emptiness, a solitary desolation, a sense of loss of all that might have been.

And at that moment the mob broke. It surged not forward, but to either side, splitting, panicking, turning to meet the attack that came from behind. There was shooting – rifles by their sharp bark – and rioters were falling and others were struggling across them to escape back up the alleyway they had emerged from.

"Don't move," Dawlish shouted to his group, "hold back!" for the few terrified men who blundered towards them were more intent on escape than on confrontation. They scurried past, opening a gap that showed the wrath that had been unleashed upon them.

For there was the half-platoon of Japanese troops that had now crashed into the remnants of the mob, immaculate and deadly in their blue tunics and whitened canvas gaiters, eyes hard and merciless beneath the peaks of their flat caps. They were bayoneting the wounded their volley had taken down and showing just as little compassion for those who were too slow to flee and who were now raising arms in surrender.

An officer was striding from the slaughter, his sword blood-smeared, pausing only by an injured Korean who was struggling on all fours in the wake of his fleeting companions. The blade came arcing down and the head tumbled free in a gush of blood. The whole action was as effortless, and as casual, as if the killer had trodden on a troublesome insect.

And the officer advanced, transferring his sword to his left hand and extending his right as if to grasp Dawlish's in greeting, as he had done once before.

Captain Shimazu Hirosato of the Imperial Japanese Navy.

10

There was no conference with the Japanese Ambassador, no polite exchange of compliments, no gracious circumlocutions, no courteous probings of each other's positions. Hanabusa Yoshitada, grim-faced and muscular, seemed more like a soldier than a diplomat and he had barely acknowledged Dawlish's thanks for his deliverance. Beneath the ambassador's impassive features Dawlish sensed not just seething fury, but the realisation that the political strategy he had planned and implemented was falling apart before his eyes, that he and his country were humiliated. The embassy compound, the focus of popular hatred of Japanese encroachment, had already withstood one half-hearted attack by soldiers of the *Muwi* Regiment. Another, possibly more determined, might occur at any time.

The small detachment of Japanese troops assigned to the compound's defence, supplemented by Shimazu's seamen, had been enough to rescue Dawlish's group from an undisciplined mob but was too small to hold it against determined assault. In the city outside the sounds of chaos continued, distant shooting, the roar of unseen mobs, pillars of smoke. The Japanese residential quarter on the hill above, the order and grace of which Dawlish had admired from afar, was now also burning fiercely. Its residents had hurried away the previous night, part of the embassy guard being detached to escort them to safety at Chemulpo, their homes and property abandoned to the looting and destruction now upon them.

"Ambassador Hanabusa is considering retreating to Chemulpo himself," Whitaker's voice trembled with pain. His right arm, broken, was in a sling. He was standing with Dawlish and watching a shallow grave being scraped for the two dead marines. Dawlish had insisted on their bodies being recovered.

"How do you know?" The ambassador had given no hint of this to Dawlish.

Whitaker nodded towards Takenaka, who was overseeing the burial.

"He got it from Shimazu," Whitaker said. "They've got a few ponies, they'll take half of the troops with them for protection. Shimazu volunteered to stay here with the remainder, and with all his seamen."

"You'll go to Chemulpo," Dawlish said. "You and Hawley." The sergeant's thigh had been shattered by a musket ball, the wound so serious that Dawlish suspected that amputation was inevitable. And that must be on *Leonidas*, if he was to have a chance. "Elton will go with you – you'll need a fit man to help you both." Elton was the remaining marine and he had come through the street battle bruised but otherwise uninjured.

Whitaker started to protest.

"You're a liability here," Dawlish motioned towards the sling.

"And you, Captain?"

Dawlish gestured towards the red sunburst on a white ground that drooped from the embassy flagpole. "As long as that Jap flag's flying here I'm damned if I'm leaving," he said. "We left ours flying at your compound and I won't be shamed by hauling it down. If the Koreans see us run at the first sign of trouble we'll never have their respect, never get those damned codicils signed."

"It's madness," Whitaker said.

"I'll get back to your compound somehow – Takenaka can talk the language, he'll get me through. And after today, maybe even tonight, more marines will be arriving from *Leonidas*. Your compound will be secure then and we'll lie low and let all this burn itself out." Dawlish's words were at variance with the doubt he felt within. But an unjustified display of confidence had carried him through dangers enough before when, as now, retreat would have meant professional suicide. "You'll arrange it with the ambassador, Whitaker? And a pony for Hawley? Otherwise a litter, though God knows it would slow them down."

The dead marines were in the ground now, their graves dug in what had been an ornamental flowerbed, their hands joined as if in prayer and their faces covered. Dawlish spoke a few words from the burial service – he had used them often enough before to remember them – and threw a handful of earth over each body. Then two Japanese soldiers began to shovel.

"Their deaths were glorious ones."

Dawlish turned to see that Shimazu had come to stand by him, hand frozen in salute.

"No servant of Her Majesty could hope for better," he said. "These men are to be envied."

*

The escape party was due to leave at dusk but the attack came in mid-afternoon. As there were insufficient men to man the entire perimeter it was fortunate that the assault was focussed on the main gate.

A hostile crowd – civilians as well as soldiers – had been gathering for several hours, standing well back from the compound. They shouted insults and beat gongs and the bodies of those killed in the earlier skirmish were dragged away. More heads were brandished on pikes and at one point a single wretch, his official status identifiable

111

by the tattered remains of the robes he still wore, was dragged to the front, stripped naked and held down while he was dismembered by deliberate sword cuts. Dawlish watched, sickened, from the watchtower above the gate as the bloody limbs were raised and flourished one by one. He raised his Snider, tried to draw a bead on the screaming victim. He failed, for the bodies of the executioners blocked the line of sight. One final howl of agony announced the end and the mob drew back, leaving the hacked remains and a head impaled on a pike like a warning of yet worse to come. Dawlish's hand moved to his holster. The feel of his revolver's butt was reassuring. If the worst came to the worst the last bullet would be for himself.

Soon afterwards the crowd parted, opening a lane through which an antique cannon could be seen, its muzzle pointed towards the gate. Another was being man-handled into position alongside it. There was a terrible fascination in watching the preparations but Captain Shimazu, who had taken control of the rear-guard, forbade any retaliation yet. Most of the dozen men left to him were concentrated on the tower above the gate and behind the walls' parapets to either side, with two others assigned to the furthest corners of the wall to watch for hostile movements at the rear. There were none as yet and though it was still light there could be no delay for getting the ambassador's party out through the small gate there. Dawlish grasped Whitaker's free hand, wished-well a semi-delirious Hawley whom Elton was supporting on a small pony, saluted the ambassador and watched the small column creep surreptitiously away between the low buildings behind. Then he walked back, climbed to the watchtower and took his place beside Shimazu and Takenaka.

The cannon were being trundled forward, the mob standing back as they passed, voices and anger growing, weapons raised, leaders whipping up a frenzy of anticipation of vengeance to come. The gunners were in uniform, red and blue tunics, one carrying a glowing linstock, others with rammers and buckets, more following behind, bowed by the weight of the roundshots they carried. Shimazu snapped a command and two Japanese soldiers dropped to their knees, steadied their rifles on the parapet and took careful aim. They confirmed in turn that they had their targets. Shimazu uttered a single word and both men fired. The Korean with the linstock spun and fell and so too did one of his followers. Already the Japanese were ejecting, pushing their next rounds into their rifles' smoking breeches, were aiming and firing again, not once but three, four, five times. More bodies fell and the surviving gunners scuttled for cover, leaving the cannon abandoned in the middle of the street. And yet the rifle-fire inflamed others. Soldiers were breaking from the mob – one was waving a banner – and urging advance towards the gate. A few joined him and they began to run, shouting as they came. There was a moment of hesitation before the bulk of the mob followed, soldiers and civilians mixed together without order or discipline.

And then they died.

The first full Japanese volley – over a dozen rifles, for Dawlish and Takenaka fired with them – tore down most of the leaders and those behind stumbled on over their fallen bodies only to be smashed down by the next wave of fire. Shimazu was standing, sword in hand, calmly calling for a deadly rhythm of spaced volleys. The charge was slowing, breaking, as the next hail fell upon it, and as more attackers fell others were already beginning to run back along the street. It had taken little over a minute but the mob's immediate resolution, if not its fury, had been spent. It surged back, stopping only beyond the forlorn cannon, as savagely resentful and as dangerous as a wounded tiger. Crawling in its wake, a few undaunted figures were dragging injured with them.

"They'll be back, Captain Dawlish," Shimazu said. "Not immediately, but when it's dark. If you want to leave you should do so now." There was no irony, no implication of insult in his tone.

Dawlish shook his head, gestured towards Takenaka. "We'll take our chances here," he said. "We're in good company."

Shimazu smiled. "The Royal Navy's presence is always welcome." He bowed. Shared danger and his calm professionalism made it easy to forget what he was.

Each hour that passed until nightfall brought increased assurance that the ambassador's party had escaped. Had they been captured they would almost certainly have been dragged into sight of the compound and butchered as mercilessly as the unfortunate official earlier. But new columns of flame-streaked smoke were rising across the city, emptied rice-stores put to the torch, government offices, homes of hated officials. A significant concentration of these fires lay between the present position and Whitaker's compound. Safe haven though it might be, and not a focus of hatred like this embassy, Dawlish realised that the chances of reaching it through the warren of alleyways, accompanied by Takenaka, a Japanese even if he wore British uniform, were negligible. And that could be the case for perhaps several days to come. He doubted if Shimazu could hold out that long, and guessed that he probably knew it, but the quiet resolution with which he and the other Japanese – including Takenaka – were accepting the reality made the topic undiscussable.

At dusk the Rising Sun flag was lowered with full military ceremony, the bugle call as it dropped as plaintive as when Dawlish had heard it in British camps. The flag was folded carefully and carried to Shimazu. He received it with a look that had something of exaltation about it. After the party was dismissed he asked Dawlish if he would join him in the guard-room, and if he objected to Takenaka joining also. No objection.

A portrait of the Emperor had been propped on the table, obviously removed from some more formal hanging place. A small lamp burned before it.

"His Majesty's image must not be exposed to dishonour." Shimazu bowed twice, first towards the portrait, then, turning, towards Dawlish. There was the slightest tremor in his voice as he spoke, enough to tell that he was forcing himself to forget the insult that had passed between them at that village on the road from Chemulpo. "I ask you as a fellow officer, Captain Dawlish, to permit my countryman assist me in a sacred duty." He gestured towards Takenaka, who also bowed.

"I will be honoured, Captain," Dawlish said. "So too Lieutenant Takenaka."

Shimazu spoke in Japanese. Takenaka bowed, then helped Shimazu remove his tunic. Then, reverently, Takenaka unfolded the flag and wrapped it around Shimazu's torso, tucking in the end so as to hold it. Then both men bowed to each other and Takenaka stepped back. Dawlish saw that tears glistened in his eyes and that he was only controlling his emotion with difficulty.

Another bow towards the portrait and then Shimazu took a razor from his pocket and cut the canvas cleanly from the frame. He spoke quietly and Takenaka came forward with the tunic. Shimazu held the canvas to his chest as the younger officer helped him put the tunic on and buttoned it.

114

"A painful duty, sir, but an honourable one," Takenaka said to Dawlish. "Should Captain Shimazu fall, his last breath will be in defence of His Majesty." He bowed at the name.

Shimazu called out and a soldier, who must have been waiting outside, entered with a flask and three porcelain cups. Shimazu filled them and gestured to Dawlish and Takenaka to take one each. They drained the rice wine together and shook hands in silence. Then they went outside, Dawlish and Takenaka back to the tower above the gate, Shimazu to inspect the sentries on the perimeter wall.

Dawlish felt proud to have been included in the ceremony. Proud even though he knew that Shimazu was still a monster.

*

Darkness came, hideous for the flickering red from the hundreds of torches that illuminated the growing crowd further down the street. The memory of the glow-worms that had bobbed so recently through the city's maze seemed to have been in another age. The sound of gongs and of wailing, that might have been of mourning, and of chanting that might have been prayer – or fury. The mob was jostling and shifting as more joined it, groups flushed with triumph from looting and rapine elsewhere, bravado pushing them to the fore.

Then the torches began to be extinguished, dying at first one by one, then the remainder in a rush, as some order was passed from mouth to mouth and the brands were knocked to the ground and trodden upon. Now only the faintest light lay across the city, the star-filled sky half-obscured by drifting smoke, its streets and alleyways black canyons between the houses' roofs. The clamour died, the hush that followed terrible in the realisation it brought to the gate's defenders that assault was imminent.

Shimazu's voice was calm and low. In the tower, along the parapets by the gate, only the slightest metallic sounds told of rounds fed into breeches. Takenaka translated for Dawlish. "They're coming now, he says. Hold fire until he commands."

Half-obscured by the darkness, the crowd moved silently down the street, separating to either side as it came to open a channel between them. And then the inevitable.

Flame erupted from an unseen cannon's mouth and an instant later its dull boom and then, with a loud crash, its missile smashing into

115

the stone wall to one side of the embassy gate. Then another blast, a second weapon, though this was better aimed. Its ball fell short, bounced on the roadway, losing momentum before it impacted against the thick wooden gate, shaking it but not penetrating. The crowd cheered but still cowered back. Shimazu's barked orders urged his two best marksmen – the men who had inflicted such destruction on the gunners previously – to shoot into the dark patch which sheltered the cannon. But this time there were no clear targets and though their rounds must have screamed close the Korean gunners' resolution held. Once more a long orange tongue reached out, illuminating briefly through rolling black smoke the cannon's crew and its companion which spoke only a second later.

Both balls found their marks, one punching through the door with a shower of splinters, the second, a lucky shot, grazing along the gateway's wall and impacting on the hinge line. The door's left-half toppled inwards, part-supported by the half that still stood to the right, but the breach had been made and the mob had seen it. Screaming, gongs beating, weapons raised, unaimed muskets blasting, it now rushed forward.

The Japanese volleys, fast, rhythmic, deadly as they were, failed to stop the onrush fuelled by so much hatred, even though semi-darkness masked so much of its cost. Bodies fell, others trampled across them and more pushed on from behind, all part of a single raging, unreasoning animal that was driven to yet higher levels of fury by every injury it suffered. It was close to the gate now, close enough for Dawlish to lay his Snider aside and blaze down with his revolver as Shimazu and Takenaka were doing also. The mob, stupidly, was funnelling itself towards the wrecked gate, only a few soldiers among it realising the threat from above and firing up with their muskets, their aims spoiled by the jostling throng around them. At Shimazu's command five of his men were sent down to stand to either side of the gate. They fired remorselessly out through the gap and were ready with fixed bayonets to strike down any attacker who managed to get through.

Still the slaughter went on, and still the mob pushed forward. Dawlish knew with dreadful certainty that no matter what losses might be inflicted the situation was hopeless. The defenders were so few, the attackers so many and so far gone in blood lust. He drew back for a moment, pushing fresh rounds into the warm revolver's chambers.

Shimazu joined him and Dawlish hesitated to speak his thoughts, reluctant to share what might be construed as fear with a man whose values he could not understand.

Yet Shimazu surprised him. "There is no dishonour now in retreat, Captain Dawlish," he said, almost shouting to be heard above the continuous gunfire "Our lives are not our own. The Emperor and the Queen-Empress have more use of us alive."

"Retreat? Where to?"

"The Palace. The *Pyolgigun* are there."

"The *Pyolgigun*?" Dawlish began, then remembered. The unit the Japanese had trained and was commanded by one of their officers.

"The King and Queen need our protection – Japan's protection. Britain's too." Shimazu paused, then said "In the interest of His Imperial Majesty. In the interest of your Queen-Empress also."

The gate at rear of the compound had still been spared attack and escape was still possible. Disengaging was now the problem. After a final massed volley from above into the churning mass below all but two of the soldiers were brought down and concentrated behind the gate. Realising that the fire from the watchtower had diminished the mob now surged into the gateway. Rifle-fire met them there. The leaders fell, but those behind struggled on, jamming themselves into the gap between the wrecked doors. There were soldiers among them, the inaccuracy of their muskets no disadvantage at almost point-blank range so that Japanese defenders were falling too even as their comrades reloaded. The gateway was half-blocked with bodies and the few who struggled across were met with Japanese bayonets as well as Japanese gunfire. Shimazu stepped forward twice, sword in hand, to slice down Korean soldiers blundering forward with halberds that belonged to earlier centuries.

At last the assault faltered and died and the mob shrunk back, shocked by its losses, even angrier than before, its leaders pondering whether another rush could succeed. This was the moment when an undisciplined force, without a hierarchy of command or authority, was at its weakest.

It was time to retreat. Time to draw back through the compound, leaving two soldiers dead by the gate and dragging two others who were wounded, one badly. Time to flit past the flowerbed where two Royal Marines lay so far from home. Time to creep past the residence from where Ambassador Hanabusa Yoshitada, now somewhere on the

117

road to Chemulpo, had planned to rule Korea for Japan. Time to file through the small rear gate on cautious steps, with empty rifle breeches and holstered revolvers and strict orders to use swords and bayonets only in the streets and alleyways ahead.

Through the dark labyrinth now, under a smoke-darkened and flame-crimsoned sky, on towards the palace of a weak king and a clever queen, with its safety assured only by the loyalty of a guard trained by hated foreigners.

But there was no other refuge to be had.

11

It was well after midnight when they reached the palace. On their way from the now-blazing Japanese compound through a labyrinth of dark, deserted streets, foul with the smell of burning and night-soil, they had encountered no opposition. A few isolated looters had scurried into the shadows as they saw the fiery sky above reflected on the party's bayonets and unseen householders cowered behind closed shutters. The noise of distant shouting and crackling gunfire confirmed that rioting was raging through much of the city.

A Japanese sergeant, obviously familiar with the route between embassy and palace, acted as guide, keeping the group to lanes and alleyways that paralleled the broader thoroughfares it was occasionally necessary to flit across. The only European in the party, Dawlish was impressed by the catlike stealth with which the Japanese moved rapidly. He made every effort to pace as silently himself, uneasily aware that he might be the noisiest of all. He was aware of Takenaka to his right, and a step or two behind, his sword drawn – just as he had been close to him throughout the earlier tumult. No word had been spoken, no undertaking given, but Dawlish knew that his navigation lieutenant was resolved, if necessary, to give his life for him.

Challenged by the same Korean troops in western uniforms who had impressed when Dawlish had made his formal visit, they were admitted through a small fortified gate in the palace wall. To their surprise there was only a corporal's guard and Shimazu questioned them in fluent Korean. He turned to Dawlish and spoke in English.

"It's bad. Very bad. *Muwi* troops have control of the South Gate. They've proclaimed their loyalty to the *Daewongun*. Only Lieutenant Horimoto and the *Pyolgigun* remain."

"And the King?" Dawlish said.

"Not here. They think he may be with the *Daewongun*, his father."

"The Queen?" Dawlish remembered his brief glance of a woman's face, small, delicate, obviously intelligent. And that her husband's father hated her, had once tried to have her killed by explosion.

"She's still here, in the *Gyotaejeon*, her own quarters. Lieutenant Horimoto is there with his men. He hasn't got enough to defend the whole palace wall." Shimazu gestured to the corporal he had just questioned. "Except at the South Gate there's a small guard like this at each entrance. They've orders to fall back and report if there's any sign of attack."

The succession of gardens and courtyards through which they passed seemed at once both deserted and haunted, the sense so palpable as elsewhere in the city that terrified eyes were watching from shuttered windows. His formal visit to the palace had given Dawlish the impression of a Chinese puzzle, of one walled compound within another, within another, but now it seemed closer to a maze, all pattern lost in the near darkness among the tiled-roof cloister walls and the curving double-winged roofs and the carefully-tended gardens heavy with the scent of flowering shrubs. And all the while there was an awareness that a few hundred yards to the south mutinous troops held the main gate, awaiting perhaps the orders of the *Daewongun* they had declared for. They seemed to be amusing themselves in the meanwhile for there were irregular sounds of screaming, terrifying in their frenzied rise and sobbing fall, of victims being subjected to torments unimaginable as scores were settled. Dawlish fought down fear, his sense of despair, and horror at the nightmare in which his sense of honour had trapped him.

Shimazu identified several of the pavilions as they passed, residences of relations of the king or queen and of senior court officials. A few lights burned inside them, gilded prisons since the palace guards had deserted and left them to the protection of a few retainers armed with antique weapons. "It will go badly with them if there's an attack," Shimazu said. "They're hated."

"They can't take shelter with the Queen?" Dawlish asked.

"No. They don't matter." Shimazu might have been talking of insects. "Only the Queen matters to us. You know that, Captain Dawlish. Only Queen Min can resist the *Daewongun*."

The Queen's quarters lay within a larger compound, its walled perimeter too long for prolonged defence with the forces available, at its centre a long single-storey hall upon a raised stone platform, a cobbled courtyard in front and a sloping garden behind. Beautiful it might be with its lacquered decorations and wave-like roofs but it was obvious that its wooden construction could make it a death-trap in case of fire. The *Pyolgigun* troops, pristine in their pressed uniforms and whitened gaiters, crouched behind the wall's ornamental stone balustrades. They were Koreans, not Japanese, and the test of their allegiance still awaited them. For all their smartness they now seemed pitifully few in number.

The smug pride that Lieutenant Horimoto had radiated when Dawlish had previously seen him at the palace was now gone, replaced by grim awareness that he was facing an impossible task with inadequate resources. He immediately deferred to Shimazu, bowing deeply before summarising the situation, nodding too-ready assent to the naval officer's curt remarks. Both men ignored Dawlish's presence.

"What are they saying?" Even as he spoke Dawlish wondered where Takenaka now saw his loyalty lying – loyalty, again that word, that vital word here – whether to the uniform he wore or to something older, deeper, beyond European comprehension.

"The Queen won't leave." Takenaka's voice was low. "Horimoto urged her to let him take her to Chemulpo, while it's still possible, to Japanese protection there. He said that ..." He stopped, listened. The exchange between Shimazu and Horimoto was getting heated despite their subdued tones.

"What now?" Dawlish said.

"Captain Shimazu wants to take her anyway. But she has told Horimoto that she doesn't want to be beholden to Japan, that she won't go, would prefer to die here."

"That's unthinking talk," Dawlish said. The screaming from the South Gate was still fresh in his memory. "Shimazu's correct. She must go now while we can still get out."

"The Queen will have poison about her, sir," Takenaka sounded for a moment as if he were stating an obvious fact to an obtuse child. "She will be thinking very clearly about it."

Horimoto was getting very agitated now, his statements low angry barks.

"He says can't answer for the *Pyolgigun* troops if anybody touches the Queen," Takenaka said. "If she wants to die here then they'll die with her. And they'll kill anybody – even Horimoto himself – who lays hands on her, even if to save her."

"Can we see her? Ask them!"

Takenaka moved towards them, bowed, addressed himself directly to Horimoto. A short discussion. "Her Majesty is not to be disturbed," Takenaka translated. "She refuses to see anybody. She's in her private quarters, with her ladies, with a few servants. She has already sent the rest away."

"So now?"

"So now we stay here." Shimazu had turned to Dawlish and was speaking in English. "And I suggest you remain with us until the rioting burns itself out. And it will. The rabble won't dare attack here – even the *Daewongun* won't countenance an open assault on the Queen. Our best protection is that the *Muwi* troops are with him and that they hold the South Gate. He'll want them to keep the mob out. And if he comes here it will be to negotiate."

"And the Queen?"

"She has Japan's protection. And Britain's also?"

"Great Britain's also," Dawlish said.

There was nothing to do now but wait.

*

Dawlish joined Shimazu on an inspection of the perimeter wall. Three sides looked out into the larger palace complex across cobbled courtyards but the fourth, the garden side, was bounded by the palace's own outer wall. There was no gate there, just a small doorway through which gardeners might pass. From the parapet above it the ground outside looked open, no huts or houses, just the sight of distant woods. There was no sign of movement, no flames flickering in the darkness and at this moment it still represented a clear path to safety. Salvation lay just beyond the small iron-studded wooden door. Only the unseen queen's adamantine resolve, and the pride that kept Shimazu and Dawlish from deserting her, made that escape impossible.

In the hours before dawn Dawlish and Takenaka snatched sleep in turns in an ornate antechamber devoid of furniture. Dawlish rolled his tunic as a pillow, his revolver beneath it, and he did not remove his boots. When he was woken, as requested, the sun was already rising.

"Any sign of trouble?" He stretched, limbs aching. He realised that Takenaka had been sitting cross-legged beside him, drawn sword across his knees.

"None, sir. It seems quiet outside now. There's been no movement from the South Gate."

The morning passed slowly. Smoke still hung over the city but most of the fires had been extinguished. Distant gunfire crackled, but intermittently, dying quickly. Another attempt to speak directly to the queen proved futile. The blue and scarlet uniforms of the *Muwi* troops could now be seen above and around the distant main gate but they came no closer. The intervening courtyards looked as empty of life as if the palace had been deserted for centuries. Half of Horimoto's force – now supplemented by the guards and seamen who had come from the Japanese Embassy – was in position on the walls at any time, the other half resting, but as they changed guard he inspected them with the same intensity he might have employed before a ceremonial parade. Dawlish saw him strike one private across the face with the flat of his sword because of a single unclosed gaiter bottom. It was the impassivity with which the man accepted the blow, rather than Horimoto's deliberate savagery, that impressed most. Well trained, well led, such men could be invincible.

Shimazu seemed to have avoided Dawlish through the day, their contacts few and formal, reviews of the unchanging situation, agreement that the situation was looking hopeful, that peace if not order was returning to the city. But in late afternoon he sent an orderly to request him and Takenaka to drink tea with him and Horimoto.

"He is honouring you, sir," Takenaka explained. And Dawlish remembered the headless corpses and crucified victim in the village square no less than the ceremony he had been included in when the flag and the emperor's portrait had been so solemnly protected. He realised that he was at once attracted and repelled by this man, perhaps by the entire world he represented.

"I will be honoured also ..." Dawlish began, and was then cut off by a rattle of musket-fire and by the roar of thousands of voices that followed.

To the south, first hundreds, then thousands, were pouring through the South Gate, weapons in hand, intoxicated by earlier rapine and revenge, their hunger for more unsatisfied, their numbers swelled by the blue and red-clad *Muwi* troops, their fury sanctioned by the king's own father.

The worst slaughter was about to begin.

*

The mob washed briefly around the walls of the queen's palace but there was no coordinated assault, only the blind milling of a crowd dazed by its sudden freedom to penetrate the forbidden, to loot the riches they had known of but had never seen. Three measured volleys from Horimoto's troops dropped dozens of them as they surged first towards the wall, and then away in panic, dispersing to find easier triumphs elsewhere. Shortly afterwards smoke began to rise from a close-by pavilion half-hidden by its surrounding wall. Its gate appeared to have held but *Muwi* troops had come forward with ladders and had smashed down the tiled roof above the parapet. Dozens were now climbing across.

Dawlish watched with the Japanese officers. Shimazu translated Horimoto's identification.

"The Tribute Bureau," he said. "We can blame all this on its director. Min Kyong-ho was known for his greed. He should have paid his troops honestly."

"Min?" Dawlish said. "A relation of the Queen?"

"A cousin. She placed many of them in such positions."

For a half-hour or more shouts and shooting issued from the compound, and the lacquered wooden structure within blazed up like a furnace until the heat forced the mob out from it, some staggering under the weight of chests and furniture, others waving bloody clothing and other objects, worse. Dawlish, sickened, looked away and handed back the field-glasses Horimoto had passed to him.

Already another compound was under assault, the mob smashing down its ornate gate and trampling through its gardens to be met by brief and futile musketry. Horimoto pointed to it and spoke rapidly.

"The Office of the Royal Kinsmen," Shimazu translated. For all his outward impassivity there was in his voice a graveness, perhaps even a fear, which had not been there before. "Lieutenant Horimoto cannot believe that the *Daewongun* could have sanctioned such an offence. The mob must be beyond his control."

From that compound also smoke was soon rising, a single vast flame roaring skywards as the exquisite wooden structure took light and its roof collapsed. Here too the heat forced the attackers to retreat, dragging several half-naked bodies with them to butcher to the delight of the baying onlookers. Except for the Queen's compound the entire palace complex was now open to looting, groups dragging booty with them back towards the South Gate and often fighting each other for possession, others moving on to smaller buildings and compounds to initiate another orgy of greed and fury. They stayed as much as possible outside the sight and range of Horimoto's troops on the *Gyotaejeon* wall.

"The Queen must leave now," Dawlish said. The violence was still confined within the palace boundaries and even as the sun dropped in the west the countryside beyond the outer wall, just beyond that single iron-studded gardener's door, was still free of threat. Escape was tantalisingly close. But only if the unseen Queen consented.

Shimazu agreed. "We'll bring her whether she wants to or not," he said. "It will be dark soon. Just her. Her attendants must stay." He glanced towards the troops on the wall. "They mustn't know," he said. "Horimoto must remain with them to cover our retreat."

Dawlish shook his head. "She may have poison. She may prefer that to leaving."

And then, unexpectedly, Takenaka broke in. "Queen Min may prefer to die than to be..." He paused, as if summoning the will to say something distasteful. "...than to be what she may construe as an instrument of His Majesty the Emperor's policy." Even now he bowed at the mention of the word. He saw the look of anger on Shimazu's face and added "She would be mistaken of course."

And now Dawlish saw a glimmer of hope. "She doesn't want to go to Chemulpo under Japanese escort." he said. "But would she consent to go somewhere else? To relations, to supporters?"

"No!" Shimazu was vehement. "Only in Chemulpo can she be safe. Only under the protection of His Majesty the Emperor."

"Let's accept realities, Captain Shimazu. She won't see you – but she might see me. And if she does I'm damned if I'll persuade her to hand herself over to you." Dawlish felt the enormity of what he was committing to without knowledge of the country or language or customs. But he was conscious that at this moment he embodied Britain. He had all the authority of the Queen-Empress's official representative, and he would use it to the limit.

"You don't speak Korean, Captain Dawlish!" Shimazu spat out the words. His eyes registered cold satisfaction. "You would need me to interpret for you. And I feel no obligation to do so!"

"I'll manage somehow, Captain Shimazu!" Even as he spoke Dawlish knew that this might be empty bravado, but he was damned if he was going to be browbeaten. Now more than ever he missed Whitaker's presence, his easy familiarity with the language. He looked to Takenaka. "You can manage some Korean, Lieutenant? At least make yourself understood?"

Takenaka flashed a look towards Shimazu that somehow combined defiance and respect. Their eyes locked for a moment before Takenaka turned to Dawlish and bowed stiffly. "I will be honoured to attempt so, sir" he said. "I will do my best."

Rifle-fire from the wall was telling of Horimoto's troops successfully repelling a half-hearted surge towards the compound gate as Dawlish and his navigating lieutenant began their slow parley with the guardian of the inner chambers where the Queen and her entourage sheltered. There was a single door to be passed, massive but beautifully carved. It was opened only a crack, and restrained by chain inside from wider opening, but it allowed speech with a smooth-faced, shrilly voiced man whom Dawlish realised must be a eunuch. Takenaka made little headway at first – his gestures towards Dawlish's now grimy and torn uniform seemed to carry more meaning than the words he spoke – and the door was closed twice, and then reopened after long minutes for further talk.

"What does he say?" Dawlish asked as the door closed again. He could hear the rumble of a bar being drawn across inside.

"Nothing, sir. Only that he must consult his mistress again."

From outside rifle-fire rippled again, then died. Darkness had fallen, emboldening the braver souls among the mob to advance under its cover. Dawlish wanted to be gone, wanted to be no part of another murderous resistance like that at the Embassy gate that seemed an age before. The small gardener's door beckoned but only the door before him now could open it for him.

Another brief but futile negotiation through the barely-opened door. As it began to close again Dawlish pushed himself forward, sensing that Takenaka's Japanese identity might be a hindrance rather than a help. Suddenly inspired, he ripped a brass button from his sleeve cuff and reached it through. Surprised, the eunuch took it and closed the door yet again. The button, with its fouled anchor surmounted by a crown and edged as if with rope, must count for something.

It worked. When the door opened again a left hand was reaching for his and pulling him inside.

"Come in, Captain," Fred Kung said.

He closed the door, shutting out Takenaka. It was not the Fred Kung in whipcord breeches and with a Paisley scarf whom Dawlish had met before, but another, clad in the dull uniform of a palace menial. But the air of self-reliance and confidence was the same and Dawlish sensed mutual respect.

"I can't offer you rye whisky or even a cigar, Captain," he said. "But you're welcome anyway."

"How long have you been here?"

"Since early yesterday, since things started going to hell."

There were several others in the small chamber, eunuchs by their looks, but Kung gestured to them to leave. None were armed and if Kung had a weapon it was well concealed.

"How did you get in?"

"The hired help never attracts much notice." Kung gestured towards his shabby clothing. "And I can cringe like the best of them if I need to. My boss wanted me to relay a message, and so here I am."

"For Queen Min?"

"For nobody else. News that a Chinese force had crossed the Yalu into Korea, was making good time, and that a cavalry squadron was pressing on before it. And one galloper got through ahead of it, confirmed the force would be here at latest two days from now. And there should be eight hundred men arriving by sea from Tiensin and landing at Chemulpo. So Her Majesty was advised to sit tight here and wait for us."

"But it's different now," Dawlish said. "There's no hope of holding out. She's got to leave. It's still possible. Just possible."

"Not with those goddam Japs outside. She won't let the mob, or her father-in-law, have her, but most of all she won't let the Japanese use her as a puppet like they'd use her husband. She knows what to do. She has her poison to hand." Kung's voice dropped. "Look Captain, you don't know us here, not any of us Asians. We look differently at death than you do."

"I want to see her," Dawlish said. "I want to tell her that Queen and Empress Victoria's emissary is here. That he's guaranteeing her

Britain's protection. That he's pledging his life to get her safely to her own people and that he'll keep her from the Japanese."

"Quite the knight errant, ain't you?" Kung said. "You believe all that stuff too, don't you?"

"You haven't chosen to run to save yourself, have you Mr. Kung?"

Kung shrugged, an American gesture rather than a Chinese one. "Yeah, I suppose so. Maybe we're two of a kind, Captain." He sounded apologetic, almost as if amused at himself. And then he said "I guess it's time we saw Her Majesty."

*

She was seated, immobile, in the centre of a small, high-ceilinged hall, furnished with nothing but the carved chair she was enthroned upon. To either side, half-a-dozen women kneeled equally immobile on the polished wooden floor. The only sound was that of rifle-fire, muffled by the intervening walls. The folds of her voluminous dress, red silk, beautifully adorned with gold embroidery, had been arranged with conscious artistry, the long sleeves brushing the ground and hiding her clasped hands. Her hair had been swept up like a massive black crown adorned with pearls and secured behind by a long a golden skewer that extended to either side of the delicate, intelligent, impassive face that Dawlish had glimpsed so briefly only once before. Cleopatra, he realised, had not faced death with greater dignity or composure.

Kung bowed deeply, Dawlish also. There was the slightest flicker of recognition, perhaps even of a smile, on the Queen's face as Kung began to speak, his words incomprehensible but urgent. There was nothing now of the informality of his American speech, and his delivery was blank-faced, as if constrained by some ancient courtly convention, and punctuated by repeated small nods and bows. He gestured towards Dawlish's uniform, and Dawlish detected his own name, and the word Victoria, more than once in the torrent of what must be Korean.

And all the time the volume of shooting outside was growing. It was almost continuous now, the sharper reports of the rifles interspersed with the duller crash of musket-fire. A small voice in Dawlish's head screamed that Horimoto had insufficient men to hold the wall, that he might have even fewer by now, that if the gate was

127

breached or the parapet crossed, there would be nothing for it but a last hopeless stand at this flimsy but exquisite tinderbox of a pavilion.

But at last the queen spoke, her voice as calm as her still-impassive face.

"Her Majesty wants to hear your guarantee from your own lips," Kung translated. "She wants you to swear that she will have the protection of her sister-queen."

12

Shimazu's face twitched with supressed fury as he strove to maintain a mask of equanimity. Dawlish had told him that an arrangement had already been agreed when he had emerged through the carved door. Behind it Fred Kung was supervising frantic arrangements. The women and eunuchs who would be left behind – and these would be the majority – must even now be reconciling themselves to their fate.

"Once outside you'll have nothing to protect her!" Shimazu spat.

"Myself, a few retainers, and Lieutenant Takenaka." Dawlish had not mentioned Kung's presence or that Kung had contacts waiting scant miles away. "And she has my word as a British officer, and as Queen Victoria's envoy, that she has Britain's protection." It meant nothing at this moment, he knew, and yet he was proud to say it. Shimazu – Japan – would not have her.

Shimazu brought his face to Dawlish's, close enough for Takenaka not to hear above the spasmodic rifle-fire from the wall. "You want to buy her escape with Japanese lives," he hissed. "Her escape, Britain's interest and your life, Captain!"

"That implication does you no credit, Captain," Dawlish said. "You've worn the same uniform that I do."

A sudden flicker that might have been embarrassment crossed Shimazu's face. "I do not forget it." He paused, and when he spoke it was with an effort. "It will be as you say. We will lay no hands on her. But I will come with you. I must live to report to my superiors."

"And Horimoto? He only needs to hold long enough to cover our escape. Ten minutes before he follows us. I don't ask for more."

Shimazu shook his head. "Lieutenant Horimoto will know how to die."

At that moment a great many-throated cry from beyond the wall announced the last assault. Stiffened by *Muwi* blazing upwards with their muskets, others running forward with ladders, yet more hurling themselves towards the gate with a battering ram improvised from a fallen beam, the mob, oblivious of its losses, was now unstoppable. Horimoto's troops were shooting down from above the gate, but others were turning with their bayonets to face the *Muwi*, first a handful, then a torrent, which had gained the top of the wall and was pressing along the parapet. There was no room for reloading now, just savage bayonet-parrying of thrusting pikes and halberds.

"Now!" Dawlish hammered on the carved door and it opened just as the gate, ornamental rather than functional, shattered under the ram's blows. "Get in," he shouted to Takenaka and Shimazu, then followed. He glanced back as the door closed and saw Horimoto laying about him with his bloody sword, his empty revolver swinging uselessly on its lanyard. Around him his *Pyolgigun* also knew how to die. He had trained them well.

Kung was already ordering servants to pile furniture against the closed door, enough only to buy minutes, perhaps even just seconds. He left them to it and led Dawlish and the others on towards the hall where the Queen had so calmly awaited death. When they entered Dawlish was taken aback even though he already knew what to expect. For a slight figure was still seated there, immobile, the folds of her voluminous dress arranged with conscious artistry, the long sleeves hiding her clasped hands, half-a-dozen women kneeling equally immobile to either side. But the face beneath the black hair fixed with a golden skewer was thinner, less intelligent, than before, and the lower jaw was trembling in terror for all the resolution and obligation that kept her waiting there for death, for her last service to her mistress.

"This way!" Kung led them through another door, into a smaller chamber, and there they found a tiny figure – she had seemed larger when on the throne – with hair dishevelled, face reddened by being scrubbed clean of powder, and clad in the plain dress of a serving maid. A broad-shouldered servant stood behind her, grim-looking and bearded.

"Yi Yong-Ik will carry her if necessary," Kung said, then plunged on through another door.

Through the wooden-panelled walls the sounds of fury reverberated, cries of anger mixed with musket-shots, no longer interspersed with the bark of rifles. Another door, and then they were in the garden behind the pavilion. The sky above shed enough red light to pass silently between the shrubs and flowerbeds towards the door in the outer wall, Kung in the lead, the Queen and her servant close behind, Dawlish and the two Japanese bringing up the rear, their swords and his revolver drawn.

Another servant stood by the gardener's door and he swung it open as they approached. There were sounds of screaming from behind now, high-pitched, agonised, women's voices crying for mercy that would never come. Figures were blundering out from the pavilion and into the garden.

"Quick now!" Kung was bundling the Queen unceremoniously through the gate, the servants with her. But a woman was blundering towards them through the garden, falling, sobbing, striving to rise though encumbered by silken robes. Two men, *Muwi* by their uniforms, were catching up, laughing. Then one had her by the hair and was holding a blade against her throat while the other was sweeping up her clothing.

"Takenaka!" Dawlish gestured towards them. Silence was essential – this was no time to use his own pistol. Already *Leonidas's* navigation lieutenant was springing forward, sword upraised, and Shimazu was close behind. Their flame-reflecting swords whirled lethally, their victims unaware of them until it was almost too late, though with time enough for one to slice the knife across the wretched woman's throat. Blood fountaining, she slumped down, drawing her murderer with her, exposing his neck to Shimazu's deadly slice. His head was already rolling as Takenaka's downward blow split the other's face. It was the work of seconds only and both their faces had a look of savage joy as they joined Dawlish at the gate.

They passed out and a servant pushed it to, locking it with a huge key. Here, outside the wall, the sounds of the slaughter inside were muffled and there was as yet nobody on the parapet above. But the ground that extended ahead, undulating slightly towards the woodland a mile or so distant, was open. It had to be crossed as quickly and stealthily as possible before some marauder discovered the gardener's gate and the identity of the loyal servant who had taken the Queen's place.

Dawlish felt his hands shaking, his heart thumping, as they started. Exposed here, obliged to scurry from one slight shadowed fold to another, towards cover that did not seem to get any nearer, was worse than facing armed opponents, weapon in hand. The Queen was tiring already but there could be no let-up in pace. Her face was drawn with effort and she was panting. Soon it was time for the servant, Yi Yong-Ik, to carry her, piggyback style, and Dawlish recognised his pride that he might do so. Fred Kung led the way – he had come this way when he had slipped into the palace – and now the pace was faster. A glance back revealed no figures on the outer wall's parapet but flames were rising from the pavilion they had so recently fled.

They paused, breathless, in a low hollow, deeply shadowed. Kung spoke to the Queen and she was nodding, smiling faintly towards Dawlish, then speaking quietly.

"She's thanking you," Kung translated.

Now, for the first time, Shimazu realised who Kung was, for he had played the role of a devoted retainer with limited English perfectly, and had kept his face lowered in humility when he had spoken before. But now he could not keep a tone of triumph from his voice and his American accent was unmistakable.

"You're Kung!" Shimazu face was contorted with fury. "I know of you!" He snarled what sounded like an insult in a language Dawlish could not recognise. The smile of amusement with which Fred Kung greeted it aggravated Shimazu's anger still further. He turned to Dawlish. "You're delivering her to the Chinese," he snarled. "So much for your British protection, Captain! She's going to the Chinese!"

"She's going where she wants to go," Dawlish said. "And right now I understand that she wants to go to her own people. And Mr. Kung is helping her reach them."

"I should have killed you back there," Shimazu's voice was icy with contempt. "You and your traitorous lackey. Nobody would ever have known." He turned towards Takenaka. "You don't just wear their uniform. You prefer them to your Emperor."

Takenaka's face hardened and his hand closed on his sword hilt. Dawlish reached out and touched it. "Enough, Lieutenant," he said. Lip quivering, Takenaka nodded deeply, the closest he could come to a bow as they crouched in the hollow. "I understand, sir," he said.

Kung had been smiling as he watched. "You'd be welcome to kill each other, gentlemen," he said. "Two fewer of your people would be no bad thing. But this just ain't the time or place." He gestured towards the woods ahead. "Not far to go now. My men are waiting there."

The last few hundred yards were the most frightening of all, for they must ascend a gentle slope that was wholly devoid of cover.

Behind them the riot still raged at the palace. Yet another pavilion was burning now but still there were no signs of detection or pursuit. They jogged on, the Queen bouncing on her servant's back, his pace relentless, Dawlish and the two Japanese again in uneasy alliance as the rear guard.

At the wood's edge they found Kung's men, a dozen of them, his blue-turbaned Uighurs, all heavily armed. Dawlish envied them their Spenser repeaters – had Horimoto's men had the same then the Queen's compound might have been held indefinitely. They led the newcomers deeper into the wood and there, at the side of a track, several sturdy ponies were tethered. With them, unmistakable by their dress, stood several Koreans. They fell on their knees and touched their foreheads to the ground as they saw the Queen. Only now was she set down. She swayed on her feet but waved away her servant's move to support her. There was no time for ceremony. Kung was issuing orders rapidly and she was being hurried to a pony and lifted on its back. Already two of the Uighurs were taking the leading reins and Yi Yong-Ik, who had carried her so tirelessly, was supporting her upright in the saddle. Two of the Koreans were also mounting, both cousins of hers, Kung told Dawlish, and eight of the Uighurs would provide the escort. Their goal was a family stronghold at Chungju, a full night's journey ahead.

Just before they started she beckoned to Shimazu. He bowed deeply, and deeper still after she had spoken.

"She says she's grateful for what his people did back there," Kung translated. "And so she should be. They died hard for her. But she reminded him that that don't alter the situation none. She's not for Japan to manipulate, nor for China either. She's only for Korea."

She gestured to Dawlish to come to her. He saw that her face was wan with exhaustion and with release from terror but that somehow she was smiling. She reached out her hand. The intake of breath around him told him that the action must be unprecedented, the shattering of centuries of tradition. She was holding the brass button he had torn from his coat. He took it. She did not withdraw her hand, small, delicate, but grimy from the escape, and he kissed it, then sank to one knee as he released it. The urge to do so was unthinking, spontaneous, yet somehow inevitable and he felt gratitude course through him that he could have served her. Then he heard her speak a single phrase, the pronunciation distorted but the English words – perhaps the only ones she knew – unmistakable.

"Thank you," she said.

Her party disappeared off down the track, leaving Dawlish and Kung, Takenaka and Shimazu standing in uncomfortable silence while the remaining Uighurs busied themselves with the two ponies that remained.

Kung broke the silence. "This is as far as we go together, Shimazu," he said. "I guess you don't like my company any more than I like yours. There's a horse here for you and you can find your own way to Chemulpo or anywhere else you damn-well like. To Hell for all I care."

It seemed for a moment that Shimazu might draw his sword but he somehow controlled himself. "You'll be paid later for the horse, Mr. Kung," he said, "and we'll have other accounts to settle with you and your countrymen. You can tell your ambassador that." He turned to Dawlish. "I'll see you at Chemulpo, Captain, but I'd prefer not to see your Lieutenant Takenaka again. The Royal Navy is welcome to him."

Shimazu took the pony that had been readied for him. It was too small for him and his exit lacked the dignity that he would have relished. His waist was still thickened by the flag and portrait he had preserved and defended so well. He disappeared off down the track in the opposite direction to that the Queen had taken.

"It's time to be getting you back to the British compound, Captain Dawlish," Kung said. "We'll take our time, let those folks in town get the anger out of their systems. Come the dawn and most of 'em will be tired of the fun and slinking back home to sleep it off."

"But the *Daewongun* holds the palace now," Dawlish said. "He must control the city too, and probably the King."

"Not for long, Captain. Not with a small Chinese Army on the way. He's welcome to the city in the meantime."

Kung's and Dawlish's small party set off to loop cautiously around Seoul's outskirts. And as they did the red glow in the sky faded slowly, and the sounds of distant tumult died. Even to murder and looting an end must come.

*

It was as if the city was prostrate, speechless and numbed from the horror of recent days. The alleyways and lanes and even the broader streets were all but devoid of movement, no stalls trading, no shops open, no oxen lumbering under ungainly loads. There were bodies slumped in unexpected places, sometimes individually, sometimes in untidy groups. Over them numbed relatives wept, still too grief-stricken to pull them free for burial. They scattered at the sight of the Uighurs, and so too did the carrion birds and dogs lurking hopefully nearby. The fires were out but the smell of charred wood and thatch was everywhere and ash-smeared scavengers were sifting through still warm embers to find anything they could of value.

The Union flag was flying proudly at Whitaker's compound and the guard could not have been more smartly turned out. Ross's small garrison had been reinforced by the dozen marines whom Watkins had been sent to bring from *Leonidas*. They had covered the distance from Chemulpo in little over twelve hours and had encountered no opposition either on the way, or at the city gate, from which its guards seemed to have deserted. The waves of rioting had lapped harmlessly around the British compound and no enmity had been directed against it. For the enraged mob only the hated Japanese mattered.

"Mr. Whitaker got to Chemulpo with the Japanese ambassador," Watkins said. "The whole party was exhausted but they made it."

"Sergeant Hawley?" Dawlish knew that for him the journey must have been agony.

"He had to lose the leg. But he's making the best of it."

"Whitaker's arm?"

"It will mend. He wants to get back here as quickly as he can."

"The ambassador?"

"He didn't wait about, not even with those Japanese ships in port. A British trader, the *Flying Fish*, had just arrived. His people chartered it even before it could unload. He was heading back to Japan with his whole party."

In anger and thirsting for revenge, Dawlish thought. "The Japanese ships, the *Haruna* and *Kirishima*," he said. "They're still at Chemulpo?"

"At the same moorings. They put marines ashore to protect Japanese property but they needn't have bothered. There was no problem there. The Koreans are terrified of them."

Dawlish was impatient to return to *Leonidas*. There was no prospect for now of any signature of the codicils. Perhaps there was not even any authority remaining which could sign them.

"Wait a week or two," Fred Kung was about to leave. "We'll have a Chinese garrison here by then and we'll have the *Daewongun* on his way to honourable detention in Peking. We'll have found the King, wherever he's skulking at present, and the Queen will make sure he signs whatever she puts in front of him. She owes you." He laughed and there was an air of triumph about him. "And those goddamn Japs are gone. I don't doubt they'll be back but they're wrong-footed for now."

Secure again and surrounded by men who were part of the service – the world – he had grown up in, men who thought and judged and behaved by its codes, Dawlish felt disgust wash through him. For Kung no less than for Shimazu. The atrocities he had witnessed were part of a greater game that took no account of individual worth or loss. Horimoto and his *Pyolgigun*, the Queen's ladies, had all been sacrificed without hesitation or remorse as pawns whose deaths were more valuable than their lives. Dawlish found his mind recoiling from the recognition that these victims had accepted their fates so unthinkingly, so willingly and that he owed his own survival to them.

There were dispositions to be made, decisions to be taken. A small guard was to remain at the compound – the flag must be kept flying there – but a reliable corporal had come from *Leonidas* and could be trusted to command it. Ross and Watkins and the remainder of the marines would return with him to *Leonidas*.

But first would come the opportunity to discard filthy clothing, to wash, to eat and to smoke a single cigar and then, most important of all, to sleep.

13

There were now five warships moored at Chemulpo when Dawlish returned, two new arrivals in addition to *Leonidas* and the Japanese corvettes. They lay almost a mile from the other ships, in deeper water, and the dragon-adorned yellow triangular ensigns at their sterns identified them as Chinese.

"They arrived yesterday," Edgerton said. He was seated in Dawlish's quarters and making his report. There was little enough to tell. As Dawlish had expected *Leonidas* had been left in safe hands. "Damn poor sailors those Chinamen are too. That larger ship made three attempts to anchor. I've seldom seen men running about on deck to so little effect and the officers only made it worse rather than better. She's called *Hi Ying*. The other looks impressive though."

The necessary courtesies had been exchanged, the contacts sufficient to establish the identity and details of the new arrivals. The larger vessel, whose handling Edgerton had deplored, a single-screw cruiser of about 2000 tons and 300 feet, flew an admiral's flag. She carried a barquentine-rig in addition to her engine but it was obvious even from a distance that the stays and shrouds were poorly set, that the mizzen missed a topmast and gaff and that the foremast's yards crossed at crazy angles. Her black sides were streaked with rust.

Dawlish shook his head as he lowered the telescope through which he was regarding her. "A pretty miserable sight," he said, "What happened to her?"

"Nothing. That's the problem. It seems most of their ships are kept like that. Built at the Foochow dockyard apparently and she'd be sound enough if properly looked after. But it seems those fellows just don't care."

And yet the *Hi Ying* could have been a formidable vessel – she carried two breech-loaders in armoured sponsons ahead of the bridge, dangerous weapons.

"Krupps," Edgerton said. "Imported from Germany. Eight-inchers. Powerful if they know how to handle them, though I doubt if those Celestials do."

But it was the second vessel that interested Dawlish more. He already knew of her through professional journals that had made much of her and her sisters. The *Fu Ching* and the two others of her class were the most heavily-armed vessels afloat for their size. They were sophisticated and expensive craft. An enterprising British yard had convinced Chinese diplomats, and naval officials who knew little of sea-duty, that they were ideal responses to growing Russian and Japanese menaces.

"You can see the Armstrongs, the ten-inchers?" Edgerton asked.

Dawlish focussed on them, two single breech-loaders from Britain's premier manufacturer, one forward, one aft, as powerful as any that the Royal Navy itself was only now acquiring. Only the muzzles were visible, protruding from the fixed steel drums, closed off by removable armoured flaps, inside which they pivoted. Four more Armstrongs, 4.7-inch breech-loaders, were carried, two to each broadside, efficient and deadly if well served. On a mere 1350 tons and little over 200 feet *Fu Ching* carried a heavier armament than many of the out-dated ironclads which were likely to remain in service for years to come in the world's major navies. Lightly armoured and of low freeboard *Fu Ching* might be, but a fearsome adversary nonetheless.

"She looks smart," Dawlish said. Men had been suspended over the side to paint the black hull and the upperworks were a gleaming white. Even the single funnel's yellow had been scrubbed clean of soot.

"There's an American on board," Edgerton said, as if in explanation. "I understand that strictly speaking he's an adviser but in practice he's running the ship."

"You've met him?"

Edgerton shook his head. "Not yet. But you will. You're invited by Admiral Shen to dinner on board his flagship tonight so I imagine this Yankee will be present."

"I'll need you with me," Dawlish said. "Sound him out, pump him. What exactly they're up to, how capable they are, what reinforcements they're expecting. We're likely to learn more from him than from any of his employers."

Afterwards Dawlish asked for Whitaker to join them. His arm was bound in a sling but he seemed otherwise unscathed by his recent experiences.

"News of the Japanese?" Dawlish asked.

Even a superficial examination through the telescope indicated that their standards of efficiency and smartness were being maintained on their moored warships. Boat crews were exercising vigorously and had even run informal races with their counterparts on *Leonidas* the previous day. One of the Thorneycraft torpedo boats had also been lowered and was also exercising, a bone in her teeth, white waves streaming back from her bows – 19 knots, maybe even 20, Dawlish thought with admiration. It was hard to reconcile this scene of systematic professionalism with the barbaric reprisal he had witnessed on the road to Seoul.

"The Japanese?" Whitaker said. "After the Ambassador left they landed marines and blue-jackets to secure Japanese property. No incidents though. The Koreans are too terrified of them and Admiral Hojo is keeping his men on a tight rein. I doubt Shimazu likes it. I suspect he'd crucify half the town if he had the chance."

"Shimazu's here?"

"He got here yesterday, before yourself. We saw him rowed out. He's back on board the *Kirishima.*"

Dawlish glanced again towards the Japanese corvette. The contrast with the *Hi Ying*, her similarly sized Chinese counterpart, was glaring, a proud young beauty compared with a prematurely aged slattern. The distance they were moored apart conveyed distrust if not hostility.

"What do we do now, Captain?" Whitaker looked away as if towards the Japanese ships, avoiding Dawlish's eyes. His tone conveyed something of relief that the decision was not his, a satisfaction that neither he nor the Foreign Office could carry blame for any negative outcome. This man had physical courage, Dawlish saw, but his career meant more to him than life itself.

As did his own...

"What do we do now?" Dawlish said. "We'll wait a little, see what develops."

For he still wanted the codicils signed, the confirmation that he could handle a diplomatic mission as competently as a naval one. Topcliffe would expect nothing less, would reward nothing less. What Dawlish had once thought a ladder was in fact a treadmill that would throw him off if he stopped climbing.

He returned to his quarters to wash and change. As he finished his steward entered.

"Beg pardon, sir. Mr. Leigh's compliments and he asked if he could speak to you. Private-like. Only for a moment, he said."

Other than official exchanges on the bridge Dawlish had spoken no word to the Sub-Lieutenant since the interview in Portsmouth. Now he was intrigued.

"Bring him in," he said.

Formalities, but Leigh seemed to be supressing a smile.

"For you, sir." He reached out an object six inches long and wrapped in paper. "With respect, sir, they're greased, so be careful not to get it on your uniform."

Not one object, but two, steel shafts, diameter varying in steps along their length. They were indistinguishable by the naked eye.

"Every dimension is accurate to within two-thousandths of an inch, sir." Leigh said.

Dawlish found himself smiling too. "I'll keep one, you the other. You can show it to your grandchildren, even bore them about it."

A nod told the young officer that he was dismissed but as he reached the door Dawlish called him back.

"Well done, Mr. Leigh," he said. "Well done."

And then it was time to visit Sergeant Hawley in the sick-bay, to offer hollow assurances that life without his leg outside the service might yet be rewarding, that a post would be found for him. And the families of the dead marines must not be forgotten. Letters were better written while faces could still be remembered.

The price of ambition was high.

*

There were still some minutes of daylight when Dawlish stepped on board the *Hi Ying*, the Chinese flagship. Whitaker, encumbered by his broken arm, boarded only with assistance, but his presence was essential as an interpreter. Edgerton was the third of the party. It was better not to bring Takenaka.

Dawlish had been unsure what to expect. He knew that China, unlike Japan, was only hesitantly and inconsistently embracing modernisation. Its attempts to develop a navy capable of defending its enormous shoreline were known to proceed only in fits and starts. He knew of a few Chinese officers being attached to the Royal Navy for training but they had earned none of the grudging respect their Japanese counterparts had secured. Several had been sent back early with a degree of ignominy and the general consensus was that they had neither the aptitude nor the dedication to make serious naval officers. Ships had been ordered in Europe, from Britain and Germany mainly, but not according to any obvious overall plan, and rumours of inflated prices and corrupt dealings between yards and Chinese officials were too persistent not to have a grain of truth. Vessels purchased overseas were usually delivered by European crews engaged by the dockyards, with perhaps a single Chinese official on board in nominal command. A few ships had been built at the Foochow dockyard – the *Hi Ying* was an example – but the design and construction-supervision had been by foreign advisers.

Yet none of this knowledge prepared Dawlish for what he found when he stepped on to a grime-encrusted deck that had not seen a holystone in months, if ever. The crew drawn up there were clad in loose blue uniforms which were more traditionally Chinese in style than the Royal Naval pattern the Japanese had adopted. Many had white cloth ovals stitched to the front of their collarless smocks, with embroidered characters that seemed to identify them by rank, as did the yellow markings on their blue turban-like caps. All seemed to have long, plaited pigtails. The officers were more gaudily dressed in long-skirted coats over which they wore wide-sleeved tunics, some extravagantly decorated, their black caps adorned with top-buttons that must indicate seniority. The unmoving array of faces was not only impassive but had also something surly and resentful about them, as if the very presence of outsiders was an offence. There was nothing about them of the cheerful pride that was so typical of the best Royal Navy crews, nor of the almost inhuman smartness of the Japanese. They had more in common with the coolies who toiled at the Hong Kong docks. Had it not been for the breeches of the massive weapons behind them, and the Snider rifles of what Dawlish guessed was the marine guard, and the smoke drifting lazily down from the funnel overhead, and for the single figure in western uniform, the tableau might have occurred at any time in the last thousand years.

Whitaker, well versed in custom and courtesies, murmured instructions at Dawlish's side during the long process of introductions and bowings. The officers' long sleeves extended over their hands and it was impossible to imagine anybody thus clad being able to act decisively in an emergency. Only one of the officers, a young man, a Lieutenant Lin, had some English, broken and hesitant as it was, and Dawlish wondered how he and his colleagues could ever have been instructed in the complexities of the heavy guns the ship carried. The answer might well be the officer in the austere blue uniform, which might have been that of any Western navy, though devoid of any badges of rank. He reached out his hand to Dawlish as they were introduced.

"Cyrus J. Lodge. Late United States Navy." He spoke the words slowly and deliberately, as if to disassociate himself from the Chinese officers he stood with. He was tall, with a rawness about his features and his hair steel grey. He might be fifty, maybe older.

"Commanding the *Fu Ching?*" Dawlish realised the impropriety of the question even as he spoke.

Lodge shook his head. "Captain Ma is in command of the *Fu Ching.*" He nodded towards the officer Dawlish had just been introduced to. "I'm on board his ship merely as an adviser." There was a hint of bitterness in his tone.

Dawlish was led aft. He noticed as he went that the peeling paint and sprung planks of several of the ship's boats indicated that they were seldom lowered from their davits. Brasswork was dull and rust abounded. On the shrouds gaps showed where ratlines were broken and the running rigging had been repaired with clumsy knots certain to foul blocks. It would take weeks to bring this vessel into fighting trim, longer still to bring this churlish and perhaps cowed crew to any acceptable level of efficiency. And yet it could be done – only two hundred yards away the smartness of the *Fu Ching* attested that Lodge had managed as much with a crew of similar background. Dawlish's mind flashed back to the squalor he had once found on an Ottoman ironclad and yet he had welded her and her crew into a deadly weapon. With discipline and training and leadership anything was possible.

Admiral Shen did not rise when Dawlish was ushered into the saloon in which he sat, as if enthroned, on a carved gilt chair. What he wore could scarcely be thought of as a uniform, shot through as was its silk with exquisite patterns like watermarks on paper. His face was plump and smooth, wholly hairless, and the hand he extended was soft and fleshy, the nails extending a full inch beyond the finger tips. The few formal words of welcome which Whitaker translated were in a piping treble. Despite the fastidious cleanliness of his silks and the scent of musk Dawlish detected a distinct odour of urine, as if the man before him was leaking. He realised with a mixture of pity and horror that Admiral Shen was a eunuch. And yet by his side the *Hi Ying*'s captain's face registered fear as well as deference. There was no doubt where power lay.

The sequence of compliments and polite enquiries seemed endless. The Admiral again introduced officers Dawlish had already met on deck and courtesies endured once-before were repeated again. Lodge too was present. He was obviously fluent in Chinese and as familiar with the protocols as Whitaker. As he conveyed the Queen Empress's compliments for the third or fourth time, but in slightly differing wording, and as Whitaker translated them with scrupulous care, Dawlish took in the surroundings. It was hard to believe that he was on board a warship. The walls – the term bulkhead seemed wholly inappropriate – were richly panelled with varnished wood and the furnishings were even more exotic, intricately carved and lacquered and inlaid with mother of pearl. The floor – no deck this – was of polished parquet, different shades laid out in complex patterns. And above the scent of musk, for Shen was not alone in liberal use of it, was the heavy, pervasive smell of opium.

Edgerton was standing in a group of Chinese officers, smiling, nodding, uttering short, quiet, meaningless courtesies as incomprehensible to them as their equally meaningless replies were to him. He was looking towards Lodge but the American was making no effort to join him.

The compliments continued and yet as they did Dawlish realised that there was nothing empty, nothing useless, in this exchange. As Whitaker translated the extravagant phrases Dawlish became conscious of the gleam in the Admiral's small dark eyes. He himself was being gauged, weighed up, evaluated as to how far he might be trusted or feared or used. The title of Admiral might be an honorary one only – and Dawlish suspected that it was – but Shen could only have come to this position of power through intelligence and ruthlessness, triumphing despite pain and mutilation and the contempt of whole men of lesser ability.

And at last words of significance.

"Admiral Shen understands that you met Mr. Kung in Seoul." Whitaker's right eyebrow flickered briefly as he turned to Dawlish to translate. *Watch out. Brass tacks.*

"Please advise the Admiral that I had that honour, that her Majesty's Government and I personally are obliged to Mr. Kung for his assistance." Shen had not mentioned the Chinese ambassador, only Kung.

The admiral was pleased to hear it. And as Whitaker translated this reply Dawlish wondered if the point of meaningful exchange might have been reached. He would chance it.

"Mr. Kung mentioned that Chinese troops would be landed here in the near future."

Whitaker's look flashed alarm. *Too direct. We don't do it like that.*

"Ask him," Dawlish said. *Don't question. Do it.*

Whitaker's translation seemed inordinately long, as if the simple question was wrapped up in endless embellishments. The faintest smile hovered for the first time on Shen's lip and his answer was short.

"Two chartered British merchantmen are due to leave Tiensin. They should be here in two days." Whitaker translated. A direct answer, no circumlocutions. "Eight hundred men."

Shen spoke again. "Not bannermen," Whitaker translated. "Men trained to use modern rifles." Shen was nodding slightly and Dawlish realised that he understood English even if he did not admit it, that he was following every word. "Two artillery batteries also."

Enough, more than enough, to garrison Chemulpo and to secure the road to Seoul. And the Chinese force on its way overland would control Seoul itself. Powerful and impressive as the ships anchored here might be, the Japanese had no regular troops here to forestall them. Short of outright confrontation, short even of war, the Chinese would have won this trick.

Shen knew it. He was nodding slightly and smiling as he looked at Dawlish. *We understand each other. Just stand back. Leave it to us. We've been playing this game for untold centuries.*

They moved to the wardroom, scarcely less ornate than Shen's quarters. The layout was no different from a British warship's, the long table in the centre, oil lamps suspended above it, the skylight's panels locked open overhead to provide some respite from the night air's steaming warmth, the sideboards and cabinets to the sides all exotic, carved, painted, lacquered as if in a palace. The table was bare of cloth but heated bronze-ware at its centre already gave off powerful smells of the food within. Each place setting was provided with its own bronze and porcelain bowls and spoons and ivory sticks. The overall impression was of infinite care that had transformed an occasion for eating into a work of art.

Dawlish was seated by the admiral, Whitaker by his side to translate. The Chinese officers took their positions in a sequence of obvious seniority and Edgerton was seated opposite Dawlish, but not directly so. Lodge was over to Dawlish's right, too far away to allow conversation. The seating might or might not be deliberate but it ensured that there was only one point of contact, the admiral himself.

"Admiral Shen has specially requested for you the banquet of the eight sea delicacies." Whitaker translated. "It's a special honour," he added. "A mark of respect."

Dawlish was effusive in his thanks, even as his mind shrank from what some of the items might be, but he was ever more vocally appreciative as the list progressed from shark's fin and bird's nest soup to dried sea cucumbers. He was even more thankful when the admiral paid him the compliment of himself lifting delicacies with his own sticks and dropping them into his bowl. As dish succeeded dish he was grateful now that he had asked Takenaka to instruct him in the use of sticks. Diagonally across from him Edgerton, unskilled in this, was trying to eat everything with a brass spoon, to the little-disguised merriment of the Chinese around him. The drink was flowing freely now, rice wine initially but soon thereafter heated cups of something that burned the mouth like brandy.

"Baijiu," Whitaker said. "It's distilled from sorghum".

Under its influence faces were becoming flushed, reserve fading, but Dawlish noted that the admiral scarcely drank. Abstemious himself by nature, and doubly so in these circumstances, Dawlish restricted himself to the slightest sips. The banquet had lasted well over an hour by now, and still more food was coming. There were several more hours to go, Whitaker told him, and cautious probing of the admiral was eliciting further scraps of information. He had twice been a provincial governor. The names Henan and Huguang meant nothing to Dawlish but he gathered they were places far inland. Though the time was not specified, Shen's appointment as admiral appeared to be recent. Familiarity with the sea and ships did not seem to be a prerequisite for senior command in the Imperial Chinese Navy. But loyalty, absolute loyalty, all too clearly was.

Another heavy bronze tureen, its contents steaming, was being lifted onto the spirit heater before the admiral. The table was noisy now, voices raised, the liquor's hold increasing, the formality relaxed a fraction. Edgerton's smile was less forced and even Lodge seemed to be relaxing. Dawlish was feigning interest in Shen's answers to his contrived enquiries about the internal economy of Henan and cautiously parrying the admiral's ornately phrased but astute questions about British intentions.

And then suddenly came the sound of a muffled explosion and a sudden lurch to starboard. A shudder ran through the ship, powerful enough to throw others as well as Dawlish from their chairs. Shen was on top of him, and men were shouting in pain as hot soup cascaded from upturned tureens. Two oil lamps had fallen and one Chinese officer was screaming as his clothes took light and a blaze had erupted, and was growing, at one of the lacquered sideboards. The ship lurched again – the list was already ten degrees at the least. Fallen men were scrambling to rise and others were rushing towards the doors leading forward at either side.

Dawlish struggled to his feet, then dragged the admiral up. He seemed uninjured and his stammered thanks sounded like a choirboy's. Whitaker had somehow risen despite his broken arm. Through the open skylight came the sounds of shouting – confused, terrified – and running feet and already an impression of chaos on deck. Lodge had torn off his tunic and was using it to smother the flames engulfing the burning man. There was a jam of bodies at both doors, all discipline forgotten. The fire at the sideboard was spreading to the panelling, its choking smoke already searing eyes and its scarlet flicker casting a ghastly light on the pandemonium.

The ship lurched again – some internal structure must have collapsed, flooding yet another compartment. There might be only minutes before the vessel rolled over, for the list was now enough to send the remaining items on the table sliding from it. With the fire growing as more panelling took light, and as the ship shuddered again, Dawlish knew that the wardroom was now all but a tomb. The panicked crush at the doors made exit by that route impossible. Whitaker seemed frozen and was grasping the table for support, his face terror stricken, as was the admiral, abandoned by his subordinates. Dawlish glanced up. Smoke and flames were being drawn towards the skylight and it could only be minutes before it was a volcano. And yet it represented the only possible exit.

"I'm here, sir." Lodge too had identified the only way of escape. The young Chinese officer, Lin, was with him.

"Hold my legs," Dawlish yelled and clambered on the table. His boots skidded on the polished surface but Edgerton's grasp about his knees somehow steadied him. He reached up, coughing in the thicker smoke above, but the skylight coaming was still a foot or more beyond his hand. His eyes were streaming, his nostrils and throat an agony from the smoke and he was trying not to cough. It seemed hopeless.

"Here, try to lift this man." It was Lodge, clambering up beside him. "Hold me!" he yelled to Edgerton, so that he and Dawlish now perched, swaying, on the canted surface.

"We can't reach it!" Dawlish shouted. Lodge was no taller than himself.

"Lin Chen-Ping can!" Lodge was reaching towards the young Chinese officer and Dawlish helped pull him up. He was light and slender and though he looked frightened he seemed to be controlling his fear.

Another arm wrapped itself around Dawlish's legs – Whitaker was using his good arm to help Edgerton hold him and Lodge steady. The American shouted in Chinese and cupped both his hands to make a step. Lin raised his foot to it and projected himself upwards. The shock of his leap knocked Dawlish and Lodge from their feet and sent them sliding helplessly down the table, but he had grasped the coaming with both hands and was swinging from it. Dawlish fought his way back to Edgerton through a barrier of tumbled chairs, Lodge close behind him. Smoke was not the only problem now, but heat also, for the panelling was blazing. The jostling dam of bodies at the doors had not broken and another wretch was screaming as his garments burned.

Dawlish would never remember the exact sequence of events that followed, only that he somehow mounted the table again, that Lodge joined him, that together they caught Lin's flailing legs and gave him enough momentum to raise himself over the coaming and disappear from view. For an instant there was a fear that the young Chinese would put his own survival first but suddenly he was back, leaning over and reaching down, and he seemed to have others with him. Smoke and heat were blasting through the open aperture but he did not flinch. He turned slightly and yelled back, and then dropped further – somebody on deck was holding his legs. His hand reached out, close enough to grasp. Then, somehow, Dawlish and Lodge were dragging up Admiral Shen and hoisting him towards Lin above. He was both heavy and bulky and his thrashing feet all but knocked them over, but in the end he was dragged from sight. Other faces had appeared now, other hands reaching down. Whitaker followed, gasping in pain as they raised him, and then it was Edgerton's turn. Without his support Dawlish and Lodge were swaying violently. If either's boot should slip again there would be no further chance since the wardroom was now a searing inferno whose breath was tearing past them like a gale.

"You first!" Lodge shouted as Lin's hands reached out to him.

Dawlish shook his head, some small part of him marvelling at the blind pride that still prevailed at this extremity.

Lodge recognised it. "Wait!" he yelled then called out to Lin above in Chinese. Another man was being lowered towards them alongside Lin, arms outstretched.

"Together now!" Lodge shouted.

There was an instant of terror as Dawlish felt hands brush past his own, miss, then somehow find them again even as his boots skidded from under him. Then he was being hoisted, Lodge too, and they were being dragged through the skylight's aperture.

They collapsed on the inclined deck, saw Shen and Edgerton grasping a stay and heaving for breath, Whitaker crouching against the bulwark to which he had slid, Lin and a half-dozen seamen clustered about the skylight. Beyond them was the chaos of an upset ant-heap. The ship lurched again, another tremor running through it.

And then, from the darkness a flash, then a second, and a double report in the instant before two explosions erupted around the bridge. The *Hi Ying* was under attack.

14

Debris scythed across the deck from the shell's impact on the bridge, mowing down anybody in its path and leaving a twisted tangle of wreckage behind.

His eyes still smarting from the smoke and straining to accommodate to the darkness that followed the flashes, Dawlish searched the darkness for the source of the gunfire. There was no moon, no natural light to identify a hull against a brighter horizon and all he knew was that the attack had come from seawards. The *Hi Ying* was heeled over to starboard, towards her assailant, and much of her deck must be exposed to it above the bulwarks. The list had already made it near-impossible to launch the boats slung on the port side but a terrified mob was nevertheless struggling to free them.

"She's finished," Lodge said, "She's going over. We need to get everybody off. I'll try to get them away from those boats." He shouted to the men around him, cuffed about the head one who hesitated, and moved forward, a dozen with him.

"Stay with the admiral," Dawlish yelled to Edgerton. "Find anything you can that'll float. Get him in the water, away from the ship." He had a fleeting vision of the masts and rigging ensnaring anything in their path when the vessel capsized — and that must now be inevitable. "You too!" he called to Whitaker, who seemed frozen in shock.

A solid column of flame was roaring through the wardroom skylight and the deck around was taking fire. The only hope of rescue must come from *Leonidas* and the other ships at anchor. Dawlish hoped there might be some chance of signalling for help if a sharp-eyed lookout could identify him. He headed diagonally towards the port bulwark, his boots slipping such that he made the last few feet on hands and knees. Beneath the mizzen shrouds he found a footing on a rack of belaying pins and he heaved himself up to the bulwark edge. He steadied himself against a block and looked seawards. At that moment there were two more flashes in quick succession, enough to illuminate for an instant what could only be one of the Japanese ships – a mile away, not more – and as the light died two reports thundered across the intervening water. The hot blast of the shells' detonations tore past him as one exploded by the base of the funnel, the other somewhere forward. A fire was suddenly taking hold there too, followed by a staccato of smaller reports as Gatling or Nordenvelt ammunition stored there ignited.

An icy beam reaching out from further inshore made Dawlish turn. It swept slowly across the anchorage, holding the stricken *Hi Ying* for a brief moment, then reached out further to sea, seeking the attacker. A second beam followed instants later, moving back and forth as if to search the waters between its source and the stricken ship. Dawlish felt a surge of hope – and pride. *Leonidas's* two arc-light projectors had been brought into action and Purdon, as gunnery lieutenant, must be directing them. The second beam's slow arc illuminated one of the Japanese corvettes, still seemingly at anchor, and so too the *Fu Ching*, the second Chinese vessel. A boat, a cutter, was already stroking away from *Leonidas* and a second was casting off.

A rending sound and an increased cacophony of despair made Dawlish turn. The foremast shrouds, already ladders of fire, were parting. As the last snapped the mast and yards swept over like a felled tree, smashing down on the water in a torrent of spray. The hull jerked back towards the vertical, then lurched again over to starboard, throwing more men into the water. Dawlish glanced sternwards – the deck was blazing furiously. He felt fury rise within him for this, he realised, must be Shimazu's doing and the shells wreaking such slaughter must be six-inchers, as deadly as *Leonidas's* own. He glanced down across the flame-illuminated deck, looking for Edgerton, for Whitaker, for Admiral Shen. There was no sign of them but with luck they might already be overboard, clinging to some piece of wreckage, paddling away from the clutching hands and bobbing heads of the men leaping into the water.

Leonidas's blinding light was locked on the *Hi Ying* now and Dawlish was dazzled as he looked towards it. He shielded his eyes with one arm, waved slowly with the other, hoped he must be visible to some lookout, perhaps even to Purdon. He turned away – it was essential to protect his night vision. The fires were more intense both forward and aft, only the ever-decreasing space between still tenable. Dozens of terrified men were crouched in the starboard scuppers, the odd one summoning the courage to mount the bulwark and leap overboard. But beyond, seawards, the *Leonidas's* other searchlight had caught the Japanese vessel which had attacked and was tracking her relentlessly as she crawled ever so slowly, parallel to the coast. And something was emerging from the darkness astern of her, illuminated briefly before it passed from sight on her other side. One glimpse of the long, low hull and the slender funnel identified it for what it was, one of the two Thorneycraft torpedo boats the corvette carried. There was the explanation of the muffled explosion that had ruptured the *Hi Ying's* hull. One fourteen-inch Whitehead fish torpedo had been enough to doom her. The shelling was unnecessary, pure savagery intended only to slaughter.

The cries of men in the water were all but drowned out by the roar of the flames. The mainmast's rigging was now ablaze and soon it too must topple over. The vessel lurched again and with a loud crack one of the funnel's stays parted, whipping like a snake, and then the other on the same side. The great iron cylinder teetered for an instant, then went crashing down on the despairing throng clustered by the bulwarks below. Thick black coal smoke and glowing pinpricks of glowing cinder rolled from the void it left in the deck.

Somebody was clawing his way toward Dawlish and calling his name. He looked down and recognised Lodge, his shirt torn, his face scorched and streaked with black. Dawlish reached down and hoisted him on to the bulwark edge to lean against the shrouds.

"I've got to get to *Fu Ching* before they hit her too," Lodge panted. Arm thrown up to shield his eyes, he was searching for the second Chinese vessel, but the glare defeated him.

A third searchlight blazed out but this was from astern and beyond *Leonidas*, and it came from the Japanese corvette still at anchor. It illuminated Lodge's vessel for an instant – "The bastards," he said, "they're going to fire on her." – but it swept on, ignoring her, locking on like *Leonidas's* to the heeling ship. It held her for a moment, then dropped slightly so as to light up the waters between. Through these waters *Leonidas's* cutter was stroking steadily forward, and a second boat was little far behind. The Japanese corvette's second searchlight came to life, illuminating the water by her side to show one boat moving away from her, as purposefully as the British craft, and two more being lowered.

"Get those men up here," Dawlish gestured to the surviving crew cowering below him. The *Hi Ying* was going to roll over and only from the high side could the water be entered safely. Lodge realised it too and he shouted down to the press of men. Dawlish recognised one raised face, still alert, still calm – Lin, the young officer who had dragged him from the blazing wardroom. He called back – he had understood Lodge and was already urging those around him to claw up the canted deck.

"Captain Dawlish, sir!" Dawlish recognised the voice of Sub-Lieutenant Leigh. Dark outlines against the icy light showed that the cutter was nearing, Leigh in her sternsheets, her oars beating rhythmically, two figures standing with boat hooks in her bows.

"Stand by!" Dawlish called back. "We'll try to get men off on this side!" Bedside him Lodge had turned away, was shouting instructions to Lin. Something slapped down on the bulwark, then whipped back and away before Lodge could catch it. "Again!" Lodge was shouting in English and this time he managed to catch the line that Lin threw to him and he began to make it fast to the shroud.

Leonidas's second boat came into sight and from it came Takenaka's voice shouting for instructions.

"Go around the stern!" Dawlish shouted. "Go to the far side, but stay well clear! Edgerton must be there, and Whitaker!" He hoped they were. "And the admiral! Admiral Shen! Find him at all costs!"

Takenaka called assent and sent his boat surging forward.

The first men to drag themselves up Lin's rope were clambering on to the bulwark. Lodge urged them over, down the exposed, curving side of the ship. They moved cautiously, some crouched, some on all fours. Several lost their footing as the slope increased and as they met the slime beneath the now-exposed waterline, others jumped out as far as they could into the waters below. More and more were coming, Lodge pushing the reluctant, praising others who had dragged an injured comrade with them. A dozen or more were already splashing in the water and Leigh's cutter was nosing among them, boathooks and oars stretched out to grasping hands, exhausted figures being dragged over the gunwales.

Dawlish glanced seawards, saw the Japanese corvette still transfixed by *Leonidas's* beam, but all but stern on now and obviously stationary as the torpedo boat that had wreaked such mischief was hoisted aboard. The shelling had finished and Shimazu must be well satisfied that the *Hi Ying* was finished – and not only the ship alone, but also the fragile, distrustful but still-peaceful balance between Chinese and Japanese power. For this was not just an act of treachery, it was an open declaration of war.

And yet...

As he helped push more men towards hazardous salvation in the waters below Dawlish forced himself to ignore the inferno raging beyond the bridge, and the knowledge that the magazines of the two Krupps there might blow up at any moment. Almost like a separate entity his mind was analysing the situation, knowing that if he got off this vessel alive he would be immediately confronted with hard decisions. The Japanese corvette – it could only be Shimazu's *Kirishima* – had now recovered the torpedo boat and was making full speed towards the horizon. But inshore, close to *Leonidas*, the second Japanese vessel, Admiral Hojo's flagship *Haruna*, was still at anchor. She had fired no weapon and her searchlights were as dedicated as those of the British ship to helping the work of rescue. One of her boats was joining Leigh's and dragging survivors from the water and her second and third were curving around the sinking vessel's stern to search for survivors there. It was just possible that Shimazu had acted without authorisation...

A rumble, and the mainmast collapsed, flailing over and leaving a trail of smoke and blazing cinders as it crashed into the sea to starboard. A cloud of steam rose from the impact and the hull jerked up violently for a moment then began to roll over slowly, steadily, offering no hope of respite. Water was flooding over the bulwark, hissing as it met the blaze, its weight dragging the vessel further over. Men hesitating beside Dawlish and Lodge were losing their balance and falling, the lucky ones down the port side towards the waiting boats, the less fortunate towards the surging foam now coursing over the deck. Still the hull rolled and Dawlish now stood upright on the outside of the bulwark and knew it was time to go. He pulled his boots off, threw them aside. He looked to Lodge – Lin, who had done so well, was with him – and he nodded as if in salute. The American returned it. Then together, they walked slowly down the curved side. When Dawlish felt the first of the slime beneath his feet he launched himself up and out, hoping that he would avoid laceration by the barnacles on the hull. He just made it, one foot grazing as he hit the water. He went under for a moment, then rose, choking. He coughed, shook the water from his eyes – it was tepid and foul-smelling but he welcomed its coolness nonetheless – and he struck out for the nearer boat. It was from the *Haruna* and already packed with survivors but the crew were still pulling more aboard. One swimmer near him was trying to support another and despite the barrier of language Dawlish managed to help him to drag him towards the boat. Nearing, he grasped an outstretched oar and was drawn alongside. He waited until the others were aboard and then was pulled across the gunwale to flop, panting, on the bottom boards like a landed fish.

"Captain Dawlish?" He recognised one of the young Japanese officers whom he had met that night of Admiral Hojo's dinner. "Shall we take you to your ship, sir?" The English was perfect, the courtesy impeccable.

Dawlish shook his head. "Not immediately…"

His words were cut off by the *Hi Ying's* final plunge. She rolled completely over, her keel now uppermost, and steam enveloped her briefly as her blazes were doused. Great dark bubbles erupted around her as water rushed into her interior, stressing bulkheads beyond endurance and coursing into more compartments as they failed. The screw and rudder rose as the bows began to sink. The forepart disappeared, but the water was shallow enough for it to dig itself into the bottom so that the remainder of the hull settled gently. It disappeared with a final lurch and shudder.

The searchlights played now on a desolation of foam and debris and drowning humanity. The boats, British and Japanese alike, moved slowly through it, searching for the last survivors.

*

"I don't need explanations, I don't want lies, I don't want goddamn excuses," Lodge's voice was cold, quiet and determined. "I want Shimazu and I want the *Kirishima*."

The preparations for departure around him confirmed his intent. The *Fu Ching's* decks were being cleared, stanchions lowered, canvas awnings struck down, a party in the bows ready to raise anchor. Already ammunition had been loaded into the ready-use lockers by the broadside 4.7-inch weapons and their crews were greasing nipples and spinning hand-wheels to check freedom of elevation and bearing. More significant still, the armoured shutters closing the drums sheltering the huge 10-inch breech-loaders fore and aft had been lowered and secured on deck. The weapons were now fully exposed to any enemy fire but they could now be brought to bear on full 270-degree arcs. The *Fu Ching's* nominal captain was dead, his body unrecovered, and Lodge had taken command in name as well as in practice. All that remained was for the boilers to reach full pressure, and that was imminent.

Standing with Lodge on the *Fu Ching's* bridge Dawlish was amazed by the contrast between the efficiency of this Chinese crew with the sullen resentfulness of the men he had seen on the ship just sunk. The uniforms might still be bizarre, the pigtails and loose garments reminiscent of a pantomime, and yet they moved with a confidence – perhaps even a pride – that was palpable. Lodge had obviously welded them into an estimable fighting unit. There had been similar men, their fathers perhaps, who had poured such deadly fire from the Taku Forts.

"Admiral Hojo is as outraged as you are," Dawlish said. "I've heard it from his own lips. I trust him, goddam it. He served in the Royal Navy!" *As Shimazu did*, a voice in his head reminded him.

Across the anchorage Hojo's *Haruna* still swung at anchor, the white canvas covers ostentatiously in place over her guns' muzzles clearly visible from this distance, advertisements of no offensive intent. Her boats had worked through the night to pluck survivors from the water and to carry them ashore and to the *Fu Ching*. It was a Japanese cutter that had found Edgerton clinging to a shattered spar, supporting an exhausted Whitaker and a semi-conscious Admiral Shen. It had deposited all three on *Leonidas*, diplomatically avoiding any potential confrontation at the Chinese vessel. Shen was now lodged in Dawlish's own accommodation, unsure of his surroundings, a dark bruise on one side of his head. Until he recovered it was Lodge who was taking decisions regarding the remaining Chinese force.

"I don't give a damn about Hojo," Lodge said. "He may be playing the innocent now but am I to believe he knew nothing about his subordinate's intentions? And even if he knew nothing of it am I to stand by when the *Kirishima* is out there searching for the transports coming from Tiensin? You sort out your Admiral Hojo, Mr. Dawlish, Royal Navy officer and gentleman that he may have been. Leave me to hunt down Shimazu and his crew of murderers!"

Yet beneath the words, beneath the anger, Dawlish detected satisfaction. Lodge was spoiling for a fight, could not keep a hungry glint from his eyes as they wandered back repeatedly to the massive ten-inchers. Dawlish knew nothing of his history. He assumed that Lodge had served in the United States Navy – in the Union forces in the Civil War, most likely, for there was no hint in his voice of a Southern lilt. But that Navy had been run down massively afterwards and many qualified officers had been cast adrift. Lodge might well be thirsting for a glory that peace had denied him. The consequences might not concern him, only the promise of battle would. The balance of Chinese and Japanese interests probably meant nothing to him.

But to Dawlish it did. He was here as a diplomat, as he had reminded himself every day since he had left Hong Kong. Commanding a ship was a role he had trained for since boyhood but there had been no preparation for navigating these shoals of Great Power rivalry. Korea as a battleground would be to the benefit of the Russians alone and only a degree of cooperation, however distrustful, between the Chinese and Japanese empires could resist the expansion of that blundering giant. There must be no war between the two Asiatic empires. That was Britain's interest, the same interest that had sent him to fight the Russians in the Black Sea under the Ottoman flag. And here, a thousand yards from a sunken Chinese warship which entombed much of her crew, an American mercenary captain was about to turn a single act of piracy into open war.

For piracy it was.

Admiral Hojo, visibly embarrassed and striving unsuccessfully to maintain his impassivity, had made no protest when Dawlish had confronted him on board the *Haruna* an hour before. In case there was any doubt Dawlish had ordered Takenaka, who had accompanied him, to translate the words. There had been no advance warning of Captain

Shimazu's intentions, Hojo said, no indication that the earlier lowering of one of *Kirishima's* torpedo boats had any purpose but to engage in exercises, no suspicion that the added activity on deck and around the guns was anything other than an increased surge of efficiency driven by Shimazu's return from Seoul. Admiral Hojo regretted the incident, regretted it deeply, would hope to be welcomed on board *Leonidas* to express his regrets to Admiral Shen personally.

He regretted everything – but not enough to commit to hoisting his anchor and setting off after the *Kirishima* to bring her to heel.

"Why not, Admiral?" Dawlish had given up on circumlocutions. The situation demanded direct answers.

Hojo did not meet his eye and looked towards the Emperor's portrait. When he spoke it was in Japanese.

Takenaka's face showed alarm as he listened. "The situation is sufficiently grave that the Admiral cannot take further action until he has consulted his superiors," he translated. It seemed like a very short summary of a long speech.

"The Admiral's superiors? Which ones? Where?"

"His superiors in Japan." As Takenaka spoke Hojo was quivering as he fought to maintain his composure. He had been humiliated and he knew it.

"Does the Admiral understand that action against a pirate will not constitute an act of war? That international opinion will favour it? That a matter of naval discipline is involved."

Hojo nodded. His English was fluent, he understood each word. He flinched at the mention of discipline. But when he spoke again it was in Japanese. Takenaka translated.

"The Admiral regrets that he must await instructions from his superiors. A small Japanese trading steamer is due here. It will be sent back immediately to Japan with a summary of the situation."

There was no more to be said and every reason to hasten across to the *Fu Ching*. Dawlish lowered his voice to a whisper as he sat with Takenaka in the sternsheets.

"Admiral Hojo is being honest," he said. "I believe his word that he has no complicity in this, but I don't understand his stance."

Takenaka avoided Dawlish's direct gaze. "Captain Shimazu is from Satsuma," he said at last.

"And you and Admiral Hojo are from Central Japan, from..." Dawlish searched his memory, "...from Mino."

"That is correct, sir."

Takenaka might be temporarily wearing the Queen's uniform but Dawlish knew he would get no more from him for now.

He knew too as he later stood next to Lodge on the *Fu Ching's* bridge that nothing was going to stop the American searching for Shimazu, ideally before he destroyed the Chinese transports which must now be at sea. But Shimazu had a head start and it was unlikely that Lodge's vessel, no matter how efficiently manned, could overtake the *Kirishima*.

Only one ship in the Far East could.

Leonidas.

15

Dawlish was fighting to supress his fatigue by mid-afternoon, not just the exhaustion itself but any sign of it his crew might detect. Years of standing watches stood him in good stead as he hastened all preparations for departure. He wanted *Leonidas* at sea before nightfall. The readying of the ship itself was in capable hands – Edgerton could be relied on for that – and the prospect of leaving the dismal anchorage invigorated the crew, even if speculation was rife as to what the purpose of that departure was. Even to himself that purpose was vague, Dawlish admitted, and his own actions would be determined by Shimazu's should the *Kirishima* be found somewhere on the sea-lane between here and Tiensin. He might have a roving commission, have full discretion, but Dawlish doubted that even Topcliffe had ever envisaged that it would be exercised in such circumstances. But Lodge and the *Fu Ching* had already disappeared over the north-eastern horizon, intent on a revenge – and perhaps on a thirst for a glory – that could plunge two empires into war. *Leonidas* had to find the *Kirishima* before Lodge did. For Lodge was no longer an adviser and was now in nominal as well as actual command of the *Fu Ching*.

Admiral Shen, still dazed, had already been brought ashore by Whitaker to be lodged in an inn in the Chinese quarter, where the *Hi Ying's* survivors had already been landed.

"Stay with him," Dawlish had told Whitaker. "I want to be sure that you'll know what he's thinking. Play up his injuries – that he's concussed, shouldn't travel."

"Why?" Whitaker was ashen with pain as well as weariness. His arm had been reset by *Leonidas's* surgeon but the night's exertions would ensure that it would never be straight again.

"Why? Because we don't know where we stand, not until after I've found either Shimazu or Lodge. Nor whatever happens after I do. Keep him away from the Japanese, even if Hojo makes approaches."

He could detect something in Whitaker's look that went beyond physical discomfort. It could be the realisation that with Dawlish absent, even temporarily, he himself would be responsible for coping with the diplomatic complexities now multiplying.

"One other thing," Dawlish said. "I've sent Lieutenant Ross back to Seoul with instructions to find Fred Kung. He's to give Kung a full explanation of what happened here – I can trust Ross for that, no embellishments – and request him to come here. Ross's got four marines with him. They'll be in Seoul by nightfall and with luck Kung will be here within twenty-four hours."

"We can't trust Fred Kung," Whitaker said.

"But I can trust him to be pragmatic. Shen's no more an admiral than my dog at home is. He's the Chinese emperor's man but I don't know how clearly he sees the situation, how he recognises our interests as well as his own. But Kung does. We can talk to him and he to us. I want him here when I return."

Dawlish had no idea how the situation might have developed by the time he returned. It all depended on whether Shimazu would find – and sink – the Chinese transports, whether Lodge would find Shimazu, whether *Leonidas* would find any of them. The possible outcomes were myriad. Speculation was useless. But in the midst of this uncertainty there was comfort in knowing that at this moment his ship's all twelve boilers had been stoked and that pressure was building, that in the charthouse Takenaka was plotting a course with meticulous care, that Purdon's guns had been checked, their crews hastily exercised, that Edgerton was making his rounds to confirm instructions fulfilled to the letter, that the crew had been moulded into a single proud and efficient unit on the long voyage from Britain.

Time now to depart.

*

The heading was slightly north of west as *Leonidas* ploughed out into the Yellow Sea and towards the great all-but-landlocked Bay of Bohai. Astern of her the Japanese *Haruna* still swung at anchor, her guns' muzzles still shrouded in canvas.

Away to the west the sun's red sphere still had half an hour to sink. The sea was glassy calm and the cruiser's speed was building so that the first log reading indicated just over 15 knots. *Leonidas* had made almost two knots more on her acceptance trials but then she had been all but unloaded. Now she carried a full complement and laden bunkers and all the provisions and munitions that made her a fighting ship. This speed and these conditions could carry her to Tiensin itself in some 35 hours, though the coal consumption would be heavy. But the Chinese transports could be anywhere inside that distance – and indeed the *Kirishima* might already have found them. If she had, then Shimazu would most likely have shown little mercy. He had some nineteen hours head-start on *Leonidas*, less on Lodge's *Fu Ching*, but his corvette, heavily armed as it was, could have made no more than fourteen knots on completion, less now, twelve perhaps, less still if her bottom was fouled. The *Fu Ching* might at best be good for the same. And *Leonidas* was only a fortnight out of drydock, her bottom pristine, her engines and her boilers overhauled, their reliability already proven, her crew at peak efficiency. And Bohai Bay was immense. Intercepting individual ships there would be far from easy. There would be many other vessels, coasters and larger steamers plying to and from Tiensin and Dalian, and each would demand investigation by *Kirishima*. There was still a chance.

Dawlish needed sleep – whatever might happen on the morrow might not only determine the fate of empires but his own further career. There would be as little sympathy for failure as there was external guidance now. He must be able to think clearly when the crisis came. He was about to leave the bridge when Takenaka, officer of the watch, drew his attention to the southern horizon. The last pink light was fading from a clear sky but there, low above the Earth's rim, was a long dark stripe.

"The glass is falling, sir," Takenaka said.

It still stood at over 29 inches but it had dropped by a half-inch in the last hour and this was the typhoon season. There might be a storm brewing to the south, nothing abnormal in itself, no worse perhaps than the foul weather *Leonidas* had thrashed through in the Bay of Biscay, but the possibility of something worse, far worse, could not be ignored. That layer of angry cloud might at worst be the advancing wall of a typhoon headed directly north to engulf *Leonidas* with its full fury, at best be the northern flank of one headed east or west, towards Korea or China, enough to bring high winds and mountainous seas. In either case preparation was essential.

The next hour was one of intense, fast and focussed activity. Loose fittings above and below decks were secured, ports and hatches too, storm plates screwed in place where necessary, boats and their fittings fastened down, hoses and buckets placed in lockers, ventilator cowls rotated to point astern, lifelines run across the forecastle and quarterdeck, men sent aloft to check the stays and yard trusses. Oilskins were issued to those who would be required on deck or in the open-backed wheelhouse. Pumps were briefly operated – no problems there – and in the engine room bearings and slides were oiled, couplings tightened, loose tools secured. Trimmers laboured to fill the fuel bins by the furnaces to the maximum, for shifting coal from distant bunkers would be almost impossible during violent motion. And all the time, as darkness fell, the long stripe of cloud to the south blackened and thickened and the glass fell still further. The calm was gone, a wind now directly from the south, quickening, at first a breeze, then growing, thrumming in the rigging, gusting occasionally, building up long white-capped waves on *Leonidas's* port quarter.

The long night began and there was no abatement.

Leonidas turned south to meet the storm head-on, speed decreased to ease the sickening combination of pitch and roll. The waves were longer now, their ghostly grey crests all but invisible beneath the dark pall of cloud overhead. Spray was whipping from them, heavy enough to make movement on deck difficult. The wind was screaming in the rigging and despite all precautions one boat was already shattered by a heavy wave. Dawlish was on the bridge, soaked and cold despite his oilskins and the meagre protection of the wheelhouse, his exhaustion no longer just fatigue but an agony in itself that he must not acknowledge or succumb to. The only consolation was that the storm was racing northwards, that *Kirishima* and *Fu Ching* must both be subjected to it too, that neither was so well placed to endure it as *Leonidas*, that both must also turn into the wind, away from Tiensin. And that wind was now a gale and continuing to rise, veering to blast from west-south-west. The cruiser was now taking the waves some three points ahead of the starboard beam and rolling heavily with them. There was nothing for it but to swing the bows around to meet them and to reduce speed still further.

By midnight the gale had grown to storm force. The crests of the waves ahead were overhanging, foam and spray stripped from them to lash *Leonidas's* bridge and wheelhouse and blot out still further whatever forward visibility remained. Noise had reduced all communication to shouts as the waves' pounding reverberated through the entire ship. The distance between the crests was longer than *Leonidas* herself so that at the crests her bows hung suspended for an instant, thirty or forty feet of her keel exposed before crashing down. At that moment a long-sloped valley stretched before her and then, as she reached the trough, a dark grey-capped mountain rose ahead and the laboured ascent of its slope commenced. Water boiled over the long bowsprit and surged across the bows, overwhelming the freeing ports as it foamed between the containing bulwarks and washing over chains and mooring bitts, thirstily seeking any gap through which it might cascade. Despite all the measures that had been taken Dawlish knew that torrents would still find their way below to slop though passages and spill down to lower levels.

Now was the time to endure, to run slowly into the storm and to accept its anger. In the early hours one of the ventilators between the funnels was torn free. Carried aft by the wave that had wrenched it loose, it smashed a boat to matchwood before it disappeared overboard. It left an open three-foot circle through which water rained down to the boiler room. A small party, secured by lifelines, took more than half an hour to plug the gap with rolled hammocks and a tarpaulin cover, fighting to keep their footing as the deck heaved and fell and heaved again beneath them and as water foamed about their knees. Yet no furnace was extinguished, no boiler's pressure dropped, and though the engine room crew steadied themselves against being hurled against their machinery, the great cylinders of the compound engines still panted calmly and the screws maintained their steady beat.

Light came at last – hardly brightness but rather a grey twilight that filtered down from the angry clouds above – and the prospect was no less dismal than in the darkness. The pewter-grey sea was strewn with pools of foam and the unrelenting wind ripped great flecks of it from the wave crests and hurled it against the wheelhouse as *Leonidas* maintained her slow, determined plod. There was still no sign of the fury lessening, only further veering that now brought the gale screaming in from the west, no longer in line with the axis of the waves' advance and inducing a corkscrew motion that combined pitch and roll and was more uncomfortable than either. Again the course was adjusted, not once, but several times, seeking the balance between the forces of wind and wave that would least strain the vessel and her engines and her crew.

The morning wore on, its monotony broken by warm cocoa heroically prepared and even more heroically transported to the wheelhouse by galley personnel. Dawlish, at the edge of collapse, felt strangely satisfied – proud indeed – that his ship and his crew were taking this battering in their stride. He had witnessed *Leonidas's* gestation on the slips at Pembroke dockyard, had commissioned her and worked her up, had brought her to maturity with the tenderness of a father for his child, had taken her across the globe with a rapidity that no other ship in the navy could match. No matter what the coming encounter with *Kirishima* would bring – and he knew he would find her, of that he was sure – he could rely on *Leonidas*.

The wind had dropped slightly by midday but it still blew hard and gusted harder, and the sea remained as turbulent as before. The heading was south-west, directly into the waves, water still cascading across the cruiser's bows as they plunged under before rising again, white foam streaming, dropping from a crest, climbing from a valley, the sequence endlessly repeated. But as he wedged himself in a corner of the wheelhouse, as he offered the occasional word of encouragement or approval to the quartermaster, as he discussed the prospects for improved conditions with Edgerton, as he heard the reports of damage sustained and of responses in hand, Dawlish's feeling of satisfaction was reinforced. *Leonidas* and her crew were passing their test with flying colours. There might be another day, maybe even two, of such weather, but the storm – likely by its power to be the outer edge of a typhoon – must be moving eastwards, towards and over Korea. It would pass and the seas would calm again and then, and even before then, *Leonidas* needed to be forging north on her search, hunting while her quarries were still intent only on survival. Somewhere up there the *Kirishima* and the *Fu Ching* must also be steaming slowly into the storm, the Japanese ship with her higher freeboard well equipped to face it, but swamping a real danger for the

Chinese vessel with her low bows. For now neither ship was a threat to the other. They must be found before they were.

Late afternoon and there were open streaks in the clouds above, the first hints of relief even if the wind remained unrelenting, the seas still high. There would be another night of this but the morrow might well bring respite. Dawlish went below, snatched four hours' sleep — essential now — and returned refreshed to the bridge. Takenaka, again officer of the watch, delivered another routine report — minor damage, two injuries from falls, one a broken leg, the other concussion, no problems with boilers or engines, spirits high among the men. The report was as exact and as succinct as Takenaka's always were, but now Dawlish sensed an even higher level of formality and reserve than he knew the Japanese officer was comfortable with. Something was troubling him, something he wanted perhaps to raise but hesitated to broach. And Dawlish guessed what it was.

"I'd like to discuss our course, Lieutenant" he said. "If weather permits I want to turn north before morning. Shall we adjourn to the charthouse?"

The noise level was low enough there to permit something approaching normal conversation. The charts and instruments had been cleared away in advance of the storm and the table was clear. Takenaka moved to produce a chart.

"I think that can wait for now, Lieutenant," Dawlish said.

"Yes, sir." Takenaka's face was blank, obviously deliberately so.

"I think you want to speak to me about Captain Shimazu. I understand the subject is sensitive."

"Thank you, sir." A slight bow, something like relief flickering briefly on his face. Then silence.

You've stood by my side in mortal danger, you've defended me, you've seen me ready to do as much for you, Dawlish thought. *You know you can trust me, not just as your commanding officer but as a man.* Yet Takenaka was still in an agony of silence, more intimidated by some concern of conscience than he had been by physical danger.

"Something to do with Satsuma?" It always seemed to come back to that.

"Yes, sir." Again that expression of relief, and this time it remained. A long pause, but one in which words were obviously being sought and weighed and carefully phrased. "Admiral Hojo is fearful for the consequences of Captain Shimazu's action. He is fearful..." Again a silent search for words. "He is fearful of civil war, fearful that Captain Shimazu has been ordered to initiate it. As it was before. For the same reasons which Captain Shimazu's father and brothers died for."

The memory now of another conversation about Shimazu, a no less troubled one, on the night of that atrocity on the road to Seoul. Dawlish could not remember the Japanese word but the English translation had stayed with him.

"Black Ocean?"

Takenaka nodded. *"Genyosha."*

It was falling in place now. It might not officially exist, but the *Genyosha* society wanted Japan to absorb Korea as soon as possible. And afterwards, Manchuria. Then China. Then all Asia. For all the progress Japan had made in less than three decades, the ambition seemed an insane one for a small island nation. And yet Britain's ambitions had once also seemed no less unrealistic.

"The *Genyosha's* loyalty to the Emperor is absolute?" Dawlish remembered the word now.

"All *Genyosha's* actions, even Captain Shimazu's sinking of the *Hi Ying*, are undertaken in all sincerity on that basis."

"That's manifest nonsense. Nobody can believe that." Yet Dawlish realised that for Takenaka or for Hojo, probably even for Shimazu himself, there was no contradiction here.

Takenaka shook his head. "Captain Shimazu's action was almost certainly approved by many powerful people. Some of them close to His Majesty." Even though wind was screaming outside and as Takenaka must brace himself against the table to maintain his balance, he bowed at the mention of his emperor.

"But surely His Majesty won't approve?"

"Nobody can know His Majesty's mind but I suspect..." Takenaka paused, as if astounded by his own temerity in such speculation "...but I suspect that His Majesty fears civil war above all else. That not only will it bring us ruin, but it will destroy all that has been achieved in almost thirty years."

And those years had seen unprecedented transition from a medieval society to a modern one, of acceptance and adaptation of modern science and industry, of economic growth, of steady progress towards Great Power status, of development that had somehow accommodated long-established tradition and culture.

"Shimazu must be mad."

"No madness, sir. I suspect that he believes, that his friends also believe, that His Majesty will authorise his actions rather than divide the country." Every word seemed like an agony to Takenaka, as if discussing the matter demanded breaking of every stricture he had ever believed in and lived by. "They know – as His Majesty must know – that war with China is inevitable sooner or later. It must, if Japan is to take its rightful place among great nations. And they want that war now, and it will be too soon, but they believe that even if His Majesty is hesitant he will accept it rather than see civil war in home."

Admiral Hojo's inaction was beginning to make sense now. "His Majesty would be happy to see Shimazu destroyed?" Dawlish asked. "But not by a Japanese force?"

Takenaka said again "Nobody can know His Majesty's mind," but he nodded nonetheless.

"When I called Shimazu a pirate Admiral Hojo did not object."

"He did not disagree, sir."

"Let's look at the charts, Lieutenant Takenaka," Dawlish said. "We have a course to plot."

*

The wind died slowly but steadily through the night, the seas less so, but still enough to allow the bows to swing northwards. The waves were rolling from the port quarter as *Leonidas* forged onwards, decks awash, thrusting foam and spray aside, wind screaming about her masts and rigging, engines panting, normal watch-keeping resumed and sleep snatched. Her present position could only be guessed at – the clouded skies had made it impossible to take fixes and the storm had made dead reckoning unreliable. Her heading was based on a guess by Dawlish, one that would take her roughly north-eastwards towards the median point between Tiensin and Chemulpo. If the Chinese transports were at sea then they must be somewhere in that vicinity. They would have taken a battering in the storm, perhaps had not even survived, perhaps had already been found by Shimazu. The possibilities were endless and he thrust from his mind for now the dilemma he would face if *Leonidas* found only an empty sea.

At dawn the wind died, suddenly, the calm almost unnerving in its abruptness. The waves began to subside and the sky above was clear but for a few streaks of cloud. The sun climbed and the temperature with it. The horizon was empty. The repair of the storm's damage commenced and there was less than had been feared, for the preparations for weathering it had been thorough. There was warm food and drink again and in all parts of the ship, as Dawlish made his inspection, there was an air of pride in a task well done. He returned to the bridge.

"Deck there!"

A call from the lookout arcing overhead.

For there, on the horizon, was a vessel, still hull down.

Armstrong 6-inch Breech-loading Rifle on Vavasseur Slide & Turntable Mounting 1880

As mounted on HMS *Leonidas* 1882

(Note that Shield is shown cut-away for clarity)

Weight: 81 cwt (4 tons)
Barrel length: 156 inches
Shell Types: 80 pounds Palliser Armour-piercing, Shrapnel, Common Shell

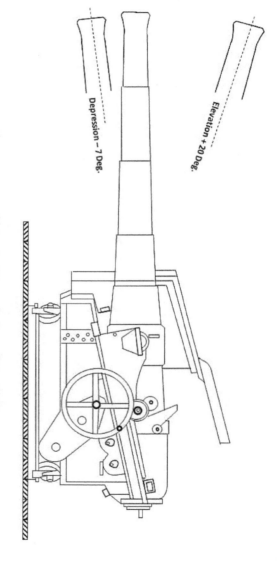

Depression – 7 Deg.

Elevation + 20 Deg.

16

The sighting was a disappointment, a large Chinese trading junk, one mast down, but the crew, when *Leonidas* drew briefly alongside, cheerful and undaunted as they engaged in repairs they seemed resigned to, having endured as much so often before. She had been coasting north from Tsingtao and had been blown eastwards with the storm, tossing like a cork. She carried no troops, no artillery, and investigating her cost a half-hour that Dawlish begrudged. *Leonidas* continued north afterwards, again at full speed once checks in the engine room had confirmed that nothing had been damaged by the storm's long pounding. Lookouts were posted on all three masts but for two, three, almost four hours nothing appeared on the horizon. All Purdon's guns were manned, their crews nervous but elated that what they might be called upon for could be in deadly earnest, not for training. O'Rourke had his torpedo crews standing by with no less earnestness. The sinking of the Chinese flagship had proved the lethality of the weapons they were responsible for – if only they could be brought into range.

At last, to the north-east, a long smudge of smoke against the clear sky. Dawlish felt his heart pound as he ordered the new course towards it.

Caught in the binocular's disc two masts, crossed but without sails set, were just visible above the sea's rim. A single funnel grew slowly up between them and then at last the black hull itself came into sight. She was headed eastwards, towards Korea. There had to be hundreds like this, thousand to fifteen-hundred tonners, trading along the Chinese coast and venturing, when the cargoes demanded it, as far as Japan. As with the vast majority of those vessels, a small scarlet rectangle fluttered at her stern. Even at this distance the Red Duster that identified her as British. As the *Leonidas* drew closer this plodding merchantman made no alteration to her course. Only a few figures were moving about on deck, obviously busy repairing storm damage. One letter of the name on her bows was obscured by rust but she appeared to be the *Kutsang*.

"Signal that I want to speak to her," Dawlish said.

A single flag, split into blue and yellow rectangles, ran up the halliard. A minute passed before confirmation was received, white, two blue stripes and one red. The steamer's pace did not decrease until the cruiser pulled on to a parallel course at a cable's separation. Dawlish needed more information than could be exchanged by speaking trumpet. Cost time though it might, there was no alternative to sending an officer across. The duty fell to Sub-Lieutenant Leigh.

The sea that might seem relatively calm from the cruiser's bridge made the sea-boat's passage across to the steamer a difficult one, made hooking alongside and putting Leigh on board more hazardous still. Two officers greeted him and he disappeared aft with them.

The delay until Leigh reappeared seemed interminable and Dawlish maintained an aloof silence, anxious that his inward fretting might not communicate itself to others on the bridge. Years of service had taught him that a captain's slightest flicker of doubt would jump like wildfire to those about him and beyond, growing in intensity as it did, destroying confidence and resolution. The strain of command, the inability to appeal for aid or advice to some superior authority, had never lain so heavily. It was a relief that it was close to midday and that the now-clear sky allowed the essential but distracting fixes to be taken and the results discussed.

Leigh reappeared and the sea-boat began its long, bobbing crawl back to *Leonidas*. It seemed another age before he stood on her bridge, the brightness of his look already showing delight that he had significant information.

"SS *Kutsang*, sir. Her captain's a Mr. Maitland and he sends his compliments. She's three days out of Tiensin, bound for Nagasaki with mixed cargo, and he says he'd have been half-way there by now but for the weather. He's been through worse, he says."

"Does he know anything about Chinese transports? Troopers?"

"That's the best of it, sir. They were still in port when he sailed, two of them, China coasters like his own, British owned, the *Singan* and the *Ningpo*. They've been chartered at high rates – it was a seller's market."

It would have seemed a good bargain, Dawlish thought, an easy voyage and a high profit and the price inflated most likely by collusion with corrupt officials. Nobody had counted on Shimazu.

"Captain Maitland's scathing about the Chinese naval people," Leigh continued. "He says they hadn't a single seaworthy vessel available for the duty and that their officers were more interested in opium and women and in selling off their own stores than in their own ships."

Takenaka was listening and Dawlish saw a faint smile of superiority on his face.

"I'm interested in the transports, Leigh, not in Chinese deficiencies," Dawlish said.

"Yes, sir. But Captain Maitland says the loading of the two ships had gone slowly and that there has been a lot of confusion – chaos he called it. Men embarked, then taken off again. Guns without ammunition and then a wait until it turned up and then it was the wrong calibre. Uncertainty about who was to do what. If it hadn't been for all the bedlam the ships would have been at sea a week earlier."

"Are they still at Tiensin?"

"Captain Maitland doesn't think so, sir. They were finally ready to leave when he departed. He's pretty sure of that, they could only have been an hour or two behind him. He knows both the captains and spoke to them before he left. He's sure they're at sea now."

So they too would have been condemned to endure the storm. It was likely that they would have survived – captains of China coasters were inured to such weather and could take it in their stride. But it would have been worse, much worse, for the soldiers packed on board, bewildered peasant conscripts who might never have seen the sea before. It would have been a hell of terror and vomit in the holds they were confined in like cattle – if indeed they had been content to remain locked in. Dawlish did not envy any crew that was so vastly outnumbered by such a frightened and potentially mutinous human cargo. And the vessels, in whatever state they might now be in, must lie somewhere to the east, almost certainly north of their original track towards Chemulpo.

Leonidas had a new heading now. The sea was all but calm and the skies clear. The sense of anticipation among the crew was palpable, an increased concentration on even the most mundane task, an awareness that action might be imminent. For many there was an eagerness for such action, tempered with unspoken fear of failure to achieve what might be expected of them. Only a handful had ever seen a shot fired in anger. The Royal Navy was a peacetime navy, the majority of her personnel concentrated in the Channel and Mediterranean Fleets in which dazzling paintwork and gleaming brass and absorption in meticulous and complex manoeuvring counted for more than readiness for combat which might never come. Only on remote stations, and usually only on small vessels, did a small fraction of the navy's manpower ever see action. But it had been in that hard school that Dawlish had come of age.

For two hours more the horizon remained clear but at last, north-eastwards, two thin threads of smoke lay low on the horizon. Dawlish restrained himself from hope – they might be any ships other than the transports. *Leonidas's* bows nudged over into an interception course. As the separation closed the lookouts' reports confirmed that the vessels were headed south-east and that they were close cousins to the *Kutsang*. Soon Dawlish could confirm it for himself through his glasses. There could be little doubt now – *Leonidas* had located the transports before Shimazu. And they were British Register ships too and there was every reason that a good lawyer might argue to justify *Leonidas* escorting them to Chemulpo, even if they were laden with Chinese troops and equipment. Around him Dawlish sensed relief among those on the bridge.

And then another "Deck there!" from the lookout.

Almost directly north, another dark smear was growing over the horizon, thickening as it advanced and as the ship emitting it emerged slowly into view. She too had spotted the transports and, truncated as her hull appeared in Dawlish's disc of vision, it was obvious that she too was swinging on to an interception course.

"The *Kirishima*, Commander Edgerton?" Dawlish knew there could be only one answer.

"The *Kirishima*, sir."

There was no mistaking the long clipper-bowed hull with the proud bowsprit above it and the three bare barque-rigged masts and the single funnel. The white foam creaming at her bows told of a higher speed and efficiency than might be expected from any Chinese warship.

Dawlish glanced towards Takenaka and saw sick apprehension on his face. Not cowardice, Dawlish sensed, but recognition of a possibility – with every further minute almost an inevitability – of hostile engagement with his countrymen.

The two transports were little over a mile distant now, the names on the bows just discernible through telescope, the *Ningpo* leading and the *Singan* trailing two cables off her port quarter. Neither could have been making more than five knots. Both were under steam only and the *Singan's* main topmast had fallen over and was suspended above the deck in a mass of tangled rigging. There were other indications too that

170

she had weathered a severe battering – no boats remained beneath her davits and the single remaining cowl-ventilator by the funnel was canted at a crazy angle. A survey of the *Ningpo* told that she too had suffered damage, though less severe. More ominous still were the black masses of men congregated on the decks of both ships. Even from this distance it was possible to see the ripples of movement that swept through them, a shuffling, jostling mob, still restrained, perhaps cowed, but on the verge of violence. Whatever discipline had existed among these Chinese troops had been broken by the storm and there was every chance that they wanted only to turn for home. Three men stood on one bridge, two on another, and for an instant it seemed that one brandished what might have been a pistol towards the crowd below and then put it away again.

"How large was the *Kutsang's* crew?" Dawlish directed his question to Leigh.

"Nineteen, sir. Captain Maitland and his mate are English. The engineer too. Then a half-dozen Lascars and the rest Chinese."

The crew composition on the *Ningpo* and *Singan* was unlikely to be much different. The Lascars might or might not be reliable, though Dawlish doubted it if it came to violence, but in any case the officers and crew were badly outnumbered. One spark, one perceived provocation – whoever it was who had brandished the pistol was a fool – and both vessels could become bloodbaths.

Leonidas's course would bring her ahead of both ships, leaving them some five cables port as she sped on. Two miles ahead, off her starboard bow, the *Kirishima* was still forging directly towards the transports. She seemed oblivious of *Leonidas's* presence. In another minute she would be directly ahead, another minute more and she would be off the port bow and steaming parallel, but on an opposite heading, to the lumbering transports. The red and white Rising Sun ensign streamed at her stern and the covers on the ports along her flank were open to reveal the muzzles of her six-inch Krupp breech-loaders. There was movement on deck and figures on the open bridge – one must be Shimazu. There was no doubt of her intent.

"Flag X," Dawlish said, not lowering his glasses. "And ask Mr. Purdon to be ready to put a shot across her bows. Wait for my word. Common shell will suffice and reload with the same."

Below the bridge, on the main deck, *Leonidas's* two forward six-inch weapons, marginally more modern than the *Kirishima's,* were mounted on sponsons that protruded from the hull sides to provide end-on fire. Purdon himself was standing by the starboard weapon, quietly approving the gun-layer's tracking.

The signal was rising up the halliard, a blue cross on a white background, its internationally-recognised message stark and unambiguous. "*Stop carrying out your intentions and watch for my signals.*"

The flag had been seen – sunlight flashing on the lenses of the glasses directed towards it from *Kirishima's* bridge confirmed recognition. But there was no acknowledgement, no attempt to alter course.

"One round," Dawlish said, and even as the message was relayed to Purdon he knew that the warning would be futile. The *Kirishima* was showing no intention of slowing, was ploughing ahead regardless of *Leonidas's* presence. And the Rising Sun streamed from her stern…

The seconds before Purdon's six-inch roared were like an aeon. For the Rising Sun proclaimed that Shimazu saw his ship as representing his nation and his emperor, and Dawlish remembered Takenaka's words, that His Majesty might well endorse any action by a mutinous subordinate rather than risk dividing his county. That approval might already have been given, tacitly. And Britain was looking for an alliance with Japan…

A line of white foam erupted as the 80-pound shell skipped and tumbled a cable-length ahead of the *Kirishima's* bows. Still she drove on, passing out of sight of *Leonidas'* starboard six-inch and half-obscured by the cruiser's foremast and bowsprit. Purdon had crossed to the port sponson and the gun-crew there were poised to track the Japanese vessel as she emerged into view. Bows-on to the *Kirishima*, *Leonidas* was exposed to the full weight of her broadside, four weapons, and of a fifth on a turntable aft, and she momentarily had nothing to counter her with. Dawlish, cold with fear he could not display, knew that one word from Shimazu could reduce *Leonidas* to a wreck.

And yet the *Kirishima* did not open fire, not as she passed the projection of *Leonidas's* axis, not when she passed into the arc of Purdon's six-inch. Dawlish lifted his glasses, caught the Japanese, swept along the hull and up to catch the open bridge. And there, on the port wing, he saw Shimazu, and Shimazu saw him, and raised his hand in salute.

Another eternity passed. Shimazu had signalled clearly that he had no quarrel with *Leonidas* but there was no doubting his intent towards

172

the plodding transports. Dawlish glanced astern and saw that both vessels had their helms over and were pulling southwards to put *Leonidas* between them and the *Kirishima*. Across the intervening water he could hear the sounds of shouting – perhaps of panic – from the nearer ship, the *Ningpo*. He looked down towards the port sponson and saw Purdon's face upraised, seeking the order to open fire.

The Rising Sun was whipping at the *Kirishima's* stern. Her attack back at Chemulpo had been piracy – even Admiral Hojo had admitted that – but the possibility existed that it might have been authorised by the Emperor. In Pekin or Tokyo declarations of war might already have been exchanged in decorous terms. If so, then action by *Leonidas* could plunge Britain into a war with a nation she desired alliance with, the only counter in the Far East to the Russian threat. Dawlish guessed that such a situation had never been considered within his roving commission. But doing nothing was not an option. Common humanity, stronger than any national interest, linked him to the eight hundred Chinese on those transports, and yet he still shrunk from the necessary decision…

Purdon's port-forward crew were tracking the *Kirishima* now, their weapon's barrel inching across as she pulled away. Dawlish could feel the tension around him, could sense that Edgerton and the others, even the helmsman and yeomen, had their eyes fixed on him. He looked astern again and saw that the two transports were stern on, their screws thrashing white foam in their wakes and black smoke pouring from their funnels as they strove for speed undreamt of in normal times.

The Red Duster was whipping at their sterns – British ships, even if they had been built in Hong Kong or Singapore, ships that had never seen Britain. Dawlish knew he had no choice.

"Port, eight points," he said.

Leonidas swung over to parallel *Kirishima*. As the cruiser pulled out of the turning-arc a mile and more lay between her and the other warship, now again off her starboard bow.

"Mr. Purdon," Dawlish called, "All starboard weapons ready for action! Common shell. But wait for my word!"

Purdon's commands were relayed aft, to three six-inchers there on limited broadside arcs and to the stern-chaser, sponsoned out like its counterpart at the bows, with slightly greater reach ahead. Yet in the present heading only the starboard bow-chaser could still hold the

Kirishima in her sights and *Leonidas* must swing to port – and increase separation – if all the guns on the starboard flank were to be brought into play.

"Captain Dawlish, sir?" It was O'Rourke, expectant, hopeful.

"Stand by the launchers." Dawlish did not add that he suspected that ranges and manoeuvring involved would rule out use of torpedoes.

Rolling smoke lanced by flame erupted from four locations on the *Kirishima's* port side. An instant later the wave of sound reached *Leonidas*, four reports so closely spaced as to be one. Dawlish's head snapped round involuntarily, knowing that the target could not be his own ship but even as he did three white plumes were erupting to port and slightly ahead of the *Singan* transport and a fourth to starboard. Shimazu's gunners were good – bracketing a target with an opening broadside demanded superlative professionalism – and even now new shells and charges were being thrust into open breeches and gun layers were calculating adjustments.

Dawlish felt his hands trembling as he lowered his glasses. It was not the prospect of action that unmanned him, but the knowledge that his next order might end in ignominy the career he had sacrificed and endured so much for, now when the prospect of flag rank no longer seemed so remote. He grasped the rail before him, called down to Purdon "Open fire!" and then ordered four points to port, but only to be initiated after the six-inch had fired. It would open the range, but would bring *Leonidas's* entire starboard battery into play. The increased range was not a problem – the six-inchers were sighted to ten thousand yards and the present range was all but point blank.

But before *Leonidas* spoke *Kirishima* blasted again, this time with her turntable weapon aft adding weight to the broadside. Shaken by the earlier near-miss, the *Singan's* helmsman had turned the vessel several points to starboard and so had laid her flank open to the hail now screaming towards her. Three shells fountained spray up harmlessly to starboard but the fourth and fifth struck almost simultaneously. An orange flash and wreckage flying from it indicated a hit at the counter and another flash, followed by billowing smoke, erupted by the storm-damaged mainmast. Stays parted, the mast seemed to shiver for an instant, then toppled forward, dragged down by the wrecked topmast hanging before it. It crashed down on the single funnel and black smoke now belched at deck level. The first dark specks began leaping from the vessel, arms flailing, Chinese soldiers driven beyond the limits of terror.

Smoke and flame erupted from Purdon's weapon and it heaved back on its recoil slope as its ear-splitting crack reached the bridge. Dawlish flinched but held his glasses steady on the *Kirishima* and to his joy he saw a flash towards the corvette's bows. A hit, a very palpable hit. He resisted the urge to cheer, saw with satisfaction that the gun-crew had already swung the breech open and were reloading with smooth efficiency gained by hours of practice. And now too the helmsman's wheel was spinning over.

Leonidas heeled in the turn, then swung smoothly to the vertical, and a little beyond, then stabilised, as she straightened into her new course. Along her starboard flank brass hand-wheels were spinning as the six-inch crews arced their barrels across to lock *Kirishima* in their sights.

"Permission to open fire, sir?" Purdon's cry was urgent, hopeful.

Dawlish hesitated. Smoke was billowing from the *Kirishima's* bows, long black tendrils streaming back along the hull, and figures were scurrying around it to bring a fire hose into play. *Leonidas's* full broadside would wreak fearful damage, perhaps even fatal, were it to crash out now, and it must be now, before the Japanese gun layers could shifting their aim to her. And yet...

"Permission to open fire, sir?" Purdon's repeated cry was on the edge of insubordination but it had an air of longing that made it forgivable. This moment was one every gunnery officer dreamed of.

But the Rising Sun ensign still streamed proudly. Still Dawlish hesitated. Shimazu's action might yet have official sanction and Japan was needed as an ally and...

And the *Kirishima* began to turn away, her bows swung to starboard, to the north, away from *Leonidas* and the transports.

Thank God!

Dawlish kept the thought to himself, kept his face impassive. This was enough, enough to limit the atrocity, perhaps even enough to safeguard his own prospects. But he saw disappointment, bewilderment, even anger, on the faces the gun-crews turned to him when the order to hold fire reached them. Around him on the bridge, from Edgerton, from the rest, he could sense frustration, of expectation raised to fever-pitch and now dashed. Only Takenaka seemed relieved. The *Kirishima* was stern on now, receding, her speed

175

undiminished, whatever damage she had sustained not mortal. Shimazu had taken a deliberate decision to retreat – and it must have cost him agony to do so – and to keep his vessel ready to fight another day. Not to fight the Royal Navy, but China, to draw it into war, not to fight *Leonidas* but to fight Lodge's *Fu Ching*. Cool pragmatism had mastered pride and that made Shimazu even more dangerous. Yet on both *Leonidas* and *Kirishima* officers and men would be wondering silently if their captains had lost their nerve. Dawlish, like Shimazu, must endure that in silence.

The leading transport, the undamaged *Ningpo,* was also receding rapidly, intent on her own escape and with no care for her sister. The stricken *Singan* was down by the stern and she had lost all way. Splashing and bobbing heads by her sides showed drowning men. Panic reigned in the black mass heaving on her decks. White steam was blasting from around the toppled funnel – somebody had the sense to blow down the boiler and the mass of tangled cordage around the fallen mast had not taken light. There might yet be hope.

"Signal for half revolutions."

"We're going alongside, sir?" Edgerton said.

"We're going to take her in tow. We've got to keep our distance for now, but be ready to drop the sea boat." It was a whaler, already swung out and hanging from its davits, ready for immediate launch. "Put Leigh in command." The young officer had done well in the rescue after the *Hi Ying's* sinking at Chemulpo but the difficulties would be even greater here in the open sea.

"Any other boats, sir?" Edgerton said. "There are a lot of men in the water." There were, but fewer every minute even as *Leonidas* drew closer.

"There won't be many by the time we get there. Drop a cutter. Pick up any left." Water was lapping now over the *Singan's* poop but the settlement seemed to have stopped. The after deck was less crowded now and the mob of frightened soldiers had congregated forward. "Send a party aft to rig a towing bridle. And another party to go across to secure the tow once we're alongside. Marines with them – it won't be easy to get through that mob to the forecastle and I wouldn't count on much help from the officers."

Another order, a distasteful if necessary one. "Man the Gatlings in the tops. We may need them". If the fear crazed mob tried to surge across to *Leonidas* there would be nothing for it but to let the spinning barrels high on the masts repel it.

The work of rescue began, slow and laborious, made more so by the fear and suspicion of the frightened men who lined the transport's rail. But the *Singan,* did not sink even though she was down at the stern, with her steering gear shattered, her boiler blown down and her fires extinguished for safety's safe. The rough kindness with which the wounded were carried across to *Leonidas* slowly conquered distrust and soon many of the Chinese soldiers were assisting with securing the tow and cutting free the toppled mast. The *Singan's* officers, fear overcome, confidence restored, were participating too and the Chinese officers were reasserting a degree of control over their men. Despite the losses overboard there were still over four hundred troops on the transport, enough with their comrades on the *Ningpo* to take control at Chemulpo if they could be got ashore. And all the while the empty horizon was scanned for signs of the *Kirishima's* return, or for a smoke trail that might indicate arrival of Lodge and the *Fu Ching*. Had she arrived then Dawlish would gladly have transferred the task of towing to her but the hope remained vain.

As darkness fell *Leonidas* was straining towards Chemulpo, across a smooth sea, the *Singan* wallowing in her wake at the end of a long cable that rose at intervals from the water, shaking silver droplets from it before it dipped again.

Dawlish looked back across the phosphorescent wake and remembered the bodies in the water and the smell of the corpses that had been retrieved from under the crushed funnel, simple, humble men who had been sacrificed like cattle in the cause of one emperor and in the name, however unjustified, of another. He felt a cold anger course through him, the same anger he had once felt in a Black Sea port when he had shorn the ear from a murderous brigand, anger that could distort judgement. He hated Shimazu and if he could he would frustrate and kill him.

But not at the cost of his own career.

17

"I haven't much sympathy," Dawlish said.

His patience was running out. For the last twenty minutes he had listened to the complaints, wails rather, of the two British merchant

177

captains, Holles of the *Ningpo* and Dugdale of the *Singan*. The *Leonidas* had not been on hand in time to protect them, they kept repeating, and when she did she was ineffectual, and it was little thanks to the Royal Navy that the two transports – British registered ships, they stressed – had reached Chemulpo.

Dawlish had received the captains in his quarters. Looking out through an open scuttle he could see the *Ningpo* swinging safely at anchor and the *Singan* beached on the soft mud on to which *Leonidas's* boats had towed her on arrival, a quarter of her crew straining at the oars. Given the damage to her rudder and screw the *Singan* was going to be there for a long time to come. The troops both ships had landed were now encamped on shore, close to the Chinese quarter, colourful banners streaming over squalor that their officers ignored.

"We were entitled to…" Dugdale began.

"No." Dawlish was trying to keep his irritation under control. "You're entitled to nothing, Captain Dugdale. You forfeited your entitlement to Royal Navy protection when you entered into an agreement with a foreign power to transport its troops." He was not sure of the legal position but he doubted if either captain was either. It was never going to come to a court anyway.

"I'm ready to sail." Holles's Glaswegian tones were full of resentment. "I've landed those Chinks and even if you're correct the *Ningpo* is now a civilian vessel again. A British ship at that. But I can't take her to sea with that damned pirate on the loose. And ye're lying here with yer great big powerful warship and devil a care you have for British interests."

"But in the meantime you're not making a loss, Captain Holles. You're claiming demurrage, aren't you?"

Holles coloured. "It's none of yer damn business." He avoided Dawlish's eye.

But claiming demurrage he was, Dawlish knew, compensation from the charterers for each day spent in port after his cargo, in this case troops, had been landed. Dawlish knew because Fred Kung had told him. And half the demurrage payment was going back surreptitiously to the Chinese officers who had arranged the charter. The same would apply to compensation for the *Singan's* damage. Fred Kung himself was probably taking a percentage too, though he was hardly going admit it.

"So what are you going to do, Captain?" Dugdale said. "Are you going to stand by and..."

Dawlish stood up. "Thank you for your visit, Gentlemen," he said. "I believe you have a boat waiting. So Good Day to you." He nodded to his writer, who had been jotting down notes in the background. The man came forwards to usher them out as Dawlish turned away.

Yet Holles had identified the same problem that Dawlish already knew was facing him. Somewhere out there was a ruthless pirate, ready and willing to inflict loss enough to trigger confrontation between two empires, even at the cost of civil war at home. Two other warships swung here at anchor, one each from those two empires, with *Leonidas* moored equidistant between them, one of them unwilling to act, the other, for now, incapable. For the Chinese *Fu Ching* had encountered the same storm as *Leonidas* had encountered and she had been lucky to survive. Her low bows had ill-equipped her for ploughing into a head sea and at times she must have been all but engulfed. Only Lodge's skill had brought her limping back to Chemulpo and when Dawlish had been rowed across to confer with him he had found the Chinese vessel's upperworks a shambles, boats and fittings smashed, ventilators swept away, the wheelhouse partly shattered. Had the *Kirishima* found her on her crawl back the *Fu Ching's* doom would have been inescapable. But she had survived and Lodge and his first officer, Lieutenant Lin, who seemed equally driven and competent, were pushing her crew to the limit to make her ready for sea again – and for battle.

Lodge, backed by Fred Kung, was in no doubt of his duty, indeed obviously longed for it. A single salvo from the *Fu Ching's* two massive ten-inch Armstrongs would be enough to smash the *Kirishima* to a hulk. But only if she could be found.

Despite Fred Kung's urgings Dawlish was in no mood to hunt the *Kirishima*. Bland Japanese assurances, meaningless for their polite vagueness, did not convince him that Shimazu's actions might not yet be endorsed, that they might not indeed have been planned as a deliberate attempt to trigger war. And Britain needed Japan as an ally – that fact could not be overlooked. If the signatures to the treaty codicils could be obtained in Seoul – and by all accounts the situation there had calmed, even if the king and queen were still absent at separate safe refuges – then *Leonidas* could be steaming south west towards Hong Kong the following day, away from this imbroglio. Too much had been invested up to now, too much risked, to sail away without those signatures. Only a few more days' wait...

The Japanese *Haruna* had all but quarantined herself. No more friendly boat races with *Leonidas*, no admiration of pet eels and chirping crickets, no more brotherly reminiscences about boyhoods in the Royal Navy, no toasts to the Emperor and the Queen-Empress in Admiral Hojo's quarters. The admiral himself was indisposed when Dawlish's invitation to dine on *Leonidas* had been declined with infinite courtly regret, even though it was Takenaka who had carried it across. And there had been no message of regret or condolence, much less of conciliation, to the Chinese.

"Hojo's playing a waiting game," Fred Kung had said, looking with calm hatred across the roadstead towards the *Haruna*. "He's damned if he's going to commit himself. He'll have contacted his masters, don't doubt it, messengers sent overland southwards to Pusan and from there it's just a day's steaming to Japan. They'll know by now exactly what Shimazu has done and Hojo will be waiting to see if they'll support it. Until then he'll be sitting tight."

Takenaka's analysis was no different, though extracting it from him was far from easy. Dawlish had invited him, alone, to his own quarters. At the end of the interview one issue could not be avoided.

"Can I rely on you to follow my orders, Lieutenant Takenaka?"

The slightest of twitch beneath the young officer's right eye betrayed an agony beneath. Dawlish realised that Takenaka had never been asked such a direct question though he might already be wrestling with its substance.

A long silence. Then Takenaka said "My oath of loyalty is to His Majesty, the Emperor." And even at this extremity of emotion he bowed slightly. Another silence, longer, then at last "I am honoured to serve in the Royal Navy." He did not need to say that he was on secondment, that he had taken no oath as a British officer.

"That's not what I asked you, Lieutenant." Dawlish's voice was gentle. "There would be no dishonour in your leaving this ship, in re-joining your own service." He was prepared to accept the responsibility of releasing him. "You would retain the respect of all on *Leonidas*, officers and men alike. And my respect also." He meant it. Takenaka had been ready to give his life for him.

Another silence. Supressed agony, painful to watch. It must have been like this, Dawlish thought, when American officers had been forced to choose between Union and Confederacy, when English gentlemen had decided between King and Parliament.

Takenaka spoke at last. "Captain Shimazu's actions are dishonourable," he said. "He cares nothing about civil war, nor about war too soon with China, nor about the disaster all this might bring." He looked straight at Dawlish. "You can rely on me, Captain Dawlish, to obey any order that helps stop him." He paused again and speaking cost another painful effort. "I apologise for my presumption in advising you, sir. But Captain Shimazu must be destroyed before his friends prevail on His Majesty to endorse his actions."

Dawlish said nothing but he stood up and reached out his hand. As he shook it he knew that the interview had been a worse experience for Takenaka than when he had faced the mob in Seoul, sword in hand.

*

Four bells of the forenoon watch had just sounded when an alert from Purdon, the watch-officer, brought Dawlish to the bridge. He found Edgerton there also, already scanning north-north-westwards through his glasses. The sky was clear, the sea glassy calm and there was the slightest wisp of black smoke on the horizon.

"The *Kirishima*?" Dawlish asked.

Purdon shook his head. "Too early to say, sir." The vessel was still hull down, only the hint of a funnel at the base of the smoke plume. "I thought it better to warn you, sir."

"Correct, Lieutenant." The hull was now rising above the sea's rim.

"It's tiny," Edgerton said. "Too small for the *Kirishima*. And no masts or yards." He looked towards Dawlish. "Clear for action?"

"We'll wait five minutes. But recall the cutter." It had gone ashore to collect fresh vegetables. Clearing for action, raising anchor and getting underway unnecessarily might be interpreted by the Japanese and Chinese vessels watching as panic.

As the small vessel neared the hesitation was justified. Labouring at a crawl that seemed disproportionately slow compared with the volume of smoke belching from her funnel was a small steam tug. It towed nothing in her wake.

181

"It's the Caledonian and Oriental's," Purdon said, and Dawlish too was recognising it, a vessel seen before, or one almost identical, just off the island of Socheong, with a coal-laden barge straining on a long cable astern.

As she neared the figures on the open steering platform could be identified – three Europeans, one the red-faced and filthily clothed helmsman, to his side a slighter figure, in grimy and sweat-stained white, the clerk in the Caledonian and Oriental's office whom Dawlish had once brushed past and to his other side the bloated features of the overseer McIver. Closer still and the glasses revealed a dark bruise on the side of the clerk's swollen face, the left eye closed and the cheek beneath bloody. He seemed crouched over, as if to find respite from pain. The expressions of all three men registered relief as their craft steered towards *Leonidas*. Relief after terror.

And Dawlish realised what must have happened. The *Kirishima* was at Socheong,

The pieces were falling into place now, the coal-mining concession onshore, the bunkering facility on the island, the armed Japanese – more accurately Satsuman – guards, the hostility of the Caledonian and Oriental's manager, Wishart, to the presence of *Leonidas*. The arrival of the Royal Navy cruiser might have alarmed a weaker man to panic, but Wishart's aggressive bluster had pre-empted suspicion. Dawlish had dismissed him a boor and had underestimated him – indeed had never considered him – as a conspirator. For conspiracy it was. There had been nothing spontaneous about Shimazu's actions. The Royal Navy had not been alone in identifying Socheong as an ideal base of operations.

"Signal that craft to come alongside." The order was unnecessary, for the tug was headed nowhere else. "Bring McIver to speak to me. In the charthouse." Dawlish had no intention of receiving the whisky-soaked Scotsman in his own quarters, even if he was the most senior man on the tug.

Ushered in, McIver's fawning thanks was even more offensive than his insolence had been on Socheong. "Thank God! Thank God, Captain Dawlish, sir, that you're still here!" He smelled as strongly as before of alcohol. "It's a hell there, sir, a hell. Thank God for the Royal Navy, sir!"

He was given coffee, black coffee, on Dawlish's instruction.

"The *Kirishima* is at Socheong?" Dawlish could already see it in his mind's eye.

"The Jap ship? She is, Captain Dawlish, sir. For two days now."

"The bay was deep enough to take her?" The space inside the coaling anchorage was large enough but the critical factor was water depth.

McIver nodded and a look of remembered horror on his face almost made him pitiable. "I didn't know anything about it before, sir. I'll swear my oath on that. It was Wishart. Wishart, and him alone."

"Just what are you talking about? What happened?"

"It's the Japs, sir. They've taken over. Wishart was expecting it. Once that Jap ship sailed in, before any of her crew had even come ashore, he'd ordered our guards to get the coolies mustered."

Dawlish could imagine it, the Satsumans in clean blue tunics, the polished Sniders, the bandoliers, the air of confidence that could so easily turn into arrogance. And the whips. Before now he had seen men enjoy using them, men themselves humble but elevated in their own estimation by freedom to use the lash

"What did he need the coolies for?"

"For the guns, sir. To get the guns ashore, sir, guns and supplies." McIver was starting to knead is hands together. "Would there be a touch of something, Captain Dawlish, sir, just a drop?" He was perspiring badly and starting to shake.

Dawlish turned to Purdon. "Have my steward bring a glass of brandy for Mr. McIver. One glass."

"Thank you, sir. God bless you, sir."

"What guns were they bringing ashore, Mr. McIver? Ship's guns? Small arms? Rifles?" Dawlish's unease was growing.

"Big guns, sir. Off the ship. But I only saw one come off. First the barrel and then the rest. They had to rig a shear-legs to get them on to a barge but they were damn fast about it. Then they were going to get the gun ashore and up the hill. Not just one, Wishart said, more of them to come. I don't know how many. That's what they wanted the coolies for, to drag 'em up."

The steward appeared with the brandy. McIver snatched it and drained it in a single gulp.

"So why are you here, Mr. McIver? You and your friends? I thought that you were Wishart's men? Loyal employees of the Caledonian and Oriental?"

"Money wouldn't pay for it, sir. Not for what they wanted." McIver's gaze was flitting from face to face, from Dawlish to Edgerton to Purdon and back again, his bloodshot eyes imploring compassion and finding only contempt. "I told you, sir, it's a hell. Not with that Jap captain around, and Wishart's shown himself no better. We had to get out. Nobody's safe there." His hands were shaking again and he reached out the emptied glass, embarrassed but obviously longing.

At a nod from Dawlish the steward, who had remained in the background, took the glass and disappeared with it.

"You were going to tell us what happened, Mr. McIver."

It cost him an effort and it took a long time, and several lengthy pauses, and another tot of brandy before it all came out. The first gun had been landed, further questioning having indicated that it was probably a six-inch, lifted from the *Kirishima's* waist. It was to be dragged on a sledge, first its barrel and then its mounting, up to the cliff top to the east of the anchorage. A rough track had been cleared on Wishart's orders several weeks previously. "He never said why," McIver said. "We thought it was for a signalling station." The sledge got stuck about a third of the way up, the coolies dragging it exhausted, unable to go on without rest despite indiscriminate blows.

"Then one of the poor devils hit one of them Jap guards. Knocked him down, he did, saw it with me own eyes. So they beat him, pounded him like meal with their rifle butts and others laid into him with their whips but that wasn't enough for that Jap captain when he heard about it. He had him carried down to the shore and, and..." McIver looked as if he was going to vomit.

Dawlish, suppressing his own nausea, knew what must have happened then. "They crucified him?"

McIver was starting to weep and at last Dawlish pitied him. "They did, sir, God forgive them. That's what they did, sir, on a cross they made of poles and then..."

"All right, Mr. McIver. We understand." Dawlish's own mind recoiled from what would have followed next, the bayonet thrusts, the glistening intestines hanging from the ripped belly.

"So then?" Dawlish was surprised at the gentleness that had entered his own voice. McIver was no longer an object of contempt.

"They hung a board around his neck. Chinese writing, or Korean, one of them lingos. A warning, and it worked. Nobody would look any of the Japs in the face after that. And Wishart, I saw him laughing with that Jap captain. But Albert Perkins, sir, he wouldn't stand for it. We never expected it of him, though we knew he was godly and religious-like. Always reading his bible."

"Albert Perkins?"

"The clerk, sir. I think you saw him on Socheong. He said it wasn't right and he tried to take the body down that night. So they beat him too, but not so badly. Wishart said he didn't want him killed even if he had little sympathy for him otherwise."

Then, without warning, McIver began to weep, silently at first, then with racking sobs. Dawlish and the others looked away, embarrassed.

McIver at last regained some measure of self-control. "What's to become of us, Captain? We've the clothes we stand up in, nothing more. We haven't a penny between us."

Dawlish turned to Purdon. "You'll talk to Mr. Whitaker," he said. "Present my compliments and assure him that he has my backing for advancing funds to distressed British citizens. I suggest accommodation of these gentlemen ashore, clothing too. And kindly arrange mooring of their tugboat." A handy craft inshore, he thought, though he did not say it.

"God bless you, Captain." McIver wiped his eyes with the back of his hand. "God bless you, sir."

The steward had returned with another glass of brandy. Dawlish caught his eye and shook his head slowly. He wanted McIver cooperative, not drunk.

"You saw them landing the gun," he said. Located on dry land, and on an elevated position, a six-inch would have the advantage of greater range and accuracy over any similar weapon mounted on a ship. "Did they land any more guns?"

They had, a second, and a third as well, with preparations commencing to lift a fourth from the *Kirishima*. A gang of coolies had been set to clearing a track up to the western headland overlooking the bay in preparation for guns to be dragged up there also. The work had gone on through the night. The lash, and the fear of yet worse, had ensured that. McIver and Perkins decided to escape if they could. "There's no trusting Wishart, sir," McIver said. "It's gone to his head."

The tug skipper, Samuel Wheeler, had arrived from the mainland, just before nightfall, towing another barge-load of coal. He too had been frightened by developments and was eager to get away before worse followed. The tug was due to return to the mainland with an empty barge the following morning and it had departed, apparently normally at first light. McIver and Perkins had secreted themselves on board. Half-way to the coast the tow had been slipped, the barge abandoned, the tug's furnace stoked to the maximum and the safety valve screwed down so as to make maximum speed to Chemulpo.

There was another piece of disturbing news.

"Them little steamboats the Jap ship was carrying," McIver said. "Torpedo boats, ain't they? They were lowered as soon as they arrived and they're patrolling off Socheong. We were terrified in case one would find us."

So it was even worse than Dawlish could have feared. Not a single cruiser wandering without a base about the North China Sea, but one with a secure anchorage, and virtually unlimited coal supplies and landed batteries that would make any approach hazardous if not deadly, and two torpedo craft for further defence, one of which had already sunk a formidable warship.

The real nightmare was just beginning and failure to act was not an option.

*

Leonidas would sail in darkness, would be off Socheong by first light. Sharp-eyed Japanese lookouts and more slovenly Chinese ones might see her slip away from Chemulpo but her goal would be uncertain and her being followed unlikely.

Alternative courses of action were swirling in Dawlish's brain, all with one objective, to eliminate Shimazu's base before it could be consolidated. It was what Topcliffe would have demanded, with every hint of further favour and advancement to reward success, with every certainty of repudiation in case of failure. For Dawlish knew the Admiral well enough by now, the old Lucifer whose position was so hazily defined but was apparently so essential to government regardless of who might be in power. And essential to Dawlish's own career as the only source of patronage for the son of a market-town solicitor without influential family connections. Patronage dearly bought, dependent only on success. But Topcliffe was in London, and even if he were here he might not commit himself in a situation this complex...

So many courses of action – and yet Dawlish forced all but one from his mind. It was too soon to plan. First he must know what was at Socheong. For one thought, one fear, nagged him. Nelson himself had once warned as much, that every sailor who attacked a fort was a fool. And Shimazu already had at least two six-inch weapons landed, and at a height also, increasing their range…

He confided in Whitaker.

"You understand that I'm not supporting what you're doing, Captain Dawlish?" Whitaker's arm was in a sling, his face still pale from pain. Foreign Office disapproval still concerned him more than closeness to death had done.

Dawlish kept his voice innocently neutral. "What could be more appropriate than for a Royal Navy vessel then proceeding to Socheong to investigate possible risks to British lives and property?"

"It's more than that, Captain. You know damn well that it's more."

"You can write me a formal warning accordingly," Dawlish said. "I'll sign that I've received it, that I've weighed your advice and that I've rejected it. My responsibility. You'll be happy with that?"

"That would be excellent. Most appropriate in fact." Whitaker looked sheepish and avoided Dawlish's eye. "You'll understand that in the circumstances…" His voice trailed off.

Dawlish broke the silence. "No word to Shen," he said. The Chinese admiral was recovered now and was installed in the camp established by the landed troops. He had been effusive in his thanks for his rescue and for Whitaker's care.

"We know he's in contact with Seoul," Whitaker said. "The first Chinese troops have got there from the north. There's talk that they may be bringing the king back to the palace. Now that there are no Japanese troops there he'll be in their pocket." He paused. "For now at least. But if Shimazu…"

"No word to Fred Kung either, nor to Lodge," Dawlish cut Whitaker off. "But keep an eye on the *Fu Ching*, on how well Lodge is getting her back to fighting trim." For the Chinese vessel mounted two ten-inch Armstrongs, the most powerful weapons north of Hong Kong.

Dawlish found himself lusting for them. He might yet need them.

18

The sea was calm as *Leonidas*, cleared for action but with her boats still stowed, crept from the western darkness. Dawlish had brought her far to the west of Chemulpo before turning north, and later eastwards, so that her approach to Socheong was blocked from view of the coaling harbour. The sky to the east lightened above the distant Korean mountains and against their silhouette the island's bulk was undetectable. Then, as the sun's burning disk heaved into sight and began its steady climb, Socheong's outline was defined. The first rays reached *Leonidas*, their warmth welcome to the group on the bridge after the night's chill. In another hour the air would be again be humid and uncomfortable, but by then *Leonidas* and her crew would have more serious concerns.

"Five miles, sir." Takenaka nodded towards the scrub-covered hills of the island's western extremity. The map he had prepared so thoroughly on the previous reconnaissance was pinned to a portable table next to the pelorus. His coloured pencils and his notebook were neatly arranged along its edge. On him in the coming hours would fall the responsibility of updating the map to reflect the island's transformation into a defended base.

Turning to Edgerton, Dawlish said "Very well. Course as decided."

Every manoeuvre in the next hour had already been thought through and would be followed strictly until and unless circumstances demanded. And "circumstances" meant Shimazu's response. That fanatical and brutally efficient mind had probably expected *Leonidas* to appear and had planned accordingly.

Dawlish moved to the port wing of the bridge, his glasses raised. Behind him he could hear the orders to helmsman and engine room that would bring *Leonidas* swinging south, then east, parallel to Socheong's southern shore. He could rely on Edgerton for faultless execution and on Latham's engine and boiler-room crews for sustaining the maximum speed the ship was building up to. Aft he could hear Leigh's instructions to the party streaming the patent log. Ten minutes passed and the island now lay to the north east. Leigh's report indicated just over fifteen and a half knots and a second run of the log confirmed it.

Socheong was now directly to the north, and the coaling harbour was coming into view beyond the high promontory just west of it. *Leonidas* would be visible from there now and it was likely that Shimazu's gun-crews on the heights would already be tracking her course. Below them the *Kirishima's* hull and masts stood out against the sheds and coal heaps behind. There was no other vessel in the anchorage, no sign either of the Japanese torpedo boats.

"They may be moored inboard of her," Edgerton was scanning through his glasses.

There was no way of knowing. Were it up to Dawlish he would employ them only by night. Any attack in daylight would be near suicidal. But that might not matter to the Japanese.

At least 8000 yards lay between *Leonidas* and the shoreline, longer by far than the effective range of either her six-inch weapons or the *Kirishima's*.

But only at sea level, a small internal voice reminded him.

The sea was glassy smooth, concealment impossible and the Gatling crews in *Leonidas's* tops were no less alert, and probably no less nervous, than those manning the main armament. The exchange of gunfire with the *Kirishima* during the previous encounter had left no doubt that action might be imminent.

Dawlish's gaze was fixed on the heights to either side of the anchorage. Judging them by the height of the *Kirishima's* masts he estimated the westerly at as much as 300 feet, its counterpart to the east perhaps a hundred lower – elevation enough to add fifteen hundred yards, perhaps more, to the effective range of any six-inch Krupps Shimazu had landed there. At worst two thousand yards advantage over *Leonidas's* comparable weapons...

He felt fear rising, a hollow ache in his stomach, his palms moistening, the signs he had learned to conceal. It was the time, he knew, when a show of outward nonchalance was essential. McIver had mentioned three weapons having been landed, perhaps even a fourth, and it was vital to know their location. There was no alternative but for *Leonidas* to trail her coat until Shimazu showed his hand. Dawlish leaned his elbows on the bridge rail and steadied his glasses, his disk of sight searching the heights. No sign of guns there. And then, uncertainly, since memory of such things was fallible, but with excitement rising, he wondered if there had been so much scrub on either height when *Leonidas* had steamed past on her previous reconnaissance. For the scrub at the summits was slightly browner than the greener shades of that further below, as if it was already withering...

A cry from the foremast lookout confirmed that another eye shared his suspicion. He called for a telescope – the magnification was greater than that of his glasses – and he scanned the lines of scrub methodically, sweeping back to probe a gap, then on again to examine an unbroken wall that seemed too regular for nature alone. Vegetation must have been cut lower down and dragged up to provide cover. Shimazu did not lack labour to accomplish that.

Then Dawlish saw movement on the western headland, an almost imperceptible shaking of foliage, a fleeting impression of what might have been a man, and there, little more than a black dot, what might have been the open muzzle and foreshortened barrel of a Krupp. And, though nothing was visible in the scrub on top of the eastern promontory, McIver had seen a weapon dragged up there. Absolute maximum range for such a weapon 8000 yards, maximum effective range half that. Then add 2000 to that half... still not enough for *Leonidas* to be in range. Shimazu would be holding his fire, keeping his guns concealed, until there was a reasonable chance of a hit, and more than one while *Leonidas's* own weapons were still outranged. Once she was sufficiently crippled he would send out his torpedo craft to finish her. Daring Shimazu into revealing his landed guns meant risking *Leonidas*.

Risking everything. Even Nelson had warned sailors of forts, and with good reason, for he had lost an eye in attacking one.

The Socheong anchorage was now squarely on *Leonidas's* port beam.

"Any change of plan?" Edgerton asked, the slightest hesitation in his voice betraying the same supressed fear that Dawlish himself was feeling. For the next manoeuvre would bring *Leonidas* closer, two thousand yards closer, to the island.

"Proceed as agreed, Commander," Dawlish did not lower his telescope. "And forward my compliments to Mr. Purdon. Advise him that I've every trust that his starboard battery is as well-prepared as his port." Purdon was on the open deck forward with his beloved guns and the message was superfluous, for Dawlish knew that each six-inch crew along the cruiser's flank had been drilled to clockwork precision, that each weapon was firing-ready, that further shells and bagged charges were stacked in the nearby ready-use lockers. But superfluous or not, the message would pass to each crew in turn, a reminder of what they were respected for, of what was expected from them. With such small gestures was morale consolidated.

Leonidas ploughed on, bow wave foaming, screws at full revolutions. The unseen stokers feeding the furnaces in the boiler rooms must by now be almost intolerably hot. Her course still lay west-east, parallel to the island, and Dawlish was scanning the tops of the cliffs that ran towards the eastern tip. No sign of landed weapons here. The rocky eastern extremity of the island was in sight off the port bow. It was now time for the sweeping turn to port.

The tension on the bridge was almost palpable as the cruiser heeled in the broad turn, a full sixteen points, that brought her on to a straight east to west heading, back along the southern coast. The reversal had reduced the distance to the island by at least ten cables, 2000 yards, and *Leonidas* might just be coming within effective range of the Krupp on the higher headland. Nervous glances were being cast towards the island, for once more the anchorage, and *Kirishima* within, were now visible. There was no sound other than the rush of water alongside, the faint throbbing of the engines pulsing through the deck, the irregular click of the wheel as the helmsman corrected to hold the heading.

To ease the anxiety around him Dawlish moved towards Takenaka's map table. The Japanese officer was bent over it, as intent on his use of a coloured pencil as he might be in his own cabin. He straightened and bobbed the slightest bow.

"That gully," Dawlish said, turning and pointing towards a cleft to the east now long passed, "I don't think it was so obvious when we were here before." It had been, and Takenaka would not have missed such a feature, but that was immaterial. "I trust you've noted it, Lieutenant."

"Assuredly, sir." Takenaka indicated the feature and as Dawlish looked he noticed also that the elevations of the headlands flanking the anchorage had just been added. The height estimates were close to his own.

Dawlish turned to Edgerton. "Ready? Two minutes?"

"Two minutes, sir".

Those two minutes would bring *Leonidas* directly south of the Socheong anchorage.

"Mr. Purdon!" Dawlish looked down on the gunnery lieutenant's upturned face. "Remember the *Toad* and the San Joac! Give me the same when I call for it! You know your target!"

"Depend on it, sir!" A look of pride but the voice tempered by what Dawlish recognised, as in himself, a fear of failing expectation.

Dawlish sensed mystification around him but said nothing to clear it. The San Joaquin expedition had been a private enterprise, a mercenary one. There had been little to be proud of on that bloody river, but it was Purdon's mastery of gunnery in the expedition's final stages that helped break enemy resistance. Now that skill was needed again.

Shimazu must surely be tracking *Leonidas's* progress now, noting the second fast sweep parallel to the island, wondering perhaps if there would be a third, still closer. He would be calculating ranges and hit-probabilities, balancing the merits of opening fire or of withholding it. And above all he would be uncertain of Dawlish's own intentions...

But Dawlish knew that Shimazu's uncertainty represented his own best advantage. For had the positions been reversed he himself would not open fire, would keep his weapons masked, would not force his opponent into a confrontation which political manoeuvring might make unnecessary ...

All the more reason therefore to force Shimazu's hand.

"Mr. Edgerton? Time I believe." For the anchorage now lay directly to the north, the *Kirishima* beam on inside the anchorage and flanked by the headlands to either side...

Now *Leonidas* sheered over to starboard, four, six, eight points of the compass, a full 90 degrees before she straightened out and ploughed across the glassy sea towards the anchorage at all but 16 knots, the range shortening by some 500 yards a minute. The cruiser must be entering the range of the unseen weapons on the headlands but her manoeuvre must have come as a surprise and end-on she represented a smaller target than before the turn.

"Ready, Mr. Purdon?" There had been time enough, almost two minutes, for the gun layers of the two forward six-inchers to fix their target.

"Ready, sir!"

Leonidas's bowsprit was lined up on *Kirishima* and both guns in her forward sponsons had a clear bearing on the Japanese cruiser. Range still closing, 5000 yards and still shortening...

"Your guns, Mr. Purdon. A single salvo."

Another half-minute, an eternity, quiet exchanges and nods between Purdon and his gun captains, last fine adjustments to elevation hand-wheels, then the crews frozen at their assigned positions, every eye on deck and in the tops above fixed ahead.

"Fire!"

Purdon's command was lost in the simultaneous blast of both weapons. Sulphurous smoke washed back across the deck as *Leonidas* rushed on and as the crews swung the breeches open and commenced reloading. But Dawlish had no care for that, for his glass was fixed on the *Kirishima*, towards which two 80-pound explosive shells were hurtling. There was no doubt now of his intent...

And then a plume of white foam erupted in the open water between the headlands, well short of the Japanese cruiser, and the identical column that rose simultaneously was shorter still. Two misses, but enough to leave no doubt as to *Leonidas's* deadly intent.

Dawlish's heart was thumping, his mouth dry. Shimazu could not ignore this threat...

"Maintain course, sir?" Edgerton's voice had an insistence that told that he too feared the mounting risk.

"Maintain Course, Commander!" Dawlish was gripping the rail before him to disguise the shaking of his hands. Those unseen weapons on the heights that loomed ever closer must be manned, must be tracking *Leonidas*, and on the *Kirishima* too, crews must... But no! He must not allow himself to be transfixed by fear of the enemy's intentions.

He looked down to the guns below. Both breeches were closed, the crews were standing rigidly – too rigidly, for it betokened fear – at their stations.

"Your guns, Mr. Purdon! Another salvo if you please!"

Both barrels were dropping a fraction to correct for shortening range ...

Suddenly a flash from the westerly headland, and smoke billowing above the withered scrub there and a sound of the report reaching *Leonidas* an instant before a raging white column burst upwards from the sea a half-cable off the port quarter. Close, close enough to make the helmsman flinch involuntarily, for his hands to jerk, for *Leonidas* to swing slightly to starboard before he could correct the course. But at that instant Purdon was ordering fire, and the lanyards were being jerked and the six-inchers were again vomiting flame and smoke and shell.

Even before one shell smashed into the face of the eastern headland, before the second fell into the sea just short of it, Dawlish knew that the current course was now suicidal.

"To port! Ten points!"

Leonidas ploughed into the turn that would carry her south-westwards away from the island, screws thrashing, deck heeling, smoke vomiting from her funnels. As she did another flash from the western headland announced a landed Japanese weapon coming again into action, and a fraction later a second, and then a third, this last from the promontory to the east. Their reports reached *Leonidas* almost as a single long bark just before their shells fell around her, two to port and one to starboard, the last close enough to drench the bridge decks with falling spray.

Three weapons landed, just as McIver had warned, their positions now known, two to the west and one to the east. But *Kirishima* carried ten six-inch Krupps...

On the deck below Purdon was hastening aft towards the sponsoned stern-chasers but Dawlish's call halted him.

"Hold fire, Mr. Purdon! And my compliments to your men." For they had done well at extreme effective range and had they met *Kirishima* on the open sea Dawlish would have had no hesitation in continuing the action. But those landed weapons, with the advantages of firm footings and increased range that *Leonidas* could not match, were deadly.

The immediate objective now was to get out of range of Shimazu's shore battery. But Socheong also had a northern coast and there, sheltered by a high curving peninsula, was a bay, a shallow one, at the point of exit of the valley that ran southwards to the main anchorage. There too Shimazu must be forced to show his hand...

The Krupps blasted twice more as the range lengthened, their first salvo straddling *Leonidas* harmlessly, and not closely, the second plunging into her foaming wake a cable and more astern. Dawlish felt relief wash through him as the cruiser – his cruiser – raced into safety, engines panting, screws beating at full revolutions, a bone in her teeth. She carried confirmation with her of just where Shimazu had landed his weapons. Damaging the *Kirishima* would have been a bonus but he had never been fully confident of achieving it. That must wait...

"A well-executed manoeuvre, Gentlemen," Dawlish said. "My best compliment is that I expected no less." He ran his hand down his tunic, still soaked from the spray hurled by a falling shell. "Not much glory in a drenching," he said, "and it'll take more than that to put us off our stroke." There were nervous nods of agreement, even slight polite laughs, but the release of tension was obvious.

Through the engine-room voice-pipe he thanked Latham, asking him to relay his appreciation to the crew there. The sun was now high and metal deck-fittings were hot to the touch. Down in the sweltering hell of the boiler and machinery spaces some men might now be on the point of collapse but there could be no let-up, not for another hour or more. A word of encouragement was cheap, the commitment it bought incalculable.

Takenaka alone seemed unelated. Dawlish gestured to the chart table.

"You've noted the gun positions, Lieutenant?"

"Yes, sir. Here sir, if you will permit." Takenaka's pencil pointed to the three locations but there was no air of pride in his confirmation and his face was a mask of supressed agony.

Dawlish nodded approval and turned away, concerned that he might have pushed this man's loyalty towards, and perhaps beyond, some invisible barrier. But for now there was nothing he could ask or say.

The island was dropping away astern but the morning's work was not yet done. Still at maximum speed, *Leonidas* swept around the western tip of the island to parallel the northern coast. The rocky peninsula that jutted from the shore – the fin on the leaping fish's back that Takenaka's map had suggested – was at least as high as the promontories to the south, maybe even higher, and it still blocked sight of the shallow bay there.

I'd have a Krupp up there, maybe two, Dawlish told himself. He was sure that the Shimazu would think the same. But to confirm it there would be no alternative to *Leonidas* trailing her coat again. There would be no advantage of surprise this time – lookouts had probably already reported the cruiser's swing around the island – and there would be no target similar to the *Kirishima* that would require opening fire to protect it. Yet Shimazu might still rise to the bait if *Leonidas* approached close enough for him to score a hit. Dawlish could imagine him, his face locked in fury and determination, hurrying across the island's narrow neck, messengers running before him to order semaphore flags to wave signals up towards any landed guns.

Dawlish could once again sense the unspoken tension rise around him on the bridge. The familiar hollow ache had returned to his stomach. There were no doubts now as to the efficiency of the Japanese gunnery, of the range advantage that height lent to any landed weapon, of the elevation-limitations of *Leonidas's* own guns that made retaliation impossible. And there was nothing for himself but to stand, apparently assured, nonchalant of danger, on the open bridge and to radiate a confidence he did not feel to the men around them and to the gun-crews furtively watching for, and fearing, any sign of irresolution. He knew that at this moment the survival of *Leonidas* and the lives of some 300 men, the happiness of as many families, depended on him, and him alone. His own ambitions seemed petty by comparison. He found himself praying silently to the God whose existence he sometimes doubted and his plea was not for himself but for decisions he must make.

"Mr. Purdon!"

The gunnery officer looked up from behind the starboard bow-chaser, his face expectant.

"Hold fire until ordered." *If ordered*, Dawlish thought. A target was unlikely.

The Japanese guns on the headlands of the southern coast had opened fire at under 5000 yards and they had been almost deadly accurate at that range. There was no option now but to swing *Leonidas* towards the island and to drive eastwards on a course that would take her at no greater distance than this to the northernmost tip of the peninsula now looming off the starboard bow.

As on the southern heights, that peninsula carried a cap of scrub, denser than the isolated patches on the slopes below. Dawlish steadied his telescope and focussed on it, searching for any signs of withering, of brown against the thick wall of green. But there was none, none at least that could be detected at this distance. There was no sign of movement there, no glimpse of a barrel, no hint that there could have been time enough to drag a four-ton weapon there and install it on a solid foundation. There was nothing to prove, or to disprove, the absence of a Krupp six-inch.

The semi-circular bay was becoming visible, fishing boats drawn up on the sand at its eastern extremity, but the greater part of the bay still masked by the peninsula. *Leonidas* was broadside on to it now, presenting a larger target than she had done when she had forged directly towards the anchorage to the south, but still Shimazu's Krupps – if there were indeed any on the heights above – did not speak. Dawlish was now resolved to take his ship on to the island's eastern tip and turn there for Chemulpo. He had learned as much as he could…

At that moment a cry from the foremast lookout drew every eye towards the dark shape that was racing out from the lee of the peninsula. Small, 60 feet long, no more, a hull that was slim and low. She was moving fast, very fast, with a white wake boiling astern and heat shimmering above her single funnel. The deck carried little more than that funnel, just an exposed steering position and a mounting above it for what must be a Nordenvelt or Gatling, and one long cylinder on the forecastle. It was obvious immediately what she was, one of the two Thorneycroft torpedo boats that the *Kirishima* carried, the same craft perhaps that had sunk the *Hi Ying* at her moorings in Chemulpo. There was no doubt of her intent as she drove towards *Leonidas*, her helm thrown to and fro to make her weave in a series of long s-shaped course-changes intended to distract the aim of her quarry's gunners. She had been designed for stealth, for attack under cover of darkness, but though that advantage had been lost, and the sun high in the sky and flashing on the waters, her commander was plunging on remorselessly towards the hail that would soon greet her.

Shouted commands. *Leonidas's* helm was over, heeling her into a turn to starboard that would bring her bow-on to her attacker and reduce her target area. From the forward top the Gatling gunner there was shouting acknowledgement of the order to open fire. None of the weapons in the other tops could be brought to bear, masked as they were by the foremast. In his disc of vision Dawlish could see the Japanese helmsman on the tiny steering platform, and the face of the officer beside him set in the same grim earnestness that so characterised Shimazu and Takenaka. The torpedo boat's gun-crew – their weapon was now clearly another Gatling – was slewing their weapon round towards *Leonidas*, striving to hold her in their sights despite their craft's bucking and rolling in her furious weaving. That they were still holding fire made their menace seem all the greater.

And on the vessel's small forecastle, three men were crouched by the single tube there. Within it the pointed nose of a 14-inch Whitehead torpedo was just discernible.

The range was dropping, the speed of closure at least 34 knots. *Leonidas's* battery of six-inchers counted for nothing now, and only the single Gatling in the foretop could offer protection. Fifteen hundred yards now, twelve hundred, and still the Japanese craft bored on. A ripple of fire, a dozen shots, blasted from *Leonidas's* Gatling as its gunner ground his crank and its stack of barrels rotated. Then a pause – continuous fire could almost certainly lead to jamming – and then another burst, and again a pause, and then another burst. All useless. The torpedo boat's writhings made holding an accurate aim on her impossible and the fire directed towards her lashed the waters to either side harmlessly.

A thousand yards separated the vessels and *Leonidas's* present course, directly towards the island, could not be maintained if she were not to run aground. In a moment Dawlish was going to have to order a turn away and he knew that in the process he must present a broadside target to the attacker. Eight hundred yards now, seven hundred and there was no option but to call the turn...

The Japanese launched. The torpedo was glimpsed for an instant as it leapt from the tube and plunged into the water ahead of the creaming bow wave. The vessel peeled away to port and as she did her Gatling crew opened fire, her discipline of bursts and pauses as perfect as that of the counterparts they were aiming for.

There was a terrible fascination in watching the thin line of bubbles that marked the torpedo's track. The moment of launching had been well judged and the aim seemed all but aligned with *Leonidas's* bowsprit. On the bridge Dawlish could sense the intake of breath around him, the expectation – the longing – for the order he must give for turning away. And if he were to misjudge...

"Hard to starboard!"

There was a long instant before the bows began to swing over. Dawlish resisted the urge to run to the port bridge wing to follow the torpedo, but Sub-Lieutenant Leigh was there, hypnotised by the streak of approaching bubbles. Aloft, the foretop's Gatling was hammering again and in her pauses an answering chatter confirmed that the fleeing torpedo boat's similar weapon was still in action.

"It missed!" Leigh was yelling. "It almost scraped down the side. But it missed!"

Dawlish too felt like cheering. *Leonidas* was well into her turn, into a reversal of course that would take her towards the safety of the open sea.

There was a cry, a scream, from the foretop, as the Gatling there fell silent. Wooden chips cascaded from the structure there as the departing Japanese vessel registered a lucky hit. Dawlish looked up and saw a body – the gunner's – falling backwards from the shattered platform, a look of horror on his loader's face as he reached out vainly to catch him. The body crashed on the deck ahead of the bridge, a ghastly circle of crimson blasting out from it. The Japanese torpedo boat was out of range now, and had found shallow water. Thwarted in her main intent she might be, but she had survived.

Now it was time to set the course for Chemulpo. Dawlish looked back bitterly towards the peninsula. He still did not know if Shimazu had a landed weapon there.

That one frail torpedo boat had seen to that.

19

Dawlish had previously officiated at burials, but whether on land or at sea the task had never become easier. The single canvas-shrouded body resting on a finely-balanced plank beneath the Union flag, the grim set of the features of the ranks drawn up to either side, the supressed sobbing of one man and the tears on the cheeks of two others, all told of shock as well as of grief, even of resentment. Most of these men had never previously seen action, nor indeed had Andrew Sturt, unmarried, twenty-four years old and with eight years' service, whose body Dawlish was about to commit to the deep.

As he reached the words *"I am the Resurrection and the Life, saith the Lord..."* Dawlish's voice caught. He coughed to cover his emotion before he continued. *"...he that believeth in me, though he were dead, yet shall he live."* He glanced up from his Book of Common Prayer and caught Purdon's eye. He saw that he too was remembering when they shared such a moment before, when they had laid a brother officer in a simple grave next to a muddy Paraguayan river. The look, fleeting as it was, offered comfort and understanding that could never be spoken. For at this moment Dawlish knew that he had never been so alone, that his innermost fears and concerns could never be shared on this ship, that his mask of calm resolution must never drop. And that Andrew Sturt had died because of his decisions.

The service ended. The moment before Dawlish nodded to the men by the plank seemed to last an eternity, a chill across the deck despite the soaking heat, the silence broken only by the rush of water along the hull, the realisation unspoken that the game was deadly and not yet finished. Then Andrew Sturt's loader and another seaman were raising the plank and the weighted bundle slid from beneath the flag and plunged into the foam.

And then the ship's routine resumed, each man more intent on his duties than before, most thoughts unshared for now, most fears unspoken, *Leonidas* steaming towards Chemulpo at minimum revolutions. Dawlish did not intend to enter the anchorage before daybreak and the night would pass in slow reversals of course parallel to the mainland. Lookouts would be doubled during darkness and crews would stand to their guns.

Dawlish found it hard to sleep, even after poring over options for long hours in the solitude of his own quarters. The only alternative to be rejected out of hand was to forget Shimazu and to leave Socheong to him. It was too late for that. Should the Japanese government choose to back him – and the possibility could not be discounted – then outright war between Japan and China would be inevitable, and a British alliance with Japan then unthinkable. The only winners would be the Russians, hungry and ambitious, an unseen but menacing presence to the north. Dawlish knew that he might have won some shred of sympathy in London had he sailed for home when he returned to Chemulpo from the rioting in Seoul. He might have pleaded that the anarchy there had made signature of the codicils impossible in the immediate term, but he had instead plunged into conflict, into what some, many indeed, would characterise as private war. The squalid piece of paper he had signed to absolve Whitaker of responsibility would represent only the first of many repudiations. And it would be no wonder, for *Leonidas* had been risked, might indeed have been sunk had that Japanese torpedo boat launched on a slightly different heading. There would be no mercy, no second chance, no future for a much-envied captain who had lost the most modern ship in the navy. He must come back victorious or not at all, and that victory must neither prevent an Anglo-Japanese alliance nor destroy British relations with China.

Dawlish's mind went back again and again to the conversation with Takenaka some days before, the only insight he had into minds and values of a culture all but incomprehensible to him. The possibility that groups around the Emperor might well secure reluctant approval for Shimazu's actions.

But only if he was still a force, on Socheong as well as at sea.

There was no alternative but to destroy him – and to destroy him quickly, before any reinforcement could reach him from Japan. Even *Leonidas's* six-inch battery, however modern, might not suffice for the task. Today's coat-trailing had proved that. Dawlish studied Takenaka's map of the island endlessly, covered a dozen sheets of paper with rough copies and sketched as many alternatives for attacking it. Each one he tore in small pieces and thrust in the waste basket. But the most promising – even if not promising enough – had a common feature, one that must be the basis for the final plan.

He needed the Chinese.

*

The *Haruna*, Admiral Hojo's flagship, was gone. Other than a handful of junks and sampans the only occupants of the Chemulpo anchorage were the two Chinese-chartered British ships and the *Fu Ching*. It was on this Chinese cruiser that Dawlish's thoughts had focussed during his wakefulness from disturbed sleep. He hungered for her two massive Armstrong ten-inchers.

"She's down at the head, badly down". Edgerton's glass, like Dawlish's was trained on her.

The bows, low at the best of times, were now all but awash and streams of foam-flecked water were pouring overboard from two points on the inclined foredeck. Men were clustered there, bending and straightening and bending again in slow rhythm.

"They're pumping," Dawlish said. "It looks as if the steam pump alone can't keep up." One stream was voluminous and steady, obviously mechanically propelled, but the second, in line with the knot on deck, pulsed more weakly. A figure looking down from the bridge was clearly Captain Lodge. He turned towards *Leonidas* and Dawlish caught him in his disc of vision. His face was haggard. No need for a gun salute. Lodge had weightier concerns.

And those concerns were suddenly Dawlish's. He had depended on *Fu Ching's* storm damage being repaired by now.

Even before *Leonidas* dropped anchor a boat had been launched to take Sub-Lieutenant Leigh ashore to fetch Whitaker. He needed to be quick about it – the tide was ebbing fast and the vast mudflats would soon be exposed. On the shore the Chinese camp now looked permanent and a grey haze from a hundred cooking fires hung over it in the morning stillness. Figures were moving about there, soldiers in half-Europeanised uniforms and the odd dash of colour of the silken robes of some official, but there was no impression of purposeful bustle.

Whitaker had received news from Seoul the previous night. "The Chinese have control there," he told Dawlish after he had been helped up from the boat, his arm still in a sling. "They were as brutal about restoring peace as you'd expect. They beheaded dozens whether they were involved in the rioting or not. They're keeping fifty alive to hand over to the Japanese for punishment. Whether or not any of them were actually in the mob that stormed the palace makes no difference. They'll be a token of apology. I wouldn't want to be in their shoes."

"Any news of the Japanese coming back?"

"None. Not yet at least. But you've seen that Admiral Hojo and the *Haruna* are gone."

"Any information about where he's headed?"

"He just disappeared over the horizon. My guess is that he'll stay at sea and bide his time out of sight until he knows how his masters in Japan will react."

Admiral Shen had gone to Seoul to confer with the Chinese Ambassador.

"To give him his instructions, more likely," Whitaker said. "The title of Admiral is nominal. I suspect that the ambassador is grovelling to him"

In Shen's absence all power at Chemulpo seemed to have passed to Fred Kung. The officers of the troops landed there seemed to defer to him – not least, Whitaker guessed, because he absolved them from responsibility for decisions. "There's hardly a single Imperial official who'll risk taking any decision unless he has got no option," he said. "It's too damn easy for them to lose their heads."

Dawlish did not remind Whitaker of the disclaimer he had asked him to sign. Whitaker's head might not be at risk but he was taking no chances regarding his Foreign Office career.

Whitaker had other information from Kung.

"You believe him?" Dawlish asked.

"Not more than I normally do. But the main facts probably aren't in doubt."

The King and Queen were back in the palace in Seoul, now guarded by Chinese troops. Whatever resolution the King had ever possessed had been lost in the turmoil. Only Queen Min's presence stopped him from automatically signing whatever the Chinese put in front of him.

"Fred's aggrieved," Whitaker said. "He won't say as much but I can read between the lines. He saved her from the mob at the palace and he expected eternal gratitude. You too helped her get away. Maybe you expected the same."

Dawlish shook his head. It was a possibility that he had already discounted. The woman who had been ready to leave a disguised servant to die in her place was hardly likely to remember lesser favours.

"She's free to play her own game now," Whitaker said. "She'll play the Chinese and Japanese against each other. It won't be easy but she's clever enough to do it. She'll see the Chinese get whatever nominal homage they want as long as they keep enough troops here to deter Japanese occupation. It's what she always wanted and now, with the King's father gone, there's nothing to hinder her."

"The *Daewongun's* gone?"

"Taken to China under armed escort. As an honoured guest of course. He'll have a palace, a retinue, concubines, anything he wants. Anything that doesn't involve coming back here."

It seemed an ideal solution, ideal for the Queen, perhaps ideal for Korea, acceptable to the Chinese, tolerable, however temporarily, for the Japanese as they built up their strength for some future contest. Ideal too for Britain since the Chinese presence would inhibit Russian expansion southwards.

Except for one consideration.

Shimazu and the *Genyosha* and the Satsuma clan all wanted war, a war that the Emperor might not like but which he might accept if it was the price of stopping Japan tearing itself apart again in civil strife.

So it always came back to the same conclusion. Shimazu had to be destroyed – and quickly.

*

Dawlish had himself rowed across to the *Fu Ching*. He did not expect to be received with ceremony, nor was he. Lodge greeted him in grimy overalls and looked as if he had not slept for days.

"You'll excuse me, sir, if I don't offer you may hand," Lodge lifted it to show it dirty.

"I'll take it anyway," Dawlish said, reaching out and shaking. A flash of memory recalled the American sailors so long ago on the bloody deck of HMS *Plover*. Time now to make some recompense. Blood was thicker than water. "Your situation looks serious. Can I be off assistance?"

Lodge led him to the bridge and they looked down on the straining backs of the pumpers rising and falling in slow unending rhythm. Many looked near to collapse.

"Eighteen hours now," Lodge said, "and we're just about holding our own. Everything ahead of the second bulkhead is flooded."

"What happened?" Dawlish tried to hide his own rising despair. He had been counting on this ship being at sea with *Leonidas*, blockading Socheong to prevent Shimazu making a sortie seawards, keeping *Kirishima* bottled up there until...

"She was strained in the storm," Lodge said wearily. "Seams opening, a few popped rivets that we could plug easily, enough for the pumps to cope with. Then yesterday she started to take on water fast, much faster."

"You know why?" Dawlish could guess the reason, one that he dreaded.

Lodge confirmed it. "Corrosion," he said. He seemed glad to have somebody to tell this to, somebody who understood. "We got a swimmer down to feel around. There's a hole a foot long and half that wide and the edges are paper thin. He broke off a piece and brought it up. The surrounding metal isn't much stronger."

It was the curse of iron ships, stagnant water slopping in the bilges and trapped in unseen crevices and corners, corrosion slowly chewing away a hull's integrity. And there was worse.

204

"Number one bulkhead failed last night – the same reason. I lost a man, drowned, in the second compartment when the water broke through. We're shoring up the next bulkhead but there's no guarantee that it won't go the same way."

"How long …" Dawlish began.

Lodge cut him off, voice angry with the rage of the fatigued and hopeless. "You mean, Captain, how long have I commanded this vessel? That I should have been aware of this corrosion before I sailed? Three months, sir, three months, and the ship I took command of was a floating slum that hadn't known proper maintenance nor been dry-docked once since she left the builder's yard. I'd challenge any officer to achieve as much as I have done in that time, sir!"

Dawlish was taken aback. He had wanted to ask how long Lodge thought the next bulkhead might be relied upon. He sensed Lodge's embarrassment, his regret already that he had spoken in anger. Better to ignore it.

"Could I see the compartments for myself, Captain? I've encountered something similar myself in the past." He had, on a rotten troop transport that had almost killed several hundred men. That vessel had all but fallen apart in the Indian Ocean. It had been a hard lesson, not a memory to be cherished.

"You'll need overalls, Captain Dawlish." Lodge seemed appeased – and relieved – by the suggestion.

Dawlish changed in Lodge's cabin, its austere comfort contrasting with the red and gold painted wooden carvings that decorated the wardroom they passed through. As he stepped out of his own uniform and pulled on the boiler suit his mind was racing over possibilities. Repair must be possible – difficult, but possible. And Lodge did not seem to be a man to accept defeat easily. And it only needed the *Fu Ching* to be capable of leaving port, of carrying her ten-inch smashers to Socheong, of keeping afloat for just another week – only that, and something more he must negotiate with the Chinese.

Together they nudged past the pumping team on the foredeck, many of them stripped to the waist. Despite their obvious fatigue their faces were blank, masks of mute acceptance that must surely hide seething resentment. Dawlish realised that it was such impassivity he found so disquieting here in the East, the more so for awareness of the fury that must finally erupt. As had that mob's in Seoul.

"Welcome, sir." Lieutenant Lin was almost unrecognisable in overalls as filthy as his captain's. He looked no less exhausted. It was hard to imagine any such dedication from the effete and long-sleeved officers who had dined – and died – in the *Hi Ying's* wardroom just before Shimazu's torpedo struck.

Lin led them below through a hatchway, squeezing past the sections of flanged iron pipe that dropped down through it and which pulsed with every stroke of the pump. They found themselves in the crew accommodation, rolled hammocks and furnishings dragged to either side. In the fetid gloom the pipe could be seen disappearing into another hatchway, past a vertical ladder, down into the flooded forepeak. Dawlish glanced down and saw brown water swirling in small vortices, various flotsam and even a wooden box bobbing there. The level seemed to drop ever so lightly with each stroke of the pump, then surged back greedily. Further aft the whirlpool above the intake to the higher-volume steam pump was just discernible. The water's surface was within two feet of the opening in the deck.

As if reading Dawlish's mind Lodge said. "It was almost a foot lower at dawn."

"You've tried plugging it from outside?" The question was all but superfluous. That would be the first action.

"We've lowered hammocks, mattresses. They seem to be holding in place. I guess they help, but not enough."

"Has it been possible to reach the hole from inside the compartment?"

"I had several men go down. It wasn't easy. Only one got to the hole, and for seconds only. But yes, it can be reached"

Dawlish forced himself to speak with a calm he did not feel. "I'm carrying standard diving dress on my ship, Captain Lodge. I've got a trained diver to wear it. It won't be easy to get him in there, but it should be possible."

"You mean it, Captain?" The first hint of hope in Lodge's voice since Dawlish had boarded. "You think anything can come of it if he does?"

"I've got skilled artificers and there's spare steel plate on board for routine repairs." Dawlish said. "There's no shortage of caulking material. We can fabricate a patch and we can lower it externally, then with luck we can bolt it secure against another patch within, bolted on from inside the hull."

A small internal voice reminded him that the surrounding plates might themselves be so weakened – also paper-thin perhaps – that they might be incapable of supporting the stresses involved at the patch's edges. But he did not share the concern with Lodge. If the *Fu Ching* was capable of leaving port, of carrying her ten-inch smashers to Socheong, of keeping afloat for just another week, that could be sufficient...

They came back on deck, blinded momentarily by the sunlight. Across the roadstead the British-owned *Ningpo* still swung idly at anchor. Dawlish gestured towards it.

"She's still being paid demurrage?"

Lodge laughed sourly. "I guess Mr. Kung's paying," he said. "I'd be damned if I'd do so myself." He looked Dawlish straight in the eye. "I do a decent sailor's job for these people but that doesn't mean that I'm involved with them any deeper or any shiftier than that. I'll be proud to go home with my salary when that job's done, and not a cent more."

"And the job's not done yet, Captain Lodge?"

"I told you before, sir, that I want Shimazu and I want the *Kirishima*. That stands."

"Then you and I need to have a talk with Mr. Kung," Dawlish said. "But first you'll need some men and equipment carried across from *Leonidas*. We can't let your ship sink under you."

Not in view of what he had in mind.

20

Fred Kung proved amenable – unexpectedly, fulsomely amenable – when Dawlish and Lodge found him at the Chinese camp. The haphazardly pitched tents there, the troops squatting idly by them in loose, shabby smocks, some cooking over small fires, the tattered banners flapping gently in the breeze, the smell of human waste, the few platoon-sized groups exercising untidily with flint locks and pikes, all gave an impression of aimless slackness. It was hard to imagine such forces facing Japanese troops with any hope of success. And yet the mob at the palace at Seoul had proved that numbers could swamp a determined defence – and there were large numbers here at Chemulpo, over seven hundred.

Only at the Korean house Fred Kung occupied at one corner of the camp was there an air of purpose. His grim blue-turbaned Uighurs guarded access and he himself was clad in the same quasi-military Western clothing in which Dawlish had first encountered him. Then he had introduced himself as a lieutenant of the Chinese ambassador, but now he was something more, a power in his own right, as if Admiral Shen had vested authority in him before leaving for Seoul and he had no hesitance about using it to the limit. Whitaker had suspected as much and Dawlish probed Lodge cautiously about it.

"He's a powerful man," is all Lodge would say. "I don't understand the half of it. It's better I don't. But I wouldn't underestimate him, captain. Don't be taken in by talk about Presbyterian colleges. He's ambitious and he's got backing in Peking, maybe even in the court itself."

Alone, with Lodge the only other present, Kung was American in speech and manner, easy, offering cigars and tea, whiskey if they preferred that. Dawlish made his proposal and Kung welcomed it, hinting indeed that he had been thinking similarly. Seizure of the Caledonian and Oriental's coal mine and loading jetty on the coast at Songang-ni would cut off the source that gave Socheong such value as a base, the first step to frustrating Shimazu's gamble.

"The King will be in favour," Kung said.

"King Gojong knows about the mine?" Dawlish was surprised that the king cared very much about anything other than his own skin.

Kung laughed. "I guess that Admiral Shen will have jogged his memory."

It had been less than a month since the King had been wholly subservient to the Japanese. Now it was to the Chinese. With the Daewongun in comfortable but firm detention in Peking they were firmly in control for now. And for now only – for it was hard to imagine Japanese acceptance of the situation, especially if one of their officers held a location as strategically critical as Socheong.

Speed was essential, they all three agreed, even if Lodge's vessel might not be ready for another five days, maybe longer. But what was required could be managed until before then without the Fu Ching. It was essential to maintain the initiative, to keep Shimazu under pressure.

They pored for almost an hour over practicalities – numbers, transportation, supplies, weapons, command, timing. That part was straightforward – practicalities always were – but more difficult was how responsibilities would be shared, what each was prepared to commit, what each was determined not to risk. Not just for this first step, but beyond. Fred Kung had no hesitation about risking others' lives but Dawlish was unwilling to risk his own ship beyond a certain point. And Lodge seemed to care neither for lives nor for his ship, not as long as he could get her into action and slake his ill-disguised yearning for a fulfilment that peacetime American service had denied him. There were wider understandings also, recognition that what was now envisaged was a first step only, that cooperation must have its rewards, that there would be no formal agreement, no signed document. And all the while Dawlish recognised that, underneath the show of easy cooperation, both Kung and Lodge were evaluating his own trustworthiness and openness, just as he was evaluating theirs. But for now there was a first step agreed against Shimazu, one that minimised risks to Leonidas. Once over this hurdle, once confidence had been justified, more could be hazarded.

It was time then to bring in the waiting Chinese officers. At once Kung was no longer the Americanised immigrant made good but a grim, blank-faced Imperial official who accepted bows and compliments with barely concealed impatience. Dawlish watched silently as Lodge quietly translated for him the convoluted evasions of Kung's demands, admiring his polite but firm demolitions of excuses and reluctance. Once, frighteningly, Kung displayed controlled fury that ended as quickly as it had erupted but which left its victim – the equivalent of a colonel, Lodge whispered – cringing as he stammered apologies and compliance. It was time that all these officers pressed for, and what they called time was obviously delay, delay in which changing circumstances might remove the need for action, might save them the risk of blame for failure. And it was time that Fred Kung would not allow them. Even as they spoke Dawlish doubted yet again how far such officers might ever be relied upon, whether fear of punishment would alone be enough for their troops to follow them, whether they could ever match the lethal proficiency of Shimazu and Takenaka and their like.

The meeting broke up in a display of fawning courtesies that Kung curtly dismissed. The Chinese officers departed, their orders unambiguous, their resentment scarcely concealed by studied impassivity. Then Captain Holles was ushered in. The Ningpo's master presented a combination of indignation – for he had been kept waiting over an hour and he clearly resented it – and of uncertainty, for the summons had not mentioned why he was needed. A strong odour of alcohol indicated that he had found a way of passing time as his ship swung idly, though not unprofitably, at anchor He must have guessed that something was afoot, for McIver of the Caledonian and Oriental, and Wheeler the tug skipper, had been his drinking companions in recent days. He probably knew that Dawlish had summoned both men to the *Leonidas* two hours before, but not what had been agreed. Their resentment about their flight from Socheong was of a depth and vehemence that had secured easy cooperation.

Fred Kung, again American, did not ask Holles to sit. "Your ship's needed again, Captain," he said. "I guess you'll be ready for sea by tomorrow night."

Holles bridled. "There's a pirate at sea, Mister. Ye're aware of that, are ye? And mine's a British ship, ye can remember that, can't ye?" He looked appealingly towards Dawlish. "I'm right, Captain, aren't I?"

Dawlish shook his head. "I think I told you before that I had little sympathy," he said. "You entered voluntarily into a charter with the Chinese Imperial Government, did you not?"

"And you hold twenty percent ownership of your vessel," Kung's voice was quiet, emotionless, "and you signed on behalf of your partners. The charter's still valid. Your acceptance of demurrage confirms that."

"I, I…" Holles spluttered then went silent, obviously unsure what he could say.

Kung fished a small notebook from an inside pocket with his good hand. He flipped it open and leafed to what Dawlish saw was a blank page, though it was out of Holles's line of sight. He made as if to read.

"There's also the small matter of the private understandings you reached with Imperial officers, Hu Han-min and Wang Ching-wei and He Yingqin when the charter was drawn up."

"But you, Mister Kung, you yerself…" Holles began, then went silent as Kung shook his head slowly.

"Two officers who will be anxious to make amends for corrupt dealings that bring shame to Imperial service, Captain Holles. They'll wish to reveal all details of their agreements with you." Kung paused – it seemed an eternity as the blood drained from Holles's face – and then said "I've no doubt your fellow owners will also be glad to learn about these agreements."

Another silence, then Dawlish said "I don't think it need come to that. I'm confident that the Ningpo will be ready to by tomorrow night."

As Holles nodded mute assent Dawlish hoped the Chinese troops would also be.

*

Leonidas sailed just before sunset, partly cleared for action and her crew on alert, weapons and ready-use lockers checked, hasty checks in the boiler and engine rooms complete, bunkers still two-thirds full. If all went well they would be soon be full again.

She left behind upwards of a dozen men under the supervision of her carpenter – a title that was increasingly a misnomer throughout the navy since the skills and responsibilities the position involved were nowadays for the integrity of iron and steel ships. The party had crossed to Lodge's damaged *Fu Ching*, taking with them tools, steel plating, bolts, caulking, even a portable forge. And, most important of all, the group included *Leonidas's* only qualified diver, together with the air pump, hoses and assistants to support him. His head encased in a copper helmet, his body clothed in a cumbersome suit of rubberised fabric, Able Seaman Jameson would be lowered into the flooded compartment. Working by touch alone in the murk he must locate and clear debris to give access to the breach in the hull plating. Dawlish shuddered inwardly at the thought of what this man must do, pushing from his own mind the recollection of himself once smothering in the darkness of a tiny iron chamber, a nightmare that still haunted his sleep. Jameson was perhaps a better man than his captain. As *Leonidas* slipped towards the open sea the disc of Dawlish's telescope showed, in the midst of the cluster of other bodies on the *Fu Ching's* foredeck, two seamen slowly and steadily rotating the air pump's handles. Jameson was already at work and the night's oncoming darkness would be no hindrance to him in the flooded compartment's blackness.

The sea was oily calm as the sun died spectacularly on a red horizon. *Leonidas* was at half revolutions, her speed and course set so as not to come in sight of Socheong before daybreak. Word of the destination had been passed around the crew. The memory of what had previously transpired off the island – most of all memory of the torpedo boat that had attacked and survived, and which must still lurk there with her sister – would ensure maximum alertness.

Dawlish made a quick round of inspection before going to his own quarters. He made a point of climbing to the now-repaired Gatling position on the foremast. He spun the weapon's barrels, checked the feed hopper, gave a curt nod of approval to the late Andrew Sturt's successor – moved there from the mizzen position – and to the dead man's loader. Purdon's beloved six-inchers also proved to be faultless. Dawlish had expected no slackness and found none. His round was intended to convey his own trust and confidence to his crew rather than check equipment he already knew to be well maintained. He passed to the engine room – pistons hissing, the atmosphere redolent of heat and oil, Latham's men so obviously proud of their craft – and on to the stokehold. It was here the greatest heroism would be demanded when action came, the begrimed trimmers toiling like miners to shift coal from the remotest bunkers, staggering with baskets and wheel barrows with each roll of the ship, and the blistered stokers shovelling fuel into the ravenous furnaces. All there were surrounded by pipes that would scald them to an agonising death if ruptured, all blind to what was happening on deck, fearful but ignorant of any threats to their lives.

Tonight Dawlish would allow himself six hours sleep. But first he spread out a chart on the table in his saloon, the one chart he had of the Korean coast, incomplete and superficial as it was. A single Royal Navy vessel had made a survey almost a decade before. Details had been added by correlation with later – and equally incomplete – French and American charts, but the hazards of venturing close inshore were still largely unidentified. And this was nowhere more so than on the broken, deeply indented mainland coast east and north-east of Socheong where shallow water extended out for several miles offshore. Shallow it might be, yet deep enough to hide hidden rocks. They could be an even deadlier menace than Shimazu's guns and torpedoes. Leadsmen alone might be no protection. He stared at the chart, his eyes riveted to one spot on the coast, endlessly debating with himself how near he might dare approach. He found himself haunted by an almost palpable fear of metal grinding against stone, of a shudder running through his ship, of a sudden check to her momentum, of masts collapsing forward, of stays and shrouds snapping, of an inrush of water. He thought briefly of summoning Takenaka, for he recognised him as one of the finest navigators he had ever encountered, but then decided not to. The decision could only be his alone.

His steward woke him at first light, as instructed, with hot coffee. Purdon had the watch when he came on the bridge and Socheong was no more than the slightest hummock on the northern horizon. The sky was clear and it would be another day of high temperature and humidity, of merciless sun beating down on a waveless sea. The conditions would be ideal, the visibility high and little likelihood of more than a slight haze. *Leonidas's* course was still directly towards the island but she would approach no nearer than five miles. At that distance, with furnaces deliberately poorly managed to produce maximum smoke, the cruiser would commence a series of slow sweeps eastwards and westwards, parallel to the southern coast. Shimazu must see her, must know that she lay there with her ten six-inchers to the six now mounted on the *Kirishima*. Landing weapons to protect the island still left her a menace to unprotected shipping but the Japanese ship would now be at a massive, and possibly fatal, disadvantage in any contest with *Leonidas*. Shimazu's game must be a waiting one, hoping for endorsement from his homeland, and he could not afford to risk his trump card, the *Kirishima*, in the meantime. And the torpedo boats that might be so deadly in darkness or inshore would be shattered by *Leonidas* if they approached across open sea in daylight.

The morning wore on, the increased level of preparedness little more than a mild complication for the cruiser's normal routine. The benefit of relentless exercising on the voyage from Britain was now confirmed as the gun drills demonstrated a level of efficiency that few ships in the navy could match. Breech-loading called for new skills, longer range required sharper perceptions of speed and relative motions. The complexity of interrupted screws and hand-wheels and Vavasseur slides demanded a new breed of gunner. They must be literate and more technically competent than men, some still serving, who had grown up with handspikes and wedges and breech ropes, with tasks that had been all but unchanged for two centuries. Cutlass drill took up an hour, Dawlish himself participating, performing the cuts and parries that had been second nature to him for over twenty years, the forward stamps and vicious chops and deadly thrusts that had served him as well as they had thousands before him. On another section of deck Ross's marines, without discharging their weapons, went through their own drills, the two-rank volley-firing sequence of such clockwork precision that made their single-shot Martini-Henrys so deadly. And afterwards there was bayonet drill, individual pairs facing each other in elegant ballets that Dawlish always found somehow more lethal, more frightening, than the cutlasses' more brutal attack.

Dawlish sent for Takenaka. "Your drawing of the island, Lieutenant. It's first class."

A bob of the head combined pleasure with pride. "I am pleased, sir."

"I need more detail. But don't risk that copy. Make an outline of it, then get aloft. Fill in all you can, hills, those headlands, the batteries' arcs of fire."

"And elevations? They can only be estimates, sir."

"Your best effort, Lieutenant, just your best effort." Dawlish knew that would mean excellence.

Leonidas left a long smudge of smoke along what would have been Shimazu's horizon, steaming slowly west, then east, then west again, far outside the range of his shore battery, a series of slow sweeps that extended through the long, hot morning and afternoon. Dawlish climbed twice to the foretop. Takenaka was perched there with a drawing board on his knees, a masterpiece of precision slowly emerging from his observations and estimates. Dawlish took a telescope from one of the two lookouts also there and gazed into the Socheong anchorage. There, flanked by the two cannon-crowned headlands, the *Kirishima* lay at anchor, the slightest wisp from her funnel indicating that her boilers were at least at harbour pressure. There was no sign of the two torpedo boats, neither there nor on the open water that intervened. The afternoon passed, only the slight breeze from the ship's forward motion contesting the draining heat that sapped men's energy.

Dawlish gathered his officers in his quarters just before sundown. Only now did he outline what was intended in the coming days, what would be required of each of them and of *Leonidas*. There could be no disputing, no questioning, of the overall thrust of what must happen – for the word of a captain must be absolute – but Dawlish demanded refinement within these bounds, identification of risks that might have been underestimated, recommendations for improved allocation and deployment of men and matériel.

The reactions were not unexpected. Edgerton was clearly focussed on risks, though he made few enough suggestions for countering them. Relieved that the responsibility for any failure would not rest with him, he had little enough to add. His response on the day would be competent, stolid and reliable, but no more than that. It was on the younger officers, on Purdon, on O'Rourke, on Ross, on Leigh, on Hamilton, all enthusiastic, that the burden would fall heaviest. Each of them was ambitious in a way that did not yet recognise how much ambition might demand of them or whether the price would be worth paying. More experience, hard-bought experience, might have prevented some of their suggestions but others were of definite value and Dawlish saw flushes of pleasure as he accepted them.

Only Takenaka looked uncomfortable, the stiffness of his posture rather than any hint of emotion on his immobile face indicating discomfort. For the first minutes Dawlish feared that he had pushed his navigating officer's loyalty too far, that the reality of facing his countrymen as enemies had stressed his conscience and his nerves beyond some limit. But as the discussion went on, as Dawlish sought and listened to the suggestions of his subordinates, he realised that it was the process itself that disturbed the Japanese, that any slight criticism of the plan proposed constituted disrespect. Reluctant to pain him further, Dawlish only asked him once for comment, and passed on when assured that his plans needed no embellishment.

Night fell. Lights were doused and lookouts doubled. Still the sequence of slow sweeps continued. The furnaces were now being nursed to allow fast increase in power when needed and the boilers were holding pressure just below relief. There was no moon and only faint rays from the thick carpet of stars above relieved the blackness. Gatling positions were manned in the fore and mizzen tops and higher still lookouts peered out into the soft gloom. Socheong was invisible to the north as *Leonidas* steamed slowly back and forth on her vigil, the wave at her bows scarcely breaking white, her wake little more than a ripple.

The cold beam of a searchlight stabbed out from the island. It swung in a slow arc across the waters closer inshore, then lifted, sweeping remorselessly from west to east to find *Leonidas* but its power was insufficient to illuminate her at this range.

"It's mounted high, sir," Leigh said. He was on the bridge with Dawlish and he too must fear the slow creep of a torpedo boat – or maybe of two – through the darkness. "It's on one of the headlands. God knows how they're powering it."

It probably had not been difficult, Dawlish thought. There would have been labour enough available to drag up a small boiler and steam engine removed from a dockside crane and a dynamo from the ship. There would have been skill aplenty in the *Kirishima's* engineering staff to mate one to the other.

Dawlish wondered if it was a diversion, a distraction to draw *Leonidas's* attention while the torpedo boats stalked her. "Maximum revolutions," he ordered and word was immediately passing down the voice pipes to set stokers flinging coal into the furnaces and throttles opening to feed more steam into the engines' cylinders. As the vessel accelerated he ordered the helm over and she creamed over to starboard, then another change of course, and another, weaving so as to frustrate the aim of any hunter. Yelled commands from the deck were telling the lookouts aloft to stare out into the darkness rather than towards the light.

As abruptly as it had sprung into life the light on Socheong died. It left *Leonidas* to resume her monotonous creep in darkness that seemed more absolute than before. An hour passed before it burst into life again, spurring *Leonidas* into further violent manoeuvres to protect herself against a threat that never materialised. She brought her own arc-lights into play, three times sweeping the calm expanse to search for imaginary torpedo boat presences identified by nervous lookouts.

The long night passed in tense alertness, in awareness that those deadly craft might still be creeping stealthily through the darkness. And yet for all the tension, for all the sense of threat, Dawlish was pleased. He knew that Shimazu was aware that *Leonidas* was on station, was ready to fight, had the greater firepower in open water.

That was enough for now. At dawn he went below and slept.

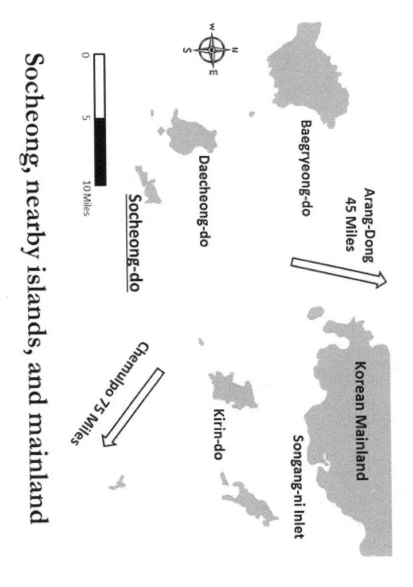

Socheong, nearby islands, and mainland

Baegryeong-do

Daecheong-do

Socheong-do

Arang-Dong
45 Miles

Korean Mainland

Songang-ni Inlet

Kirin-do

Chemulpo 75 Miles

N
W E
S

0 5 10 Miles

21

The second day of blockade was no different from the first, the same slow sweeps along the Socheong coast, closer inshore than during the night but still far out of reach of Shimazu's landed guns, the same long streak of smoke to emphasise *Leonidas's* presence. Another day of routine, of holystoning, of polishing and painting, of oiling bearings and trimming bunkers, of cutlass and bayonet drill, of tedium mixed with apprehension. The officers now knew of the plan that would be implemented during darkness. The men, who as yet did not, sensed that some action was imminent. Through the long day the waters stretching towards the island remained empty, and the *Kirishima* remained immobile in her anchorage.

In the first hours of darkness on the second night the same routine was adopted as before, lights doused, the furnaces efficiently stoked to minimise smoke, only the slightest glow above the funnels, the occasional stabs with the searchlight, the answering icy sweeps from the island. Again there were the false alarms – better these than complacent ignoring of the slightest hint of enemy presence – and again the sudden evasive manoeuvres. Already refreshed by daytime sleep, Dawlish snatched another two hours while the ship slid slowly back and forth on her monotonous patrol.

He was awoken as directed just as the four bells of the middle watch sounded, two hours after midnight. He came to the bridge. Darkness was almost total. Edgerton had the watch, Takenaka by his side.

"Any sign of our friends?"

None. Still no sign of those dreaded torpedo boats. Only another sweep of Shimazu's searchlight but it had died quickly and had not been repeated. The operators ashore might just be getting complacent.

"All's ready, Gentlemen?" he asked. The question was rhetorical. He knew that every man was now at his station. "Then let's proceed as planned." He walked to the bridge wing and lit a cigar as orders were passed quietly by messenger and voice pipe and as *Leonidas* swung around from her westerly heading, a full sixteen points. Engines throbbing slowly, screws at quarter revolutions to avoid betrayal by bow wave, the cruiser crept eastwards towards the Korean coast. With luck her absence from her station would not be noted before dawn.

Boats were swung out in almost total silence and readied for dropping. *Leonidas* did not carry a launch but the cutters and Dawlish's own gig could carry fifty men comfortably between them in addition to their pulling crews. The tiny open pinnace scarcely deserved the name, but her two-cylinder steam engine made her as useful as a tug. Swung outboard, her boiler had been fired up and was being kept replenished to maintain pressure. One cutter carried a rocket-tube in her bows, capable of hurling a powerful 24-pound Hales projectile, though not with any great accuracy. It was unlikely to be needed, and the men who would constitute the landing party might prove equally superfluous. Dawlish had no intention of sending them ashore if it could possibly be avoided. They would be present as a reserve, as an assurance, not used in action unless there was no alternative. But the men did not know this and the prospect of landing had sent a thrill of excitement and apprehension through the vessel. The expectation of close action, the possibility of face-to-face combat, so different from the more impersonal demands of ship-to-ship engagement, must mean for many, perhaps all, the unspoken, unadmitted fear of showing fear.

First light found the islet of Kirin-do five miles on the port beam. Directly ahead, still shadowed by the hills beyond, lay the long bay with its jagged coastline and treacherous shallows that led towards the day's intended target at Songang-ni. But it was not eastwards that Dawlish searched through his glass but south, towards Chemulpo. And the horizon there was empty, without even the faintest black wisp to confirm the arrival he had hoped for. It was as he had feared. The *Ningpo* had not been ready – Captain Holles could probably have found reasons enough to ensure that – or the Chinese officers had proved masters of delay despite all Fred Kung's threats. It didn't matter what the reason might be. The rendezvous had not been met.

Leonidas loitered off Kirin-do for another hour, until the sun was fully up and the dank, heavy heat building again. Still the southern horizon was unbroken by sight of sail or smoke and there was nothing for it but to turn west again, now at maximum revolutions, to regain the position south of Socheong. Dawlish did not leave the bridge. He masked his disappointment and drank his coffee and smoked his cigar in silence, ignoring the questioning glances shot towards him by Edgerton and the others there. The possibility that Shimazu had detected *Leonidas's* absence, that he had slipped away with the *Kirishima* to surprise unsuspecting shipping along the Chinese coast, was a slight one. Yet such an escape was however more likely with every hour until the slow sweeps parallel to Socheong's coast could resume. But the greater worry was that a day had been wasted – and perhaps there might be more days like this unless Kung and Lodge could get the reluctant Chinese forces into motion. Delay meant that Shimazu's allies in Japan had yet more time to gain the Emperor's support, time even to get reinforcements on the way.

On station south of Socheong, furnaces again stoked to guarantee maximum visibility by a smoky trail, the slow monotonous patrol recommenced. *Kirishima* still swung at anchor, the intervening sea was still empty. Anti-climax dispirited all.

And so the long day passed.

*

The night passed as before, searchlights probing from ship and from shore, apprehension and alarms about torpedo boat attacks that never materialised, unspoken nervous tension. The impression of growing complacency on the island was reinforced, the sweeps of icy light almost perfunctory. It seemed that on Socheong *Leonidas* was expected to be offshore, night or day, and that her presence was not feared. It was faintly reassuring that even Shimazu's ruthless efficiency had its weakness.

Dawlish again made a point of going to his quarters, though the sleep that came was intermittent and comfortless, and he was woken once more at the fourth bell of the middle watch. He went to the bridge, sensed the tenseness there, and ordered the turn directly towards the mainland. He prayed inwardly that the rendezvous would be met this time, that the troop-laden *Ningpo* would make her appearance. Astern, Socheong's searchlight swept briefly, then died.

Leonidas steamed silently and darkly eastwards, boats swung out, gun-crews alert, seamen told off for landing and lining up for issue of cutlass or axe, the marines oiling rifles already oiled a dozen times, checking ammunition and fingering bayonets. Dawlish passed among them, his occasional inspection of a weapon allowing a simple word of approval. It was above all important that the men should see him, should feel his confidence in them no less than in himself. He had no belief in inspirational speeches – the men saw through them too easily and needed no reminding of what they owed themselves, their comrades and their ship. Example was the greatest source of inspiration. The memory of the mud before the Taku forts flashed in his mind, the recollection too of his terror, of that unnamed seaman who had heartened him, of the slaughter and the failure. He forced the demoralising remembrance away. What was now planned would be little more than a demonstration and had nothing in common with the Takus. And there would be no mud.

Kirin-do was again to the north as the sky lightened, a lower island than Socheong but its coasts no less rocky. Beyond it lay the long stretch that *Leonidas* must advance across northwards so cautiously, for the available chart told almost nothing of water depth. The sun rose above the hills and now huts could be discerned on the headland that shielded the interior of the curved inlet at Songang-ni from view.

"Nothing yet, sir." Takenaka handed the telescope back to Dawlish. "There's still time, sir. We cannot expect absolute promptness." *Not from the Chinese*, Dawlish knew he meant but hesitated to say. The concern in the navigating officer's tone seemed not just for the operation in hand, but also for Dawlish's frustrated expectation. It seemed as touchingly close to an expression of personal regard as Takenaka might permit himself.

Two hours of cruising slowly south of Kirin-do, and still no sign of the longed-for *Ningpo*. Then a third hour, one more than he had intended, and there would be no fourth, for it would be bright then and necessary to turn, dishearteningly, for Socheong. The fear of Shimazu having realised *Leonidas's* absence, and of *Kirishima* taking advantage of it to slip out to sea, was stronger than on the previous day. To disguise that fear Dawlish went to his quarters in a deliberate show of confident nonchalance – he had papers to attend to, he said – but the tension he left behind on the bridge was tangible. The papers remained unattended to, for he found it impossible to concentrate on worthy administration at this moment. He forced himself not to look southwards through the open scuttles for some trace of smoke.

The word came at last. That the news was good was told even before he spoke by the expression, part relief, part trepidation, on the face of the seaman who brought Mr. Edgerton's compliments and a request to come to the bridge. Dawlish snapped his watch shut as he hurried on deck. Ten minutes remained before he would have ordered the return to Socheong.

There at last was smoke on the southern horizon, not one source but two, the larger by far than the other, the vessels still hull down. For long minutes Dawlish nursed the silent hope that Lodge – and *Leonidas's* carpenter and diver – had done the impossible in the time available and had readied the *Fu Ching* to accompany the laden transport *Ningpo*. But as first the masts and then the hulls raised themselves above the sea's rim it became obvious that the second smudge was from the Caledonian and Oriental tug in which her skipper Wheeler had fled from Socheong with McIver and the unexpectedly heroic clerk Albert Perkins. A cluster of sampans bobbed in her wake at the end of a towline. The *Ningpo's* sides were streaked with excrement and vomit and her decks were crowded with men, the banners fluttering above them confirming that they were troops. Captain Holles and the Chinese officers had conformed with Fred Kung's directives, even if they were a full day late.

"Muster the landing parties and take us a half cable alongside." Dawlish nodded towards the *Ningpo*.

At Edgertons's direction the quartermaster spun the wheel over and *Leonidas* leaned out of the turn. The gun-crews were standing by their weapons, the marines and bluejackets detailed to land were assembling in silence by their allocated boats. Amid the shuffling of feet and the odd bark of command or reproof the sense of apprehension must be unbearable. There was no doubt among them now that action of some sort was imminent.

Leonidas drew parallel to the labouring transport and at Dawlish's order moved closer still. Captain Holles stood on the bridge wing with a speaking trumpet and Fred Kung was by his side, his crippled arm thrust into his tunic in Napoleonic style, a blue turban on his head similar to those of his Uighur guards. Two of them were close behind him on the bridge and Dawlish could see two more at the base of each of the ladders leading to it. Kung was taking no chances.

In the exchange shouted through speaking trumpets Kung indicated that Lodge's *Fu Ching* was still under repair. The Chinese troops on the *Ningpo* were ready to land. Even from this distance they gave little confidence. They shuffled in an amorphous mass on the decks, without sign of organisation. Their mix of traditional uniform and medieval weaponry and scattering of modern rifles was in stark contrast to the smartness of those Japanese-trained troops who had died so hard at the palace. But little was being asked of them and the greatest hazard they might face could be transfer to the sampans that trailed astern of the accompanying tug.

"We're glad to let the Royal Navy lead us safely!" As *Leonidas* pulled away the sarcasm in Holles's parting shout was unmistakable. "It's yer responsibility, Captain! I'm not risking this ship, not for you and not for a bunch of Chinks!"

Leonidas drew level to the tug and dropped a boat. It pulled across and Sub-Lieutenant Leigh boarded with a seaman, a signaller, and an engine-room artificer. Wheeler, the tug's skipper, was carried back to the cruiser and brought directly to the bridge.

Dawlish welcomed him, introduced his officers, made a show of formality and respect that obviously pleased Wheeler. "She'll be in good hands, Captain Dawlish, I can see that," he said, nodding towards his little craft. "That young man you sent looks very well able, very able. And I'm proud to be here, Captain, proud to render assistance, proud to tread the bridge of a Queen's ship."

"You know these waters well, Mr. Wheeler," Dawlish said.

"None better, sir! None better!"

"You have our fullest confidence, Mr. Wheeler. Take us to Songang-ni. We know what's to be done there and it's time to do it."

*

They moved slowly, north-eastwards, at quarter revolutions, through the four-mile wide channel that lay between Kirin-do and a similar island to its east. *Leonidas* led, two leadsmen in the bows searching for bottom but not yet finding it, caution essential as she nudged into uncharted waters. Invaluable as Wheeler's familiarity with this approach might be, the fact remained that though he had followed it a hundred times or more, it had been in a shallow-draught vessel towing only slightly deeper barges. The mainland was still several miles ahead but darker patches in the water's blue betrayed rocks close to the surface. As she threaded slowly between them *Leonidas* still had six to eight fathoms beneath her keel, but at any moment that might change.

The *Ningpo* followed two cables astern and the tug chugged in her wake. The land ahead was a succession of hills, some wooded, many showing signs of cultivation. Long strips of beach fringed the coast, most with cliffs rising behind.

"There's Songang-ni." Wheeler pointed to the headland to the north that Dawlish had viewed the previous day. It lay on the eastern side of an inlet about five-hundred yards wide. "You won't see the jetty or the mine until you're well inside. They're tucked in behind that hill, the village, the barracks, the workers' compound."

Dawlish could visualise the interior it in his mind's eye, with no need to look at the sketch map that Takenaka had so carefully drawn up on the basis of Wheeler's description. He looked again towards the headland. Even a single six-inch Krupp installed by Shimazu on those heights could have *Leonidas* in range long before she could fire back. There had been no such weapon landed when Wheeler had last been here, but there had been time enough since...

The silence was broken only by the muffled beat of the engines, by the lap of water sliding alongside and by the leadsmen's calls confirming that Wheeler's directions were keeping *Leonidas* in sufficiently deep water. She was crawling due north now, directly for the inlet's entrance, and like the other officers on the bridge Dawlish was searching the headland with his glasses. Purdon had ranged the five six-inchers on the starboard flank on the headland, elevation close to maximum, and their barrels arced slowly to keep it in their sights as the vessel moved forward. The Gatling crews in the tops were no less alert – the possibility that a torpedo-boat might speed from cover could not be ignored. In the landing parties waiting on deck by their boats each eye was riveted on the shore. O'Rourke would be in one cutter and in overall command, Ross in the other with the marines.

And still there was no sign of opposition...

The headland slipped past – harmless, no gun landed there from the *Kirishima* – and as it did the inlet curved away to starboard, north-eastwards, and narrowing to its end not above a mile distant. From the bridge a river estuary could be seen entering from the north but a long, low spit of sand blocked its direct access. The land beyond was low, patched with paddy-fields. So too was the terrain to the east, beyond the head of the inlet, where beaches extended along the shoreline. The water here could only be shallow, very shallow.

But for Dawlish *Leonidas* was his first concern. The leadsmen were still calling five fathoms under the keel. Wheeler was convinced that another quarter-mile advance could still be made in safety. There was however no sense in risking the ship. Dawlish's orders were passed to the engine room, the quartermaster instructed. With her engines at dead slow the cruiser would loiter here, just inside the entrance, circling slowly but not venturing further.

"Signal the *Ningpo* to heave to." The flags ran up the halliards as Dawlish swept his binoculars along the inlet's eastern inner shore. "Give Mr. Wheeler a glass – and you, Mr. Wheeler, tell us what we see."

"There's the jetty, sir." It was a twin of that at the Socheong anchorage, its surface carried out from a narrow beach for some hundred yards on wooden piles, black coal-mounds on the shore behind. "No sign of life that I can see, not that they've much call for it without my tug."

Several flat-top barges were moored there, some heaped with coal, and there was no wisp of steam rising from the crane near the end. Figures were moving there, four only, one running, and Dawlish fancied that he glimpsed a blue cotton uniform and peaked cap such as the Satsuman guards at Socheong had worn. Wheeler had seen them too.

"How many there normally?" Dawlish asked.

"A hundred and twenty, maybe a hundred and fifty. I didn't go ashore much – I slept at Socheong. But I'm surprised there are any still here. Probably just a few to guard the place. Not that they need to. The Koreans are so scared of them that they'd steal nothing even if there were no guards about."

It made sense, Dawlish thought. Shimazu must need every man to defend his base and three rapid trips by his torpedo boats could easily have transferred a hundred and fifty men back to Socheong.

On a gentle slope to the right of the coal heaps thatched roofs rose above the walls of a compound similar to that which accommodated the workers at Socheong. Here too there seemed to be only a single gate. It was closed.

"And you see them rails, sir?" Wheeler indicated two parallel strips which were catching the sun's reflection and running southwards from the jetty. "At their other end, about a quarter of a mile away? That's the mine."

There was no mistaking it. Above the cluster of corrugated iron sheds and further heaps of coal rose the dark lattice, topped by a spoked wheel, now stationary, of the colliery's winding gear. Large numbers of thatched huts were scattered around it, some in clusters, some individual. By the sheds stood what looked like a long wooden

225

house, a smaller counterpart to the Caledonian and Oriental's office on Socheong. Here too no sign of life and, better still, no sign of landed weapons.

Leonidas's own boats had been dropped, and boarded by bluejackets and marines, long before the *Ningpo* managed to get the first sampan loaded. Leigh had brought the tug alongside the transport, ranging the string of sampans along its side, and troops were being lowered into them on ropes. There was little short of chaos on the decks, men shuffling and pushing, tripping over pikes and muskets, banners dropping, rising again, weapons falling into the water as they were passed down. Identifiable by their uniforms, Chinese officers were gesticulating wildly as they urged the men over the side, only too conscious that they were close to losing control. Dawlish shifted his disc of vision towards the bridge, saw a smirk of satisfaction as Holles's face was turned to him and sensed something of Fred Kung's fury as he spoke rapidly to two of his Uighurs and sent them aft to impose order there.

Her pulling boats, all laden, hovered close to *Leonidas*. Dawlish glanced down at the smart little steam pinnace now moored alongside, heat shimmering above her polished brass funnel and carrying only her own three-man crew. He considered for a moment sending her across again, this time to assist Leigh with the sampans, but decided against it. The pinnace would accompany *Leonidas's* boats, ready to tow them in case of necessity. And Leigh was being given the sort of opportunity to demonstrate his ability that every young officer dreamed of. Getting those troop-laden sampans to the shore and jetty was a task he was well capable of.

It took over an hour, one of concealed frustration for Dawlish, before the tug drew away from the *Ningpo's* side, a dozen overladen sampans strung out on towlines from her stern. A forest of pikes rose from two and banners fluttered above them all. The troops inside them, some hundred and fifty in all, crouched silently, their features blank and impassive, and Dawlish detected something of the same resignation that he had seen on the faces of Paraguayan conscripts packed on to barges on a far-off river. Like them, the Chinese soldiers knew that they were valued less than beasts of burden, that their destiny was to endure without hope, to be expended without conscience.

The tug strained past *Leonidas* at a cable's separation. From her tiny bridge Leigh saluted and Dawlish and his officers returned it. The string of sampans drew slowly away, curving as it turned eastwards up the inlet. Even at this pace the jetty would be reached within ten minutes. And all still quiet.

"Our boats, Captain?" It was Edgerton. "Should they follow, sir?"

Dawlish nodded. "Let them follow at two cables length, then stand off while the Chinese go ashore. Leigh should have his day."

Like every young officer, he deserved the chance to distinguish himself.

22

The tug strained slowly up the centre of the inlet, Leigh on her tiny bridge, the string of sampans snaking in her wake. There was dead silence in the midday's humid heat, no sound from the packed troops, none either on *Leonidas's* bridge, from where a half-dozen telescopes scanned the shoreline for signs of movement. There was no further sign of life ashore, not on the jetty, where a few figures had briefly appeared earlier, nor among the coal heaps, nor near the sheds and the pit's winding gear. The stillness had an ominous quality about it, the apparent absence of life somehow threatening, portentous, and it worried Dawlish. And what was happening out on the smooth stretch of water was so slow, so agonisingly slow. The packed sampans looked infinitely vulnerable and so too did *Leonidas's* little less-heavily laden boats which were stroking steadily behind them, the steam pinnace circling, as instructed, to their rear. If Shimazu had landed even a three or six-pounder...

"Nothing to the west, Commander," Dawlish said to Edgerton. "We can be thankful for that."

"A man called Conroy is on the mizzen." Edgerton sensed Dawlish's need to break the tension. "He's said to have the sharpest eyes on board and he's been warned not as much as to blink eastwards." That lookout westwards was vital. It was possible that *Leonidas's* absence might have been detected. Shimazu might have taken the *Kirishima* to sea. The possibility that he might head towards this coast could not be ignored.

Purdon was moving between his gun-crews, alternately starboard broadside and bow-chasers, port broadside and stern-chasers, again and yet again, as the cruiser crawled repeatedly through an anti-clockwise racetrack course at the inlet's mouth. The six-inchers' barrels swung slowly over to hold the jetty and mounds of coal in their sights, the crews that served them silent.

The tug was heaving to, a cable's length off the jetty. Now there was confusion. The sampans bunched together when they detached themselves from the tow, reluctance to head for shore obvious. Sounds of shouting, of the repeated beating of a gong, of a musket inadvertently discharged, carried to *Leonidas*. At last the first sampan broke from the knot, banners flapping limply, men in dark blue smocks with yellow ovals front and back crowded within. It crawled slowly towards the end of the wooden pier. A laden ship's boat from the *Ningpo* followed it. Another sampan broke from the huddle, then a third, and finally the whole cluster seemed to disintegrate. All the individual craft were now heading either for the jetty or for the narrow beach to either side.

Still no sign of guards or workers ashore. That was more ominous than any actual show of force.

"What do you think, Mr. Wheeler?" Dawlish gestured shoreward.

"There can't be nobody there, sir," the tug skipper said. "They can't all be gone."

The first sampan reached a ladder at the jetty. Two men climbed it and helped others up, ten, fifteen, before they started to advance slowly, over-cautiously – and therefore dangerously – towards the coal heaps. The *Ningpo's* boat also grappled on to the piling and more troops were clambering up, their movements hampered by their loose clothing and their long pikes. Scarcely half carried muskets, flintlocks no better than ones that might have served at Malplaquet, and only a handful had modern Sniders. The first of the remaining sampans had grounded on the beach to the right and troops were splashing unwillingly into the shallows. The other craft followed in ragged sequence, gongs beating for encouragement, and from them also soldiers waded towards the shoreline. There they hesitated, reluctant to break from the groups they had landed in until the officers moving among them began to organise them in a long, straggling line. There was little impression of urgency, none at all of dash, no indication of intent to push on as quickly as possible to occupy the colliery or to

228

secure the walled compound. The men who had landed at the jetty had come to a halt at its landward end, neither seeking cover nor pressing forward among the black hillocks.

Dawlish felt his heart thumping, his mouth dry, a sense of dread rising in him though he strove not to show it. But his was not the only unease. He could sense the others around him, Edgerton and Takenaka, Wheeler, and the quartermaster and the yeoman and signallers, even Purdon from the deck below, all flashing apprehensive glances towards him, eager for reassurance he could not give.

Edgerton broke the silence. "Should we signal to Lieutenant O'Rourke? Should he remain standing off?"

The question was superfluous, stupid even, for it had been made clear that *Leonidas's* party should not land without a clear order. Dawlish found himself snapping "No!", then instantly regretted the sharpness in his tone. The concerns around him were well justified. "Better hold off for now," he added. There must be more than the single Satsuman guard and the few others first spotted on the jetty. Shimazu must surely have hung back from bringing them all to Socheong, if only to prevent resentful workers wrecking the colliery equipment here. And not just the absence of guards either – what of the workers themselves? Were they gathered, incarcerated even, in that walled compound?

The ragged line of troops along the beach was at last on the move, hesitantly, bulging forward here as the ground was more open, falling back there as some ditch offered minimal, easily-crossed, obstruction. The pikes, carried high, and the waving banners were reminiscent of a schoolbook illustration of Crecy or Agincourt. The first huts were reached – no sign of resistance, or even occupation, there. The line broke and flowed around them, coalescing into irregular knots of men beyond. By now all cohesion had been lost, two groups heading directly for the walled compound, a third, the largest, outflanking it to the right and moving towards the colliery buildings, gongs beating irregularly. The greater part of the troops landed at the jetty had found some excuse to remain huddled there and only a few were advancing between the coal heaps.

It was slow, agonisingly slow. Dawlish knew that if he had landed marines and bluejackets – more admittedly than he had been prepared to commit – they would have gained their objectives by now. Gained them, or be fighting hard for them had there been opposition. But for now there was no opposition, might never indeed be any at all and everything might be occupied within the hour. He glanced towards *Leonidas's* three pulling boats, now stationary, and the steam pinnace hovering just beyond. Even at this distance they seemed to radiate quiet competence and discipline. Only if they were needed would...

A loud chatter broke the silence, shocking in its suddenness, more shocking still when recognised as the unmistakable stammer of a Gatling. Two, three seconds and then it died. Dawlish swung his glass along the line of Chinese troops – all movement had frozen – but as yet he could see no casualties, could not detect where the fire was aimed on. Edgerton was already calling to the maintop and receiving no indication from the gunners and lookouts there of any sighting. Then the unseen Gatling opened again, another three-second chatter, a pause, and then another burst. Now Chinese were falling in the group on the left, closest to the walled compound, though there was no sign of the weapon there – it must be positioned somewhere yet further to the left, within a hut perhaps, and firing obliquely across the line of troops. Within his disc of vision Dawlish saw bodies jerking in that same dreadful convulsion which he seen so often in that ghastly fighting in Paraguay two years before. They fell, three or four in a single burst of gunfire, clothing shredded and blood erupting, and the men to either side turned away in horror and began to run.

It was well done. Seen from almost a mile's distance a terrible efficiency could be discerned, even admired, as the hidden weapon opened again, the aim slightly different, the range lifted to catch the fleeing Chinese troops. Another burst and another, none longer than three seconds lest the breeches jam, a pause, and then yet another. The loader would be feeding rounds into the Broadwell hopper, the gunner counting the seconds slowly as he ground the firing handle slowly, and then another pause as the stack of barrels was loosened from its base, tapped across along a new line of sight, then locked, and the terrible sequence commenced again.

The group advancing on the left towards the compound was breaking, a quarter perhaps already slumped lifeless or trying, in agony, to crawl rearwards, the remainder rushing back towards the shoreline, throwing down their banners and tripping over pikes, discarding weapons, any weapons, in a headlong flight that was led by their officers.

Dawlish sensed the shock around him. Edgerton turned to him, his expression asking mutely for guidance and decision – long peacetime service in the Channel and Mediterranean Fleets was no good preparation for this. But Dawlish knew that there was nothing to be said, not yet at least, for the setback need not be fatal, even without *Leonidas's* support. For the second Chinese group heading for the compound was still moving forward, now at a run. Some officer, more resolute than his fellows, must be driving it on towards the shelter of its walls. Over to the right the larger group that was heading for the colliery had already passed the compound and was still moving towards its objective, banners still waving, but more quickly now. A scattering of huts lay before them, separated from each other by vegetable patches and small ditches, across which the leading men were now leaping. The organisation might be poor, the discipline ill-directed, but there was no doubting the courage of the Chinese troops when given even a modicum of leadership.

"I'm depending on the lookouts, Commander Edgerton." Dawlish did not lower his glasses as he spoke but he guessed already that the enemy Gatling was too well concealed for easy detection.

"And the boats? The landing party?" Edgerton's voice had the slightest quaver. A good executive officer as an administrator, a weak one in a crisis, though this was not one. Not yet.

"Orders unaltered, Commander. Boats to continue standing off." But Dawlish's mind was churning options over. Ross's marines might well be capable of finding and eliminating that Gatling, though with losses, and O'Rourke had four Hales rockets...

There must be an end now to *Leonidas's* racetrack circling. Dawlish felt a temporary relief in ordering for the cruiser to heave to, to admire the precision with which Takenaka's careful juggling of engines and rudder held her almost stationary, to enjoy however briefly the normality of the well-practised manoeuvre. Now the jetty and colliery lay exposed to the six-inch guns of the starboard battery.

The retreating Chinese on the left were now crouched in the shelter of an irrigation ditch. The ground between them and the compound was littered with dead, wounded and discarded banners. It would be foul there, Dawlish knew, as foul as in that ditch before the Taku forts, but its cover would be just as welcome, and the terror would be as great as his own had then been. The Gatling was still ranged on them, but less deadly now, the spurts of earth its intermittent hail threw up before and behind the ditch immobilising rather than killing. And then an interval of silence, a silence dreadful for its promise of death should anybody leave that ditch, a silence as effective as gunfire for pinning them there.

The second group had reached the compound, from which no fire came, no sign of life. They crouched along the base of the high mud wall facing the inlet, sheltered there from the Gatling's line of fire. The single massive wooden gate was closed and no attempt was made to break it down. Two officers seemed to have control. Under their direction the troops were filing rightwards along the wall to join the group yet further right which was now moving between the huts there towards the colliery.

"Captain Dawlish, sir?" Dawlish's attention was called by Purdon on the deck below. "I'll lay the bow-chaser myself. When we have a target that is." There was no disguising his frustration.

"Just stand by, Lieutenant. I'll rely on your best when the time comes." For Dawlish recognised that Purdon too must be remembering the men who had died on the Rio San Joaquin and how only gun power, heavy gun power, had prevented yet greater slaughter. But that had needed targets, and for now there were none.

The hidden Gatling had been silent for almost four minutes but now it stuttered into life again.

"On the jetty, sir! There!"

Edgerton's pointing finger was directed towards the cluster of troops that still had not moved from it. Close packed, a half-dozen were down with the first burst of fire. Then the instant silence, the few seconds before the spitting gun-barrels would grind around again, the survivors dashing for the scant cover offered by the steam crane there and the stationary coal trucks by it. Then fire again, scything down fleeing men, driving others to hurl themselves into the water below. And as before there was no sign of the weapon's location – it could be secreted in any of a score of sheds or huts. There could only be one, Dawlish thought, for the long silent interval before the jetty had come under fire must have meant relocation – otherwise two targets would have been engaged simultaneously. Shimazu had sacrificed only a single Gatling from his ship but it was enough.

Another ripple of gunfire – not a Gatling, for this was irregular but sustained, unmistakable as rifle fire. It was from to the right, where the Chinese advance was now largely lost from sight among the huts there. Other than individual figures scurrying rearwards there was no sight of the troops and Dawlish realised that the initial shock must have driven them also to seek cover, any cover. This was the moment when resolute leadership was essential, when determination to hold was essential at the very least, when advance was perhaps less dangerous than retreat. But it needed fearless officers and the Chinese officers had all seemed more committed to personal enrichment than to risking themselves.

Dawlish glanced towards *Leonidas's* boats. O'Rourke had pulled them back, out of Gatling range. There were fifty men out there ready to land, the worth of the marines proven by the heroism of some of their fellows during the rioting in Seoul, the bluejackets less expert perhaps with rifle and bayonet, but dreadfully effective with their cutlasses in close action. It could be time to commit them…

Edgerton was obviously thinking the same, looking questioningly towards Dawlish but hesitating to give words to the thought. A signaller was positioned on the bridge wing, his semaphore flags held low before him and by him the yeoman was watching the boats through a telescope. A signalman was standing on a thwart in O'Rourke's boat and he too held his semaphore flags ready for use. It would be so easy to pass the order…

The firing on the right was now almost continuous. The riflemen, well trained, could only be Japanese, most certainly the Satsuman guards, stiffened perhaps by a handful of the *Kirishima's* marines. Now they were flailing the Chinese into retreat. At first individual soldiers, then twos and threes, were scurrying back from the huts, now seen in the vegetable patches between, now lost behind cover. There seemed at first to be some order to it, a fighting withdrawal, with a few men, rifle or musket-armed, shooting back and holding ground. But others were in headlong flight, their useless pikes and banners cast aside, and soon the rout was total. The group that had skirted around the compound's walls had now emerged into the open and they too were under fire, their leaders falling, those behind wavering for an instant, then streaming back across open ground towards the beaches. Here the Gatling opened on them again, smashing three or four down with each burst until they, like the group to the left, had gained the sanctuary of an irrigation ditch. There they cowered, too terrified to retreat further.

For the first time the Japanese forces were emerging from the colliery area and darting among the huts and gardens from which they had driven the Chinese. They could only be glimpsed briefly, for they moved from cover to cover, but those who could be seen were dropping calmly to one knee to aim carefully, calmly, and to shoot before rushing forward again. Their blue uniforms and peaked caps identified them as the Oriental and Caledonian's Satsuman guards but even from *Leonidas's* bridge their discipline and skill were obvious. These men had been trained well, and not recently either, as soldiers. Before them the panic-stricken Chinese fled towards the beaches to join the broken remnants already there. They streamed past the walled compound and as they emerged from its shelter the Gatling opened on them also. Behind them the Satsumans were emerging from the hutted area but now they were driving white-clad figures before them.

"Sweet Jesus! They've got women there. Children too!" Edgerton, horrified, was pointing and Dawlish was swinging his glass towards them.

There, in a shambling, tripping, terrified throng, Koreans in shabby white, not just men but women too with exposed breasts and even clutching babies, were being herded forward. The Satsumans were interspersed between them, dropping calmly to loose off aimed shots, then pushing forward again. A Korean – he looked like an old man – fell, and tried to rise, but a rifle butt smashed him down again. A woman rushed back to try to help but was driven forward, screaming, at the point of a bayonet. The ragged line advanced, the guards firing steadily, the Koreans cowed and stumbling, but it lurched to a halt a hundred yards from the ditches where the Chinese remnant sheltered. There was return fire, little and ineffective, from the ditches, but it was the civilians who were going down, blood erupting against their clothing's shabby white. Many were trying to lie down between the kneeling or lying Satsuman marksmen but they were clubbed immediately to their feet again.

Dawlish was in mental agony, even though he kept his silence and held his face as expressionless as Takenaka's. For this was failure, total and undeniable, and he remembered an unarguable maxim learned in youth. *Never reinforce failure.*

But troops were dying in his sight, poor men with no say in the matter whose fate had been determined at least in part by him. He had fifty well-armed and reliable men of his own in boats just off the beaches and they might make a difference...

"God help those poor buggers!" The signalman spoke for all on the bridge before the yeoman beside him snapped "Belay that!"

Dawlish felt the attention of all focussed on him. Edgerton was glancing obliquely, questioningly, towards him. Takenaka's rigid features and fixed gaze told more eloquently of embarrassment than words could ever do. Purdon was looking back from the bow-chaser, the telescope through which he too had seen the horror grasped white-knuckled, pleading silently not to be ordered to fire.

Never reinforce failure...

"O'Rourke's man is signalling," Edgerton said. Dawlish could see for himself, the flags snapping in fast well-practised movements. It was torture enough to witness the slaughter and the hostage taking helplessly from *Leonidas*, a hundred times worse when seen from close inshore.

"Permission requested to use rocket," the yeoman relayed. A pause. "At discretion. Repeat. At discretion".

Discretion or not there would be no way of avoiding injury to those wretched Koreans. The Hales rocket was devastating in effect but difficult to range from a boat with any great precision.

Dawlish shook his head. "Permission denied." The signal flags snapped the reply. Silence on the bridge, silent, agonised expectation.

"Boat coming across." A cry from the maintop. "From the *Ningpo*."

"Let it come alongside." Dawlish saw that other than the rowers the craft only carried Fred Kung. "Bring the gentleman here." He guessed already what he must expect.

The rattle onshore was intermittent but more than enough to keep the Chinese force pinned down. An eternity passed – three, four minutes – and men were dying, now perhaps women and children also. And there was only one choice that could be made.

Never reinforce failure. The lesson of the Taku forts.

His damaged hand made it hard for Kung to ascend the Jacob's ladder lowered for him and a seaman descended to help him up. He was led straight to the bridge. He brushed past Edgerton, who had advanced to greet him, and made straight for Dawlish

"You think you're going to stand here and watch this goddam slaughter?" Fred Kung, the American Fred Kung, showed no hint of oriental reserve and made no attempt to hide his anger. "You're letting them bastards hold the mine? You agreed goddam well that you'd support us!"

Dawlish contained his own rising anger. "Please step this way with me, Mr. Kung". He directed him to the port bridge-wing, out of direct sight of the action ashore. Kung's fury radiated from him like a physical force.

"You're on a Queen's ship and you're on my bridge, Mr. Kung." Dawlish's kept his voice low but spoke slowly, deliberately. "I can have you flung in a cell or I can have you thrown overboard and I've got two hundred men here who'll jump to my order. The process would be undignified. I trust you'll remember that, won't you?"

"I want that mine!" Kung was forcing himself to be calm. "You agreed to help me take the mine, the colliery, everything. I want to hold it before..." He cut off his own words.

"Before what, Mr. Kung?"

Kung ignored the question. "Are you going to send your men ashore? You've guns enough on this ship to clear every one of those goddam Japs before the first of them reach the beach!"

"You've seen the hostages they're holding?" Dawlish found himself chilled by the sheer callousness of the suggestion.

"I want that goddam mine!" Kung had again evaded the question. "I want it today at the latest! It can't wait, not longer!" he forced himself to speak slowly, quietly. "It must be today. You've got to send your men ashore. You owe me your life, Dawlish! You'd be dead back at the palace if I hadn't saved you. I want that mine and it's time for you to pay me back!"

Dawlish sensed something personal about Kung's concern. It had been agreed that action should be at the earliest possible, but no question of this day being the latest acceptable. There was no time to consider that now. He glanced across Kung's shoulder and saw that the officers and men gathered by the wheel and on the further bridge-wing had their backs turned diplomatically. At that moment the yeoman glanced back and Dawlish gestured to him to come across. Kung was trembling now, his anger so palpable that Dawlish wondered if he might be struck by him.

"My compliments to Mr. Edgerton, and tell him that Mr. Kung will be returning to the *Ningpo*," Dawlish told the yeoman. "He's to be escorted to his boat." He turned away and walked to the starboard bridge wing.

Never reinforce failure. But failure to rescue survivors was unacceptable.

"Signal to Mr. Leigh. Take tug inshore to take off the Chinese force." It was going to be difficult, and more men would die before they could reach the beach, but there was no help for that. "And to Mr. O'Rourke. Send in the pinnace only. No landing."

And so the long, slow, bloody evacuation commenced. Dawlish watched it all from *Leonidas's* bridge, impassive and silent but for the occasional order. Within him despair attacked like a gnawing louse which he tried to ignore but could not.

Failure was never palatable.

23

The sun was setting when *Leonidas* finally turned westwards from Songang-ni, the leadsman in her bows calling monotonously until she crept into the safety of deep water. Behind her she left the *Ningpo*, now headed south to Chemulpo with its freight of wounded and defeated. Well over a hundred dead had been left on shore. It had taken courage for the survivors to break from shelter under fire from the Satsuman riflemen crouched between the hostages and to make towards the sampans at the beach, even more courage to wait long enough to drag others on board to fill them. Leigh's tug and *Leonidas's* steam pinnace had darted in again and again to tow them out to safety. Without them not a single man might have escaped and their crews had performed unflinchingly as they came under fire. Leigh's signaller had been killed and another seaman had been wounded – not enough to kill him but enough that he must lose his arm. The second death had been on the pinnace when it survived a raking by Gatling that had somehow missed the boiler. *Leonidas's* other boats had remained impotently in the centre of the inlet, just outside effective range of the Japanese onshore, unable to do more than gather the escaped sampans around them and render what succour they could to the wounded. Prevented from firing back by the shield of Korean hostages, the marines and bluejackets could only helplessly watch the slow butchery at the beach.

The last craft to be towed away was the *Ningpo's* own boat, taking with her the remnants of the men who had landed on the jetty. Towed by the pinnace, she followed the long trail of sampans that Leigh drew slowly back down the inlet, each with its cargo of suffering. *Leonidas's* other boats followed, not a shot fired throughout the action, a Hales rocket unignited in a launching trough, rifles undischarged, bayonets and cutlasses unbloodied, men more demoralised by uselessly watching slaughter from a distance than if they had been launched into action. There was sullenness about them when they again came on board *Leonidas* again, a sense of shame perhaps, their glances towards Dawlish on the bridge conveying something between resentment and reproach as they filed below.

It hurt.

Even though he did not betray it, Dawlish felt wounded by the furtive looks and nudges, by the suspicion that he had lost his nerve at the critical moment, that he had shrunk from action. He sensed it most of all from the marines, from men who had seen him incapable of stopping the crucifixion on the road to Seoul, almost as much perhaps from those who had not been there but who had heard a tale that had lost nothing in the telling. He sensed it too – perhaps imagined it, though he could not be sure – in the manner in which his officers addressed him, in the brief and over-formal phrases in which O'Rourke and Ross reported what they had witnessed. The achievements that had bought him accelerated promotion had been shrouded in secrecy and he was largely known for his earlier service as a junior officer and latterly as an instructor in the torpedo school. He had no generally-known reputation as a commander to draw upon and the suspicion that favouritism alone had won him captaincy of *Leonidas* must still linger. The fear that he might have lost the confidence of his officers and men tormented him but most of all he was oppressed by awareness that he could not discuss the matter with anybody on board.

And yet…

He knew that he had done the right thing, had not reinforced failure, had avoided an even greater bloodbath. Now it was for him alone to carry the weight of his decisions, the weight of distrust too, in silence and without explanation, until trust could be won again. And only action could accomplish that.

It took almost three hours to get the wounded transferred from the sampans to the *Ningpo,* all the more terrible for the mute endurance of suffering that had more about it of acceptance of personal unimportance than of conscious stoicism. Tadley, *Leonidas's* staff surgeon, had done the best he could – and Dawlish suspected that some of the medicine he administered had brought quicker deaths for the worst-injured than nature on its own might have granted – but the numbers were too great for him to achieve much. There would be more deaths, if not before the *Ningpo* reached Chemulpo, then in the days after. Mortification of wounds would see to that.

Leonidas's boats were recovered, the men who had sweltered all day in the open boats were sent to eat and rest, the furnaces stoked for the dash to come. Kung had returned earlier to the *Ningpo* and there had been a cold exchange of notes before the ships parted company. Of one thing Dawlish left Kung in no doubt. Today had seen failure, abject defeat even, but Shimazu's destruction was still the goal.

The *Ningpo's* lights receded as *Leonidas* drew away into the darkness. Her wardroom table had already been cleared and covered by a white sheet, the surgeon's dreadful tools laid at one end, Tadley himself preparing for the amputation of the seaman's shattered arm.

Leonidas ploughed westwards at full revolutions, back to the interrupted blockade.

Towards Socheong.

*

It was another calm night, no moon, the darkness velvet-soft, a phosphorescent wake marking the cruiser's passage at full revolutions. Normal watch-keeping had been resumed but full gun-crews were posted at the bow and stern-chasers and the lookouts above had been doubled. Dawlish passed through the ship in his usual way, a word of approval here, a frown there, but he encountered little of the normal cheerful pride, little more indeed than cautious, formal respect. The worst was the visit to the sick berth. Tadley's operation had gone well and a pathetic canvas-wrapped object had been cast over the side. The seaman was becoming restless in his cot as the effects of ether wore off and in another hour he would wake to weeks of pain and to the reality a lifetime without his right arm.

The sail maker and his crew were still busy, silently, pensively, in a circle of yellow light. The dead signalman's body was already weighted and neatly parcelled, but the second man's was still being washed. His cheeks had already fallen in and it was impossible to believe that he had been a living being only hours before. Dawlish forced himself to look at the exposed wound – it was to the chest - and to confront the consequence of his own decision. He had seen the

239

signaller frequently on the bridge, had known him to be efficient, though he had never exchanged more than a few words with him. But this second man – Arthur Chambers, Able Seaman – had been little more than a name on a register, a face half-remembered from inspections, no charge against him ever, no mark of distinction either, nothing to indicate that he would behave with exemplary courage when getting the sampans off the beach. Now dead, another service to be read, another letter for a grieving family. The sailmaker asked Dawlish if he would lead them in the Lord's Prayer, and he did, then laid a square of cloth on the dead man's face. The burials on the morrow would be no easier.

Dawlish felt oppressed, bowed down in spirit, as he returned to the bridge. *Leonidas's* voyage from Britain to Hong Kong and back had been intended to test her engines and boilers to the limit, to accumulate statistics on coal consumption, to gain insights that would allow design-optimisation of her successors. It was to have been a peacetime cruise with no expectation of action, less still of casualties. But for the odd rupture or broken limb or bout of recurring malaria the ship's company could not have been more fit and healthy.

Until Korea.

Since then the slow drip of casualties, the marines buried so incongruously in the flower bed at the Japanese Embassy, the marine sergeant who had lost his leg, the Gatling gunner swept from the foretop, now these two men, and the seaman whose arm had just been sacrificed. All to such little effect, the only achievement the driving away of the *Kirishima* from the Chinese transports. Because the expectation of a fast return home had been universal until scant weeks before, the shock of the losses had been all the greater. For Dawlish himself as well as for the crew.

It was a relief to discuss the next day's plan with Edgerton and Takenaka. It would be a repeat of the monotonous station-keeping south of Socheong.

"How long more?" Edgerton asked.

"Until Lodge has the *Fu Ching* ready for sea." Dawlish said. And that depended on what *Leonidas's* diver had found in the flooded compartments and whether *Leonidas's* carpenter and his men could effect repairs.

"It could be another week, maybe longer." Edgerton seemed oppressed by the day's setback.

"Then we'll be on station for another week, Mr. Edgerton," Dawlish said.

But it did not just depend on Lodge. It depended on Fred Kung also, and whether he would be prepared to commit Chinese forces again. And after today… It was better not to think of it now. He turned to Takenaka, who was officer of the watch. "I'm going below. I'll sleep a while. Have me woken if you think it necessary."

"We should be off Socheong at least two hours before dawn, sir," Takenaka said.

The scuttles were open but it was still oppressively warm when Dawlish lay down in his cabin, removing only his tunic and boots. The rush of the water outside, the distant pant of the engines, the throbbing of the screws lulled him into shallow sleep.

Only minutes seemed to have passed before his steward was rousing him, lantern in hand. He struggled to his feet and saw a seaman standing at the doorway

"Mr. Takenaka's compliments and he requests your presence on the bridge. Urgent he says."

Dawlish flipped his watch open. Just short of three o'clock. Socheong must be close, but that had been expected. Takenaka's request implied something more. He pulled on his boots and went on deck, now fully awake, apprehension growing. He found the night still dark.

On the bridge Takenaka only said "There, sir," and pointed slightly to starboard of the ship's heading. He handed Dawlish the large night-telescope. "It may be nothing," he added. "But the lookout has seen it too."

It took a full half-minute's searching of the darkness before Dawlish detected the single faint pin-point of reddish light ahead. It was blotted away for an instant, then appeared again. Not a navigation light, just a very slightly flickering glow, again fading, disappearing briefly, then returning.

"You see it, sir?" Takenaka's voice was urgent. "It's been there for ten minutes now, and not getting any closer."

There could be no mistaking what it was. Dawlish glanced aft towards *Leonidas's* funnels. A reddish glow hovered above each and she was making smoke as the stokers below fed the furnaces for maximum speed. Seen from a distance *Leonidas's* own presence would be betrayed by similar glimmering which would be obscured irregularly by her own smoke.

"Where's Socheong?"

"About five miles off the starboard bow, sir." The darkness still hid it.

"You saw the light come from there?"

"Impossible to be sure, sir, but probable."

"Has it got any nearer?"

"No, sir. The light's no brighter, no darker."

The vessel must have turned away, heading eastwards, and its speed was close to, almost identical to, that of *Leonidas*. There could only be one explanation.

The *Kirishima*.

"Extinguish all lights on deck." Dawlish's first reaction. *Leonidas* might not yet have been detected and her smoke might mask her for a little longer. "Summon Commander Edgerton."

The "night quarters" order that flashed through the ship sent men spilling from hammocks towards their allocated stations. It was a drill practiced several times since leaving Britain but now there was a deadly urgency about it, a seriousness tempered by fear, a shocked awareness that this was real, and all in stricter silence than in any exercise. Crews now stood by the broadside six-inchers as well as at the bow and stern weapons and the checking of breeches, of traverse and elevation hand-wheels, of ready-use ammunition had commenced.

"Clear ship? Completely, sir?" The idea of stripping the vessel obviously shocked Edgerton. Drills had never gone that far.

"As much as possible." Dawlish had seen Krupp quick-firers wreck the upperworks of a Russian warship even if they could not destroy its armoured hull. Flying debris killed as effectively as direct shell-fire.

"And the boats?"

"Retain two cutters only. Fill them with water. Drop the others overboard. We can pick them up afterwards." *If there is an afterwards*, Dawlish thought. This measure, more than any other, would leave the crew in no doubt as to his resolution.

A maelstrom of activity. Stanchions, davits, hinged bulwark flaps, anything that marked the fire of Purdon's guns was being stripped away, wooden ladders removed and stacked in the boats dropped overboard, rope ladders fitted in their place, splinter nets rigged transversely across the deck, hoses snaked out, pumps tested, tubs of drinking water lugged by the stewards to the gun positions. Tadley, roused from exhausted sleep, was again setting out his instruments on the wardroom table and his assistants were breaking out wound dressings and distributing them through the ship. But it was in the boiler and engine rooms that the greatest efforts were demanded, gauge needles trembling at the edge of their red danger zones, safety valves close to lifting, blackened trimmers hurrying with laden wheel barrows to the sweat-drenched stokers feeding the furnace maws, artificers cautiously feeling shaft bearings for overheating.

Yet more was needed. Dawlish glanced up towards the foremast's crossed yards, aft towards the gaffs on the main and mizzen. These heavy spars could disable guns and crews if they were to smash down, could be deadlier still for the splinters that they might shatter into. *Leonidas* had crossed half the world without their aid and they were a liability now, a lethal one.

Dawlish turned to Takenaka, whose telescope seemed glued to his eye. "Are we gaining?"

"I think so, sir. But I estimate that she's still upwards of six or eight miles ahead."

The *Kirishima* was still running westwards and even if she had detected the *Leonidas* it made no sense for her to turn to fight, weaker as she now was by the three guns – perhaps even four – landed at Socheong. She had escaped from her anchorage to create chaos among unarmed merchant shipping on the China coast, not to engage a warship. *Kirishima's* best option now was to pile on speed. She was doing it well, maintaining a lead that would take *Leonidas* hours to reduce. But those hours could provide the time for clearing the masts also.

Caught in the open, *Kirishima* would fight at a potentially fatal disadvantage. As *Leonidas* closed from astern she could bring her two sponsoned bow-chasers into play, two to the Japanese's single stern-chaser. And if *Leonidas* could overtake *Kirishima*, and parallel her course, she would match five weapons on her broadside to her adversary's three, diminished as she was by landing the shore batteries. Shimazu had gambled on being undetected when he left the protection of his anchorage, but he was doing so with a fatally-weakened vessel.

It was no time for half-measures, time indeed for *Leonidas* to move in for the kill, to finish this affair for once and for all.

"Mr. Edgerton – all yards and gaffs to be struck down. Cast them overboard."

Ghostly in the faint binnacle-light, Edgerton's features registered shock. "Overboard, sir?"

"Overboard, Commander."

Dawlish had no intention of recovering them even if all went well. *Leonidas* would fight under bare poles, as a pure steam vessel, almost certainly the first time a Royal Navy ship had done so. No captain had yet had a better excuse for such a decision. The drill for striking down had been a common one, essential indeed, when warships depended on sail as their primary means of propulsion. As a midshipman Dawlish had been aloft, at first to learn, later to supervise, as spars and even topmasts had been lowered, then raised and secured again, activities measured in minutes for well-trained crews as agile and fearless as gibbons. He was thankful now that he had put *Leonidas's* crew through the exercise three times on the voyage out, his intention each time to reinforce discipline and smartness rather than with any great view as to utility.

It went well, fast for such a skilled and brutally laborious job, a raw-throated, eye-smarting one for the men on the main and mizzens, enveloped as they were in hot, acrid smoke and almost total darkness. It took little over half an hour – though that would have been considered disgracefully long in Dawlish's youth – and the last yard splashed overboard as the sky began to lighten.

As the sun rose above the distant mountains on the eastern horizon Socheong was already falling away off the starboard quarter and the Japanese ship ahead had not deviated from her westwards course. Black smoke vomited from her funnel but her hull gleamed white, as if her paintwork had been renewed to ready her for her foray. The frothing wake she left across the calm sea told of maximum speed – that was fourteen knots, two less than *Leonidas* could manage at her best. Three more hours at least before getting in range. And Dawlish knew that his crew's efficiency might well ebb in that time, that the enthusiasm generated by clearing ship would dissipate during the waiting, that awareness of the two bodies whose burial had been deferred might sap morale. He ordered streaming of the patent log.

All eyes now on the fleeing *Kirishima*, Edgerton and Takenaka in oppressive silence on the bridge, Purdon by the bow-chasers, Hamilton, the junior sub-lieutenant, endlessly checking the pumps and fire hoses, Ross's marines in the now-unobstructed tops. And Dawlish, on the bridge wing, more alone than he had ever felt in his life.

Long minutes passed before Leigh returned to report just under fifteen and a half knots. Good, but not good enough. Dawlish's mind raced. The engines were at their limits, the boilers almost dangerously so. He felt the deck throbbing beneath his feet, looked aft to see smoke vomiting from the funnels like never before, the wake frothing, the water rushing past the side in a long wave streaming in a narrow vee from the bows.

And then the idea!

"Mr. Edgerton! Get every available man aft!"

A look of surprise.

"I want the bows lifted. A foot, even six inches, might help. Get them aft! Marines, gunners too, all except bow-chaser crews and engine-room staff."

Almost three hundred men. The average weight must be about twelve stone. A quick mental calculation. Over 20 tons. Not a lot but, concentrated at the extreme stern, it could only help, not hinder.

"Mr. O'Rourke's crews?"

Dawlish shook his head. He did not want sun-dazzled torpedomen blundering back into the gloom of their positions on the lower deck. Their arming and launching tasks were intricate enough already. "But all others. Every man possible."

Commands passed and then bellowed instructions, the sound of bare feet thudding on planked decks. Men still grimy from their labour aloft in the smoke hurried towards the quarterdeck, and with them gunners warned by their captains to stay together, then cooks and stewards rushing from below, and sailmakers and paymaster's men and any others not needed to feed and serve the boilers and engines. A sense of urgency seemed to flash between them, a realisation that even the act of standing still was as valuable this moment as manning a weapon. Watkin, the paymaster, was in control, packing them against rails and stanchions. They jostled ever closer, greeting with a derisory but good-humoured cheer each tardy joiner, their cheering heartfelt when the two surgeon's assistants came struggling towards them with Hawley, the one-legged Marine Sergeant, carried between them.

Dawlish glanced aft and felt a surge of satisfaction, something too of pride, even of love, for the rough, profane and yet superbly skilled men crowded there, as ribaldly jovial as if on a bank-holiday excursion. These men were with him heart and soul now, and would be with him in the hours to come, even though recent losses had left no doubt of what the price might be.

He looked forward, almost afraid to do so, but Yes! - the bow wave was different, slightly, ever so slightly so, the angle it streamed at off the side marginally more acute. He hesitated to run the log again — indeed it demanded shifting of the men from the extreme stern and he did not want the slightest drop in speed. A gain, however small, had been made and *Leonidas* had nothing more left to give.

And slowly, very slowly, the gap separating her from the fleeing *Kirishima* narrowed.

24

Ten thousand yards was the six-inchers' maximum range, five and a half miles, and the distance separating the fleeing warship from *Leonidas's* relentless pursuit was less than that, less by a mile and more. The sea was calm, scarcely rippled, and the sun beat down from a cloudless sky. Visibility was perfect as the bow-chasers, sponsoned out on either side of the foredeck, held their target steadily in their sights. The Japanese ship was also cleared for action, hinged bulwarks at her stern dropped down, half-obscuring the characters of her name, to expose her Krupp six-inch stern-chaser. Its crew were stationed by it like impassive and white-uniformed automatons and there could be no doubt of its being ranged on *Leonidas*.

But Dawlish still withheld the order to fire — *Leonidas's* guns' effective range was half, even less, than their maximum. The first salvo must be accurate, must be landed squarely on the *Kirishima*, for that alone might settle the issue and convince even Shimazu that battle was futile. There was no doubt now that the weight of the seamen crowded on the quarterdeck had given *Leonidas* an advantage. Small though the increment of speed might be, it was a margin sufficient to allow her to out-run and out-manoeuvre her quarry.

The Rising Sun ensign was still flying proudly — the flag of a desired ally, even if flown by a rebel. An opportunity remained to prevent bloodshed and it must be taken. "Flag X," Dawlish said, as he had once before, the blue cross on a white background, the request as unambiguous as it had been then. *"Stop carrying out your intentions and watch for my signals."*

The yeoman's telescope, Dawlish's and Purdon's glasses, were all focussed on the *Kirishima's* halliards.

And as before, no acknowledgement.

"Signal again."

The flag drawn down, a twenty second pause, and then it rose again. Still no acknowledgement.

Some five thousand yards now, less than three miles, still closing... Dawlish's trust in Purdon was high and practice against towed rafts had demonstrated that a hit was possible, just possible... Another five minutes and...

A flash at the *Kirishima's* stern and then she was blotted from view in a rolling cloud of yellowish brown. A fraction of a second later came the sound of stern-chaser's report and the realisation that a shell was screaming towards *Leonidas*. Dawlish forced himself not to flinch, the others round him also, though hearts raced and white-knuckled fingers tightened on glasses and telescopes and wheel.

Dear God let it not...

Then a skidding plume five hundred yards ahead and slightly to starboard of *Leonidas'* axis. It collapsed to leave a trail of foam and with that came relief. *Not this time...* But the range was closing and the sea was smooth and the sun was bright and the Japanese gunners must now be correcting for the leftward drift of their shell...

"Mr. Purdon!" Dawlish looked down to the bow-chasers, no need for further words, his expression enough.

"Not yet, sir! The range is still too long for accuracy! Another two or three minutes!"

"Your guns, Mr. Purdon! Your decision!" For Dawlish trusted Purdon for accuracy, just as he had once staked his own life on his expertise on the San Joaquin. He turned to Edgerton. "Other crews to their guns! And all hands away from the stern and back to their stations!"

A flurry of activity on the Japanese quarterdeck showed the weapon there being reloaded. If they had sense – if Shimazu had it, and there was little doubt of that – they would hold their fire until the range closed further. Just as *Leonidas* would hold her fire too, and then there would be two of her weapons to the enemy's one. The silence was now broken by the orders relayed from the bridge, by feet drumming on decks as the knot of men at the stern disintegrated. Gun-crews dashed to the stern-chaser and broadside six-inchers and other men to ammunition hoists and hose positions. Marines shinned aloft with rifles to supplement the Gatlings there. Ross was heading for the foretop, O'Rourke down to his beloved torpedo launchers, the surgeon's men below to Tadley in the wardroom.

Long minutes more and the range was still closing, little over three thousand yards now. A quiet again hung over *Leonidas*, a quiet agonising for its expectation, for the certainty of what must come. Her broadside six-inchers had trained out but none could yet bear on the target ahead. Purdon was crouched over the starboard bow-chaser, his whole being concentrated on his view along the sights. Then he stepped back, glanced up towards Dawlish for an instant, giving the slightest nod, then called the command to fire. The barrel leapt back along the inclined slide of its Vavasseur mounting as flame lanced from the muzzle. Choking smoke obscured the view ahead for an instant before the vessel's forward motion rid her of it. The missile was still in the air when the weapon in the port sponson also fired. Ignoring the barks that pounded his ear drums, Dawlish held his glasses fixed on the end-on white hull ahead.

In the instant before *Leonidas's* shells fell the Japanese fired again. As it did a long streak of white spray marked the fall of *Leonidas's* first shot a half cable short – an aim so perfect that it might have ploughed destruction along the target's centreline had the elevation been a half-degree higher. *Leonidas's* second shot had perfect elevation but the aim off by a fraction that brought the shell skipping harmlessly past the enemy's port side.

The Japanese shell impacted. It smashed into a water-filled cutter on *Leonidas's* starboard side, the explosion's flash briefly orange, then damped by the liquid and wooden fragments bursting from it like a fan. Dawlish glanced aft and saw the hail of droplets and splinters showering down abaft the after funnel. He heard screaming – the sort of inhuman screaming that told of injury too dreadful to conceive of in any normal circumstance – and saw wreckage fallen across the midships six-inch mounting, its surviving crew staggering back from it in shock and bewilderment.

One six-inch out of action, four now on starboard instead of five… It was her port battery that *Leonidas* must now bring to bear if her advantage was to be maximised. But first she must draw level with the Japanese vessel…

Leigh and Hamilton already had men dragging debris away from the six-inch and injured men were being helped below. Scorched paintwork but no fire, no need for hoses. With luck the weapon's shield might have protected its training and elevating bearings from damage. It might yet be brought back into action. Up forward the bow-chasers' smoking breeches had been swabbed. Into them massively built and muscled loaders were manhandling new eighty-pound shells followed by twenty-pound silk-bagged charges. Then the breeches were slamming closed, a twist of their interrupted screws locking them ready for firing. Purdon was again at the starboard piece's sights, his calm instructions directing his layer's minute hand-wheel adjustments for range and aim. And on the ship ahead another crew, equally skilled – and encouraged by their hit – must be no less intently focussed.

Takenaka yelled as Purdon's guns lashed out again. His words were lost but he had lowered his glasses and was reaching out to grasp Dawlish's sleeve – an action unimaginable at any other moment. Dawlish glanced towards him and saw horror on Takenaka's face but his gaze returned to the ship ahead – that alone counted at this instant. Purdon's range estimation had been all but perfect, the port weapon's no worse, but the slightest aiming error had saved the Japanese. The plumes thrown up on the vessel's port side were close enough to shower its deck with spray – close, but distant enough not to injure. Almost instantly the enemy's transom was again engulfed in smoke as the stern-chaser blasted. The thunderclap report reached *Leonidas* an instant before the shell screamed over her bridge, low enough for the suction of its passage to be felt, then shaved past her funnels without effect and plunged into her wake in a cascade of foam.

Half-deafened by the bow-chasers' blasts, Dawlish turned to Takenaka, who was still jerking on his sleeve, his composure gone and mouthing words temporarily inaudible. Then, as Dawlish's ears cleared he made out the words and his blood ran cold.

"It's not the *Kirishima*!" Takenaka was shouting. "It's another ship!"

"The *Haruna*?" Dawlish's mind recoiled. If Admiral Hojo had thrown in his lot with Shimazu...

But Takenaka was shaking his head, "Not the *Haruna*! I can make out part of the name..." The vessel was close enough for the bottom of the characters on her stern to be visible, enough for a literate Japanese to deduce the full name. "She's the *Tatsuta*!"

"*Tat...*" The name meaningless.

"The newest ship built for Japan in Britain!" Takenaka shouted. "She was due for delivery!"

A sudden memory of Takenaka's mention of her at Chemulpo, of Admiral Hojo speaking of her imminent arrival in Japan, and with admiration of her improved-model Krupps. He remembered now.

Tatsuta.

"What..." Dawlish cut off his words as the vessel ahead slewed over to port in a tight turn, no longer intent on escape but on turning at right angles to *Leonidas's* course. As she did the full sweep of her side became visible – almost identical to the *Kirishima* and *Haruna*, but not quite, for in place of their single funnels she carried two. Worse still, her flank was pierced with five ports to *Leonidas's* four, a six-inch barrel run out from each. With the bow and stern-chasers she could deliver a full broadside of seven Krupp six-inchers, two more than *Leonidas* could bring to bear to port, three more than her injured starboard side...

Purdon's bow-chasers roared simultaneously and this time both shells found their marks, an explosion on the hull just below the *Tatsuta's* stern-chaser and another at the base of the mizzen mast. Shrouds and stays whipped through the smoke of impact like black serpents and the mast itself canted slightly off vertical, then held. An instant later the entire side of the Japanese ship was obscured, orange flame lancing through the rolling smoke that vomited from her gun ports. Had it not been for Purdon's salvo the broadside might have been decisive, but his hits must have thrown off the Japanese gunners' aims. Even so a single shell smashed against *Leonidas's* port side, just below the bridge wing. An armour-piercing round would have punched through, would have created untold damage before its kinetic energy was spent, but this was common shell which exploded on contact. Smoke and searing flame fanned up along the vessel's side and a shock rippled through the hull. Dawlish felt the bridge decking heave beneath his feet and grasped the rail ahead to steady himself. He glanced around. Others around him had been knocked off balance and were struggling to their feet. He looked aft – no sign of damage there – then down to see Purdon and his gunners also apparently unhurt.

The *Tatsuta* was broadside on now. A huge black smudge on her white side marked Purdon's strike, and the mizzen was holding, though its gaff had dropped to hang limply against it. But otherwise the

Japanese ship seemed as little injured as *Leonidas* was herself and just as battleworthy.

Two and a half thousand yards.

The *Tatsuta's* gunners must be reloading with the grim machine-like efficiency that Dawlish now associated with the Japanese navy. Their next full broadside might tear along *Leonidas's* axis. The only option was to bring *Leonidas's* own full battery into play.

"Helm over! Four points to Starboard!"

As the wheel spun and in the long moments before the rudder bit Dawlish called down to Purdon. "Your full broadside! Then independent fire!" This was no time for the steady rhythm of simultaneous fire. Several of the gun-crews were faster in their reloading than others, faster by eight or ten seconds in some cases, and those seconds might make all the difference. Dawlish moved to the voice tubes, pulled the stopper from that of the torpedo position.

"Mr. O'Rourke!"

Acknowledgement from the position below just ahead of the forward funnel's uptake, crews standing there by each of the two torpedo-launching carriages on either side.

"Be ready to launch either to port or starboard." Dawlish forced calm into his voice, hoped that it betrayed no sense of the fear he felt. "At my word but on your aim."

Mounted on cradles that could be hurled forward by pneumatic impulse, the self-propelled weapons would be thrown out from the hull to plunge into the water below. But calculation of the angle of aim was critical, so too allowance for the relative courses and speeds of both launch ship and target, for the drag of the water racing past the hull as the torpedo entered. And only O'Rourke could make that calculation, sighting through the narrow port before him. He alone must judge the angle and the instant of discharge.

Leonidas was into the turn now, drawing astern of the *Tatsuta*, and first the sponsoned stern-chaser, then her three broadside mountings, were taking their target into their sights.

"Gatlings to engage!"

The range was extreme for Gatling fire but Dawlish could spot movement around the base of the *Tatsuta's* mizzen, desperate efforts to stay it to prevent its collapse. His words were barely out before the Gatling in the foretop stammered into life, a perfectly timed three-second burst, two seconds pause, and then another. Its companion in the maintop opened an instant later, the same controlled staccato. There was no opportunity to see the effect however, for the Japanese's side was again lost behind an erupting wall of flame-pierced smoke, seven weapons blasting out as one. The aim was near perfect, five shells screaming low but harmlessly above *Leonidas* to throw up geysers three hundred yards beyond, but the two others smashed into the port flank. The hull shuddered under their explosions, both abaft the second funnel, close enough to the gun mounting there, third from the bow, to hurl its crew from their feet. Dawlish glanced aft and saw that though the yellowish smoke of detonation was clearing it was being replaced by a rolling black cloud that spurted from the ship's side. One round had penetrated, or at least had torn a plate free, and had pulverised the coal stored in the bunker there.

"Get hoses down there!" Edgerton was calling aft to Leigh, but the chances of ignition were low. The coal stored between the sloped outer edge of the armoured deck and the ship's side had acted as had been intended, as a degree of additional protection. *Leonidas* might take a dozen or more of such hits, her upperworks might indeed be reduced to wreckage, yet the boilers and engines would remain unharmed beneath the unseen domed armoured-deck.

The two ships were now on diverging courses, the *Tatsuta*'s heading close to south, and *Leonidas*, now straightening out of her turn, forging towards the northeast. Through his glasses Dawlish saw that the lengthening separation was now masking the *Tatsuta*'s broadside weapons. Their barrels had been arced aft towards the sides of their ports limit and could slew no further. Only her stern-chaser could bear.

Leonidas's starboard battery blasted out, four guns together on Purdon's order, the fifth, that close to the impact amidships, ten seconds later, its crew's shock overcome and once more active. A flash aft, close to the *Tatsuta*'s stern, registered one hit, even if white columns rising beyond her wake showed that the other shells had missed. *Tatsuta*'s stern-chaser was lost in the billowing smoke of the explosion of *Leonidas*'s shell and above it the mizzen was toppling over to starboard, its remaining shrouds snapping. Dawlish felt a surge of exultation as it fell, smashing down into a wall of spray. The *Tatsuta*'s bows slewed over to starboard and her forward momentum, though not stilled, was suddenly reduced. She lay stern on to *Leonidas*'s full broadside, a broadside composed of individual weapons loading and firing and loading as fast as possible, raining shells towards the crippled

Japanese. More flashes indicated hits against the target's flanks and upperworks, but all activity on her decks was hidden in the rolling smoke. Men must be hacking through the tangle of fallen shrouds and stays, heaving to lug the lower section of the shattered mizzen overboard. Until they did their ship, impeded by the drag of wreckage, would continue to lurch drunkenly to starboard.

Purdon's guns were barking at a rate never achieved on exercise, their crews in a controlled frenzy that fed on its own success. The ready-use rounds were already used up and chain hoists were dragging reloads up from the magazines below. Throats rasping from their own gunsmoke, red-eyed from its acrid breath, the crews' speed of fire was braked only by the murk intermittently obscuring the aim.

The *Tatsuta* was not replying, wallowing as she was with the fallen mast still dragging her and unable to turn to bring her broadside guns to bear. Her stern-chaser, the only weapon that could menace *Leonidas*, seemed out of action. Smoke engulfed her after end and fire was now licking through it, not the sudden flashes of the shells flailing her but lazily dancing and flickering flames that told of wood burning.

"Engines to Dead Slow." Dawlish wanted to stay in the enemy's blind spot, *Leonidas* broadside on to the *Tatsuta's* stern. He was unwilling to advance into the area her hitherto inactive starboard battery could command. "Hold her here."

"If you will permit me, sir?" Takenaka's voice metallic, almost inhuman. "May I take the helm?"

Dawlish hesitated for the briefest instant, sensed reluctance among the others around him. There was no doubt of Takenaka's skill in juggling rudder and engine. But there was more involved here, a matter of conflicting loyalties, dilemmas almost incomprehensible to a European. Yet this man had stood by him at death's threshold, had been ready to give his own life for his...

"Carry on, Lieutenant Takenaka." It was no gamble.

Takenaka motioned to the helmsman and took the wheel in his right hand, his left on the telegraph. He ground it back and far below, beneath the armoured deck, a bell would be ringing to announce the command. Throttles would be closing and the long sequence of juggling engines and rudder would commence.

Leonidas was slowing and still Purdon's six-inchers were pouring a merciless hail on the stricken ship, the individual reports almost impossible to distinguish as the guns roared in irregular order. At least one shell in three, perhaps even one in two, was striking the *Tatsuta*. Foam boiled under her counter as her thrashing screws sought to rip her free from the encumbering mizzen. White-uniformed figures were toiling on deck, now visible against the rolling smoke, then hidden from view again. Another shell burst among them, hurling bodies as well as wreckage into the sea alongside.

"It's murder, sheer murder." Edgerton's voice was hushed and his face was ashen when Dawlish turned towards him. Routine service in European waters had not prepared him for this enormity.

"She's not beaten," Dawlish said. He could see the Rising Sun still fluttering defiantly over the rolling smoke. "She hasn't struck."

"She'll never strike, sir," Takenaka said and for the first time ever Dawlish heard a quaver in his voice and saw tears running down his otherwise impassive face. "It is an honour to die like this. No man can hope for more." But even as he spoke *Leonidas's* wheel was slipping easily through his hands, a slight correction to port, and then, as the rudder answered, a quick flick to starboard to maintain the heading. Weep as he might, there was no faltering in his dedication to the task in hand, his handling of the ship as deadly for his countryman as Purdon's gunnery.

There was a slowing of *Leonidas's* barrage as exhausted men lugged new shells and charges from the hoists. The acrid fog of gunsmoke that had intermittently blotted the *Tatsuta* from view was clearing. Through the drifting wisps Dawlish's glasses confirmed that the stern-chaser was disabled, its barrel canted at an impossible angle, flames from the deck's blazing plankwork engulfing her. The fire was eating its way forward and several hoses were in play, but the barrels of the broadside guns, however far astern they were arced, were still incapable of training on *Leonidas*. With Takenaka expertly maintaining position in the victim's blind spot astern the punishment could be continued indefinitely and without risk of retaliation. Dawlish felt a glow of relief as well as satisfaction. It was all going to...

And at that moment the *Tatsuta* bounded forward, shaking off the trailing wreckage. Her helm was over, pulling her into a wide sweep to port. As she built speed, and as she turned, the broadside weapons that had been masked for long minutes were uncovered and the barrels were swinging round towards *Leonidas*.

"Full revolutions!" Dawlish yelled.

Seconds passed, long seconds, as Takenaka rammed the telegraph forward, as the engine-room staff rushed to comply with its demand. Longer seconds still for the steam throttles to open fully, for the pistons and their flailing rods to build up speed, for the churning screws to accelerate four thousand tons of metal, coal and men. *Leonidas* was still clawing for speed as *Tatsuta's* flank was obscured by the discharges of her broadside guns. Their shells were still in the air as her bow-chaser also fired. In that brief instant Dawlish knew that hits were inevitable. He found himself ducking involuntarily – and stupidly, for nothing could give protection on the open bridge – as did the others round him. Then the rush of missiles close overhead, and one shearing two feet from the top of the second funnel, though not detonating, and then an explosion far aft, just above the waterline. This last must have penetrated before exploding, flinging out a volcano of flame and coal and torn plating horizontally from the side.

Fanned by the wind created by her forward movement, the fire on the *Tatsuta* was now raging over a third of her length. There must be damage below for she could be making little over five knots, and that sluggishly. But she still had fight in her and she was dying hard.

That death must be hastened.

Leonidas was now at full speed again and Dawlish knew that he could dictate range and bearing. On his instruction Takenaka brought the vessel over in a wide swing to port again, blocking her from the arcs of the *Tatsuta's* weapons.

"Mr. Purdon!" Dawlish had to shout twice more to get the half-deafened gunnery officer's attention. "No further common shell! Palliser shot!"

It would mean a delay of minutes to get the glass hard, non-explosive rounds hoisted from below, but it would be worth it for their eviscerating capability. It took longer than Dawlish would have wished, but the gun-crews were fatigued to near-collapse now and other hands had been drawn away to support Leigh's control of damage in the pierced compartments. But in the meantime *Leonidas* was circling the stricken *Tatsuta*, the radius of the turn increasing, lengthened range and speed frustrating the enemy gunners' aim. It must be hell on the Japanese ship now and it was going to get worse.

"She must strike!" Edgerton said, his tone half-pleading for a mercy he hesitated to ask for openly.

Takenaka said nothing but his face was set in pride, even though his eyes glistened with tears, and it was his touch on wheel and telegraph that was guiding *Leonidas* remorselessly to the butchery of his compatriots.

"Palliser loaded!" Purdon was looking up and shouting, then bending over the port bow-chaser's sights.

Now came the *Tatsuta's* dismemberment, shot after shot on low trajectories smashing into her side, gouging through the structure within, tearing through whatever opposed it, metal or wood or flesh. The fire raged ever more fiercely, reaching down and feeding on the shattered interior. Ten minutes passed, upwards of a dozen salvos. The Japanese vessel now a wreck, its mainmast also collapsed, gaps punched in her flanks exposing fierce red glows within. Steam was gushing near a fallen funnel and in such quantities that a boiler must have been breached. The ship was almost dead in the water, with only the smallest rippling at the stern indicating one engine still in feeble action. But the Rising Sun still flew bravely, carried aloft to the foretopmast and streamed there in suicidal defiance, and a few of the guns were still firing as the *Leonidas* passed through their arcs.

"Won't they strike, Lieutenant?" Dawlish was asking the question now, eager himself to end the agony on the dying ship. It might burn for hours yet and the crew with it.

"It is not our way, sir." Takenaka's tone indicated that no more need be said.

"Take us in close, dead slow, two cables off the starboard quarter." Dawlish had decided on his own mercy and there was little risk from the burning stern. He shouted down to Purdon to cease fire, up to Ross in the foretop to still the Gatling crews, then down the voice pipe to O'Rourke. "Launch when you're satisfied. Two torpedoes."

Leonidas was close enough to feel the heat and hear the roar of the *Tatsuta's* agony as the two weapons splashed into the water. Both 14-inch Whiteheads ran as straight as rudder adjustments that had been refined through endless test launchings could make them. Two trail of bubbles bored towards the target. Dawlish was counting silently – a mental calculation told him it would take about eighty seconds. There was dead silence around him now, silence too among the gun-crews and in the tops overhead, all half-hypnotised by the torpedoes' remorseless advance. The minute was passed, then the sixties, seventy seconds, seventy one, seventy two...

Two fountains of tortured foam erupted along the *Tatsuta's* side. Her hull convulsed like a living thing in agony. The foremast, the only mast left standing, whipped like a sapling in a gale, her standing rigging parting, her yards breaking free, and began to topple over. The columns of spray seemed to hang frozen for long seconds, then they too came cascading down, hissing in great clouds of steam as they hit the burning deck. As they cleared the great rent torn close to the stern showed itself, its edges marked by twisted plating, water pouring into the dark void within.

The bows began to lift and the *Tatsuta* lurched over, then stabilised herself. The poop submerged, the blaze there suddenly extinguished. Men and debris were spilling into the sea as the bows climbed higher still. The forefoot was rising clear and exposing the keel. The entire hull jerked sternwards, then seemed to check itself and hold as the bows swung towards the vertical.

The final plunge left nothing but a circle of foam and debris and bobbing heads through which great bubbles erupted. At last they too were stilled.

It was time to pick up the survivors.

25

Now the dreadful aftermath.

Leonidas had no boats available to lower immediately. One had been smashed beyond repair and the remainder were still water-filled. It would take too long to empty them and in that time upwards of two hundred men clinging to floating wreckage could die. Still at the helm, Takenaka brought the cruiser slowly, ever so slowly, into the foam-streaked circle of flotsam and stricken humanity. Filthy black smoke drifted overhead and carried with it the smell of charred wood, and worse. Fragments of boats, of planking, of hatchways and deck-house panelling, of masts and yards enmeshed in tangled rigging, all wallowed in the coal-dust and cinder-strewn waters.

Along *Leonidas's* sides men were being stationed with heaving lines and three painting floats were being readied for dropping. They worked largely in silence, oppressed by the enormity of what they had done, the initial elation of victory well-gone by now and horror mingled with pity now dominating. Edgerton and Leigh were supervising the rescue operations while O'Rourke and Hamilton had teams working below in the damaged compartments – their reports confirmed that there was no threat to the vessel's integrity.

Dawlish watched in silence from the bridge wing. Only now, with the need for immediate response to danger past, could he reflect on the full significance of what he had done. He had chased a ship he had believed was the *Kirishima* – a pirate, it could fairly be argued – and when he had challenged her fairly he had not hesitated to respond to her defiance. He had fought her and he had sunk her – efficiently and at minimum cost in British lives or material – and in abstract terms his management of the action would earn the respect of every naval professional.

But she had not been the *Kirishima*.

She was another ship of the Japanese Navy, proudly flying the Rising Sun until her last plunge, and she might well have been here with the full backing of the Emperor himself. That she was heading away from Socheong was not in itself proof positive of collusion with Shimazu. And if there had been no such collusion...

He felt almost physically sick, his mouth dry and his hands shaking as they had not done in the heat of combat. There could be no forgiveness from London had his assumptions been wrong, not just ignominious dismissal from the service but almost certainly criminal prosecution as well, the charge of piracy now levelled against himself. He might hang for this.

Dawlish felt it all the worse as *Leonidas* nudged towards the first knot of survivors clinging to the remains of a shattered boat. The once immaculate white Japanese uniforms were sodden rags now, some streaked with red, and what looked like one hideously burned man was being held on the wreckage of a boat by his fellows in the water. Further off, other closely cropped heads were glistening in the sunlight, many stroking steadily away, not towards, the *Leonidas*. An hour before they must have been like those smart and cheerful men he had admired on the *Haruna*, they too perhaps keepers of crickets in bamboo cages. There was satisfaction in vanquishing a ship but none in smashing lives and modest aspirations, none in inflicting pain and hideous injury on living bodies.

Leonidas slowed, then lay stationary. The first painting float was in the water, propelled unhandily by oars used as paddles and slowed by a line linking it to the ship. There were survivors in the water at *Leonidas's* side, some only feet away, but they seemed too exhausted even to look up much less swim towards it. Heaving lines splashed into the water close to them – "Here, mate! Grab this!" – but nobody seemed to have the energy to reach out. Dawlish looked down and saw one face raised towards him from directly below, a young face, and all the sadder for the absence even of despair. The man looked strong and healthy, and he held Dawlish's gaze as he calmly raised his hands above his head and sank out of sight. Further out from the ship other arms were being raised also, other heads disappearing, and yet more swimming steadily away from succour. Still the heaving lines plopped down within easy reach and yet no hand grasped them. A seaman had been lowered, a line passed under his armpits and he was stroking towards a Japanese who had gone under twice, had come up again each time as if life was still dear to him. Men were shouting encouragement from the deck as the seaman neared the exhausted man but even as he tried to grab him the Japanese turned his face away, shouted something, then disappeared.

Takenaka was at Dawlish's side, the wheel once more entrusted to a quartermaster. There were no tears now. He was watching without any sign of horror, with the slightest hint indeed which might indicate admiration.

"Don't they want to be saved?" Dawlish could not keep the exasperation from his voice. This steady, deliberate, ritual of self-destruction was worse than any fury of battle.

"They failed, Captain Dawlish," Takenaka said. "But death can still buy them honour. You'll do them no favour by troubling their last moments."

Dawlish felt his anger rising and fought to contain it. "I've no damn sympathy with that sort of talk, Lieutenant. This is a Queen's ship and we don't leave men in the water. They're fellow seamen and they've got lives ahead of them."

Takenaka looked him straight in the eye, unwavering. "They cannot surrender and they must not be prisoners," he said, "Their lives belong to His Majesty, the Emperor. They are honoured to offer them." He paused, then said deliberately "Would you begrudge your life to the Queen Empress, Captain?" His tone was even but Dawlish sensed contempt and resentment that must have been kept hidden for months, perhaps years.

"You'll take yourself down there, Lieutenant Takenaka," Dawlish ignored the challenge and pointed to where the second painting float was about to be lowered overboard. "I want to see you on that float and three men with you, and I want survivors. You'll talk to them, convince them, get them aboard whether or not they want to die. You understand that this is a clear order, don't you, Lieutenant?"

"Assuredly, Captain." He saluted and turned away.

"And Lieutenant Takenaka?" Dawlish called him back. "I want an officer prisoner, two, three if you can. I don't care a damn whether or not they want to die. I want them alive and I want answers."

The first painting float had reached the shattered boat and a scuffle had developed there. *Leonidas's* seamen were trying to reach the burned man on the wreckage but the men in the water were reaching out to drag them from the float or to rock it and spill them over. A seaman overbalanced and fell into the water and the men he had been trying to rescue were grabbing and pummelling him, trying to push him under. His British comrades on the painting float were beating the men in the water with their oars or trying to push others away, finally managing to drag him back on the float again. The urge to save was now replaced by anger and they hit mercilessly at the survivors splashing below them. Repulsed by the blows of the oars, the men in the water began to swim away, but not before they dragged the burned man with them and thrust him under.

Not a single man had yet been plucked from the water and the number of bobbing heads was already noticeably fewer. Another painting float had been got off, with as little effect as the first, and a third, Takenaka's, was paddling towards another knot of survivors.

"Over there, sir!" A call from the foretop, a finger pointing to a figure balanced precariously on wreckage a cable and more distant to starboard. He was waving something that glistened as the sun's rays caught it. Dawlish swung his glasses over and in their disc recognised red and white on the flapping and sodden sheet – the Rising Sun. The man holding it was capless but his uniform was clearly an officer's. This was what Dawlish needed. He rapped quick orders.

Leaving behind the painting floats, and a score and more of men close enough to have been pulled to safety, and were perhaps grateful for being abandoned, *Leonidas* crept towards the ensign-waving officer. He was standing on a half-submerged hatch cover and his face carried a look close to exaltation.

"Get Egdean up here," Dawlish said. There was no man better for what he had in mind. Powerfully strong, a good swimmer – and a man to whom Dawlish owed his life in other times and places.

When he came up – dripping, for he had already been over the side, fruitlessly – he looked oppressed by the presence of so much futile death. Egdean took his religion seriously, was perhaps already praying inwardly for the redemption of the men who had rejected his aid.

"We'll take you alongside." Dawlish gestured towards the officer's defiance. "I want you down on a line, and I want you to overpower that man." He hesitated for a moment. He already owed Egdean so much, was perhaps asking too much of a man who already looked exhausted. "You're sure you can do it?"

"I'll do it, sir. Happy to do it." No hint of reluctance. He hurried from the bridge.

Close now, then a half-cable, then sixty, fifty yards, and the Japanese officer was now holding up the dripping ensign before him, his face obscured by it. Egdean was at the edge of the starboard bow-chaser's sponson, head and shoulders through a bowline, the gun's crew ready to lower him, Purdon supervising. *Leonidas's* screws had been stilled and she was gliding forward under her own momentum at less than walking pace. The quartermaster was making the slightest adjustments to the helm so that the bows would just graze past the floating wreckage. Dawlish was at the bridge wing, no need for glasses this close, and the survivor's face was still hidden from him. He hesitated to hope but there might be a chance that this one man might choose to cling to life, might accept surrender as honourable.

The wreckage was scraping along the ship's side and Egdean had been lowered to dangle with his feet just above the water. A moment more and he could be on the flotsam and grappling the survivor into submission.

And suddenly the ensign was being flung aside and the officer was thrusting his right hand inside his clinging tunic. He was dragging something out – it caught on the wet folds – but Dawlish already knew that it must be a pistol. He forced himself not to flinch or duck as he saw the man's eyes locked on him – on *Leonidas's* captain – and not on Egdean or on the men on the sponson edge above. It was time to stand and receive fire as a thousand captains had done before him, as Hope and Willes had shown him so long ago on the *Plover*. The pistol was out now, a revolver, a small one, and it was sweeping up. The first shot was wild, the second and third wild also as the Japanese fought to keep his balance on his lurching raft while madly recocking, but the fourth was close enough for Dawlish to feel its passage close to his left ear.

The flotsam was almost under the sponson and Purdon's men were swinging Egdean like a pendulum so he could grapple with the officer. He did not seem to sense Egdean's proximity, had eyes only for Dawlish. Their gazes locked as Egdean crashed on to the wreckage, his weight upsetting it. It lurched over and the Japanese fell to his knees.

Then he raised his revolver one last time. He looked up towards Dawlish – no hatred, but certainly pride – and thrust the muzzle in his mouth and pulled the trigger.

Egdean was pale and blood-spattered when they dragged him back on board. It was up to Takenaka now to secure a prisoner.

*

Five living men were recovered from the water, five only from a crew of over three hundred. All were unconscious and only one wore an officer's uniform, by his insignia a lieutenant. He had a large bruise across his left face and temple but he emerged into dazed and mumbling awareness as he was carried down to the sick berth. He began to struggle, weakly but determinedly, as the full realisation of where he was dawned upon him.

"Tie him down if necessary," Dawlish said, "But give him every attention he needs. And you, Lieutenant," he turned to a dripping Takenaka, who had brought back two of the survivors, "I want you to stay with him, get all you can from him. What was his vessel doing? Who commanded her? Was her captain working in concert with Shimazu? Had he got official backing?" He tried to keep from his tone the worry now gnawing him. If the *Genyosha* had prevailed with the Emperor, if this ship's mission had been authorised...

"I will honour your instructions, sir." Takenaka snapped into a bow but conveyed no enthusiasm. In the last hours he had seemed more alien – more Japanese, more incomprehensible – than he had ever been on the long voyage from Britain.

Leonidas's bows swung again towards Socheong, still at half-revolutions until Dawlish had satisfied himself that there had been no impairment of integrity. The damage on deck and to the upperworks was superficial – though the loss of a cutter would be inconvenient – and parties were already at work clearing debris. In the two compartments which shells had struck the injury had been less than expected. The hull's half-inch steel had proved tough enough to detonate the projectiles on impact. Rivets had been sheared and plating driven inwards but not penetrated. Choking smoke and black dust filled both compartments but hoses were being played on the smouldering coal. Rolled hammocks had been stuffed into the rents and, as the breaches were above the waterline, that would be sufficient for now. The carpenter and his men would have work aplenty once they returned from the *Fu Ching*.

Casualties were light, no deaths, not yet. One member of the starboard six-incher's crew who had been trapped beneath the fallen cutter had a badly crushed chest and was choking on his blood. Tadley gave the slightest shake of his head when Dawlish visited the wardroom where the seaman was stretched on the table, the sheet beneath him crimson. Dawlish realised that the words of comfort and gratitude he spoke to the dying gunner were hopeless, empty – the man was already passed beyond the reach of platitudes, however heart-felt. The other injuries were recoverable – two broken legs, a broken arm, heavy concussion and superficial splinter wounds. By some mercy no trimmers had been in the coal bunkers which had been hit. The only other injury was a stoker who had fallen against a furnace door as the ship manoeuvred tightly – the burns, though painful, were not extensive.

Dawlish returned to the bridge and ordered full revolution, glad to leave the drifting fields of death and wreckage behind. It was late afternoon now and Socheong's western cliffs were just visible on the eastern horizon. Shimazu and the *Kirishima* might still be there – and probably were – and the blockade must be resumed. Dawlish felt a hollowness, a near-despair, even slight nausea. The game had not ended and he could not envisage any easy end. Not any one that might not involve shame and failure for himself.

Takenaka joined him, still wet, his voice devoid of emotion. He saluted, then bowed.

"The prisoner is Lieutenant Oyama Kunimoto, gunnery officer of His Majesty's corvette *Tatsuta*." He said no more, gave the impression that he had no more to say.

"And? Is he capable of telling what we need to know?"

"Lieutenant Oyama wishes to die, sir. He refuses to say anything more." Takenaka paused, then said "We can expect nothing else from an honourable officer."

"Oyama? Could he be from Satsuma?" A straw, but all that Dawlish had to grasp at.

"It is very likely, sir. I know of three officers of that name from there, but not this one." Takenaka was looking straight at Dawlish but his eyes betrayed no emotion.

A long and uncomfortable silence. Dawlish's mind touched for an instant on something that should be unthinkable, then shied away. He would not exploit his prisoner's agony. But he felt his heart beating loudly, his palms sweating as the silence continued.

"Is there anything we can offer him?" he said at last. Futile words, but all he could think of.

"Lieutenant Oyama wants to die, sir." Takenaka said it slowly, patiently. As if trying to convey something very complex to a child.

Yet Dawlish understood what was implied even as he mentally recoiled from it. Five hours before he had been striving to kill this man and hundreds like him, but that had been in honest combat between well-matched opponents. And this was... He shrank from the word.

At last he spoke. "It's not easy for an officer to be confined." He realised that even now he could stop here, not bring it further. But still he continued. "I understand that Lieutenant Oyama's injuries are relatively light. That he is capable of walking perhaps?"

"The concussion is wearing off. Lieutenant Oyama is well capable of walking."

"Perhaps Lieutenant Oyama would welcome the opportunity to come on deck after nightfall?" Dawlish knew that he would never forget this moment, this proposal, that it would lie on his conscience for ever. "On the quarterdeck, to take the air perhaps? In your company, a fellow countryman's?"

"Lieutenant Oyama would most certainly welcome that opportunity." Takenaka's tone was even, his face wholly blank. "Have I your permission to inform him, sir? And to have him moved to my cabin?"

Dawlish nodded. No need for further words.

*

Sunset was still an hour away, and the boats abandoned before the action had been recovered, when *Leonidas* once more resumed her vigil three miles south of Socheong. Dawlish, fighting exhaustion, climbed to the foretop to study the now-familiar coastline. And there, seemingly never having raised anchor, the *Kirishima* lay as before between the anchorage's flanking promontories. If Shimazu was still there then the sound of distant gunfire must have been reported to him. He might perhaps have ascended to one of the headlands to scan the western horizon, might have seen the cloud of rolling smoke that had marked the *Tatsuta's* demise, might have hoped that *Leonidas* had been the victim. He might at this moment be studying *Leonidas* through his own glass, confused by the now yardless masts but then recognising her by her hull. And he would know that the game was not yet over, was yet harder now. There was some bitter satisfaction in knowing that.

Another round of the ship by Dawlish as darkness fell, concentration not now on damage and material integrity but on the crew itself. All on board needed sleep but, with a return to normal watch-keeping essential, it must be denied to many. Everywhere Dawlish encountered an air of gloom, of acceptance of grim reality replacing fading excitement, of weariness replacing shock, of bleary-eyed men working like silent automatons, of no sense of triumph. Dawlish spoke with every party on deck, most of all with the gun-crews now cleaning their weapons under Purdon's unremitting supervision. He visited every compartment, had special words for the cooks and others whose tasks seldom brought them on deck and he spent most time in the boiler and engine rooms. The one space did he not visit was Takenaka's cabin, its door firmly closed, a marine sentry outside. His limbs were leaden by now but still he forced cheerfulness into his voice and still he continued the round, his thanks heartfelt no matter how inadequate his words, pride welling in him that all had done so well. Even should he be broken for the day's action the glory of his men's grim efficiency could never be gainsaid.

It was close to midnight when he at last retired. His steward had cleared the fitments shaken loose by the guns' thundering and had swept away broken glassware but the compartment had an uncomfortable feel about it now. He did not care. He stripped, sponged himself and pulled on clean underwear, a shirt, duck trousers, then lay down, fully dressed but for his boots. Every muscle seemed to scream with exhaustion and his brain still churned and fretted, so that he feared he might not sleep. The memory of the men in the water haunted him, as he knew they would in countless other sleepless nights ahead. It was the futility that was so oppressive, a futility so unquestioningly embraced. Even on the Rio San Joaquin life had had some value – even if only as forced labour – but the *Tatsuta's* crew, men who wore uniforms based on the Royal Navy's, who trained with it, who modelled their organisation and expertise on it, had counted life as less than nothing. And Shimazu's own crew would fight with no less ferocity. The thought of what might lie ahead chilled him, the possibility of his own disgrace paling beside the lives that might yet be squandered. If God existed – as he wanted to believe yet so often doubted – then someday he would have to stand before him to explain those deaths. It was not a comfortable thought.

Yet at last he slept and the sleep was deep and dreamless and infinitely welcome.

The call came three hours later, as he had expected, as he had hoped and dreaded. The steward was shaking him gently awake and a seaman was standing in the corridor outside.

"Mr. O'Rourke's compliments, sir, and he requests your presence on the quarterdeck."

Dawlish pulled on his boots. He sensed that the ship was leaning over in a tight turn, then straightening out again. The distant panting of the engines was slowing – half revolutions, then dead slow. He followed the seaman and, as he expected, found Takenaka with O'Rourke, the officer of the watch. They were standing in silence and looking back out into the darkness. Dim streaks on the sea below told that *Leonidas* was creeping back into her own wake. The searchlight burst into life and began to sweep to either side.

"An untoward incident, sir." O'Rourke was looking very uncomfortable. Takenaka was expressionless.

"I'm sorry to hear it, Lieutenant." Dawlish feigned surprise. "What happened?"

"The fault is wholly mine, sir," said Takenaka. "I misjudged. Your prisoner – our prisoner, sir – Lieutenant Oyama. I tended him myself in my own cabin, as you directed. He asked me if I could bring him on deck. He wanted air, he said." He paused. "He was a fellow Japanese officer, sir, a fellow countryman. I saw no harm in it."

"Where is he now?"

"He leant sometime over the bulwark and watched the wake." Takenaka motioned to the stern. "He found it very beautiful, the phosphorescence, the silence, the darkness. It brought him tranquillity. He told me that."

"And then, Lieutenant?"

"He must have felt lightheaded. He overbalanced, sir." Takenaka's face was without expression, his voice without emotion. "Lieutenant Oyama fell overboard. I raised the alarm immediately."

"I ordered an immediate course reversal," O'Rourke said. "And we're launching a boat. Thank God it had been drained."

"Very correct, Lieutenant O'Rourke," Dawlish said. "The appropriate action. Let's hope we find the poor wretch."

"I assume full responsibility, sir." Takenaka bowed. "I would be honoured if I could take charge of the boat. I wish to make amends, sir."

"That's not necessary. Sub-Lieutenant Leigh is already doing that," O'Rourke said.

The searchlight's icy beam was sweeping hopelessly. Leigh's cutter was dropping into the water, her task equally futile.

"You'd better come with me to my quarters, Lieutenant Takenaka," Dawlish said. "This is a sensitive matter. I need to get some more details from you."

And in his quarters Dawlish got them.

26

The sun rose over a calm sea, the steaming heat with it, and *Leonidas* continued her slow crawl to and fro five miles south of Socheong. The prospect of the funeral at midmorning cast a gloom over the entire ship. There were three to be buried now. The injured seaman had died in the night and was already another pathetic canvas-wrapped bundle lying next to his comrades killed at Songang-ni. Dawlish was dressing in full uniform for the service, and mentally rehearsing the words he already knew too well, when he was summoned to the bridge.

A smudge of smoke was rising over the southern horizon. Slowly, tantalisingly, a foreshortened hull emerged above it. Dawlish watched it grow, uncertain at first, yet with hope increasing…the narrow hull, the low bows, the forecastle awash, the scant upperworks and single funnel, the bare pole masts. Nearer still and there could be no doubt of it, the *Fu Ching*, ploughing purposefully northwards. *Leonidas's* diver and carpenter must have served her well. And she was bringing with her two Armstrong ten-inchers, powerful enough to dismember the *Kirishima* with a single salvo should she come in range.

Signals exchanged, a welcome flag-semaphored from *Leonidas* and acknowledged by the *Fu Ching* by incoherent flapping – Lodge had obviously not yet added competent signalling to his crew's skills. The vessels drew together, both at minimum revolutions, and the Chinese craft dropped a boat. As it stroked across Dawlish recognised Lodge in the sternsheets and a few minutes later he was welcoming the American on board.

"Your men did me proud, sir," he told Dawlish. "She's patched up better than I could have hoped and in half the time."

The American accent brought back a fleeting memory. "Blood is thicker than water," Dawlish said.

"You've seen some action, sir." Lodge was taking in all the signs of a vessel transformed since he had last beheld it yet the sight did not seem to cheer him. "A satisfactory outcome, I'll wager."

"Most satisfactory, Captain." Dawlish did not want to discuss the matter on deck. "You'll join me below?"

He led him to his quarters and ordered his steward to bring coffee. He lit cigars for himself and Lodge.

"I take it you've done the job without me." Lodge's tone hinted at disappointment, maybe resentment.

"There's still trouble enough for both of us," Dawlish said. "Shimazu may still be at Socheong. The *Kirishima* certainly is."

Lodge looked confused. "You damaged her?" he said. It was obvious that he was assuming that *Leonidas* had engaged the *Kirishima*.

Dawlish did not yet disabuse him. "Do you know of another Japanese ship in the area?" he said.

"The *Haruna*. She hasn't returned to Chemulpo. I guess that Admiral Hojo is still keeping out of sight and waiting until he knows which way the cat will jump."

"Not the *Haruna*, though very similar. Two funnels rather than one."

"Nothing like it that I've heard of. And if Fred Kung had word of her I guess he'd have let me know."

Then Dawlish told him what Takenaka had learned from Oyama, the prisoner who had disappeared into the night. That senior Japanese naval officers – probably *Genyosha* sympathisers – had ensured that key personnel sent to Britain to take delivery of the *Tatsuta* were from Kagoshima. That there had been no hint of their disloyalty since suppression of the Satsuman revolt five years before. That the *Tatsuta's* officers had been as exemplary in demonstrations of reverence for the Emperor as they had been in professional excellence. That several had trained with the Royal Navy. That after commissioning in Hull the *Tatsuta's* copper-sheathing had assured an unfouled bottom and a rapid passage to Japan. That she had remained at Nagasaki only long enough to re-coal and to receive instructions – from a higher level, too high for the late Lieutenant Oyama to be permitted to identify – to proceed to Socheong. That there had been a conference with Shimazu, who had remained at the island, and that the *Tatsuta* had left there with the mission of destroying shipping off the Chinese coast, anything, large or small, identifiable as Chinese. And that Oyama had known Shimazu, had been distantly related to him, had revered him for his fidelity to Samurai tradition, had been honoured to support his actions.

"So has Shimazu the Emperor's backing?" Lodge asked the same question that had nagged Dawlish.

"It doesn't seem so," Dawlish said. "Takenaka doesn't think so either. If Shimazu has official backing then some different ship would have been sent to support him, not one that had just arrived after voyaging half-way round the world. Not one that spent less than twenty-four hours in port. It seems more hurried than if it had imperial backing." He paused, then added. "But no, we still can't be completely sure."

"This *Tatsuta*," Lodge said. "You engaged her?"

"I sunk her." For all his doubts Dawlish felt a surge of pride as he spoke. He outlined the action.

Lodge listened hungrily, enviously. "You won't take it amiss if I'll ask you to leave the *Kirishima* to me," he said when Dawlish finished.

"You can take over the blockade?" Dawlish asked. "Hold her there for now until..." His voice trailed off. For *until* was uncertain, with no guarantee of resolution. *Until* was on Shimazu's side, *until* might buy time for the Emperor to back his adventure. The more so since a Japanese warship, however unauthorised her actions, had been sunk. *Until* was not on Dawlish's side.

"I've coal enough to patrol here for the next three weeks," Lodge said. It was obvious that he wanted *Leonidas* to be gone, that he wanted *Kirishima* only for himself.

But Dawlish knew that neither the *Fu Ching's* two ship-smashers nor *Leonidas's* six-inchers could decide the matter. Shimazu could sit tight under cover of his shore batteries and neither the British nor Chinese ships' weapons had the elevation to reach them. Shimazu's landed guns on the headlands were vulnerable only to attack from the land side. And that meant getting men ashore.

"You saw the troops who got back from Songang-ni?" Dawlish asked. "They're still at Chemulpo?"

"I saw Confederates who surrendered in '65 who had more fight left in them," Lodge said. "I've never seen such a mob of whipped curs. And Kung's ordering of half-a-dozen officers to be beheaded didn't raise fighting spirits any."

"Beheaded?" Dawlish felt repelled.

Lodge nodded. "Two took poison to avoid it. Fred was mightily angry that they didn't take the colliery and jetty at Songang-ni but he was even angrier when he learned that forces from Seoul occupied them that same night. Effortlessly too, killed a few Japs and that was it. Fred wasn't happy about it."

"What forces from Seoul?" This was a surprise.

"The troops who'd arrived overland from China. Manchurians, both infantry and cavalry. Very effective, very well trained, I'm told, western weapons and western discipline, a few of the officers qualified in the Prussian War Academy. It seems they made short work of taking the place. They force-marched from Seoul, then waited until the men you had landed from the sea were taken off, waited until the Japs were off guard. Then they struck."

Dawlish was taken aback. "Kung told me nothing about any such plan."

"He wouldn't, would he? Me neither. But Fred Kung knew that Admiral Shen wanted the mine and the coal concession for himself, just like Fred wanted it for himself. Shen probably did a deal with the Chinese Ambassador – whom he outranks anyway – and split some too with the Manchurians' general. It's theirs now, their private property, a formal transfer of concession already signed by the king and Fred Kung has no look-in. It isn't a gold mine but in the absence of one it's worth having."

It fell in place now, Kung's urgency, his need to force the issue on the day, regardless of human cost. Fred Kung had wanted the mine as his personal property.

"What's happening now?"

"Delay. The plan was that we'd have troops ready to land on Socheong now – that was the plan, yours as much as Fred's. But he saw how they behaved at Songang-ni and he's holding back and hoping the executions have encouraged them to show some backbone. By rights they should have been loading on the *Ningpo* transport by now. But they're not."

"I doubt they'll do any good, even if we get them ashore." Dawlish knew that he was stating a brutal truth. He remembered the hesitant advance into disaster at Songang-ni. Even had he landed his own blue-jackets and marines it would have made no difference. He would have committed them to stiffen the attack had it been shown to have some prospect of success. But he had refused to sacrifice them to support the half-hearted, incompetent, advance that had stalled so easily. *Never reinforce failure.* It was inconceivable that such men – beaten curs as Lodge had called them – could capture Shimazu's batteries, inconceivable too that they could be landed at some point remote from the batteries' reach and kept together as a disciplined force as they advanced along the rugged island. The opportunities for cowering in gullies and scrub would be too great.

"But what alternative is there?" Lodge asked.

It was a question that so often led to answers doomed to failure. Yet doing nothing was not an option either. Not if Dawlish was going to avoid ruining his career without making a last effort to save it.

There was one last possibility open, a desperate one.

"I'll be obliged if you'll maintain the watch on the *Kirishima*, Captain Lodge," Dawlish said. "If she does come out then she's all yours."

"And you, Captain Dawlish?"

"I'm returning to Chemulpo."

*

The prospect was as depressing as ever, the yellow silt-laden water, the mile of foul mudflats extending from the shore, the setting sun throwing harsh light on the dismal collection of buildings and the

271

squalid Chinese camp. Dawlish saw that the *Ningpo* still swung at anchor – no sign of activity there, no indication of troops being loaded – and that her damaged sister transport still lay beached on the flats. The tide was out and the long pull to shore up a winding sewer-like channel with high mud banks added even more to the despondency that Dawlish had been unable to shake off since the burial service. He had wanted to get here quickly and even though he had conducted the ceremony with heartfelt reverence there had been no slackening in *Leonidas's* speed as the bodies plunged overboard.

Dawlish had spent most of the hours since in his own quarters. It was hard to fight off depression, even despair. Self-doubt gnawed mercilessly, made worse by disgust that the command he had lusted after for a quarter-century should have led to so much suffering. He forced himself to ignore the sense of desolation and to concentrate on identifying the alternatives available. None was attractive. At last he satisfied himself that he had identified the least worst and sent for Takenaka to join him with his drawn maps and annotations. They spent another hour poring over them, searching for advantages of terrain and elevation, for approaches hidden from the fan-like arcs of Shimazu's landed guns. Three deadly six-inchers on the southern coast, two of them on the western headland flanking the anchorage, one on the easterly. And above the headland west of the shallow bay on the northern coast no certainty, only a suspicion, of another weapon, its range, like that of its fellows, extended by altitude. Meticulous as Takenaka's drawings and estimates might be, so much uncertainty still remained, so much essential information still lacking, so much to be left to chance.

And yet the possibility of success was there, however slim…

Ross was summoned. He had proved his courage and competence in Seoul, the more so since he had never experienced combat previously, but what was needed now was an ability to weigh risks and to plan at a level that might tax a more experienced officer.

"No word of this discussion is to be shared until I permit it. You understand, Lieutenant?" Then, with broad strokes, Dawlish indicated his intent. He sensed Ross's unease growing, an obvious awareness that the risks might border on the suicidal.

"Now tell me the weaknesses," Dawlish said. "You can speak freely. But remember that this plan, in the detail finally agreed, will be executed. There's no question of that."

Hesitant at first, unwilling to correct or to challenge anything Dawlish had proposed, Ross gradually relaxed. And there were weaknesses, ones that seemed obvious when explained by a man trained for combat on land as well as sea, yet ones which Dawlish had overlooked, bland and incorrect assumptions that he and Takenaka had made about topography and movement. Changes were needed – not radical as regards overall purpose, but vital regarding detail and feasibility. Yet through the discussion, through amendments, through refinement, Dawlish's confidence did not increase. The possibility of success remained but it was still slim, very slim. And one vital resource was needed even for that, one that Dawlish and the *Leonidas* could not provide in sufficient quantity. Brute muscle power.

The thought nagged Dawlish as his gig's bows grounded on the mud of Chemulpo's foreshore and he worried also that Whitaker might have returned to the comfort of his residence in Seoul. He needed him badly now, needed him as the only one he could trust to navigate political complexities and to break the barrier of language for him. With four marines as escort Dawlish hurried through the fast-falling dusk to the inn where Whitaker had ensconced himself before. He found him there, more colour in his cheeks than when he had last seen him but with his arm still in a sling. He was wearing a silk gown.

"You're looking comfortable here, Mr. Whitaker." The place had been cleaned, though there was the faintest whiff of opium.

Whitaker shrugged. "I've rented the whole place. Some of my people came down from Seoul to look after me. Even if it hadn't been for this" – he nodded towards his arm – "it would be better to stay away from there until the situation is more clear."

"Do you know of another Japanese warship? Not the *Haruna*, some other?" The same question Dawlish had asked Lodge, and the same answer. There had been no inkling of any other ship's presence. "Any other news of the Japanese?"

"None. No trading vessels either. At any other time there would be several here to load rice. Now, none at all. But absence isn't inaction. The Japanese aren't people to let things slip. You can depend on it that they've got something in hand."

Dawlish outlined the events of the last days. Whitaker knew of the disaster at Songang-ni, had seen the defeated force's return – "I wasn't surprised in the least" – but the encounter with the *Tatsuta* was new to him. He paled. "You've exceeded your authority, Dawlish," he said. "You've exceeded it badly. You've probably destroyed years of careful diplomacy."

He's only the first to say this, Dawlish thought, *and the others who'll say it will be a lot more influential.* He could see his career, his prospects, his reputation slipping from him, his ambitions reduced to ashes.

"I had no part in this, Dawlish, and you can't say I didn't warn you," Whitaker paused and then, almost to himself, he said "Thank God I asked you to sign that paper."

There was no value in pursuing the point. Dawlish needed him.

"Is Kung still here?"

"Licking his wounds and damned bitter about it too. You've heard that a force from Seoul took the Songang-ni mine? It seems like Kung wanted it for himself."

"But it isn't much use to anybody unless they hold Socheong also. It's got a deep enough anchorage to be a coaling station. Songang-ni has not," Dawlish said. "Admiral Shen will need to sell his coal. Kung can offer him a deal if he has Socheong."

"He'll never take Socheong now, not even with Lodge's ship to support him. I saw those men who came back from Songang-ni. They were a rabble." Whitaker was obviously assuming that Dawlish had decided to play no further role.

Dawlish cut him off. "I want to see Kung tonight."

"Why, Dawlish? He won't be glad to see you. Better we leave him be. Better that we make one last attempt to get the codicils signed – Admiral Shen owes you for his life and he'll bring pressure to bear at court. You'll have the queen's support also. There'll be ways of contacting her. She won't have forgotten you and the king will do her bidding. And then you can be on your way." Whitaker gave a clear impression that he would be glad to see *Leonidas* sailing into the sunset.

"I said tonight." Dawlish's tone indicated no tolerance for argument. "I can sign another one of those wretched disclaimers of yours if that will keep you happy, but I want to see Fred Kung tonight."

Whitaker sighed. "I'll need to change," he said, glancing down on his robe.

Dawlish hoped he was disguising his own desperation as, lit by lanterns carried by Whitaker's servants, they walked towards the Chinese camp. He hated the entire business now, longed only to be rid of it, loathed himself for the slow drip of death and injury he had imposed on his own crew, felt guilt for the Japanese – hundreds of them – who had died with the *Tatsuta*. The possibility of an ignominious end to his own career seemed almost trivial by comparison – though he knew the shame would kill him, would ruin Florence's life no less. He was already far down that road of disgrace and the only way to avert what lay ahead was to gamble all on one last throw. A gamble of lives…

Whitaker's skill in Chinese convinced the guards to summon an officer. A long sequence of bows and apparent compliments followed. Dawlish, mystified, bowed and smiled in imitation of Whitaker. At last they were escorted through the camp, even more squalid, more chaotic, than on the previous visit. Kung's Uighur guards proved even more difficult to get past. Dawlish recognised one he had seen previously by a facial scar and the man recognised him, but it made no difference. Fred Kung was taking no chances. Toing and froing by guards followed while Dawlish and Whitaker waited in patient exasperation.

"He knows damn well we're here," Whitaker said. "He's keeping us waiting, he's letting his people know – and us too – just how damn powerful he still is. He's smarting that he lost face at Songang-ni. He needs to regain it."

"Which Fred will we see? The American or the Chinese?"

"Don't be fooled, Dawlish," Whitaker said. "There's one only, and he's always Chinese."

Yet the Fred Kung they found at his commandeered house could have passed as American. No florid compliments, no bows, no expressions of exaggerated respect. No dissimulation and no concern for face – Dawlish's face

"You're a son of a bitch, Captain," he said when they entered. "You left me in the lurch." It was like a clear statement of fact, with no tone of animosity, even though is eyes conveyed no warmth.

Dawlish bridled, felt Whitaker's restraining hand on his arm, choked back his fury. His mother had died when he was a child and he had loved her. At this moment he would gladly have thrashed Kung. "Good evening," he managed to say. "I trust you're well."

Kung reached out his left hand and Dawlish took it. "And you, Mr. Whitaker. Gettin' used to one-handed life, are you? Not as difficult as you might have thought?" He gestured to ornately carved chairs that had not been there before. "Sit down, Gentlemen."

Tea appeared, an exquisite porcelain pot and cups, bottles too, western drinks. The guards and servants were dismissed. Whitaker took whisky and Dawlish asked for tea. In silence Kung poured two cups, one for Dawlish and one for himself.

"I guess you're not here to apologise, Captain," he said. "There's none worth making. If you'd landed your people we'd have the mine by now."

"We? Mr. Kung," Dawlish said. "I suspect that you mean I."

Kung smiled for the first time. "Yeah, Captain. Of course I mean I. I want that goddam mine. It's not unreasonable to want riches." He held up his mutilated right hand. "What else is life about?"

"I'm here to talk business," Dawlish said. "I'm still able to help you get rich. Richer, I'd guess."

"And take a cut yourself, Captain? It's too late for that."

Dawlish ignored the implication. "You can still have Socheong," he said. "The anchorage, the loading jetty, everything the mine is useless without. If you hold it you can do a deal with your Admiral Shen, with your ambassador too, split the profits, enough for everybody. And you can still get it."

"With this bunch?" Kung's good arm swung out as if to encompass the whole camp and all in it. "You saw them at Songang-ni? Useless, goddam useless."

"I don't need them just as troops, Mr. Kung. I want labourers, porters."

Kung's forced smile hid obvious anger. "Coolies, you mean. That's what we were called on the Central Pacific. Chinks, Celestials, Coolies. What I shipped home in boxes."

"You can call them what you like, Mr. Kung. We still need them if we're to take the island."

"We, Captain?"

"That's what I said, Mr. Kung. Together we'll take Socheong."

27

It was Takenaka who found what Dawlish needed, an island, separated from the coast by a four-mile strait. Arang-Dong was larger than Socheong, twice the area at the least, and some fifty miles due north of it.

"How reliable is the chart?" Dawlish asked, his fear of uncharted rocks unspoken

"It was trustworthy as regards Socheong and Songang-ni, sir. We've got to assume the same now." The chart had resulted from a preliminary Royal Navy survey several years earlier. It had little detail.

"Inhabited?"

"Possibly, sir. But there can't be more than a few fishermen." Takenaka pointed to a narrow neck of land that joined a tiny lobe on the south west to the main island. "If we go ashore here there would be a good chance nobody would be aware of us. Most of the island seems to be hilly and forested."

"Plot me a course there, Lieutenant," Dawlish said.

The *Ningpo*, the chartered transport, was essential to the plan and must be readied for sea. Anticipating that her captain, Holles, would be happier to be paid demurrage rather than take his vessel from her moorings, Dawlish undertook to put his paymaster on board to oversee the operation. He could spare no other officer, but Watkin had done well during the action with the *Tatsuta*. Supported by a half-dozen seamen, he would be well capable of demolishing Holles's inevitable plethora of excuses. An armed guard in the engine room would deter any attempts at immobilisation. Dawlish estimated three days for the *Ningpo's* preparation and loading but knew that this might well be optimistic. One factor however favoured speed. Kung's Uighurs and their vicious swords would guarantee compliance from the Chinese. Once loaded the *Ningpo* should reach Arang-Dong in a day, two at the most and then...

At the earliest action would be possible in just under a week. All that while Lodge must maintain the Socheong blockade, outside the range of Shimazu's landed guns but haunted every night by the spectre of torpedo-boat attack. But as the days slipped by and as Shimazu remained snug in his island fortress, his *Genyosha* supporters in Japan might be gaining the Emperor's approval. The *Haruna* was already somewhere in the area, neutral for now, but ready with merciless efficiency to do any bidding received from Japan. And other Japanese warships might already be at sea.

Dawlish allowed for one day only at Chemulpo, long enough to take on fresh provisions – vegetables and unpalatable ox-beef could be purchased at exorbitant cost ashore – and to continue repairing battle damage. He needed *Leonidas* to be away from here quickly, and not just because he did not want to be found anchored in the roadstead should the *Haruna* or other Japanese ships appear. His plan demanded skills that the fast cruise from Britain had allowed his crew no opportunity to practice. They had come aboard as individuals, experienced in such abilities from previous ships, but they had never worked together onshore as a team. Now there were only a few days to remedy the deficiency.

*

The gloom that had pervaded *Leonidas* in the aftermath of the action and burials dispersed in the bustle of readying for sea. She seemed a different ship, leaner, somehow more menacing now that she was incapable of carrying sail, her masts mere poles crossed with slim signalling yards. The carpenter and his crew, flushed with pride for the job they had done so rapidly and so effectively on Lodge's vessel, had worked tirelessly to rivet new plates over the rents the *Tatsuta's* shells had torn in *Leonidas's* side. Other repairs were in hand, and scorch and blast marks were being painted over. The decks were washed – there were more urgent requirements for now than for holystoning to recommence – and men and clothes could be washed also, and hammocks brought on deck for airing. In the boiler and engine-rooms bearings, valves, seals, gauges, pumps were all checked and adjusted, parts replaced where necessary. Dawlish demanded that the dynamo and the small steam engine driving it received especial attention, so too the cabling leading to the searchlights, and the carbon rods that fed the arcs were replaced. While Shimazu still possessed two torpedo boats *Leonidas's* survival might depend on the reliability of this one piece of equipment alone.

When *Leonidas* sailed an hour before sunset she had spent little over twenty-four hours at Chemulpo. Darkness fell as she steamed north-westwards, a darkness relieved only by the faintest sliver of a crescent moon above the mainland. At fifteen knots she should be eight miles west of Socheong shortly after midnight.

On the starboard side Egdean was supervising the swinging of Dawlish's 30-foot gig out on its davits, ready for lowering. Dawlish found him meticulously checking the slight, elegant craft's twin masts and sails, not yet stepped.

"Like old times, sir," Egdean said.

"But not much prospect of slavers or prize-money tonight."

They had first met when chasing captive-laden Arab dhows in the Zanzibar Channel six years before. And since then, so much had been shared that could not be spoken of to others, so much trust and respect, so much mutually owed. Yet still the invisible barrier of class and rank remained that could never be breached.

"We could do with a stronger breeze, sir." It was barely enough to ripple the calm sea, breathing rather than blowing out from the mainland.

"It will serve. It's enough." Dawlish hoped he was correct.

The conference was held around the wardroom table, again polished and pristine with no hint that men had suffered on it only days since. Parts of the plan had been communicated to some of the officers, but this was the first time that all heard the totality. Uneasy glances passed between them as Dawlish pointed to features on the large-scale sketch of Socheong which Takenaka had drawn on the back of a large chart. Nobody had expected anything like what was now proposed. Dawlish outlined the role of each officer, emphasised that each was critical. He was frank about the risks, about unavoidable weaknesses in the plan – and there were still so many – and about how he proposed to address them. He would hear suggestions for refinement but was clear that the operation would proceed, that his decision was unchallengeable.

Hesitation and silence. Edgerton looking troubled, Takenaka impassive, Ross sombre, the others torn between excitement and supressed fear.

"Can there be more time available, sir?" O'Rourke glanced around to see if others were backing him and saw that they were avoiding his gaze. "The men, the marines most of all, they need ..." His voice trailed off.

Dawlish shook his head. "I'd like to have more days too. But no, we can't."

Yet O'Rourke's question had broken the ice. Discussion was now easier – numbers, selection of men, equipment, boat-loading, rations, signalling. Minor improvements, small modifications, but the overall plan unchanged. Yet still an unavoidable level of risk remained. A high one. The responsibility for success or failure would be Dawlish's but the price for it would be paid by officers and men alike.

It was Purdon who at last raised the question that had hovered unspoken. "The Chinese, sir. Not just the troops. The ship, the *Fu Ching*, her guns. We'll be relying a lot on her, sir."

He did not need to say more. The carpenter's party that had returned to *Leonidas* it had brought stories stories of brutal discipline. Without it even the simplest tasks were avoided by the Chinese crew.

"We'll be relying on Captain Lodge," Dawlish said. "I believe he knows how to run and fight a ship." He hoped he sounded confident and that others did not see that the same question worried him. Of all the weak links in the plan the *Fu Ching* was the weakest.

Dawlish asked Edgerton to join him in his quarters afterwards. He invited him to sit.

"You're not happy about these plans, Commander," Dawlish said. Better to be direct.

"Your instructions will be followed to the letter. You can depend on that, sir."

"That's not in doubt, Commander. And you're aware that there's a possibility, a remote possibility, but we can't discount it, that something could happen to me tonight."

Edgerton shifted uncomfortably in his chair. "I may speak freely, sir?"

Dawlish nodded. Edgerton had performed well in the heat of action, had not flinched, had demonstrated admirable professionalism, but Dawlish had guessed what was coming. He was correct.

"I'm concerned about you leaving your ship, Captain Dawlish. If something, God forbid, did happen, it would be a very difficult position, very irregular. It would be…" Edgerton left the sentence uncompleted, confirming Dawlish's assessment. A competent follower but not a leader.

"If I don't return then the plans we've just discussed are void," Dawlish said. "No further action against Shimazu. No joint operations with Lodge. You don't start searching for me until first light the day after tomorrow. In the meantime stay far enough west of Socheong that not even a masthead can be spotted from there. You'll have twenty-four hours to find me – and for that you'll need to make contact with Lodge – but after that the time is up. You'll have command of this ship and you'll take her directly to Hong Kong. You'll make your report to Admiral Willes and you'll a hand him this letter." Dawlish reached out a sheet of paper.

Edgerton began to scan it.

"I've absolved you and every other officer on board of responsibility for all that has happened and most of all for the sinking of the *Tatsuta*," Dawlish said. "There may be serious repercussions but you'll bear no responsibility for them." He handed over another sheet. "That's also for the admiral, commendations of the behaviour of several officers and seamen, yourself not least."

"It's handsome, sir," Edgerton said. "Very handsome indeed. And I trust it won't be needed."

"So do I, Commander. So do I." He meant it, though he wondered if Edgerton did also. "One other request, Commander." He reached out an envelope with Florence's name on it. "I'd be grateful if you could bring this to my wife. If circumstances so demand, that is."

Edgerton took it. The letter, a single page, had been hard to write, its words inadequate, the phrases incapable of conveying all that was meant. And yet he knew that Florence would keep it by her and read and reread it until her own death.

After Edgerton left, Dawlish changed into a duck shirt and trousers. He wished they were not white, but there was no help for it in the time available. He went on deck, checked that all Egdean's preparations were complete – as they were, faultlessly, as he had expected. Then he went back to his cabin, checked the action and ammunition of his revolver, and lay down.

It felt as if only minutes had passed when the steward awoke him. Commander Edgerton's compliments. It was time.

The night was all but black with only the faintest moonlight over the land to the east. Socheong's profile was undetectable. *Leonidas's* course had brought her some ten miles south of the island before curving to the north. Now she lay stationary, eight miles due west of it, all lights doused, she herself merging into night.

The gig was lowered, slim and graceful, made for speed under oar or sail, her duty as captain's harbour-craft ensuring gleaming varnish and immaculate paintwork – too immaculate, yet even for this night's work Dawlish could not bring himself to have her whiteness daubed black or grey. He dropped down into her – five men selected by Egdean were already on board with him, insufficient to pull her as fast as she was capable of with full manning but better than nothing should the breeze die. All had cutlasses and Egdean, like Dawlish, carried a revolver.

An icy white light, little more than a pinprick, blinked into life on the horizon to the east, grew in intensity and faded again, then waxed and waned once more, then finally died. Lodge's *Fu Ching* was there, five miles south of Socheong, her steady vigil marked by intermittent sweepings with her searchlight. As it faded into the darkness again a similar light came briefly to life to the north. Shimazu's and *Kirishima's* presence and defiance were being proclaimed. Dawlish knew that Lodge was not expecting him but the *Fu Ching's* spasmodic illuminations would provide a sure navigation goal. He snapped his prismatic compass open, ready to take a bearing when the distant searchlight came to life again.

The gig pulled away from *Leonidas* and the cruiser crawled away into the western darkness on slowly churning screws. While the masts were being erected and the sails set – the gig was ketch-rigged – the *Fu Ching's* light showed itself again and Dawlish got the fix he needed. He settled in the sternsheets as the sails grasped the faint breeze. The craft came to life, water gurgling along her side, her crew silent but watchful. Her speed was low, very low, and a long series of tacks would be required to reach the Chinese ship. The tiny crescent moon over the distant mainland brought only the slightest relief to the darkness. As the gig glided through the glassy calm she encountered drifting wisps of mist, enough to block sighting of the *Fu Ching's* spasmodic flashes and the answering pinpricks to the north.

An hour passed, and another, the tacks executed in near silence, commands only a whisper. The *Fu Ching* had receded, for when first seen she had been close to the western extremity of her patrol but thereafter she had turned to crawl eastwards. She must now be close to the turn back to the west. With only the odd sweeps of her searchlight to identify her it was difficult to judge distance but Dawlish reckoned that she was still five to six miles away. He knew that the greatest danger would be when she was approached – Lodge had no reason to expect his arrival in an open boat and the searchlight activity told of lookouts on their mettle to detect the presence of Shimazu's torpedo craft. The *Fu Ching's* greeting might well be in the form of a lethal hail of Gatling fire. But there was no alternative to making contact with Lodge in this way. It was essential to keep Shimazu unaware of *Leonidas's* presence, to keep him hoping that Dawlish had perhaps given up the game, was already en route back to Hong Kong, that only the *Fu Ching* now confronted the *Kirishima*.

The breeze had all but died, was now only the slightest breath, barely enough to keep the gig underway.

"Time to pull, sir?" Egdean's voice a whisper, his presence only a darker outline against the darkness beyond.

"Wait," Dawlish said. "Wait a little longer." He was unwilling to ship the oars and tire the crew.

The gig crawled on. Dawlish reached his hand over the side and felt it scarcely dragged by the passing water. He glanced forward. Drifting mist, thicker now that the breeze had almost died, obscured the *Fu Ching's* light. Dawn was few hours away and the prospect of daylight revealing the gig's presence was daunting. He waited five minutes more and was about to order the oars shipped when suddenly he felt air brush his cheek. The breeze was picking up again, not much, but enough to urge the gig forward again. The mist too seemed to be thinning and in one brief interval of clarity he spotted the *Fu Ching*. Close now, very close, less than two miles, he estimated.

"Get the lamps ready," he told Egdean. "Don't light them yet but be ready." A thrill of fear ran through him as he spoke. The sight of two lamps waving in the darkness might as well invite defensive gunfire as cautious investigation.

At that moment came an urgent whisper from the bows.

"There's something ahead, sir!" A tremor in the voice, rational fear. Nothing should be expected here, nothing afloat until the *Fu Ching* drew close.

Eyes straining into the blackness and seeing nothing, Dawlish hissed "Go forward, Egdean!" He took the tiller and felt his heart pounding and his hands trembling. He opened the flap of his holster and felt the butt's reassuring solidity, yet knew it could be only meagre protection at best.

"There's something there." Egdean's whisper. "Just an outline. It's not moving."

"How far?"

"Half a cable."

Even at this crawl the gig would be upon it in little over a minute. Dawlish was about to put the helm over, to allow the craft's paltry momentum to carry her back into the darkness astern when a fleeting gap in the tendrils of mist showed what lay ahead.

It was the slight glow above her funnel, the odd fleeting spark flying up and dying above it that revealed what she was no less than did the long low lines. It was a torpedo boat, unmistakable, perhaps the same that *Leonidas* had engaged north of Socheong, perhaps her mate. A figure was moving on deck, then another briefly glimpsed before the mist enshrouded it again. They gave no hint of alarm, no awareness of the gig gliding silently towards them. Stationary in the mist, every eye on the Japanese craft must be intent on detecting the Chinese cruiser they lay in ambush for.

And Dawlish knew that at this moment there was only one option open to him.

"Cutlasses ready! Egdean – you've got your pistol! Prepare to board!"

Dawlish's mind raced. Two revolvers, five cutlasses – and surprise. The only weapons. An officer at the torpedo boat's con, two, maybe three, deckhands doubling as Gatling gunner and loaders, perhaps two men below to tend the tiny combined engine and boiler room amidships. A single ripple from the Gatling could tear the gig asunder, a single throw of the steam throttle could send the torpedo boat churning away into the darkness ...

The dark outline was resolving itself into detail now – the gig was bearing silently down on the torpedo boat's starboard quarter and had not been detected. He could see the Gatling mounting clearly now, a small platform just ahead of the tiny funnel, just abaft the steering position and raised above it. His heart leaped. For it was not just unmanned – there was no sign of a weapon. Other than any small arms the boat carried nothing but its torpedo. Hope soared.

"Bolton!" Dawlish remembered the name of the nearest man. "You're with me!" He feared his whisper might be loud enough to alert his quarry. "Egdean! The others forward with you!"

Ten seconds more – the gig still undetected – and Dawlish shifted the tiller ever so slightly to bring it directly astern of the torpedo boat. He had his revolver out, a tug on its lanyard assuring him that he would not lose it. His moment of fear had passed and his whole being was focussed on prevailing. At the instant that collision was imminent he nudged the tiller over to bring his craft parallel to the torpedo boat's starboard side. "Let go all sheets!" he called in a loud whisper. The sails flapped into idleness but the gig's momentum still bore her forward.

There was a cry from the torpedo boat in the instant that the gig came grating along her side. The difference in freeboard was minimal and Egdean's men were already leaping across. The bark of a pistol shot, a brief flame lancing in the semi-darkness, more shouting, and another shot. Dawlish was already scrambling across also, Bolton close behind him. The torpedo boat was small enough to rock as the seven men pounded on to her side and Dawlish almost lost his balance. He looked down and saw a small open cockpit below him, a bench along either side, a companionway, door open, at its forward end – the entrance to the engine compartment. There was shouting forward, another pistol shot, one more, swearing in English, a cry that could only be Japanese, the dull chop of steel against flesh and bone, a scream of agony. Dawlish jumped down at the moment a head was thrust out from the companionway. He swung his pistol up, then realised that the boiler lay beyond, that a shot might penetrate it. Instead he flung himself towards the open door, letting his revolver drop to swing free on its lanyard. His hands reached for the close-cropped head that was already disappearing back inside. His fingers locked on squirming flesh wet with sweat. The man screamed. Dawlish released one hand, sought with the other for the shirt collar, found it, locked on it and dragged the man out. He flung him down. As the Japanese fought to rise Bolton began to hack at him.

From the bows came the sound of more shooting and yet more shouting. Bolton's victim was stilled now and Dawlish peered into the small engine room. It was lit only by the glow from the open furnace grate and he could see the boiler, coal, the engine itself and no room for another man to cower in.

Then silence.

Dawlish looked forward. "Egdean! All clear?"

"All clear here, sir!"

Clear it was, five bodies slumped at the steering position and by the breech of the torpedo tube, two taken down by gunshot, the others hacked by cutlass. None had managed to grasp a weapon though the dead officer by the helm had half-dragged a revolver from his holster.

"Anybody wounded?"

"Nobody, sir. A few bruises." Egdean shifted his feet to avoid a rivulet of blood and nodded to the corpses. "They never saw us coming. Poor wretches, heathens though they be."

No time for sentiment. Dawlish was already feeling the reaction in himself, the trembling hands, a relief that he was alive so intense as to dominate all thought. The others would be experiencing the same and action was the only antidote.

"Get these bodies overboard. Take that man's pistol." He gestured towards the dead officer. "And secure the gig."

Beyond that was the need to signal to the approaching *Fu Ching*. If Lodge did not blast the torpedo boat to fragments, if he was to heed the lanterns Dawlish set his men to wave, then he would have another weapon at his disposal. A functioning and armed torpedo boat.

28

Dawlish was back aboard *Leonidas* some twenty-three hours after he had left her. The gig had departed from the *Fu Ching* after nightfall and sailed smoothly westward ahead of the night's offshore breeze. It displayed no identification lanterns until well clear of Socheong. *Leonidas*, unlit, emerged from the darkness and the gig and her occupants were taken on board. Edgerton's welcome seemed forced – Dawlish sensed that he might have been relieved if he himself had not returned – but the other officers seemed pleased with the order to head for Arang-Dong.

Lights still doused, *Leonidas* ploughed north-eastwards at increased revolutions. Over to the east, intermittent searchlight stabs identified Lodge's *Fu Ching* still on her monotonous patrol and Shimazu's force's no less watchful vigil on the headlands of Socheong. A few hours' sleep could at last be grasped – Dawlish's exhaustion was extreme now and he had fought to keep awake as the gig had slipped easily through the night.

Surrounded again by the normality of shipboard routine Dawlish felt as if he had never left *Leonidas*, as if the brief, murderous violence of the torpedo boat's capture and what had followed had been a dream. He was confident that his own passage to and from the Chinese vessel had been wholly undetected, was certain too that the torpedo boat's loss was probably still inexplicable to Shimazu. After coming alongside the *Fu Ching* – a nerve-racking proceeding, with maximum suspicion on one side, maximum fear on the other – he had convinced Lodge to turn south, towing the captured craft with him, far enough from Socheong for only the *Fu Ching's* upper masts to be discernible above the horizon in first light.

That light showed a ship reasonably well maintained and a crew that seemed more alert, less slovenly, than that which Dawlish had seen on the *Hi Ying* before her sinking. The flaps over the apertures of the fixed armoured drums, within which the ten-inch weapons fore and aft pivoted, had been lifted to clear full arcs of fire. Brasswork gleamed on the 4.7-inch breech-loaders, two on either side. Men were already on their knees, holystoning planking with as much energy and as little pleasure as their Royal Navy counterparts. Paintwork had been freshly washed. The furnaces were efficiently stoked – there was little smoke and indeed more would be desirable at this time to remind Shimazu of the Chinese vessel's presence. Lodge had not matched the level of smartness the Japanese had achieved, but he was coming close. He was not however convinced that he should take over the captured torpedo boat.

"I can't spare the men," he said, "not any who're any good. And it's a complicated weapon. Nobody on board has any experience of it."

"It can be another string to your bow." Dawlish said it reluctantly. The prospect of taking over the craft himself, of putting O'Rourke and five reliable men on board, of penetrating Shimazu's anchorage, was almost irresistible. But Lodge needed her more.

"If – when – the *Kirishima* comes out you'll need all the weaponry you can get," Dawlish urged. "That young officer of yours – Lin, isn't it? – he proved his mettle when the *Hi Ying* was sunk. He's intelligent, he speaks English and he's got a score to settle. He could do it."

Dawlish did not press it – not immediately – and he concentrated on talking Lodge through the plan he had already been committed to without his being consulted.

"It sounds like suicide, probably is," Lodge said, "but it's your neck, Captain Dawlish, not mine."

"Can you think of any other way of engaging the *Kirishima*?"

And Lodge could not, nor any alternative for getting the Japanese cruiser within range of the *Fu Ching's* ten-inch Armstrong ship-smashers. Dawlish had risked *Leonidas* once before and he had been lucky. He had no intention of trusting to luck a second time. He was ready to risk lives, but not his ship, even though one of those lives would be his own. Lodge was welcome to the *Kirishima* – and the torpedo boat could only help him, however inadequately manned.

At last Lodge yielded the point and Lin was sent for.

Dawlish sensed something different about him than about other Chinese officers he had met, none of the unwillingness to avoid responsibility, no elaborate evasion, perhaps even less dedication to self-enrichment. The fact that Lin had chosen a western uniform like

Lodge's rather than flapping sleeves and embroidered silk spoke of efficiency.

"Do you know anything about torpedoes?"

"Nothing, sir." Lin's honesty was at least welcome. "I've had no opportunity, sir. *Fu Ching* does not carry any."

"You know that launching one would mean closing with the enemy? Very close. Two or three hundred yards." Dawlish immediately regretted his phrasing. He was presenting Lin with a challenge he could not refuse without losing face.

"I understand, sir. The Japanese came that close to attack us at Chemulpo. We anticipated nothing. I expect that the Japanese will be taking more precautions than we did." There was an edge to Lin's voice that conveyed clear appreciation of the risk, a hint too of shame, of determination to expunge humiliation. Dawlish's challenge was minor by comparison with the indignity of the *Hi Ying's* unpreparedness.

"This may even be the same boat Shimazu used that night," Dawlish said. "You'll only have a few hours' instruction from me. It won't be enough – you understand that?"

"I understand, sir."

It wasn't long enough, a week would not have been, but before nightfall Lin had some perception of the basics. The single torpedo was a standard 14-inch Whitehead and it looked well maintained when Dawlish had it extracted from its tube. The arming lever and firing pistol had been set – the *Fu Ching* had had a narrow escape – and Dawlish decided not to open the weapon to check the depth-keeping mechanism. Japanese efficiency could be relied on for that. The air reservoir for launching was at full pressure and the cap over the tube-end protruding through the craft's stem had been hinged up – best leave it that way. Practice runs with the *Fu Ching* as target attested to the reliability of the torpedo boat's engine even if closing on a target making anything over twelve knots proved impossible. It was clear that a deflection launch would be beyond Lin – that took long training, much trial and error – and nothing short of point blank range could offer a glimmer of success. There was no gauging how Lin's nerve might hold, no way of conveying to him the terror of being caught in the blinding iciness of searchlight beam. Yet perhaps that didn't matter. Even a distraction might be valuable enough.

There was one last conference with Lodge, one last review of the plans, agreement on signals, frank acknowledgement that so much could go wrong.

Dawlish grasped the American's hand before he stepped into the gig. He had not warmed to him, and he sensed that Lodge was equally cool to him, but he recognised a feeling of mutual professional trust.

"You know that even if Shimazu doesn't come out half the Japanese navy could appear to support him. What then?" Dawlish said.

"Then I'll go down fighting."

And the grim set of his features told that Lodge meant it. He might have been preparing for this moment since the end of his country's Civil War. For seventeen years.

*

There was no sign of life or settlement when *Leonidas* dropped anchor after midday in ten fathoms off the western coast of Arang-Dong. Before her lay the narrow isthmus – little more than a low sand bank – that linked the tiny lobe to the south, a scrub-clad hummock, with the more densely forested hills of the main island. The calm was still holding, the sea glassy, the heat steaming, clothing already sodden as the landing party pulled away, the disassembled seven-pounder field gun stacked in the leading cutter. Fifty men went ashore – all Ross's marines and twenty bluejackets with them. Takenaka was in overall command. Dawlish knew that the crew had been repelled by the Japanese self-willed mass drowning. He had feared that Takenaka might be distrusted, yet the men seemed to regard him as just another officer. "A decent man for a heathen. Strict, fair though. The men like him," Egdean had said when approached in confidence.

On the first day Dawlish landed only briefly, content to leave Takenaka and Ross supervising the exercises. The smaller group, Ross's, four marines and a dozen seamen, busied themselves with the seven-pounder. They assembled it at one end of the beach. Then it was broken down into its components and lugged six hundred yards to the other end. Four men carried the carriage, one each dismounted wheel, two the barrel, while individuals laden with two shells and charge canisters ran alongside and acted as reserves when the carriers tired, Ross urged them forward, stop-watches in hand. No rest at their destination, the weapon reassembled, sights mounted, charge and shell

289

rammed down the muzzle, the loading and aiming sequence stopping short only of actual firing. Then the whole process would begin again, back and forth, muscles screaming, breath rasping, skin glistening with sweat, the marines comfortable in their boots but the seamen's feet rubbing raw in unaccustomed plimsolls.

Takenaka oversaw the drilling of the remainder. Egdean, ever reliable, and Shand, a Scots marine-corporal temporarily promoted to sergeant to replace the now one-legged Hawley, proved relentless in exercising bootnecks and bluejackets alike – no live fire, but bayonet and cutlass practice brought to a new level of intensity, individual movements initially, then man matched against man. The men had a grimness about them now, a determination to leave as little possible to chance. Sitting helplessly in their boats, they had watched the butchery inflicted by the Japanese Gatlings at Songang-ni. The story of the empty mount on the captured torpedo boat had flashed around the ship, bringing with it the likelihood that at least one Gatling could have been landed on Socheong. That knowledge had brought a dour ferocity, a resolve not to go like lambs towards slaughter.

There was no rest on *Leonidas* either, a sense of urgency and purpose almost palpable, an awareness that further action was imminent. Accounts of the close-quarters killing in Seoul and on the Japanese torpedo boat, the details both horrifying and fascinating, had gained in each telling. Recollection of the sea-burials had also underlined the possibility that the corpses that had slipped overboard had not been the last. As Dawlish moved about he sensed from furtive glances that he himself was under the scrutiny of every man on board. They knew that on him most of all their lives would depend.

The shore party returned, wholly exhausted, at nightfall. Three men had already been brought on board with heat-stroke, a fourth with a bayonet-ripped arm, another suddenly and painfully ruptured. There would be more casualties on the morrow, weakness better exposed in training here than in action later. A quiet night followed, no hint of lights on the horizon or on the island, *Leonidas* herself darkened, lookouts alert.

The cutters ground again on the beach at first light, new men added to make up for the injured. The seven-pounder no longer shuttled to and fro along the level beach but was now urged up and down the slopes of the southern lobe, the crews disappearing for minutes at a time into hidden ravines, reappearing again to drag their loads towards the brush-clad summit and to assemble the seven-pounder there. Dawlish joined them in the afternoon, accompanying the gun team on yet another heart-bursting, breath-rasping ascent, throwing himself on a line to help drag the barrel up a gully wall, carrying ammunition to relieve a man gasping under his load, satisfying himself that the assembly was correct, unhappy that there was still too much noise, urging greater silence. And checking the aim on *Leonidas*, two hundred feet below and half a mile distant. That most of all.

He weighed a shell in his hands. Seven pounds. It felt — it was — so puny, but it would have to do.

Rest, twenty minutes, before the descent commenced, the gun once more disassembled, the beach reached again in three minutes less than the first descent that day despite the men's growing exhaustion. Regardless of their normal roles on *Leonidas* – one powerfully muscled seaman was a cook, another a stoker – the landing party were no longer individuals but part of a team that was settling into smooth, almost unconscious, mutual reliance. A half-hour break, enough for essential rest, but deliberately too little for lassitude. Arms were distributed now, cutlasses and pistols only, but enough to encumber further on the next scaling of the hill. The ascent was in silence, broken only by hissed orders, by heaving breaths, by scraping of wood or metal on rock, by feet dislodging miniscule avalanches of loose soil. Dawlish timed with his own watch – a minute and a half shorter than before. It was satisfactory, but this was in daylight. Then a descent again to the beach and a long rest until sundown, food brought across from the ship and heated over brush-fed cooking fires, tea brewed, no rum ration. Men lay down and slept in whatever shelter they could find. Looking at their recumbent forms Dawlish felt as content as he dared. His plan was desperate but he could not have hoped for a better group than this to implement it.

It was an hour before sunset. "It's time to waken the men," Dawlish told Takenaka. "Get them into the boats, the gun also."

"The gun also?" Takenaka had not anticipated this, for Dawlish had not mentioned it.

"Exactly as it will be on the night."

Two cutters sufficed for the entire landing party. Dawlish accompanied the craft which carried the disassembled seven-pounder. Both craft stroked slowly out and around *Leonidas*. The sun was dropping, fifteen minutes to darkness.

"We're to land there, Gentlemen." Dawlish pointed to low cliff that fell almost vertically into the sea from the hills on the northern lobe. It was broken by a narrow cleft that reached to the water's edge. "Mr. Takenaka, kindly take bearings. Bring us in after dark."

Time passed slowly until soft darkness fell, the men resting in silence on their oars. The clear sky was light enough now, studded with thousands of points of starlight, and the crescent of the growing moon was appreciably larger than two nights before. Dawlish waited another quarter-hour, then ordered the approach to the island's black mass, Takenaka conning by hand-held compass.

The landfall did not find the cleft and in the blackness there was no way of knowing whether the craft were to the north or the south of it.

"As it may be on the night," Dawlish said. He said no more, left it to Takenaka to find by trial and error that the ravine was less than a hundred yards to the south. Ten minutes lost but a good lesson learned.

The gash in the cliff was narrow, too narrow in places for three men to stand abreast. Its steep incline, winding and half-blocked in places by fallen boulders and clumps of brush, made porterage of the gun's components a brutal struggle. But once gained, the gully's top opened on to a scrub-covered slope, not unlike what they had laboured through all day, and the progress to the summit proved easier than expected. The seven-pounder was assembled in three minutes, was ready for firing one later.

"Ten minutes' rest," Dawlish said. "Then break it down again. It should be easier on the way back."

And after that one more ascent, more familiarisation with manhandling the components over obstacles in darkness and in silence, more adeptness in assembly when touch counted for more than vision. Then back down again. The party was back on *Leonidas* by midnight. Everybody could have the sleep they craved and deserved.

They did not know it, but for some it would be the last they ever had.

29

Leonidas raised anchor and moved slowly seawards, guns manned, as the morning sun revealed masts and a smudge of smoke rising over the western horizon. The *Ningpo* was expected but it could not be taken for granted that she was the approaching vessel. It was better to meet her in open water. The ships drew closer and then, to Dawlish's relief, the ugly lines and dark squat hull confirmed that the newcomer was indeed the transport. Between them, Watkin and Kung had got her loaded and to sea faster than had been hoped.

The *Ningpo's* decks were packed, as before, with Chinese troops but even from a cable's distance it seemed that an air of dejection, of mute, hopeless resignation hung over them. Among them were the survivors of the merciless hail of the hidden Gatlings at Songang-ni and they had no illusions about the competence of the officers – those who had survived Kung's merciless retribution – who led them. Escorted by *Leonidas*, the transport plodded towards the island and anchored, like her, off the beach.

Dawlish had himself pulled across. The meeting with Kung was brief, enough to confirm the numbers he needed, better estimated now in the light of the last days' exertions. Watkin had used his time on board the *Ningpo* well and had devised simple tests of strength to select the physically strongest. Dawlish was satisfied with Watkin's choice. Their very sullenness, the sense of mute misery they radiated, promised that they would be as silent as was essential for what lay ahead.

"Feed them. Let them rest through the day," he told Kung. "I want them transferred across an hour before sundown. No weapons." A refusal of orders was less likely without them. He turned to Watkin. "You'll double check, Lieutenant. No edged weapons, no firearms."

Within his cabin Kung was once again the down-to-earth American. "No weapons for my Uighurs also?" Two would accompany the party to ensure discipline.

"Swords only," Dawlish said. They would be a painful necessity, a reminder to the unarmed Chinese that noise, reluctance or refusal could mean another severed head. "And Captain Holles. You're sure of him?"

"He's been promised twice what the ship's insured for," Kung said. "And if he gets second thoughts I'll deal with him myself."

Dawlish stood up to leave. "No landing until you've had the signal. Even then it may not be easy. It's essential to keep your men moving no matter what. If they go to ground the game's up"

"You don't need to worry about that, Captain." Kung gestured towards the forward-facing pistol butt in the holster on his right. Then he shook Dawlish's hand with his left.

"Give me that island, Captain," he said. "Give me that Jap bastard too if Lodge doesn't see to him first. My Uighurs will know what to do with him. Give me him and give me the island and you'll have your codicils signed within the week."

*

On *Leonidas* all attention was focussed on preparation for departure. The boats were readied, the disassembled seven-pounder and her munitions in one cutter and small-arms ammunition, stores and rations, segregated into individual one-man loads, were divided among the other craft. The two landing parties were mustered and a last check made of equipment. Ross had twenty men, marines only. Each carried a Martini-Henry rifle and its bayonet, fifty rounds in a bandolier and a water bottle – nothing more. Their extra equipment would be carried by ten of the Chinese provided by Kung.

Dawlish had agonised over who should command the party with the seven-pounder. Takenaka was the ideal choice – he had the cold mind and ruthless dedication to victory that were required – but the burden of success or failure, either of which would earn him the enmity of so many of his countrymen, was too much to lay upon him. Purdon and O'Rourke he also considered, Edgerton not at all. Always the choice came back to one man only – himself. And not just because of competence only, though he knew he had more experience of successful combat ashore than perhaps any other officer in the Royal Navy. It was because the plan was his and his alone, the gamble on which he was risking his life and his career, the strategy for which simple men might lose their lives. These men must know that he would run no lesser risk than they did.

The decision was made. He would command the second party and Takenaka would support him.

Thirty men, bluejackets and marines, would accompany the seven-pounder, the majority armed like Ross's party, the seamen, under Egdean with cutlasses in addition. The gun-crew itself, all marines, carried revolvers. So too did Dawlish and Takenaka, one with a cutlass, the other with the wickedly curved sword he had used to such lethal effect in Seoul. The party would be outnumbered by forty unarmed Chinese soldiers – coolies now – and by the two Uighur guards who would ensure willingness and silence. They would manhandle everything but the seven-pounder itself. Dawlish as determined to entrust it to nobody but the men who had trained so hard with it.

The coolies to be ferried across. Watkin had searched them well. Not one carried the means of defending himself.

It was two hours to sunset when *Leonidas* headed westwards, leaving the *Ningpo* still swinging at anchor. Dawlish, on the bridge, felt a lightening of his spirit, a release from the doubts and worries and fears he had endured in recent days and could share with nobody.

It was a relief to have only a single purpose in the hours ahead.

To prevail.

*

A long loop to the west and then south at twelve knots, the sea barely rippled by the night breeze, five hours to carry *Leonidas* to a point off Socheong's western tip. She carried no lights and Dawlish addressed both landing parties on a deck illuminated only by the faint light of the waxing moon. Some shivered in the night chill, the marines' red coats and the bluejackets' jumpers discarded for greater freedom of movement, all in boots and with trousers gathered in by canvas gaiters and without the too-conspicuous sennet hats to which seamen were so attached.

Dawlish could feel the men's unease as he outlined what was involved, what was expected of them. A skilful and determined enemy – he didn't need to tell them that, but he knew they'd be its match. Nothing they had not trained for, and trained well. They'd already shown what they were made of, some in Seoul and all of them in the sinking of the *Tatsuta*. Surprise would be on their side. Unhesitant execution of every order. The necessity of getting loads in position even if the Chinese labour – gathered in mute hopelessness on the quarterdeck – should falter. No wounded, British or Chinese, to be abandoned. Take no chances when it came to combat, it was the choice between your life, or your shipmate's, and the enemy's. He avoided the words "no prisoners" but a few nodding heads confirmed that he was understood. Above all silence, silence during the landing, silence in the climbs and manhandling, silence in the reconnaissance entrusted to the six-man marine section under Shand. And last of all he would be with the seven-pounder party himself. A few weak smiles when he said he was too fond of his own skin to land if he was not sure of success.

He had half-hoped that someone would have called unprompted for three cheers for the *Leonidas*, perhaps even for himself.

Nobody did.

In real life men did not greet the prospect of death in the way they did in accounts written by those who had not been there.

Leonidas hoved to, just before midnight. Seen end-on to the east Socheong was a dark mass on which no light was visible, the heights on its western end hiding the anchorages on the north and south and masking the training arcs of Shimazu's landed six-inchers. To the south a light flashed into brief life, sweeping the waters round it and dying just as suddenly. Lodge and the *Fu Ching* were on station.

The boats were lowered and Dawlish's party boarded the three boats to be towed by the steam pinnace. Leigh had charge of the string but Takenaka was on board to con her to the first landing place. A Gatling had been mounted on her bows, the only protection for the entire party should Shimazu's remaining torpedo boat be encountered. The boats were laden almost to the gunwales with men and equipment, packed so closely that there would be no chance of using rifles effectively. The Chinese were divided over all three boats, uncomprehending and fearful, knowing only that they must be uncomplaining beasts of burden in the hours ahead. Dawlish shook hands with Edgerton and the other officers remaining on *Leonidas*, and with Ross, who would land later near the eastern end of Socheong. Then he dropped down into the first cutter.

The approach, first to the western tip and then on along the cliffs of the northern coast, seemed endless, each man isolated in the cell of his own thoughts. No sound but the wash of water alongside, the odd gasp of discomfort as someone tried to flex cramped limbs, the smooth beat of the pinnace's engine, no light but the faint glow shimmering above the small brass funnel. Dawlish's stomach was knotted, his mouth dry. Fear had come upon him again, no longer of ignominy and dismissal but of something more insidious, not of death itself but of loss, of the news reaching Florence, of the outward dignity and the inward agony she would receive it with, of perhaps dozens of similar tragedies, of lives ruined by his decision. Such fear, he knew, was perhaps the most deadly enemy of all and he forced himself to ignore it. He concentrated on visualising every detail of Takenaka's map, pushing from his mind the knowledge that a mistake in a contour, or in an elevation – and all were estimates only – could spell disaster. And all the while, as the string of boats passed into the dark shadows thrown by Socheong's northern cliffs he held himself outwardly impassive, conscious of, but ignoring, the sidelong glances directed to him.

The pinnace slowed, the tow slackened and the cutters maintained momentum until they bumped together. Takenaka nudged the pinnace closer to shore. The cleft must be close now but it was hard to discern any detail on the island's dark walls. Individual rocks protruded from the sea, some a cable and more from the shoreline, and the pinnace and her following-string threaded carefully between them. Still no sign of any light, of any hint of human presence. Still forward. Then suddenly a notch of moonlit sky opening in the cliff, hearts leaping that the landing place had been found, disappointment following so quickly after with the realisation that its inverted apex ended fifty feet above a vertical cliff face. On again.

It was too shallow to sound with a lead but a seaman in the pinnace's bows was probing with an oar as it crawled forward. Then, suddenly, the moon's crescent floated into sight, trapped between the walls of a deep gully. This was the landing place. Rocks had spilled from the ravine on to the foreshore and lapping waves showed others extending out to disappear below the water. The pinnace hove to and the cutters drifted forward to cluster by her. Five feet of water under the keels but no sense in risking the steam-craft closer inshore. Her night's work was not over. The tows were slipped and the cutters were poled shorewards with oars until the first grating sounds told of grounding.

Dawlish was first over the side, water to his thighs and filling his boots, the footing beneath uneven. No more than twenty feet to the shore and his gaze was riveted on the gully ahead. There was enough light to see that it was narrower and more debris-filled than he had hoped. The ascent would be harder than anticipated. Others were coming ashore now. Shand's marines began moving up the ravine. The sound of boots dislodging tiny pebble-avalanches, and of metal chinking on rock, seemed like thunderclaps in the surrounding silence. In scarcely two minutes the marines had disappeared into the cleft's darkness, glimpses of them caught only briefly as a head and shoulders were silhouetted against the moon. Egdean was supervising the offloading of the seven-pounder. Chinese labourers were struggling through the shallows from the other cutters, heavily burdened. Seamen were sorting the loads as they were landed, laying them out on the foreshore in order of priority, shells and charges first, then the half-dozen Hales rockets and their launching frame, two boxes of rifle ammunition, last of all the meagre rations. Within ten minutes, silent but for hissed commands and gasps of effort, the cutters were bobbing empty. Takenaka had come ashore and he joined Dawlish. A last check that all needed was ashore.

"May we release the boats, sir?"

"Signal Mr. Leigh that he can leave."

Leigh must rendezvous with *Leonidas,* then tow Ross's party - a single cutter would suffice – to their landing place south of the island's eastern extremity. They would be lucky to make their landfall, at another ravine, before sunrise. The pinnace disappeared back into the darkness, the empty cutters bobbing astern. The die was cast.

A single whistle from the darkness above told that Shand's marines had reached the top of the ravine, that it was clear, that his men had fanned out to provide a defensive perimeter. The first loads up must be the seven-pounder's components. Dawlish went with them. Valuable as the training ashore at Arang-Dong had been, familiar as the men allocated to portering the weapon had become to their loads, it had still not prepared them fully for the confusion of tumbled boulders over which they must now climb. The carriage and barrel proved the greatest challenge, scraping on rock as they were manhandled upwards by men who were maintaining their footing with difficulty. Gasping, leg and arm muscles screaming, knuckles skinned, feet scrabbling for footing, they somehow struggled upwards, followed by their mates lugging the scarcely less cumbersome wheels. As men paused, panting, to regain their strength, others took their place and the pitiless advance did not falter. Already the first of the Chinese carriers were moving up behind them, bewildered but resigned under their loads of shells and charges.

Dawlish reached the top ahead of the gun components, a half-dozen seamen with him. It was a small plateau, scrub patched, and the dark outline of a ridge lay less than a mile to the east. Beyond and below it lay Shimazu's anchorage. It was to that ridge that the seven-pounder must be shifted.

Shand approached. "No sign of them, sir. We've caught 'em napping."

"We can't be sure of that," Dawlish said. Overconfidence was as dangerous as fear. The seamen could guard the gully-top for now. He wanted the marines out in front. He gestured towards the ridge. "You see that high point to the right, Shand? Get your men up there, observe what's beyond. Cautiously, dead silence. If you run into anything it's bayonet only, no shooting. Get word back once you're in position."

"Very well, sir." Shand moved off into the darkness.

The gun's parts were up now, the first of the individual loads following. More carriers were straining out of the cleft, given a minute or two's respite, then hustled back down again. It took another twenty minutes to get the last of the stores up but already Dawlish was pushing forward with the gun-crew towards the ridge. The going was relatively easy now, a gradual slope, patches of open ground, uneven underfoot and interspersed with scrub. Five rifle-armed seamen were a hundred yards in front, on the lookout for obstacles as much as for the enemy, one flitting back at intervals to warn of a low ravine ahead, of the need to move further to the right to avoid it, of an easier path through a thicket. The gun carriers had settled into an effective if not easy routine, men changing position every hundred yards or so to ease aching muscles, and in places their pace increased to a jog-trot. The advance was more silent than Dawlish could have hoped, little more than of loose pebbles cascading, of metal grating on stone, of gasps of effort, of the odd low curse of frustration, all deadened by the continuous chirping of unseen crickets.

Shand and his men must be close to the ridge crest now. Beyond it the sky was lightening ever so slightly. Full daylight was still an hour ahead and Dawlish wanted to be in position by then. He glanced back, could see the nearest of the carriers at the head of the column behind him shambling under their loads, the remainder lost in the darkness and the scrub. Along the column's length he guessed the Uighurs would be ranging back and forth, cuffing frightened wretches to greater effort as he had already seen them do at the water's edge, two seamen following at the rear to deter stragglers. Takenaka and Egdean had brought the majority of the bluejackets forward and were pushing ahead of the column towards the crest.

A wall of brush ahead – the only way around would mean a long detour, a scout warned. There was nothing for it but to hack a thirty-yard path through with cutlasses, fifteen minutes lost and the resulting passage so narrow as to slow progress as loads and clothing snagged. Word back from Shand now, a panting but elated marine confirming that the summit had been reached – "We could see both sides, sir, north and south, and that Jappy ship's still in the bay, sir, and the buggers don't know we're there, haven't got a clue, sir."

The last section was the hardest, the slope very steep, littered with boulders, scree shifting underfoot as they toiled upwards, ledges and shelves in places up which the loads must be lifted individually and passed to be received by men above. The pace slowed, all the worse for the pink glow now rising beyond the crest and the imminence of daylight. Dawlish longed to be up there and looking down on the valley bisecting the island, but he restrained the urge to race ahead. Takenaka would be there by now, and establishing a protective screen, and he could be trusted for it. It was better to stay with the gun, to keep the now-exhausted seamen and marines moving it forward, to lend his own strength when the carriage was stuck on an obstacle, to hearten and cajole, to communicate confidence and resolution.

All but at the top now. Takenaka, a dark silhouette against a brightening sky, came down to meet him. "There's a small plateau over there, sir." He pointed to the left, a section of the ridge, lower by fifty or sixty feet than the summit.

"Any masking?"

Takenaka shook his head. "There's a clear view of the *Kirishima* and the buildings. And the slope on the other side is steep, almost a cliff, and there are bushes along the edge. It can't be seen from below. It's ideal."

The final manhandling, the axis of advance shifted to the left, slow, difficult, because of the steepness and the exhaustion of the carriers. Dawlish left them for the last hundred yards and climbed with Takenaka to the top. It was as he said, a natural platform, open, little over thirty yards along the ridgeline, half that wide, higher ground on either side, a fringe of brush obscuring the view down into the valley. There was no sign of either marines or seaman – Shand's section was unseen on the higher summit to the right while the bluejackets were disposed in a screen ahead and to the left. The sun was up now, still low, but climbing, the shadows from the brush still long. Dawlish moved forward, pulling out his field glasses.

"With respect, sir. Be careful," Takenaka gestured towards them. "The sun may reflect upon the lenses."

Dawlish pushed them back in their case and edged forward with Takenaka, crouching, into the scrub. The sun was a shimmering white ball flickering through the foliage. He dropped to one knee and parted the leaves and branches with infinite care.

A surge of delight and apprehension. There below him, five, six hundred feet below, and a half-mile distant, lay Socheong's narrow neck, the valley connecting the northern bay with the southern anchorage. There, in that harbour, still in the shadow cast by the headland to the east, the *Kirishima* lay serenely at anchor, the mirror-smooth waters around her rippled only by a cutter stroking unhurriedly towards her from the coal-loading jetty. Alongside her lay the remaining torpedo boat. On the eastern headland itself, lower than Dawlish's vantage point for a hundred feet or more, the single landed six-inch could be clearly seen, boxes stacked close by, a large awning stretched over what must be makeshift accommodation, the searchlight that had probed so intermittently through the night mounted on a tripod to one side. Men moved about unhurriedly and a faint wisp of smoke told of breakfast.

"They're in range, comfortably in range," Dawlish tried to keep the elation from his voice. Those were Takenaka's countrymen over there and he was required to be complicit in their cold-blooded destruction. For all his outward calm the choice of loyalties must be agonising.

Only a few figures moved among the coal heaps and sheds and wooden houses, none at all near the walled compound where the labour was accommodated, though there seemed to be guards at the entrance. The Caledonian and Oriental's activities were at a standstill.

"There's a problem, sir." Takenaka pointed to the right. The headland on the anchorage's western side was blocked from view by the curving sweep of the ridge. Two guns were mounted on that headland. *Leonidas's* coat-trailing had flushed out that certainty.

Dawlish glanced up towards the summit Shand's men had occupied. It was all but conical and the top was wholly exposed. There was no possibility of concealing the seven-pounder there.

The view to the north was better and the headland, almost a peninsula, to the west of the northern bay lay at least two hundred feet lower than the ridge. The mystery of whether a six-inch had been landed there was solved. It was there, at the head of a track snaking up from the foreshore, mounted so as to give an almost perfect arc, almost a full half-circle, to command the entire northern coast from west to east. It had been a wise decision to keep *Leonidas* far offshore. There too was a small camp close to the gun – an awning, piled stores, figures moving in calm ignorance that they were being observed, smoke drifting from a cooking fire.

The sea to the north stretched empty towards the two islands there. The troop-laden *Ningpo*, was lurking behind them, so also *Leonidas*, which had headed there after dropping off Ross's party. Both ships were under orders to stay hidden there until midday. And by then it must have been made be safe for them to approach, safer still for Kung to get his demoralised troops ashore. There must be no repeat of the massacre at Songang-ni. There were five hours only to ensure that.

A pall of dark smoke to the south identified the *Fu Ching* steaming slowly parallel to the coast, outside the range of the landed six-inchers. Dawlish was confident that Lodge's ten-inch Armstrongs could finish the *Kirishima* if she could be deprived of the cover of Shimazu's landed batteries. He had not however anticipated the ridge's forward curve partly masking the western headland. He had banked too much on a map based on assumptions and estimates alone – a good map, the best that could have been made in the circumstances, but not good enough. Two of the four six-inch weapons Shimazu had landed on the island were visible from this hidden plateau, one on the north coast, one on the south, and so too was the *Kirishima* herself. But the other two guns, both on the western headland overlooking the harbour, could not be seen from here, could not be brought under the seven-pounder's puny fire.

The sun was climbing and Dawlish wanted to trust only to the minimum on movement in daylight. He looked to the summit on the right where Shand and his men were ensconced, no sign of any level space around it for the seven-pounder. But there was a possibility, another gamble to lay upon the others, narrowing the margin for success yet further…

There was a choice – a hard one. Forget the northern coast, for now at least. Without the *Kirishima* Socheong was just an island. Her destruction must come before all else.

30

The seven-pounder had been assembled, a ridiculously small weapon in the light of what it was being matched against. The ammunition – the full fifty rounds and charges, all that *Leonidas* had carried for it – were stacked by it. The gunner, a marine corporal, had carefully laid it first on the *Kirishima*, then on the six-incher on the eastern headland. The position of its wheels and trail were marked – it must be restored to the same position after recoiling from every shot – and wooden stakes had been hammered into the ground at a distance to mark the target bearings. That much at least could be as accurate as possible but the estimation of range would be a guess. The first half-dozen rounds on each target would be wasted until the correct elevation was found by trial and error. As much was done as was possible for now and the gun team was resting around the weapon. So too, behind them, were the Chinese carriers.

Dawlish was going to take the remainder of the force with him, eighteen men, all seamen, plus himself and Takenaka. The gun-crew must provide its own close protection. Dawlish's observation of the gunner and his team on the exercises on Arang-Dong had satisfied him that they could be relied on. He called Egdean over to join him.

"Select ten – no, a dozen – of the strongest of these people," he gestured towards the Chinese. "Get six loaded with a rocket each, and one for the launching frame. The rest to carry rifle ammunition. I want them to move quickly."

"Aye, aye, sir. And those too, sir?"

"The Uighurs?" Dawlish saw that the carriers were avoiding so much as to look at them. "They'll come also. But no loads." Their vicious short-bladed swords could be useful and there was no doubt about their willingness to use them.

A last word with the gunner-corporal, assurance that his role was clearly understood. Takenaka had assembled the bluejackets, a round in each Martini-Henry breech, bayonets fixed, cutlasses at the hip. Egdean had allocated the loads to the dozen carriers and by signs had impressed the need for speed and silence on them and on their Uighur guards.

They moved off, Dawlish with the larger group, ten men, including Egdean, Takenaka had six only, and two seaman were accompanying the carriers following behind. They advanced quickly through the sparse scrub just below the ridgeline. One of Shand's men met them at the base of the steep climb to the summit. He led Dawlish up, leaving the others below.

"You'd better get down here, sir," the marine said as they approached the summit. "There ain't much room on top." He dropped to a crouch and Dawlish followed.

The level area on top was smaller than a good-sized drawing room and there was no shred of cover. Shand and his men were lying behind low boulders but rising into even a kneeling position would have exposed them to view from below. Dawlish wriggled towards him and his gaze followed the corporal's pointing finger.

No need for words.

The western headland was scarcely a half-mile distant, though a scrub-filled gully stretched between. But it was lower than this vantage point by a hundred feet at least. The two six-inch weapons there were trained seawards and their crews, like those on the other headlands, were going about their morning routines, oblivious of being observed.

"Send your men down, Corporal. And my compliments to Mr. Takenaka. Ask him to join me here."

The targets – the two six-inch guns below, the single weapon on the eastern headland, the *Kirishima* herself, all unaware of threat – looked infinitely vulnerable to attack from above. So too they would in fact be if there was more to bombard them with. The Hales rockets, effective though they might be if landed on target, were notoriously inaccurate and little more could be expected from the seven-pounder. But the rockets could deliver surprise and confusion and Ross's unseen party must now be in position in the hilly ground to the east of the anchorage …

A few words only with Takenaka, the details settled. His small party would be left here at the summit with the rockets, the launching frame to be erected at the last moment. For one brief moment Dawlish felt a surge of doubt and Takenaka must have noticed it. He spoke as Dawlish turned to crawl back.

"Those men's behaviour dishonour His Majesty." Even when prone he attempted to bow at the mention of the sacred monarch. "I shall have no hesitation, Captain Dawlish. You have my loyalty."

The attacking force was divided in three, the seamen divided equally between Dawlish and Egdean, the Uighurs with Dawlish, Shand and his five marines a third group. They moved along the ridge, just below the crest, but the moment of danger came when its shelter had to be abandoned to cross over to descend into the gully beyond. Two Chinese porters followed, each hefting a box of rifle ammunition, more obviously fearful of the Uighurs than of any other danger. The other Chinese were sent back.

The marines went first, singly, and were exposed as they crossed the skyline and slid down the steep, bare, downward slope beyond. They gained the scattered scrub in the gully floor, flitting between it to hold a position at the base of the opposite slope. Two interminable minutes' wait, the sun broiling, the drone and twitter of insects, sweat in rivulets, fear. Dawlish, peering over the crest, saw that the Japanese gun-crews were standing by their weapons and one was being trained around to track the *Fu Ching* steaming slowly, out of range, across the southern horizon. The impression was of a morning drill, motions gone through, but no action expected. Best of all, the gunners seemed unaware of what was happening at their backs.

Two minutes up now, no sign of alarm, and then Egdean's men were across the crest also and reaching the cover below without detection, sheltering over to the right of Shand's. Another two minutes, still no indication of an alarm, and then Dawlish gestured for his group to follow him one by one. He crawled over the crest and went half-slithering down the exposed slope to the cover below, the sound of dislodged pebbles beneath him as loud as thunder in his ears. For terrifying seconds he could see Japanese backs turned towards him a scarce three hundred yards away and knew that if even one man were to turn there would be nothing to hide him from view. Then he gained cover, to Shand's left, and the remaining seamen, and the Uighurs with them, followed individually.

The patches of brush in the narrow gully offered scant cover from observation from above. The steep slope ahead – the rear of the western headland – was almost bare of vegetation and above it were the guns. The last approach must be made without cover. Dawlish glanced at his watch. Just after eight. Ross's men should be similarly close to the rear of the eastern headland by now – there had been no sounds of shooting or alarm there.

Hand signals only and the order for Shand's men to move out of the scrub and start the cautious climb. Two hundred yards at most to the edge of the headland's plateau, almost every yard exposed, the slope never less than one in one. Dawlish watched with pounding heart. The marines were well spread out and hugging whatever meagre shelter a fissure or jutting boulder might afford. He suddenly felt a tugging at his sleeve and turned to see one of the Uighurs. There was the slightest indication of what might have been a smile and the man was gesturing upwards, then running his finger lightly along the edge of his sword. The plea was unmistakable – *Let us do this. We're good at it.* Dawlish hesitated for a moment, then nodded. Both men glided from cover, supple as cats, and followed Shand.

The marines were half way up now and a signal to Egdean started the similar advance on the right. There were almost a dozen men on the slope now, the seamen's white shirts and the marines' grey ones standing out glaringly against the slope's dull brown. In the minutes ahead they would be as much at the mercy of a deviant rocket as from the Japanese above them, but there was no help for that now. Dawlish, revolver in hand, led his own small group from cover to follow them.

Shand's marines were crouching ten yards below the plateau's edge, Egdean's thirty further back, and Dawlish's men were still edging upwards another fifty to the left and rear. In less than two minutes…

Then movement above, a figure appearing at the edge, nonchalant, his clothing not unlike that of the men below him, and fumbling with the front of his trousers, his intention to urinate obvious. Dawlish froze – so too every one of his men – and for one instant of irrational hope he thought that they might not be seen. Then the Japanese started, surprise on his face, and he stepped back, out of sight, crying out as he did.

Dawlish stood, raising his pistol in his right hand, gesturing with his left for the others to stay low. He turned back, saw the summit where Takenaka's group huddled unseen, and fired twice into the air, the agreed signal. Noises now from above, shouting in Japanese, the sound of running feet. Figures appearing at Takenaka's position, a spindly object manhandled into view – the rocket-launching frame. Dawlish dragged his gaze away – it was all in Takenaka's hands now – and looked towards the edge above. He felt an urge to turn, to run back, yet though his heart was racing and his mouth dry he knew at he would go on and up, so too the men glancing towards him for some indication of intent. It calmed him to shake out the smoking cases from the revolver's chambers, to insert two new rounds – the work of seconds, yet it seemed centuries. Exposed as his men now were, it was safer to stay still for now than to advance.

Suddenly a hissing sound overhead, an object elongated like a shell, but plunging slowly enough for the eye to follow, a trail of smoke and sparks marking its passage. The spin imparted by the vents in the rocket's base were stabilising the trajectory – Takenaka would have aimed directly for the guns and there was not even the slightest breeze to correct for – but the launching elevation, and the resulting range, could only be guessed. Luck alone would ensure its point of impact on the plateau.

Dawlish's heart soared as the missile was lost to sight. Then the sound of explosion, but no way of knowing the effect, and already the second rocket was streaking over, somewhat to the left of the first. It was dropping more steeply but it too fell on the plateau above and burst there. Two rockets only – the most that could be afforded for this target. Dawlish threw himself to his feet and yelled the order to charge – shock would be at its maximum in the seconds after the second explosion. Even as he scrambled upwards he heard a crack from behind, the report of the seven-pounder, it too called into life by his pistol shots. There was no time to observe its fall of shot, whether it had dropped close to the six-inch gun on the eastern headland or not. It was now up to the gunner alone, and he had rounds enough to correct his elevation, and soon too it would be up to Ross as well if he had brought his men to where they should be.

Shand's men had disappeared over the plateau edge and rifle-fire, individual shots, were crashing out. Dawlish's and Egdean's men scrambled up behind them, driven by awareness that only in attack lay safety.

On to the plateau now, an open space, undulating, a hundred yards and more across, smoke drifting from the two craters blasted by the rockets – no direct damage done but shock achieved. A large canvas awning stretched to the right, small tents around it, a pile of boxes directly ahead and beyond them the two six-inch guns trained seawards, twenty yards apart. Shand's marines were already half-way to the guns and leaving two Japanese bodies slumped behind them. The gun-crews were forming a defensive line by their weapons. An officer's upraised sword flashed and a voice yelled defiance. Two men were sprinting from under the awning, each laden with what looked like three or four rifles. Caught at their morning drill, the Japanese gunners were all but unarmed and Shand's marines had already disposed of the sentries. Shand called his men to a halt, to drop to a kneeling position and they were already raising their rifles. The Uighurs were sprinting towards the running men, swords upraised. One of their quarries attempted to shear away but he tripped, the rifles he carried dropping, and a Uighur was on him, sword sweeping down, up again – red – then down in another lethal slice. The other Japanese was throwing down his rifles but it was too late. He glanced back to see the second Uighur bearing down on him and he froze. The sword flashed in a horizontal sweep and blood fountained from the neck. The body tottered for an instant as the head bounced away, then fell.

Shand's men were firing by volley, he himself calling the rhythm as calmly as on a parade ground. The range was fifty yards and the gun-crews were scattering for any cover they could find, behind the guns themselves, disappearing over the plateau's lip beyond, bodies on the ground behind them. Egdean's bluejackets were forming a line to the right of the marines, they too dropping to knees, their fire less regular, less rapid, yet no less deadly. Dawlish was jogging in front of his own small group – close enough to the headland's edge to glance the *Kirishima* in the anchorage below from the corner of his eye. Three Japanese were rushing towards him, the closest obviously an officer, his curved sword upraised, his face contorted in fury, the men behind him armed only with ramrods. Dawlish stopped, swept up his revolver, drew back the hammer, inhaled and held his breath, lined up the foresight on the officer's chest. Twenty yards – better to let him come closer – and though the seamen behind Dawlish were fanning out to right and left the sight did not deter the three men's onslaught. Suddenly a bluejacket was pitching forward by Dawlish's side, gasping he fell, blood erupting from his leg. Dawlish glanced involuntarily towards the fallen man – stupidly, and for an instant only, but enough for his aim to wander. The swordsman was almost on him now, hilt grasped with both hands, blade drawn back almost to his right ear.

Dawlish corrected his aim and even as he squeezed the trigger he realised that it was not enough. The revolver kicked – and as his hand rose with it he was already recocking – but as he swept it down to aim again the sword was arcing towards him. He pitched himself down, firing blindly as he fell, knew he had missed, felt the blade's breath as it swept past. The impact with the ground winded him but worse was the pistol falling from his grasp. He rolled on his back, above him saw a dark outline silhouetted against the sun behind, sword raised high for a downward chop. Time stood still – he knew that his scrabbling fingers would never find the revolver in time – and he knew that Death was on him and that he longed only to live. Then another body was blotting out the sun, light flashing on the bayonet it drove before it, and the sword was dropping and the figure that held it was doubling over with a scream and crashing down on Dawlish. He wriggled from beneath it, heard the scream cut off as a boot crashed into the head and the bayonet was jerked free by the bluejacket who wielded it. Dawlish struggled to his feet. One of the men who had followed the swordsman was already down – still, obviously lifeless – and the second was flailing with a ramrod towards two bluejackets standing back from him, one parrying with his bayonet, the other raising his rifle to his shoulder. The range was point blank and the man went down, blood bursting from his shoulder, but even then he tried to rise again, falling back as both seaman drove their bayonets into him.

"Over there, sir," the wounded bluejacket – Shepton, an older man – had raised himself on one elbow and was pointing as a mate was trying to get a belt around his thigh as a tourniquet. "The bugger who got me is over there, below that rock, sir." As he spoke a head and shoulders emerged, a rifle too.

"Get him," Dawlish yelled. He had recovered his revolver. The range was too great for accuracy, but he fired anyway, once, twice, his shots close enough to make the rifleman duck for cover as the seamen made for him. Two darted around the rock, a third went vaulting over, a single shot, another, a cry of agony cut off, then the bluejackets calling back "We got him, sir. We got him!"

Silence now, then the sharp bark of the distant seven-pounder. Seconds for the flight of the shell, then a small column of smoke and soil blasting upwards on the eastern headland, harmless, far from the six-inch there but enough to drive its crew under cover. In the excitement of his own assault Dawlish had no idea how many shells had landed there but the gunner had the range. It had been agreed that half-a-dozen rounds were to fall before Ross was to launch his attack.

Egdean's men had cut down the awning and tents and were probing them with their bayonets. One body at least was there, slumped in an ungainly heap. All was quiet over at the guns as well, bodies littering the ground before and around them. Dawlish crossed to them and Shand met him

"Hot work there, sir." He looked pale, the excitement of action fading.

"Any left?"

Shand shook his head. "They didn't give up easy, sir, only a few of them armed but it made no difference. Like bloody tigers, sir. One of them, bloody big hole in his belly, lying there, you'd think he'd have given up, but he sunk his teeth in Beasley's leg." He shook his head. "Wouldn't let go, we had to put the bayonet in him. Two more of them shamming too, they…"

Dawlish cut him off. "Get your men over there, Corporal." He gestured towards the edge overlooking the anchorage and down the access track that snaked up the slope. "Cover the approach." He glanced back to see that the Chinese porters had arrived with the rifle-ammunition boxes, a creditable performance. "Keep those boxes close. You're going to need them."

Again the seven-pounder's bark and an instant later the flash and smoke of impact just short of the gun on the eastern headland. The awning there was burning and figures were scurrying around it like frightened insects. As the smoke cleared rifle-fire crackled, a single volley, then individual shots as half of Ross's men gave cover to the others racing into the open, bayonets fixed. Dawlish tore his gaze away, already confident that the six-inch there was as good as won, its crew silenced. The greater challenge, at both headlands, was to hold them against the attempt to recapture them that must surely follow. He called Egdean over.

"Get your men under cover with Shand's. Do as he directs." He pointed to the brush-dotted slope on either side of the track. "The Japs will probably come up through the scrub, will try to outflank us. Don't expect them in the open."

Below in the anchorage the *Kirishima* had come to life, men rushing purposefully towards the deck guns – not that they were a threat, for they did not have the necessary elevation – and others were swarming up to the tops towards the Gatlings. A cutter was racing back towards the landing jetty and the torpedo boat was moving out towards the open sea. Isolated rifle-shots only from the eastern headland, then silence. Somebody was being hoisted up to stand precariously on the six-inch there. Dawlish raised his glasses and saw it was Ross, waving triumphantly. Then he dropped and his men were moving, like Shand's and Egdean's, to establish a defensive line above the approach.

Dawlish turned to his own men. "Get over to the guns. Take Shepton with you, make him comfortable." The wounded seaman was the only casualty but he had lost much blood and his face was already pallid, his eyes great with fear. There was nothing more that could be done for him for now.

Several bodies were dragged away from the bases of the six-inchers. They had been mounted on carefully-laid cement into which foundation bolts had been set – as professional a job as might be seen in any coastal fort. It would have demanded bringing the necessary materials here, confirmation that there was nothing unplanned or spontaneous about Shimazu's seizure of the island. The guns were Krupps, their sliding-wedge breeches different from the interrupted screws of the Armstrongs that *Leonidas* carried, but Dawlish was familiar with them from his Ottoman service. A single shell and bagged charge was positioned by each weapon, obviously for the morning drill, and two open crates of shells lay behind. All were fused – a dangerous practice but one that would facilitate rapid fire. A large metal box, open, contained tools, spanners, hammers, screwdrivers, essential maintenance items. Fifty yards to the right he saw the entrance to an earthen hummock that could only be an improvised shelter for the bagged charges. He sent two men to fetch them, then satisfied himself that the dead gunners had had no time to disable the guns. The breech wedges slid to and fro and locked easily and the barrel responded smoothly to spinning of the elevation and traversing wheels.

He looked seawards. The *Fu Ching* was still four miles distant but her hull was foreshortened, black smoke billowing from her funnel. Alerted by the gunfire – the only signal Dawlish had undertaken to give him, and trusting that the shore battery had been neutralised, Lodge was heading straight for the anchorage, bringing two massive ten-inch Armstrongs with him.

Dawlish had two six-inch Krupps – he could not count on Ross to operate the one he had just captured and he realised that he should have added some of Purdon's gunners to both landing parties. It was too late for regrets. He was capable of laying and firing the weapons himself. If the *Kirishima* could be driven from the anchorage, out into the minimum range of the Krupps, she could be caught between two fires.

Takenaka had four twenty-four pound Hales rockets left – every one must count – and the unseen seven-pounder, whose crew must take from him their lead in shifting target, had upwards of three dozen shells.

Time now to use them.

Dawlish turned and saw Takenaka standing on the summit by the rocket frame. He waved slowly, received an answering wave.

A half-minute later a rocket was dropping towards the *Kirishima*.

31

A white plume rose twenty yards seawards of the *Kirishima*, froze for a moment, then collapsed. Close, but not close enough. And only three rockets remained...

Figures were moving out of the sheds by the coal dumps and from the building beyond, hastening into groups, not drilled or formally arrayed, but with a terrible sense of purpose as they divided into loose knots. Dawlish swung his glasses towards them and recognised the blue tunics, the diagonal bandoliers, the air of confidence and alertness, the straw sandals, of the Caledonian and Oriental's guards. Eighty of them, he remembered – Satsumans, disciplined, Snider rifles – and among them he could pick out what must be naval personnel, an officer, two, three petty officers perhaps, sunlight flashing on their swords. He counted – five groups of similar size, three heading towards the base of the slope he stood above, the remainder towards the eastern headland Ross now held. The range was too far yet for effective rifle-fire but in minutes they would be disappearing into the slopes' scrub, pushing upwards stealthily, probing for any weakness in the screens which Shand's and Egdean's men – and Ross's men too – had established above them.

Takenaka's next rocket blasted from the summit, its initial trajectory almost horizontal due to the shortness of the range. It began to drop, its parabola marked by billowing smoke, and its flight was slow enough to allow following by eye. It was on track as it bored towards the *Kirishima* and only a miscalculation of launching elevation could spare her unarmoured deck. Dawlish watched, breathless, fists involuntarily clenched, willing it to find its mark.

It struck just abaft the mizzen – a flash, smoke, splinters, debris, whipping cordage. The mast shuddered, swayed, but held. Figures rushed towards the impact, others, fewer, to the bridge and it took no imagining to know the decision Shimazu must now be facing.

Another rocket – and after this only one would remain – was already in the air. Its plunge brought it close enough to the ship's starboard side for the geyser it flung up to shower the deck with spray. A sharp crack from the left announced the seven-pounder having shifted aim. The shell's flight lasted seconds only, then it too was throwing up a small harmless plume just short of the *Kirishima*. A pause, then the last rocket whooshed down its descending arc – and Yes! By God! It was a strike! Flame and wreckage – rent planking, an entire ventilator – exploding on the port side just ahead of the funnel, close enough perhaps to damage the broadside six-inch nearest the impact, sufficient at least to scythe down anybody close. Again the seven-pounder, its shot this time falling harmlessly beyond the *Kirishima*, but the gunners had their target bracketed and the next round must surely find a home.

Shimazu would have no idea of how long this bombardment could last but he must know that even from the lightest shells his decks offered no protection to the boilers, machinery and magazines beneath them. The *Kirishima* was armoured – and lightly at that – to resist horizontal fire only and the ordeal she was now subjected to was one never envisaged by her architects. Shimazu – he must be one of those figures now standing steady on the exposed bridge – had made his choice. A dark knot of men was gathered in the bows and the chain stoppers were being struck free. Black smoke was vomiting from the *Kirishima's* funnel, her furnaces, stoked for harbour pressure only, unable to cope yet with the fresh coal hastily fed them to enable escape. Another small column of spray rose off her starboard flank, another miss by the seven-pounder, but the threat of a luckier shot to follow.

Even from this distance the rattle of the anchor chain falling through the hawse hole was audible. Shimazu had let his cable run out in his urge to get away. Water churned at her stern and her bows nudged seawards. And out there was the *Fu Ching*, white foam at her bow, a bone in her teeth, long v-like ripples streaming out as she rushed on, liberated at last from the threat of the landed guns. A cable off her starboard quarter the formerly-Japanese torpedo boat Lin now commanded was keeping pace.

Dawlish had one over-riding concern now, to bring the Krupps into play at the moment when the *Kirishima* would enter their range – elevation was now an enemy and they could not depress enough to engage her until she was at least a mile offshore. A smooth lever-motion threw open the breech of the first weapon. The shell that had been reserved for gunnery drill – bursting charge, not armour-piercing – was lifted on its stretcher-like carrier and its eighty pounds were rammed home until the copper driving band locked in the rifling. The bagged charge followed – finest silk, the Japanese would have no shortage of it, chosen to flash cleanly away – and then the wedge slid across again to lock the breech. The second weapon was also loaded and the wait began.

Kirishima edged past the loading jetty, her speed still low and lacking time to build it. She was heading directly towards the approaching *Fu Ching*, her two six-inch bow-chasers matched with the single ten-inch Lodge could yet bring to bear, her faster but lighter fire matched against slower ship-smashing potential. The headland now blocked the Japanese cruiser from the hail the seven-pounder had maintained. There was another sound now, closer, single aimed shots, irregular but with increasing frequency. Shand's and Egdean's men, and Ross's marines on the headland opposite, were firing on glimpses of the Satsuman guards who had now reached the base of the slopes, and were flitting between cover there in preparation for advancing up.

Dawlish must himself aim and fire the Krupps and could only rely on the men with him for loading. He spun the traverse wheel of the first weapon. The barrel moved over slowly until the *Kirishima* was hidden beneath it. The weapon was at maximum depression but the ship was still so close that a shell fired would plunge hundreds of yards ahead of her. Dawlish moved across to the second weapon, trained it also. Elevation would have to be judged by trial and error, the chance of a hit would be minimal, but the threat would be there, another distraction as Shimazu manoeuvred for advantage against the *Fu Ching*.

The rattle of rifle-fire was rapid now, urgent bursts, brief silence, then shots again. The marines and seamen were in cover just below the plateau edge but the advance of the Satsumans below them, brief rushes from one patch of concealing brush to the next, was obviously relentless.

The *Kirishima* was now clear of the jetty end by a cable or more, and still bow-on to Lodge's steady advance. On both ships gunners would be squinting through sights, estimating the closing range, edging hand-wheels around to adjust elevation. On both bridges the commanders, Japanese and American alike, must be weighing up the moment for opening fire, conscious that their opening salvos would almost certainly do no more than establish range, knowing that only rapid recalculation and reloading could make the second salvos effective. It was now that unremitting training would pay off…

Smoke erupted from the *Kirishima* and she was thrusting through it as the reports reached Dawlish, the unmistakable crack of Krupp six-inchers similar to those he now manned himself. Two skidding plumes of white marked the shells' low trajectory as they hit the water a half cable ahead of the *Fu Ching*, then died suddenly some twenty yards off her starboard bow. The *Kirishima* began to nudge over eastwards, exposing her full starboard broadside, three Krupps only due to the loss of the landed guns, but the Chinese vessel was all but unarmoured and the Japanese gunnery was likely to be superb.

Flame stabbed though the smoke that enveloped the *Fu Ching* as her massive forward Armstrong blasted. A half minute earlier her aim might just have been correct but the *Kirishima's* turn had saved her and the shell tore a long track of foam astern of her. Then, abruptly, a bright flash and a vast plume of spray and black fragments as the shell crashed into what must be a rock shelf just below the surface. It must be shallow here, and Shimazu must know it, and though he was now conning his vessel south-eastwards, towards open water, he obviously did not dare to hug the coast more closely to escape eastwards.

Dawlish had continued to slew his Krupp across to keep the *Kirishima* hidden beneath the barrel. It was still on maximum depression but a glance along the side told him that his target would pass into sight ahead of the muzzle in the coming minute. Time now for a ranging shot.

He stood clear, fired, the report ear-splitting, billowing smoke blotting the view ahead, the weapon heaving back on its inclined slide, then easing back into firing position.

"Reload!" Dawlish yelled as he dashed towards the second Krupp. Clear now of the choking smoke, he saw a white plume rising a cable ahead of the *Kirishima's* starboard bow. He did not touch the elevation – the barrel was at maximum depression – but he spun the traversing wheel to hide the fleeing ship under the barrel. She was turning again, yet more to the east, and he advanced the wheel another half-turn to track her, then fired. He rushed back to the first weapon – "It's ready, sir!" – and saw his second shell plunge uselessly astern of the Japanese ship.

A broadside now from the *Kirishima*, the three guns blasting simultaneously. This time the aim and ranging were perfect. The *Fu*

Ching had altered course slightly to remain bow on to her adversary and the foreshortened target she presented was a difficult one. Despite this a single flash – somewhere abaft the funnel, Dawlish thought – registered a hit on her even as two fountains rose harmlessly off her port flank. It was a hit, but not one which had disabled the forward ten-inch, for again the bows were once again blotted out by its discharge. Another miss, the shell this time tearing a foaming track a hundred yards ahead of the *Kirishima's* bows and ending abruptly, without exploding, in now deeper water.

The *Fu Ching* thrust through her own gunsmoke. As she pulled over more to starboard, to parallel the *Kirishima* and to unmask her Armstrong aft and her two 4.7-inch breech-loaders amidships, a dark shape was emerging from behind her. Captained now by Lieutenant Lin, the torpedo boat which Dawlish had captured was racing forward on a course that would take her ahead of her former parent, *Kirishima*. Amateur torpedoman Lin might be, and with a scant few hours tuition to prepare him, but he was thrusting for his quarry with as much determination as if he had years of training. Dawlish felt a surge of admiration for he saw that Lin's decision was all but suicidal. There was still upwards of a mile to be covered before any effective launch was possible. He himself had impressed on Lin that only point-blank launching had any hope of success but any Gatling remaining on the *Kirishima* was capable of shredding the torpedo boat long before that. Lin needed support...

Dawlish was at his second six-incher, raising the elevation slightly now, tracking the barrel over, holding the *Kirishima* in sight just above the muzzle. She was moving faster now, her speed still building up, her funnel smoke less dense. Dawlish fired.

He had overestimated the elevation – slightly – but the shell that tore a plume a half-cable off the target's starboard bow masked the advancing torpedo boat. Another shell like it, yet another if possible, could throw up a curtain of foam which might just buy Lin time. And buy it for Lodge too, for the Japanese helmsman must have been disconcerted. The *Kirishima* lurched violently to port, closer to the treacherous coast, then corrected, her snaking wake demanding constant re-laying by her gunners.

The first Krupp was already reloaded. Dawlish had recognised that his inability to judge correct elevation made any direct hit on the *Kirishima* unlikely and he traversed now towards the narrowing gap between her and Lin's frail craft. He stepped back as the gun roared, began to move towards the second weapon. He saw a seaman before him – he recognised him, though his face was powder-blackened, as one of Egdean's section. In the instant before the man spoke, and in the momentary break in the blasting of the great guns, Dawlish realised that the rifle-fire from the left was now continuous.

"Mr. Egdean's compliments, sir" The seaman's fist rose briefly to his forehead in salute. Even at this juncture the forms were being observed. "He says we're hard pressed, sir. That we won't be able to hold much longer. He says you should know, sir."

If Egdean had said it then Dawlish would take him at his word. He glanced seawards, saw the white circle of foam that his last shell had thrown up dissipating between the *Kirishima* and the inexorably advancing torpedo boat. At that moment spears of flame lanced from the *Fu Ching*, first from the forward Armstrong, an instant later from that aft.

Either of the Chinese shells could have dismembered their target but they fountained harmlessly a half cable astern. Smoke was still drifting clear of the *Fu Ching* – foul yellow gunsmoke, for the *Kirishima's* single hit on her did not seem to have initiated a fire – when her two 4.7-inch weapons amidships lashed out together.

Oblivious for a moment of the almost continuous rifle-fire, and with his heart leaping, Dawlish saw flame and debris thrown out from the *Kirishima's* flank. The hit looked to be amidships, lucky enough perhaps to disable the six-inch Krupp there, better still if fragments blasting inwards might damage piping or boilers or engines.

And still Lin's boat was hurtling on, dead straight for an interception, the wedge of water between her course and the *Kirishima's* shortening by the second. A tiny figure – it must be Lin himself – was discernible on the exposed steering platform and below him two or three more were gathered around the rear of the torpedo launch-tube.

"Mr. Egdean's compliments, sir," the begrimed seaman had no concern for the drama on the water, was intent only on the severity of the threat he had been sent to communicate. "Mr. Egdean says…"

Dawlish ignored him even as he knew the situation on the slope must be critical, that Death might come storming on to the plateau behind him at any moment. But Lin was within two minutes of success and the *Kirishima's* destruction outweighed all else. Dawlish sighted down the second Krupp's barrel, raced the traverse hand-wheel to bear on the gap between the nearing vessels, then fired.

Shimazu was swinging the *Kirishima* over to starboard to meet the oncoming torpedo boat bows-on and so reduce the target size. Lin must launch now if he was to have any hope…

Dawlish's last shell was still in flight – it fell uselessly a half-cable beyond both vessels – as the Gatling in the *Kirishima's* foretop opened fire. The reports from its spinning barrels were inaudible above the clatter of the close-by rifles but the Gatling's fearsome .45 inch rounds were slamming into the torpedo boat. She lurched away, as if drunkenly, control obviously lost but the figure on the steering platform still upright and defiant.

Then Lin, and his craft, and all aboard her, died. An incandescent ball of flame engulfed her as the torpedo exploded in its launching tube, shattering the tiny vessel, flinging out wreckage and bodies from the glowing white heart that itself died almost instantly. Nothing remained.

The *Kirishima* was maintaining her turn, arcing back to reverse her course. Smoke was pouring from the point amidships where the *Fu Ching's* shell had struck, tongues of flame licking through it. Shimazu's ship was injured and now she was straightening out, parallel to the Chinese vessel but steaming in the opposite direction. It was a desperate manoeuvre, one that brought her closer into the range of Lodge's ship-smashers, exposing her to the rapid fire of his 4.7-inch weapons, but the only option she had if she was to bring the three guns of her port broadside to bear. The hit on her starboard side must have indeed knocked out at least one of the guns there and Shimazu must be bitterly regretting the loss of his landed weapons.

Shouting amid the fusillade to the left, Dawlish's own name called out. He glanced around, saw heads and shoulders, then full bodies, thrusting up above the plateau's lip – a sword-flourishing officer leading eight or ten Satsuman guards. They had outflanked the defenders and were now rushing forward across the open ground with levelled bayonets. Other bodies were rising too, over to the right, marines, Shand among them and bellowing a warning to Dawlish, rifles swinging towards the running men, gunfire crashing out, two, three of the Satsumans falling, yet the remainder, six or seven, pounding onwards towards the Krupps.

"Get that man behind the guns!"

The half-conscious seaman with the bloody leg was dragged there by two of his mates and Dawlish's other shouted orders were unnecessary. The seamen around him had grabbed their Martini-Henrys and some were already dropping to one knee for more certain aim. Dawlish had his revolver out, stood still – exposed, no time to dive for cover behind the guns – and raised it, cocked, locked fore and back sight on the officer with the sword. He recognised him – he remembered his name, Yamada, with sudden clarity, had seen him standing with the same sword, bloody then, over a headless body in a Korean village, calmly smoking a cigarette. He was drawing ahead of the men with him and screaming the same cry as had praised his butchery then. Still Dawlish let him come on. He wanted point-blank range, absolute certainty.

Rifle shots now, one, two of the attackers falling, but the onward surge unchecked, the seamen realising that there was no time now to eject and reload, some crouching now into bayonet-practice stance, others throwing their rifles down and drawing the cutlasses they trusted more. A seaman was rising from his knees and he lunged with his bayonet towards Yamada, who saw it just in time and jerked to one side. In that instant Dawlish fired and his round took the Japanese in the right shoulder. He reeled, blood already soaking his jacket, but trying to raise his sword, his eyes locked on Dawlish. He did not see it as the seaman's bayonet caught him from the side, gouging into his belly and ripping outwards. He halted, tottered, looked down on the entrails torn from him like glistening ropes, tried to shout as Dawlish's round took him full in the face. He did not rise.

The combat was a melee, bayonets, cutlasses, the advantage with the seamen against attackers still winded from their storming up the slope. Dawlish blasted with his revolver, counting his shots. His last took down the one surviving attacker.

Then suddenly it was over, what seemed a sudden stillness even though gunfire still rattled from the slope and louder reports from the sea, an awareness of survival, of relief beyond imagination. Bodies lay sprawled or humped, bloodied by cut or thrust. There had been no attempt at retreat, even when it was obvious that the attack had failed. The Satsumans had embraced death willingly.

There was another casualty now, the seaman who had carried Egdean's message, a bayonet thrust through his lung. Blood welled through the puncture when his shirt was torn away, the chance of survival minimal. He was carried to lie alongside the other wounded man. Neither could be much helped for now.

"You – stay with me!" Dawlish pointed to the most powerful-looking seaman. "You'll load for me. And the rest of you – join the men over there! Keep under cover and don't waste ammunition!" He gestured towards the plateau's edge. Beyond it Egdean's and Shand's unseen men were maintaining an irregular fire, much slower than before, the breaks in between individual shots longer. The Satsuman advance had stalled. For now.

He turned seawards, heard the bark of Shimazu's six-inchers, the yet sharper crack of Lodge's 4.7s, saw both vessels engulfed in smoke, probably all but blinded. On opposite but parallel headings, three cables, perhaps four, separated them. The *Kirishima's* mizzen had fallen and was dragging on her starboard quarter, slowing her almost to a halt. Men swarmed at the shattered base and bulwark, hacking through wood and cordage to cut it free. The fire amidships seemed to be under control and the three weapons on the port side were maintaining a steady fire. Plumes of white water were skidding and rising around the *Fu Ching* and a sudden flash in the smoke wreathing her, brighter than the stabs of her own 4.7s, marked a hit. Another hit, it seemed, for a fire was blazing abaft the funnel and the Chinese vessel had slowed perceptibly.

It's time to disengage, Dawlish wanted to yell at Lodge, to head seawards out of the *Kirishima's* range while she was all but stationary and still encumbered, to concentrate on fighting the fire that threatened to engulf the *Fu Ching*. Yet Dawlish realised that even had he been by the American's side his advice would be ignored, that Lodge at this moment was oblivious to anything but the glory of immediate victory.

Flame and rolling smoke vomited from the *Fu Ching's* forward Armstrong. Its shell ripped a white furrow just astern of the *Kirishima* – twenty yards closer and it would have carried away steering ability, perhaps propulsion too. The Chinese ship was lost now in a murk that was lit from within by the developing inferno amidships. Lodge's gunners must be all but blinded, the ten-inchers' slow rate of fire made worse by the necessity of sighting through the yellow fog.

And then Dawlish wanted to cry out, to warn of what he could see but Lodge could not. A slim and deadly form – the *Kirishima's* surviving torpedo boat, the craft that had slipped from the anchorage ahead of her parent and which must have lurked undetected close to the coast, was now racing towards the *Fu Ching's* stern. She plunged and bucked as she hit the larger vessel's wake, and three cables still separated them, but she was coming on with no less determination than Lin had shown. She was manned by a crew who knew their weapon, who had launched and re-launched perhaps a hundred times in relentless training, and of her approach her target seemed wholly unaware.

The *Kirishima's* toppled mizzen had been chopped free and she surged forward again, her guns still blasting, reloading, blasting again, the range short enough now for every second shell to slam into the *Fu Ching,* their impacts flashing in the smoke cloud.

Yet the Chinese vessel was still potent, vastly so. Her forward movement was thrusting her from her own smoke, superstructure ablaze, but her Armstrongs fore and aft were still bearing on the *Kirishima.* The after weapon fired – a brutal ten-inch killer forged in a British yard, its bore machined and rifled there with mathematical precision, with one objective only, an objective now realised. The shell punched through the *Kirishima's* side slightly abaft the foremast, just below the port bow-chaser, and it exploded in the space beneath. From his high vantage Dawlish saw flame and debris erupting through the deck like a volcano, saw the mast lurch forward as the backstays snapped, saw it sweeping down to crash on to the long bowsprit and somehow lodge there. The *Kirishima* shuddered, then slowed, flames engulfing the fallen rigging.

Lodge might now have had his moment of glory – perhaps the forward Armstrong was already trained to deliver the coup-de-grace – were it not for the still-unobserved Japanese torpedo boat. She was swinging out of the *Fu Ching's* wake, creaming away to starboard, then a wide turn that brought her directly towards her target's starboard side. She straightened out – the Chinese vessel was beam-on to her now – and she drove on to within two hundred yards before Dawlish saw the white plume ahead of her bows as she flung her torpedo, then sheared away.

Long seconds…

Dawlish had launched as many torpedoes in trials – and in anger – as any man alive and knew that the slightest disturbance could deflect a weapon from its track. Now, for the first time, he was praying for just such a miss…

For one last moment the *Fu Ching* was still a living ship, still steaming, still fighting, still governed by a fierce will to victory despite the pyre raging amidships.

Then she was gone, consumed in a single vast magazine explosion that ripped her apart, that spewed vast rolling black and yellow billows upwards and outwards, that hurled wreckage out in great smoking arcs. Dawlish saw an entire 4.7-inch mounting thrown from the inferno and his mind recoiled from acceptance of what the flailing black shapes that accompanied it might be. The flash was over in a second, the fires that followed scarcely longer, and through the churning smoke what remained of the *Fu Ching* was disappearing from sight.

The *Kirishima* still survived.

She was injured, badly injured, down by the head and sinking yet further, a fire roaring through her rent foredeck. But she was still under way, crawling, but crawling purposefully, her damaged prow aimed back towards the anchorage.

Dawlish recognised that Shimazu was doing what he would have done himself. He would not just beach the *Kirishima* – he would bring two hundred or more men with him, men trained to believe that Death was an honour, self-preservation a shame.

The Krupps were useless now – the *Kirishima* was too close for them to bear. Dawlish had nothing left to match Shimazu with.

Nothing but the few men he had brought ashore.

32

The *Kirishima* was wallowing towards the coal-loading pier with hoses playing on the fire on her foredeck and Dawlish realised that there was no value in maintaining this position on the headland. Shimazu clearly intended to hold the island, no matter how desperate his situation, hoping that his *Genyosha* confederates would have prevailed at the imperial court, that reinforcements would be on the way.

Dawlish had lost all sense of time. He glanced at his watch. Almost ten-thirty. The only hope of opposing Shimazu's force – half at least of the *Kirishima's* crew must still be effective – was to get Kung's Chinese troops ashore from the *Ningpo*. Ineffective they might be, but numbers were on their side, and driven by fear of Kung and stiffened by bluejackets from *Leonidas* it might be possible that...

His train of thought was halted by one brutal reality. The single landed six-inch Krupp still in Japanese hands dominated the approach to the northern coast, could reduce the *Ningpo* to a wreck with no more than three or four hits and plunging fire, would render *Leonidas* scarcely less vulnerable...

Egdean's and Shand's defenders were quiet now, not even single shots, indication that the Japanese assault on the slope had been suspended for now. In the brief interval before Shimazu could land his crew withdrawal was possible.

There was no alternative.

"Get those men ready to be carried" Even as he gestured towards the wounded men Dawlish knew the jolting would probably kill them but they could not be left. "And you," he singled out a seaman, "get across to Mr. Egdean. I want his men back here, one by one, quietly, stealthily. The marines last."

He turned towards Takenaka's summit, saw him outlined there, sunlight flashing on his field glasses. Dawlish waved, indicating retreat, Takenaka waved back. Understood. He would provide whatever covering fire was needed.

One last task before leaving. Dawlish examined the nearest Krupp. Three large brass nuts secured the lever that slid the breech-closing wedge open and closed. Without the lever the weapon would be inoperable. He turned to the box of maintenance tools and pulled out three spanners – all looked close enough to fit – and a hammer.

The first of Egdean's men had arrived and a litter was being fashioned from the remains of the fallen awning to carry the wounded men. Another seaman, and another, crawled up cautiously from the slope. Occasional rifle-fire by the marines, unaimed at any human target, gave notice to the Satsumans sheltering below them that the slope was still defended.

A glance down to the anchorage. The *Kirishima's* bowsprit was underwater, but she was still afloat, still moving. Dawlish suddenly realised that the torpedo boat should have been with her now to help get men ashore, but there was no sign of it. He looked seawards. A circle of dying foam sprinkled with wreckage and a thinning column of smoke above it marked the *Fu Ching's* grave. Beyond it, two, three miles beyond it by now, a tiny dark hull, a white streak in her wake, was heading southwards. Towards Chemulpo. Bearing news of Shimazu's plight.

The first spanner was too large but the second fitted perfectly. Dawlish hammered and broke the nut's grip. A seaman spun it free as Dawlish attacked the next. In less than a minute the lever was off. He cast it out as far as he could down the headland's steep seaward drop and saw it disappear among a clutter of rocks at the base. He moved to the second gun, made equally short work of its lever. He counted on Ross taking similar action on the opposite headland. The marine officer could be relied on for initiative and he and his men now seemed, wisely, to have retreated.

The litter bearers disappeared down into the valley separating the headland from Takenaka's position, one of their burdens already unconscious, the other, Shepton, barely stifling his gasps of agony. Egdean would hold the edge of the plateau with his seamen until the remainder of the force could pass through. The marines joined Dawlish, faces drawn, sweat and smoke-stained, but with a palpable awareness that they had done well, could do as much again.

Shand was last. He looked down, saw Yamada's crumpled form, the sword still grasped in his hand.

"Perhaps you'd like this, sir." He pointed to it, a trophy he probably hungered for himself, one he might one day show proudly his grandchildren.

Dawlish shook his head. "Go ahead, Shand. I'll follow." When the marine turned away he reached down and wrenched the sword free. Yamada's grip was powerful in death. Dawlish felt loathing, felt befouled by touching the weapon – a thing of exquisite beauty – which he had seen behead those Korean peasants for sport. He strode to the seaward edge and flung it out as far as he could. It fell, twisting and flashing, and disappeared like the firing levers among the rocks.

Then it was time to go.

The wounded men slowed the retreat even though their comrades, even the two Uighurs and the Chinese carriers, took turns with the litters. The descent back into the gully was difficult, the ascent the far side worse still as the bodies slid and lurched on the now blood-soaked canvas beneath them. There was no respite for them at the ridge beyond – they must be hurried on to the relative safety of the seven-pounder's position. Shand's marines were the rear-guard, lurking in one scanty clump of brush after another until the men behind them had reached the next cover. And still no pursuit.

Dawlish pushed ahead, joined Takenaka on the eminence he still held. From here the *Kirishima* could be clearly seen. She had not reached the jetty but seemed grounded in the centre of the anchorage. Men were moving ashore on anything that floated – most seemed to be bringing rifles with them. Many were being supported by their companions, exhausted, shocked, dazed, some injured. Those who had landed were being marshalled near the coal heaps, the injured carried there and then ignored, the fit mustering in a ragged line. A glance to the left showed that *Leonidas's* seven-pounder and its crew were still in position.

"How many rounds did they fire?" Dawlish had lost count.

"Twenty-four, sir."

So twenty-six remained. And so too did the single Krupp on the headland above the northern bay. It was just visible, its elevation a hundred feet or so lower than the seven-pounder. A rush by Dawlish's force would have no chance now of catching its crew napping. The gunfire from the south would have alerted them and they might indeed have been reinforced. It would be up to that puny weapon and her twenty-six shells.

"*Leonidas?*"

"There, sir."

She had slipped out from behind the shelter of the islands to the north and the transport, the *Ningpo,* was following. Dawlish had hoped that the Krupp dominating the approach to the small bay on the northern coast would have been eliminated before noon, that troops would be landing soon after. At least Edgerton's caution would keep *Leonidas* out of range, but that would be little help to the small and – Dawlish hesitated to admit it – desperate group ashore.

"Down there, sir," Takenaka pointed down into the valley that bisected the island. "In those huts just north of the walled compound. By that one on the left."

Dawlish swung the glasses towards the cluster of shacks roofed with rusting corrugated iron. For an instant he saw a movement, a figure flitting from one hut to the next, a stealthy disappearance into an open door.

"It might be my imagination, sir, but…"

No imagination. Something thick and stubby protruded from the northern wall.

"I think it's a Gatling, sir."

Dawlish focussed, studied. No more than a foot length was visible but there was no doubt of the ribbed appearance of the barrel stack. The field of fire had been brilliantly chosen, open ground in front sloping down towards the curve of the northern bay. The Gatling was not sited at right angles to the beach but rather to sweep along its length.

"One only?" Dawlish remembered the empty mounting on the torpedo boat he had captured. If one craft had given up its weapon then it was likely that the second had also.

"Possibly there, sir." Takenaka pointed towards the headland overlooking the bay. "There, in that gully below the six-inch, a little to the right of the track. You see it, sir?"

As on the headlands on the southern shore a rough roadway snaked up the nearer slope, its surface furrowed by the sledges that had carried the Krupp to the summit. The gully was a gash that extended from the shoreline almost to the top. It was partly filled by brush and heavily shadowed.

It would be a good position from which a weapon could also rake along the beach, but from the opposite end. But there was no giveaway, no sight of a multi-barrelled snout projecting from the scrub.

"I don't see a damned thing," Dawlish was uneasy as he spoke, the recollection of the Songang-ni massacre strong.

"With respect, sir. Just focus on the track. Half-way up, where it doubles back on itself as it climbs. And look slowly to the right of it, from the outside of the turn."

It was faint, and it might have been made by a goat or other animal, but there was the slightest disturbance of the soil, of vegetation trodden down and withered. Dawlish scanned along it several times, convincing himself as he did. It was a pathway and it led into the gully. It could have only one purpose.

One Krupp to dismember the *Ningpo* if she were to approach, two Gatlings to butcher the troops she carried even if they could be got ashore.

Three targets.

Dawlish rapidly weighed alternatives, gauging the sufficiency of his resources for each, finding all wanting, aware that momentum was still with him, but a diminishing asset as his men tired, as the involuntary moans of their wounded shipmates gnawed at their resolve. Ross's group must be hidden somewhere among the brush-strewn hills on the other side of the island's neck across the valley, a powerful asset if it could be located. And there was the seven-pounder…

He glanced at Takenaka, had a fleeting recollection of that moment in Seoul when he had drunk a cup of rice wine with him, and with Shimazu too, before going out to face near-certain death. He sensed Takenaka's resolution as well as his competence and courage. He could never know or understand this man fully, but he was lucky to have him. Now he must depend on him even more.

It was clear now what must be done. He explained it to Takenaka. A few questions, some changes of detail, then he called Egdean and Shand to join him. Lying prone, he showed them through the glasses what would be required of them.

Time then to leave, a last glance showing two separate groups of *Kirishima* survivors moving to the bases of the headlands flanking the anchorage, obviously intent on recapture of the Krupps. They were welcome to advance cautiously up the slopes, Dawlish thought. They would find the summits deserted and the guns useless. By sending men there Shimazu was diverting effort from what was now the key sector, the northern end of the island's thin waist. Shand and his marines stayed behind, well hidden, their responsibility to block any eventual Japanese move along the ridge from the Krupp positions, to delay any move towards the seven-pounder a quarter mile behind. Dawlish's remaining force hurried just below the crest line towards the weapon itself.

The small field gun's crew had already hauled it around to bear on the single Krupp to the north. There was no sign of movement around it, its crew obviously staying under cover. Only the appearance of a vessel offshore would draw them out to serve it. From the seven-pounder's position it was impossible to see the deep cleft which was suspected to contain a Gatling. There could be no hope of lobbing a shell into it.

There was no sign of movement in the valley below, only an ominous stillness, an impression of men well-hidden and waiting patiently. The huts concealing the other Gatling could be better observed now. These shacks clustered on open ground to one side of the track linking the northern and southern bays, but the ground on the nearer side, sloping at first gradually, then more steeply, towards them was studded with clumps of scrub. It should be possible to get within a hundred yards before emerging from cover. The Gatling there was likely to be the more difficult target. It must be Dawlish's own.

He selected three seamen – Nuttall, Bolton and Glover – men who had charged with him towards the Krupps and had withstood Yamada's frenzied attack. They looked exhausted but were young and fit enough to give yet more. He hesitated, then decided to take the two Uighurs also, knowing how deadly they might be at close quarters. It would be difficult to keep a larger group concealed on the approach. Takenaka, supported by Egdean, would have the remaining men.

"You've done well," Dawlish told the marine gunner. "Now you've got to do better. Don't open fire until you get Mr. Takenaka's signal. Three revolver shots – there'll be dead silence until then. Once you've got the range, hammer them with all the shells you've left."

A glance seawards. *Leonidas* was crawling slowly parallel to the northern coast, well outside the Krupp's range. A quick grasp of Takenaka's hand – no need to reiterate his orders – and a nod to Egdean. No need for words – example was the surest motivator.

Down on to the slope, sliding on loose soil and pebbles, one man at a time briefly exposed as the others crouched in patches of concealing scrub. Dawlish, armed with revolver and cutlass alone, and the sword-armed Uighurs, moved more easily than the rifle-equipped seamen. The chatter of insects was loud in the intense heat, yet even so the sound of every disturbed branch and leaf sounded like betraying thunder. It was impossible to gauge time – each crossing of an open patch, even if it was yards only, seemed to last an eternity.

The slope was evening out and the scrub was more sparse, movement yet more nerve-racking. The track, and the huts beyond, though still hidden, could be little over two hundred yards ahead, at the foot of the slope of the valley's other side. Still undetected, still no three shots from Takenaka to announce that his men were in position. It was time to rest briefly among the brush, to gather strength for the rush that would come. Water bottles were drained thirstily, then laid aside as an encumbrance. The Uighurs had none and before he drank Dawlish raised his own and offered it to one of them. The man shook his head, unwilling perhaps to touch what an infidel's lips had defiled even if they might die together within minutes.

Rifles rattled from the south in brief bursts, then died completely. Shimazu's men must have reached the top of one of the headlands and found it empty, the guns disabled. If it was the western headland, which Dawlish had fired from, there would be every chance that they would now start to move north along the ridge. If so, then only Shand's tiny force would stand between them and the seven-pounder.

The last part of the approach was the worst, the scrub thinning out, then ending completely some fifty yards short of the track. The huts, rusting corrugated-metal ones that must have been for storage, were the same distance beyond. From an opening in the northern wall of the shack on the left the muzzles of the protruding Gatling stack were unmistakable, an indication that there must also be men inside. Dawlish left the others under cover, then crawled – totally exposed for twenty yards – towards the last patch of meagre brush. He gained it, heart pounding, fear rising in him.

He looked to the right along the track – the walled compound three hundred yards to the right, silent also, but with three, four men just visible above the parapet, obviously Satsumans and rifle-armed, positioned to cover the Gatling's rear. They, rather the men in the hut, represented the greatest threat to the assault and they might be reinforced at any moment by *Kirishima* survivors. To the left the track led down a gentle gradient to the northern bay and beyond could be seen *Leonidas*, carrying so much gun-power and yet at this moment so impotent.

Hesitation meant certain failure. Dawlish gestured to his men to join him. He watched, mouth dry, as they slithered towards him one by one across the open ground, pausing in each tiny dip they encountered, then crawling slowly forward again. Two of the seamen, Glover and Nuttall, reached him, one of the Uighurs also, and still they were undetected.

Three revolver shots from the left and rear. Takenaka's group had reached the bottom of the headland. An instant later came the crack of the seven pounder, a pause, then the sound of the shell's impact. It was impossible to see if the top of the headland had been hit but a half minute later – and during it Dawlish and his men had frozen – came the next report.

"That hut! Rapid fire!"

Nuttall and Glover had rounds in their Martini-Henry breeches. They fired, ejected, pulled from their bandoliers, loaded, fired again and again in the steady rhythm they had practised dozens of times. Dawlish beckoned to the remaining seaman and Uighur to join him – they came at a run across the intervening ground – then turned and began to empty his revolver towards the hut. He saw dark spots appearing in the metal sides as rounds punched through, knew that the men inside, if not hit, would be cowering for protection. He pushed more rounds into his pistol's cylinder and steeled himself for what was to come.

Something ripped through the brush, showering fragments of branch and leaf. The men at the compound to the right had seen the gunsmoke, were taking it under fire. Only in offence lay safety.

"Right, lads! With me!"

Dawlish flung himself to his feet and burst from cover. He sensed the others pounding forwards around him, was vaguely aware of rifle fire and of the distant crack of the seven-pounder, had his whole being focussed on the hut ahead. A cry behind told him that one of his men was down. He was across the track now and a Satsuman was emerging from a hut to the right – not the Gatling's – and dropping to one knee to aim his rifle with greater accuracy. Another followed. The first man fired, missed, then fumbled to reload as the second rushed forward with bayonet extended. Dawlish stopped, crouched, cocked, levelled, aimed for the midriff, then fired. The body crashed down and to Dawlish's left a Uighur's sword was hacking at the first man.

Another ten yards brought Dawlish to the door of the Gatling's hut. Conscious of firing behind him, of close combat melee with bayonet and cutlass, he flattened himself against one side of the open door. Sounds of moaning within, the hint of somebody moving stealthily, awareness that the thin metal wall offered him no protection.

"I'm with you, sir!" Glover, rifle cast aside, bloodied cutlass in his hands, reaching the other side of the doorway.

Dawlish reached around the doorpost, fired blindly, fired again, heard a scream, nodded to Glover and then threw himself inside. Flame spat from a rifle raised clumsily by a bloody figure sprawled against the opposite wall. Dawlish blasted at him, saw him jerk, saw another movement to his left, another wounded man, Glover over him, chopping. Two other bodies, slumped untidily below the perforated metal wall, and another fallen over the Gatling's breeches, throwing the barrels skywards.

The sounds of close-by combat were suddenly stilled. A glance outside showed five or six bodies – one a Uighur. Nuttall appeared at the doorway. "Bolton's copped it, sir." A bald statement of fact. Mourning could wait. Rifle fire sounded from the compound to the south and pinging sounds announced holes neatly punched in corrugated metal walls. This position was untenable.

"Get up there! Find cover! I'll follow!" Dawlish pointed to the slope to the south. The scrub there was thin but better than nothing. "And Glover! You'll need your rifle! And give that man Bolton's!" He pointed to the Uighur.

The Gatling must be disabled. He dragged aside the body hunched over it, saw the single nut holding the firing crank on its shaft. There were wooden ammunition boxes to either side but among them he saw a smaller metal one. He threw it open, found the tools he expected – Shimazu could be relied for demanding meticulous maintenance – and grabbed a wrench. More holes were being punched in the walls and throwing up spurts of dust as they impacted around him. He strained at the nut, slipped it in his pocket as it came free, then dragged off the crank. He was taking it with him.

He paused, crouched by the door. He could hear Nuttall calling from the scrub fifty yards distant – fifty open yards. He knew that he could not remain here but he could not resist a single look towards the northern headland. It was wreathed in smoke and dust. A brief flash as another seven-pounder shell landed and, as the soil it had blasted skywards fell, the small weapon barked again. The marine gunners had the range and, whether hitting the Krupp or not, were making it impossible to serve it. Rifles crackled from that direction also – Takenaka's men were firing, or were under fire.

Dawlish thrust the Gatling crank inside his shirt, then sprinted. The dash seemed endless. He crashed between two bushes, heard rifle-fire close, could not know if it was directed at him, saw thicker foliage ahead, threw himself down and scrambled forward on all fours.

"Over here, sir." Nuttall's voice.

He crawled towards it, found Nuttall and Glover and the remaining Uighur in a dry ditch, overgrown so as to be almost a tunnel. They hurried, crouched, along it and found a cleft running down to it from the right – good cover, a place to make a stand if the Satsumans were to follow. They gained it, chests heaving, found it scrub and rock-filled, a steep gash torn by winter floods. It deepened as they climbed – sixty, eighty feet, before resting.

Dawlish peered above the edge and could see the huts he had just left. Armed men – fifteen or twenty, spread out, not bunched – were moving from the walled compound. He glanced northwards and his heart leaped as he saw *Leonidas* forging towards the northern shore, emboldened now to approach by the dark plumes rising on the headland – the-seven pounder must be down to its last rounds, but it was still firing. The *Ningpo* transport was following in *Leonidas's* wake, her boats hung out to either side on davits, ready for launching.

A cloud of flame-shot smoke suddenly enveloped the cruiser. Another followed. The bow-chasers' dual report reached Dawlish an instant later, just after a geyser of dark earth told of a shell landing on the headland while another jetted out from the cliff-face below.

"They're coming, sir! Down there, sir!" Glover was pointing back towards the huts they had left.

There were Japanese seamen, and one officer with a sword, among the advancing Satsuman guards. They were skirting around the huts and heading for the scrub that had sheltered Dawlish and his men so briefly. They must surely find the ditch, must find their way towards this gully.

Two rifles, his own revolver, their cutlasses and the Uighur's sword. Time to die, as he had once accepted in another hollow, on an icy slope above the Black Sea, outnumbered, the prospect then more bitter for the knowledge that Florence Morton would never know he had loved her. At least now there had been four years together...

The first Japanese had disappeared into the scrub below.

"Keep your heads down. Hold your fire." Every round must count before it came to naked steel.

Mouth dry, heart thumping, terror hidden behind a mask of resolution, the prayer for strength only and for it to be quick...

Foliage rustling above the ditch, a figure emerging, pointing towards the gully, disappearing again. A head and shoulders briefly seen, a sun-flash on a sword blade, the officer ducking back under cover. A long wait, an aeon.

Then they came. They burst from the scrub into the open and headed up the slope, avoiding the direct route up through the ravine, bayonets levelled, the officer leading, shouting.

"Now! Rapid fire!"

Too far yet for Dawlish's revolver but the seamen and Uighur were taking aim across the gully's edge. A report, Nuttall swearing as he missed, Glover firing also, another miss, and they were reloading as the onslaught came on unchecked. Another minute and ...

Rifles crashed out from somewhere behind and above, sustained rapid fire. The officer went down, men fell around him, the charge collapsed.

Ross and his marines had reached the slope above.

Salvation.

33

Dawlish struggled into wakefulness, blinking, joints aching, saw Takenaka prodding him respectfully. Long shadows confirmed that the sun was just up, that he had slept for little over an hour. He smelled coffee, recognised his steward offering him a mug – he must have come ashore in the night and had brewed over a fire of twigs. Dawlish stretched and pulled himself to his feet by the low parapet he had slumped against.

"Any movement, Lieutenant?" Looking south from this point on the wall of the compound that had housed the Korean labourers, the wooden administrative buildings were less than two hundred yards distant. Beyond them lay the coal heaps, the jetty and the harbour with the half-sunken *Kirishima* at its centre. No sign of life, no gunfire, but the certain awareness of armed men crouched there under cover and ready to sell their lives dearly.

"Over there, sir," Takenaka motioned to a patch of scrub to the right. "There's a report of three more dead. Two throats cut, one beheaded. Nobody saw or heard anybody come or go."

It had happened earlier in the night also, Japanese finding their way silently into the positions now held by the Chinese force landed the previous afternoon. They were small victories but enough to engender fear and nervousness. Even though driven back, almost surrounded, Shimazu's mixed force of guards and seamen was still to be reckoned with.

The humble seven-pounder had proved the decisive factor, silencing the Krupp position on the northern headland and allowing the *Ningpo* to come close inshore to launch her troop-laden boats. The first Chinese ashore had fallen to the Gatling that had remained silent and untaken in the ravine beneath the Krupp – Takenaka's attacking force had been driven back by the dozen rifle-armed Japanese who defended it. Kung himself had landed from the first boat that ground ashore but as the Gatling lashed the beach even he was unable to get

333

the men moving from any illusory cover they had cowered in. It was Edgerton's willingness to bring *Leonidas* close enough inshore for her guns to bear, and Purdon's skill in serving them, that had sent five shells gouging into the ravine, obliterating the Gatling, its crew and its defenders.

In the hour that followed all the Chinese troops had landed. Lacking they might be in training and resolution but they had numbers on their side, and with them came another thirty bluejackets under O'Rourke. They had surged southwards until halted by the fortress the walled compound had now become. Direct attack had proved futile and only *Leonidas*, firing down the valley, had broken the stalemate. Emaciated wretches had poured through the breached walls, starving labourers who had been immured there for days past, while the Japanese defenders steamed southwards. Shand's marines had blocked attempted outflanking on the southern ridge, and had held out, just, until Takenaka had reinforced them. By nightfall Shimazu's force was confined to the harbour area and the fighting had halted for the night. Except for the posts infiltrated, for the ghostly killings.

Now, in daylight, the worst must be yet to come, slow elimination of one pocket of defenders after another, certainty of suicidal determination to resist, acceptance that losses would be two or three to one in Shimazu's favour. The plan for the day's assault had been agreed with Kung in the early hours, his troops to drive directly towards the harbour, the marines and bluejackets hooking around them to the right. And all through the conference the unspoken and unadmitted awareness that failure was still possible, that Chinese morale, already tested to the limit, could be pushed only so far.

The assault would start in one hour. All that could be done was already done. Dawlish felt oppressed by awareness that the butcher's bill was already too high, that the signature of the codicils that Kung had assured him was now certain – the Chinese Ambassador would see to that – would be too dearly bought. And even if victory came today Shimazu might be triumphant even in failure should his *Genyosha* allies already have the Emperor's ear.

"Captain Dawlish! Over there, sir!" Takenaka, pointing.

A single figure was walking hesitantly from the wooden office building. He was carrying a long pole with what looked like a bed sheet drooping from it – a white flag. He glanced back towards the building's veranda, then plodded on when a figure there waved him forward, then disappeared inside.

Before he even raised his field glasses, before he saw the gaunt features, the peeling red skin, the ginger moustache and the great buck teeth, Dawlish knew it was Wishart, the Caledonian and Oriental's manager. "Make sure he isn't fired on," he said. "Send for Mr. Kung," This could not be surrender, he thought. It was perhaps some bizarre gesture of mercy by Shimazu, or a reluctance to allow a non-Japanese to share in the glory of the final hecatomb.

Kung was pleased. There was something of Shimazu about him now, not ruthlessness alone but a grim pleasure in strength and power. "We can do business with your Mr. Wishart," he said. "I guess you'll want to extend him protection as a British citizen. I'll have no objection to that."

Wishart looked shrunken, arrogance and insolence gone, his hands trembling, the smell of alcohol overpowering. "It's none of this is my doing," he blurted. "I never expected anything like this." He looked beseechingly at Dawlish, the only Briton of the three men confronting him, and extended his hand. Dawlish ignored it.

"What do you want, Mr. Wishart?"

"It's not me who wants it. It's that Jap bastard Shimazu." He glanced at Takenaka. "No offence, sir. No offence."

"Shimazu? He wants to surrender?" Dawlish found it hardly credible. He sensed Takenaka stiffening at his side, shock and disgust obvious in his intake of breath.

Wishart shook his head. "He just says he wants to see you, Captain Dawlish. And the Japanese gentleman." He seemed to find it hard to look Takenaka in the eye.

"Not me?" Kung's tone was icy, his face all the more intimidating for its lack of any expression.

"No, sir. Sorry, sir. Not you, sir."

"You're the Caledonian and Oriental's manager?" Kung said. "You've got other Europeans here too? Mechanics, supervisors? Are they still here?"

"They are, sir. Down there, sir. They're safe, sir, they're under cover." Wishart pointed towards the sheds by the harbour. "We didn't give them Jap buggers any more help than they forced us to. None of us touched a weapon, sir, we drew the line at that. And no…"

Kung cut him off. "You've been running this place well, I understand. Profitable, very profitable?"

"I was, sir. Profitable too, like you say." Wishart's voice was wheedling, his hand kneading unconsciously. "That's all the company wanted, sir, profit. Not this sort of thing. Not at all, sir. But I hadn't much say in the matter, sir. That Jap devil gave me no option."

"So you're out of a job now, and your company has lost an asset. I'm confiscating it on behalf of His Majesty in Seoul." Satisfaction was just detectable in Kung's voice, tables turned, Wishart the scapegoat for a thousand petty humiliations in the Sierra Nevada. "I think you'll need a friend in court, Mister, because nobody there will think kindly of what you've been party to. And I don't think you've got any such friend. It could be painful, Mister, mighty painful."

A dark patch was spreading around Wishart's crotch and a trickle was running from around one foot as Kung turned towards Dawlish. He nodded towards the white building Wishart had come from. "You want to trust that bastard, Captain, or we just go ahead and finish the business like we planned?"

Likely losses two to one in Shimazu's favour, maybe worse. Already too many dead.

Dawlish looked over to the right, to the left, towards the humble men, Chinese and British alike, now being marshalled for the assault. Still living.

"I'll see him," he said.

*

The walk was two hundred yards. It seemed like two hundred miles.

Dawlish felt ashamed of his clothing – ragged, filthy, no tunic, no badges of rank, not even a cap – and hoped Shimazu might not take it as a gesture of disrespect. Despite all that had passed he was worthy of honour as a brave enemy. Dawlish was unarmed but Takenaka had insisted, politely but firmly, that he himself should carry his own sword.

"Shimazu Hirosato will expect it," he said and Dawlish did not press him.

They walked in silence, oppressed by the yet greater stillness around them. Dawlish's mind raced over the terms he would offer, something he had not considered until minutes before. Surrender must be absolute and no facilities were to be damaged beforehand. He had gained Kung's reluctant but quick assent to humane treatment of prisoners. No beheadings. Britain, Dawlish would tell Shimazu, would stand guarantor for that. Yet, occupied as he was, he could not but sense in Takenaka a tension, a supressed passion, perhaps even an agony of spirit, for all that his face was set in an expressionless mask, his tread steady.

No sign of life, but awareness of observation by hundreds of hidden eyes, until they were close to Wishart's old office. A young officer came down from the veranda to meet them. The insignia – identical to the Royal Navy's – on his scorched and torn tunic confirmed him to be a lieutenant.

He bowed. Dawlish did likewise, but clumsily, Takenaka gracefully. A quick exchange in Japanese.

"Lieutenant Kirino presents his captain's compliments," Takenaka said. "He requests us to enter alone." He paused, then said. "There will be no treachery, sir. Not at this moment. There is nothing to fear."

The veranda was stacked with furniture, not systematically as if to aid defence, but haphazardly, as if cleared out in haste, office desks and chairs and cupboards, ledgers and files.

They entered what had been the large office outside Wishart's inner room. It was empty now, wholly bare but for a single square of canvas – its edging showed it to be a fragment of a sail – and a single chair in the centre of the floor. On it was propped a portrait of the Emperor and before it, eyes fixed on it, kneeled Shimazu. He was erect, sitting back on his heels, the skirts of a blue silk kimono fanned out around him, broad stiff wings extending from the shoulders of a yellow sleeveless jacket over it. The only other object was a short dagger, wooden handled, the blade pointed and edged and highly polished, on a cushion to one side, out of Shimazu's reach. He did not look up, said nothing.

Dawlish felt revulsion, horror, rising in him. He realised now what was coming, what Takenaka had told him of that night in a Korean village. *Seppuku.* Now he was to be a mute participant.

"We must kneel, Captain." Takenaka motioned to Shimazu's left. He was trembling, fingering his sword hilt but again he said "There is nothing to fear." He bowed towards the portrait.

They arranged themselves on the floor, Dawlish mimicking Shimazu's and Takenaka's posture as best he could. He noticed that the window behind the portrait faced to the east and the sunlight streaming in from it was bright on Shimazu's expressionless face.

When he spoke it was in Japanese, brief phrases, bitten off, face expressionless. Takenaka's answers were equally curt. He turned to Dawlish. "Shimazu Hirosato has honoured me by requesting a service for him. I have assured him that you will not object."

Shimazu spoke again and Takenaka translated. "Shimazu Hirosato recalls the night we three shared in Seoul." More words. "He would have been proud to die with you that night. And he has been proud since to have had you as an enemy. He is honoured to have you present at this moment."

Again the terrible silence, time standing still, inevitability, dread. And yet an awful fascination and beyond it, something indefinable, an awareness of the value of life itself, never more intense, of – Dawlish's racing mind found the word and half-shrunk from admitting it – of brotherhood.

At last Shimazu reached inside his kimono and took out a folded paper. He opened it to show black brush-drawn characters in perfect columns. Then he produced a second paper, the cursive script obviously European. He reached across and handed them both to Dawlish. Unsure what to do with them he laid them before him and sensed that he had done the right thing. Shimazu would have chosen each word with exquisite care and they would need no clarification.

"Lieutenant Kirino has my full authority and my instructions to surrender my force." Shimazu spoke in English now. His voice trembled slightly. "I have assured him that there is no shame in this. His life, my men's lives, are the Emperor's to dispose of thereafter as he sees fit."

He nodded to Takenaka, who rose to his feet and went to the cushion with the dagger, a folded white cloth lying next to it. Takenaka wrapped the cloth around the hilt – for better grip, Dawlish realised. Every detail had been thought out, had perhaps been fixed for centuries.

Takenaka handed it to him. He received it with both hands, reverently. He seemed to relax slightly as Takenaka helped him remove his jacket, then loosened the kimono to bare his upper body, and tucked the long sleeves under Shimazu's knees, pulling his torso forward and holding it inclined. *So he will fall forward*, a small, horrified, internal voice told Dawlish.

338

"I, Shimazu Hirosato, took action without the authorisation of His Majesty, Emperor Meiji, one hundred and twenty-second Emperor of Japan," Shimazu spoke in English, the pronunciation perfect, the pace measured, only the slightest tremor in his voice. He was perfectly still, his body hard-muscled, beautiful. "My actions were motivated by loyalty to His Majesty. The officers and crew of the *Kirishima*, with the command of which he honoured me, bear no responsibility for my decision. They acquitted themselves as bravely as His Majesty would have expected and I crave his clemency for them. My brother captain of His Majesty's ship *Tatsuta* would have done likewise had he survived." He glanced up briefly to Takenaka, the message clear. *Not yet. Wait.* "For my crime I disembowel myself and I beg you, Captain Dawlish, to do me the honour of witnessing the act. I am indebted to Takenaka Katamori, for performing the duty of *kaishaku*."

Dawlish bowed, almost instinctively. He realised that killing in the heat of battle, or remotely, by gunfire, was never so terrible as this measured ritual that could be halted by will at any moment. He had wished for this man's destruction, and had worked unhesitatingly for it, but now he was struck only by the beauty of the living body, the knowledge that vitality and intelligence and will still coursed within it. He did not know what to say – words would be insufficient even if he could find them – but he forced himself to look up, not to shrink from what was to come. Dreadful as the moment was he knew that this was inevitable, that this was how it had to end, that this could only be the best possible end. For Shimazu. For himself.

Shimazu was speaking in Japanese now, the same statement, Dawlish guessed, that he had just made in English. Takenaka had moved to Shimazu's right side, his sword drawn and grasped in both hands, its point lowered to the floor. Shimazu finished, glanced briefly up at Takenaka, nodded, then turned the dagger point towards him.

He did not cry out as he stabbed low into his left side, just below the waist. His eyes were bulging and he gasped slightly as he dragged the knife slowly to the right, but only when he drew it out did his face betray pain. He rocked forward slightly and stretched out his neck, perhaps involuntarily.

Takenaka's sword was a flashing blur.

34

Leonidas departed from Socheong early the following morning. It would never be a British base now. The fiction that China administered it on Korea's behalf would be maintained for long enough for Fred Kung to make a fortune from the coaling operation. Caledonian and Oriental shareholders might fret and protest, and maybe sue somebody, but to no avail. Wishart, Kung's man now, well-remunerated even if never fully trusted, would manage a venture no less efficient and profitable than before. Uighur guards would replace Satsuman guards and the Korean labourers would know little difference.

The dead had been brought on board, five in total, another miserable addition to the tally accumulated since *Leonidas* had first sighted the coast of Korea. It was better to bury them at sea, a cleaner element than the soil of an island where near-slavery was being re-established. The cruiser nudged slowly across the waters where the *Fu Ching* had come to her fiery end. Only scraps of wreckage had been found, charred planking, a splintered remnant of a mast, a few items of clothing, scattered fragments that the mind recoiled from identifying but which sea birds circled and dived for. Dawlish wondered if Lodge or Lin would have thought themselves to be pitied. One had found the glory his own nation's war had denied him and the other had given his countrymen an example of selfless professionalism, a challenge to their image of weakness and corruption. *Leonidas's* crew was mustered in salute as she ploughed through the dispersing debris, five canvas-wrapped bundles of her own waiting with endless patience on her starboard side beneath Union flags.

Dawlish made a round of the ship afterwards, expressed appreciation and admiration, listened to anecdotes that would grow into epics in years to come, visited the mercifully-few wounded in the sickbay. Everywhere he encountered a quietness, a pensiveness – not depression, for there was too much pride for that – an awareness of mortality, maybe even of futility. He maintained a brave face, tried even the odd humorous remark that was too-forcedly laughed at, but when he retreated to his own quarters afterwards he felt heart-sick, empty. The euphoria of battle that had carried him through the recent days was gone, the victory somehow lessened by Shimazu's triumph in his own end. He had little joy in Fred Kung's assurance that the Chinese ambassador would get the treaty codicils signed within a week, the wretched formalities that now seemed so trivial but which had drawn him into this tragic imbroglio. And the stance of the Japanese government was still unknown, the possibility that, even yet, support might be underway for Shimazu. If so, he could see no outcome for himself but repudiation and disgrace. Japan was too valuable a counter to Russian ambition for Britain to antagonise for the sake of a single over-zealous naval officer. He sat down to begin his report but found he could not concentrate. He went on deck again to seek comfort in observing the routines that made the ship a living being.

Long before *Leonidas* nosed into the great stain of yellow silt-laden water extending from Chemulpo the masts and yards of shipping moored there were just discernible.

"I think you should see this, sir." Edgerton handed Dawlish his telescope. "I can't be sure, but it could be…"

There could be no mistaking the barque rig that towered above those of smaller vessels there, nor the long, white, elegant hull that slowly revealed itself above the horizon. The *Haruna*, the *Kirishima's* sister, flagship of Admiral Hojo which had been so conspicuously and un-committedly unseen in recent weeks. And carrying her full armament of ten six-inch Krupps, not weakened by any landing of shore batteries.

"Do we stand offshore, sir?" Edgerton's tone told that he feared the same as Dawlish. That the nightmare might be beginning all over again.

Dawlish shook his head. "We'll enter port," he said. "But ready the guns."

"Clear ship?"

A pause. At last Dawlish said, "No, Commander." Doing so might be provocative, not doing so would increase vulnerability. A final gamble.

Leonidas advanced as slowly as when she had first approached this desolate roadstead. The *Haruna* was at anchor, swinging calmly with a flowing tide, as immaculate as before. Two pulling boats were moored alongside and her steam pinnace was chugging unhurriedly from shore. There was movement on deck but there was no unusual sense of urgency about it. And yet *Leonidas's* onset had been noted. Sun flashed on telescope lenses turned towards her, first from the tops, then from the bridge.

Closer now, silence broken only by the panting of the engines, the slight rattle of halliards, the crews standing by their loaded guns, Purdon sighting his beloved bow-chasers, the Gatlings already raised into the tops. Dawlish stood on the port bridge-wing, heart thumping, yet outwardly as calm as he had remembered Hope had been on the *Plover*, knowing that every eye on deck was on him, that on his judgement alone life or death might hang. This was the burden he had ached and striven for since boyhood and the reality was more terrible than he ever could have imagined in those long years.

Dawlish raised his glasses, scanned the warship again. There was another craft alongside, moored inboard of the pulling boats, the hull invisible but for a single tiny funnel rising from it. Before the funnel a small railed platform, one that should have carried a Gatling, but didn't, because it had been the one he had disabled in that hut at Socheong. This was the torpedo boat that had done for the *Fu Ching* and she had reached Chemulpo with news of the Socheong battle.

Then suddenly a puff of smoke from the *Haruna*, little more than a wisp from a small weapon. The report that followed was a sharp bark. Then again, and again, in respectful welcome.

Dawlish turned. "Be so good as to return the salute, Commander Edgerton."

Leonidas's acknowledgement came a minute later, not the vicious crack of a six-incher but the harmless yap of the blank-loaded saluting gun.

"Lieutenant Takenaka?" Dawlish saw that he was smiling, with relief, with gratitude. "You'll oblige me by crossing to the *Haruna*. Present my compliments to the admiral and advise that I wish to visit him myself in two hours." The same words he had used once before. "And..." He did not know how to phrase this, knowing now how little he still knew of Japanese etiquette. "And if you can do so, if you find the right moment, sound him out. Not directly, you'll understand..."

"I understand, sir."

Takenaka was back an hour later.

"Admiral Hojo presents his compliments and looks forward to your visit, sir. He hopes that you and your senior officers will be pleased to dine with him this evening. He mentioned that his cook would be preparing plum duff."

"Did he mention Shimazu?" There had been fury and bloodshed, ships destroyed, lives taken, lives sacrificed when they might have been saved, families devastated, wounds, misery, suffering…

"I alluded to the subject, sir." Takenaka's tone had no trace of irony, even if his eyes betrayed it. "Admiral Hojo assured me that there was no Japanese naval officer of that name."

"And the *Kirishima*, the *Tatsuta*?"

Takenaka's tone did not change. "When you go on board the flagship, sir, it might be appropriate to offer the Royal Navy's official condolences for the loss of two Japanese warships in the recent typhoon. Admiral Hojo confided that two vessels of the names you just mentioned were lost with all hands."

"Thank you, Lieutenant. You'll be accompanying me to dinner tonight."

Dawlish knew that he himself would be reminiscing with Hojo about boyhood hardships, would be admiring miniature trees, marvelling at a tame eel, hearing the chirping of pet crickets in bamboo cages.

*

Again the official Korean escort, pike-armed palace guards in red or blue knee-length tunics. Again the grooms in faded robes leading the horses sent from the royal stables to carry Dawlish and Whitaker through Seoul's streets, now even more miserable than before with squalor, resentment and fire-gutted houses. Again through the palace's south gate, the red and gold and turquoise carvings of the structure above it mocking with its magnificence the city's poverty. Again along the stone-flagged roadway lined by troops in uniforms and with weaponry unchanged for centuries, men who might have participated in rapine and massacre here only weeks before but now sullenly returned to duty. Through the inner wall with its tile-roofed cloister and yet more immobile troops lined up beyond. Sight then of the flowering shrubs and pagoda-like pavilions of the gardens beyond and of the charred remains of buildings where terror and horror had reigned so recently. Ahead to the two-tiered stone platform, blindingly white in the sunshine, and up the steps towards the huge and intricately decorated wooden building with its soaring double-roofs. Finding there, as before, the royal guard lined up, but no longer in European-style blue uniforms, but clad instead in flowing silk, Manchu bannermen carrying muskets, swords and halberds. No Japanese, not even Koreans trained by them, only Chinese.

Dawlish recognised the court chamberlain who awaited him by the entrance – a signal honour this, for this man had greeted him inside on the previous occasion. It took longer to identify the extravagantly clothed figure in Mandarin dress that stood next to him as Fred Kung. No flicker of recognition, only the most formal bow.

Into the gloom. There was the high red-painted dais and a slight figure was sitting as if frozen on his throne, his face blank, his eyes staring at some point above the heads of his courtiers. By the foot of the dais a figure stood who looked like Yi Yong-Ik, the servant who had carried the Queen to safety but who was now gorgeously arrayed. And behind was a carved wooden screen, an opening in it large enough only to allow a single person to pass.

The presentation once more of the credentials of Queen-Empress's envoy, the document heavy with red sealing wax, the King's inaudible reply relayed by the chamberlain and translated by Whitaker, Dawlish's no less elaborate reply.

As he spoke Dawlish glimpsed a woman's face in the opening in the screen behind the throne for a brief instant. Yet long enough to recognise features small, delicate and so obviously full of the energy and intelligence her husband so clearly lacked.

The translated compliments droned to a conclusion and at last an ornate table was carried forward. Upon it lay the codicils in neat columns of beautifully brushed characters and the more mundane blocks of text in English and in French. Then the signatures. Two carved onyx seals inked on soft pads for China as nominal overlord. Shen, the eunuch admiral, and Fred Kung, watched each other carefully and without sign of emotion so that their seals touched the thick paper at the same instant, precedence un-conceded. Their contest for supremacy was not yet over. Another seal, of lapis lazuli, for Korea, and then the Queen-Empress's envoy signing with the quill pen provided for him. Other seals, smaller, were pressed into heated wax.

One last formality, an unexpected one.

"You're honoured, Dawlish," Whitaker said when he translated the chamberlain's transmission of the King's murmur. "It's unprecedented, could not be better."

The robes that were carried out by an official were unfolded. Both looked scarcely less splendid than those worn by the king himself, gold thread on red silk showing dragons, flames, pheasants, mountains, even a tiger and a monkey on the upper, rice grains, grass, axes and bows on the lower.

"For you, His Majesty says, to thank you for your friendship," Whitaker translated, "so you will never forget Korea."

It was a gift beyond price, one that could be admired but never worn, one to be treasured and transmitted perhaps through generations yet unborn.

Dawlish looked up from it, spoke his thanks for Whitaker to translate, and once again he saw the face behind the throne, the power rather, the exquisite features of a woman who owed him her life but who had not hesitated to sacrifice a faithful servant who impersonated her to save her own. He nodded slightly, saw her head incline before it was withdrawn. He sensed coldness in the acknowledgment despite all the richness of the gift, a settlement of account for services rendered, no further obligation. He too had been her pawn.

At last back through the courtyards and past the motionless troops and the burned-out pavilions and on into the squalor of Seoul beyond. With him Dawlish carried the right of entry for any British warship to any Korean port to take on water and supplies and to conduct maintenance, the right too to survey the coast, for it was indeed a dangerous one and needed charts.

But there was more.

Koreans and Chinese and Japanese would still contend for control of this kingdom, but it was the frail and deadly Queen Min who would hold the balance between them. It wouldn't last of course. Were she somehow to be removed – as they surely would engineer someday – the Japanese would be back, dominating not just Socheong but all Korea. But whether they or the Chinese did so did not matter. The Russians would not have it.

All dearly bought.

The End

Historical Note

The Background to *Britannia's Spartan*

The repulse of British and French forces at the Taku Forts in 1859, as part of the so-called Arrow War, was as disastrous as it is depicted in the opening chapter. Willes of HMS *Opossum*, who as an admiral was to negotiate the British treaty with Korea in 1882, did indeed behave as heroically as described, as did the future Admiral Fisher and hundreds of others now forgotten. The Taku Forts were to fall in a second, equally bloody, assault in 1860, thus facilitating the advance on Peking that brought the war to an end. During the 1859 attack Commodore Josiah Tattnall of the United States Navy did indeed render assistance when it was most needed, and his men did man a gun on HMS *Plover*, even though they were neutrals. His decision to do so was occasioned by his view that "Blood is thicker than water", a phrase that entered the language thereafter. Tattnall had fought against the Royal Navy in the War of 1812 and he was to serve in the Confederate Navy in the American Civil War. Two ships of the United States Navy have been named in his honour.

The newly-created Imperial Japanese Navy did model itself on the Royal Navy, with which many of its officers trained, and it had already reached a high peak of efficiency by the early 1880s. Single-minded concentration on the pursuit of excellence made it the decisive factor in Japanese victory over China in 1895 and, even more impressively, over Russia in 1904/05. Britain and Japan were to remain formal allies until 1923 and in the First World War Japanese naval forces were to be stationed at Malta. The island of Socheong was not developed as a Royal Navy base but one was briefly maintained at Port Hamilton, on the small Komundo island group off Korea's south coast, in the mid-1880s.

Korean resentment of Japan's ambitions to control the country did lead to the explosion of violence in mid-1882 which led to the sacking of the palace at Seoul. The *Pyolgigun*, the Korean unit trained by the Japanese and commanded by Lieutenant Horimoto Reizo did sacrifice itself heroically to cover the escape of Queen Min. The servant who carried her to safety on his back, Yi Yong-Ik, was later to become a trusted minister. Over the next decade Korea was to remain the focus

346

of Japanese, Chinese and Russian attempts at control. Queen Min, the single most influential figure on the Korean side, was to play one group off against another very effectively. Japanese interests orchestrated her savage assassination in 1895. With her eliminated, Japanese domination then became only a matter of time. Her husband, the weak and pliable King Gojong, later took the title Emperor but was afterwards forced to abdicate under Japanese pressure. He died in 1919, by which time Korea had been under full Japanese control for nine years. The experience of rule as a colony of Japan was a brutal one and it lasted until 1945. King Gojong's father, the *Daewongun*, returned from China in 1885 and, despite opposition from Queen Min, continued to plot to return to power. He allied himself with the Japanese – who, not unwisely, did not trust him fully – and may have been involved in Queen Min's murder. He died in 1898.

Already badly damaged in the events of 1882, the Gyeongbok Palace in Seoul was systematically all-but destroyed by the Japanese after 1910 because they viewed it as a symbol of Korean independence. Reconstruction commenced in 1989 and the restored buildings are now among the most spectacular sights to be seen in East Asia.

And the *Genhosha*, the Dark Ocean Society? It grew to be a major force in Japanese politics and many cabinet ministers, members of the Diet and senior political leaders were to be members. It continued to exert considerable influence on the politics and foreign policy of Japan – not least in relation to overseas expansion and conquest – until the end of World War II. It was finally disbanded by the American authorities during the Occupation of Japan in the late 1940s.

A personal message from Antoine Vanner

I hope you've enjoyed *Britannia's Spartan* and that you've also liked the previous books in the series, *Britannia's Wolf, Britannia's Reach* and *Britannia's Shark.*

You probably know how important reviews are to the success of a book on Amazon or Kindle, especially for a writer publishing a series. If you've enjoyed this book then I'd be very grateful if you could post a review on **www.amazon.com** or **www.amazon.co.uk**.

Your comments do really matter and I read all reviews since readers' feedback encourages me to keep researching and writing about the life of Nicholas Dawlish.

If you'd like to leave a review then all you have to do is go to the review section on the *'Britannia's Spartan'* Amazon page. Scroll down from the top and under the heading of 'Customer Reviews' you'll see a big button that says 'Write a customer review' – click that and you're ready to get into action. You don't need to write much – a sentence or two is enough, essentially what you'd tell a friend or family member about the book.

Thanks again for your support and don't forget that you can learn more about Nicholas Dawlish and his world on my website **www.dawlishchronicles.com**.

You might also 'like' the Facebook Page 'Dawlish Chronicles' or want to follow my weekly blog on **dawlishchronicles.blogspot.co.uk** in which I write short articles based on material found during my research but which is not necessarily used in the novels.

And finally – I can assure you that further Dawlish adventures are on the way. I hope you'll enjoy them, even though Dawlish himself might not!

Yours faithfully: Antoine Vanner

About Old Salt Press

Old Salt Press is an independent press catering to those who love books about ships and the sea. We are an association of writers working together to produce the very best of nautical and maritime fiction and non-fiction. We invite you to join us as we go down to the sea in books.

On the following pages are details of some recent offerings – and more are on the way.

Some recent offerings by the Old Salt Press

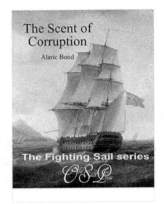

ISBN-10: 194340402X

By Alaric Bond:

**The Scent of Corruption
(The Fighting Sail Series Book 7)**

Summer, 1803: the uneasy peace with France is over, and Britain has once more been plunged into the turmoil of war. After a spell on the beach, Sir Richard Banks is appointed to HMS *Prometheus*, a seventy-four gun line-of-battleship which an eager Admiralty loses no time in ordering to sea. The ship is fresh from a major re-fit, but Banks has spent the last year with his wife and young family: will he prove himself worthy of such a powerful vessel, and can he rely on his officers to support him?

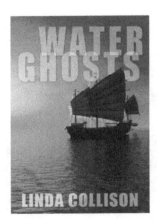

ISBN-10: 1943404003

By Linda Collison:

Water Ghosts

"I see things other people don't see; I hear things other people don't hear." Fifteen-year-old James McCafferty is an unwilling sailor aboard a traditional Chinese Junk operated as adventure-therapy for troubled teens. Once at sea, James believes the ship is being taken over by the spirits of courtiers who fled the Imperial palace during the Ming Dynasty, more than 600 years earlier, and sailing to its doom. A psychological nautical adventure with strong historical and paranormal elements.

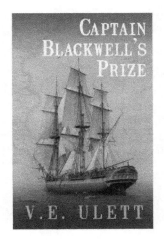

ASIN: B00E82DH2Y

By V.E. Ulett:

Captain Blackwell's Prize

A small, audacious British frigate does battle against a large but ungainly Spanish ship. British Captain James Blackwell intercepts the Spanish *La Trinidad,* outmaneuvers and outguns the treasure ship and boards her. Fighting alongside the Spanish captain, sword in hand, is a beautiful woman. The battle is quickly over. The Spanish captain is killed in the fray and his ship damaged beyond repair. Its survivors and treasure are taken aboard the British ship, *Inconstant...*

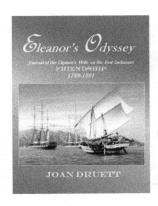

ASIN: B00Q2E992S

By Joan Druett:

Eleanor's Odyssey: Journal of the Captain's Wife on the East Indiaman *Friendship* 1799-1801

"New Zealand-based novelist and maritime historian Joan Druett is one of this generation's finest sea writers ... This book is recommended for anyone who seeks adventure at sea."
    -- Quarterdeck (Editor's choice)

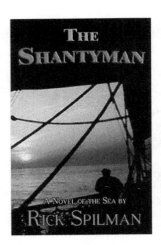

ISBN-10: 0994115237

By Rick Spilman

The Shantyman

He can save the ship and the crew, but can he save himself?

In 1870, on the clipper ship *Alahmbra* in Sydney, the new crew comes aboard more or less sober, except for the last man, who is hoisted aboard in a cargo sling, paralytic drunk. The drunken sailor, Jack Barlow, will prove to be an able shantyman. On a ship with a dying captain and a murderous mate, Barlow will literally keep the crew pulling together. As he struggles with a tragic past, a troubled present and an uncertain future, Barlow will guide the *Alahmbra* through Southern Ocean ice and the horror of an Atlantic hurricane. Based on a true story, The Shantyman is a gripping tale of survival against all odds at sea and ashore, and the challenge of facing a past that can never be wholly left behind.

ISBN-10: 0992263697

By Antoine Vanner:

Britannia's Shark
(Dawlish Chronicles series, Volume 3)

1881 and the British Empire's power seems unchallengeable. But now a group of revolutionaries threaten that power's economic basis. Their weapon is the invention of a naïve genius, their sense of grievance is implacable and their leader is already proven in the crucible of war. Protected by powerful political and business interests, conventional British military and naval power cannot touch them. A daring act of piracy drags the ambitious British naval officer, Nicholas Dawlish, into this deadly maelstrom. For both him and his wife a nightmare lies ahead, amid the wealth and squalor of America's Gilded Age, and on a fever-ridden island ruled by savage tyranny…